JUICE

True Homosexual Experiences
from S.T.H. Writers
Volume 5

Editor: Boyd McDonald

Gay Sunshine Press
San Francisco

ISBN No. 0-917342-36-4

A complete catalogue of Gay Sunshine Press titles is available for $1 ppd. from Gay Sunshine, P.O. Box 40397, San Francisco, CA 94140.

Navy Sex Hound

I. AN ASS-LICKER IN MIAMI

NEW YORK – Couldn't make it Saturday. Maybe next week. Have your letter in front of me. You want to hear about the Navy. I'll begin by commenting on the sample headline you published:

YOUTH WANTS HIS SHIT-HOLE LICKED
BUT WRITER FEARS IT'S TOO DIRTY

The example tells me two things about the youth. If he wants his shit-hole licked he's a queer youth. If the writer thinks it is too dirty then the youth is not a sailor. Sailors clean their assholes very well and the rest of their bodies. They shower when possible twice a day. Their underpants are G.I. white boxers – the only underpants allowed on shipboard or base. They sleep in their underpants and are fully clothed during the day. They go from locker room to shower with white towels wrapped around their middle. The edge of the towel reads USN in large blue letters. They do their laundry fully clothed on deck in buckets of soap and Clorox. The only hard on I ever saw (except my own) was while on nightwatch I surprised a young seaman jacking off in his sack. His sack happened to be in a single tier against a bulkhead so I suppose he felt safe. I turned off my flashlight so he could finish and nothing was said about it. Most tiers of sacks run double in the center of a compartment so jacking off in the sack is restricted. This sailor was laying on his back with his meat straight up in front of him. There is little privacy aboard a ship and most sailors probably jack off on liberty. I did. The best way to do it in the sack is to lay on your belly and press it into the canvas. But you have to do it slowly without too much movement. It's not a bad way when you get used to it and I did it that way sometimes after I left the Navy. Sailors being so clean never smell bad aboard ship; the closest they come is returning from liberty with their breath stinking of booze and whatever sex they had and their uniforms rumpled. With the open showers everybody gets *particular* views of everybody else. There is the usual horseplay, the usual talk of pussy and queers.

Back to assholes: You can sometimes rim straight men but if you go beyond the edge they withdraw. Men who let you suck their shit-holes are queer. If they let you eat it tonight they'll let you finger it tomorrow. Next night they're ready for your prick. Example: Sailor (me) meets queer in Miami park. Sailor wants blow job. Sailor goes home with queer. Both strip down. Queer has good body but too much jewelry. Too much perfume. Too perfect tan. Sailor in T shirt and underpants stretches out on bed. Queer in Jockeys kneels before him. Queer licks sailor's dick. Sailor lets him. Queer works his tongue up inside sailor's shit-hole. Sailor *lets* him. Queer eats sailor's asshole.

Sailor LETS him. Queer wants to fuck sailor. Sailor says no. Queer pleads. Sailor says he's not pogey (sailor term for guys who take it in the ass). Says blow job or nothing. Queer sucks off sailor. Sailor dresses. Queer asks him to stay. Sailor drags his ass back to hotel.

II. SAILOR TURNS QUEER.

I called you yesterday (Sun.) but no answer. Were you photographing yet another asshole? I don't know what you've got against hairy ones. I think they're fine. Let me go over the items I already submitted. The item SAILOR FUCKS HIS BUNK: I kept my shorts on for two reasons. It is against NAVY REGULATIONS for a sailor to lie in the sack without his shorts on. The other reason is that when you cream your shorts you can drop them in the laundry bag (I told you we did our own laundry). You may not have the time to change your sack-cover next day and those spots show. Which brings me to item 2: Sailor Gets His Asshole Sucked. You asked me if this item (queer and sailor in Miami) was real. It was real. The only thing I could add is that that queer gave me one of the best blow jobs I have ever had. Here's another item: my sucking off a sailor outside the base. You could call this one "Sailor Turns Queer," because it was my first suck job. Two sailors walking back to the base; no sexual innuendos that I remember. He was blond, midwestern, sturdily built and said he had to pee. I accompanied him to the park outside the base instead of saying goodnight. His prick was ramrod stiff and there was no way he was going to pee, just yet. I said, "Maybe I can help," and went down, like it was an everyday occurrence. You want me to do a letter on blow jobs good and bad – well this was bad. I went down on my knees, the way cocksuckers were supposed to do. I was too eager. He wanted relief and I was so amateurish that I came before he did. I finished him. We walked back toward the base gate. I said, "If you see me..." he said, "We were horny, that's all." I never saw him again. The dialogue sounds tacky but it's what was said. I left one thing out which has nothing to do with the item. It is that a cocksucker going down on his knees is the queer version of the "missionary position" of straights. So that cocksuckers expected to go down on their knees as did straights expect them to. It doesn't always work. The sailor I was sucking off was standing. On my knees, I was going UP on him, not down. On your knees in the front seat of a car or in the balcony of the Adonis [theatre in Manhattan] is good. In the bushes or in doorways, it won't go.

III. "THAT'S A NICE JOCK STRAP."

I wrote last night. I'm writing again. I feel coarse. You said the reason men reject may be that they feel sweaty; dirty; not up to it. BULLSHIT. Item: YMCA. Queer making the rounds of the shit-houses. (Queer is

6

me.) On the floor above my room, enters softball player. Did nine innings. All that uniform. Came in to piss. Athlete: "How's it going?" Queer: "Thought I might find something to read in here." Athlete: "I got a couple of sports magazines in my room." ATHLETE'S ROOM: a few magazines on dresser. Athlete says he is going to take a shower, proceeds to strip. Queer checks out the mags. Athlete has removed baseball jersey and pants and is standing in his jock strap. Athlete is built: broad shoulders, narrow waist — all that shit. But the ass: well-formed and jutting out from his jock. Athlete throws himself across his bed; hands behind his head. Tufts of hair under his arms; bulging muscles. Athlete says to queer with magazines: "Anything else in the room you want." Queer says: "That's a nice jock strap." Athlete removes it, hands it to queer, saying, "Anything else?" Queer checks out athlete's prick. It's tattooed. On the head is a miniature parrot. Queer says, "Didn't it hurt?" Athlete says "Nah." Athlete says, "Anything you want, neck down, is yours." Queer is fascinated by the parrot but (here is the point) intoxicated by the sweat, all nine innings of it. Queer starts with sweaty armpits, then to sweaty left nipple down to belly button and kisses the parrot. Parrot spits, queer swallows. Athlete satisfied. Wants to get rid of queer. Says he better take that shower. Queer takes magazines and jock strap which athlete wiped his dick with and goes down to his room. Queer puts jock strap under his pillow. Next time athlete encountered queer he said "hi," but they had had it. When queer says he finished mags, athlete just says, "Drop 'em under my door." Queer sniffed jock strap for a week or more before he washed it and wore it when he cruised. In Navy experiences sailor is me; after that Queer is me.

IV. "I WAS BLOWING COCKSUCKER BREATH INTO HIS HOLE."

You say as editor you survey how men taste, smell, etc. As a queer I do the same thing. So I was rimming a guy one night. He was a night watchman and loved the suck-hole: shit-hole ratio. We were locked together. I was blowing cocksucker breath into his hole. Men like this, I find, and so do I. Anyway, while we were locked in this operation he farted. Sound disgusting? It wasn't. When a guy lets a fart it can be nauseating. I've suspended operations. But when he farts directly into your mouth it's like personal, like popping a popper. Anybody else in the room wouldn't smell it because it was going from asshole to suck hole and it hit my throat, my nose, my belly and I never felt so alone with a man. I don't think he did it on purpose. It just happened. It excited me and I did the rest of the shit well. I should tell you more about him if I can dig up some paper. Got together with the watchman several times after that but it was never as good. Watchman apologized for farting. I wished he would do it again. It was the only interesting thing he ever did. He was a beefy Irishman in his twenties and guarded the brewery across the street until about one in the morning. He started coming over after work a couple of nights a week. Don't know if he had a family but every time he came he stayed all night. After a couple of weeks I felt married to him. He wasn't very attractive – fat ass, paunchy. Had two things going: his uniform (they turn me on) and a big dick. But all he wanted was for me to lick his asshole. He'd say "that's lovely," not as a queer would but as the Irish do. His shit-hole was clean but that gets boring after awhile. I probably could have fucked him but didn't want to. He wouldn't fuck me. Said he didn't want to hurt me. So after a long time I'd get on his dick and suck him off. Then he'd go to sleep. He took up most of the bed and all the covers and I'd wind up sitting in a chair reading for the rest of the night. He wasn't interested in any sex in the morning. After a couple of weeks of this I decided it was time for a divorce and made a point of being out when he finished work. These details you might not want but that fart was "lovely."

V. "HEALTHY, HETERO, HORNY AND HUNG."

Enjoyed Sat. A lot comes to mind from the chat. I'll only do dialogue when I remember it exactly because otherwise it stinks. Marines, in order: the one in uniform that got away. He was on Park in the Fifties. I cruised him. He rejected and got ugly. He said he had one thing for my mouth, a fist, if I liked that. He took a swing, missed and I hustled my fag ass uptown. He could have caught me but probably figured why bother. The other two were ex-Marines. One picked me up in Wash. Sq. I was standing at the rack on the So. side and he drove up. The stuff about "you got a light" and then I got in the car. We drove to the area near Peter Cooper [apartments] and parked. It took an hour of small talk because of shyness. He was out of the Marines and was selling encyclopedias door to door. When I finally went down it took almost another hour to get it to spit. He drove me back to Wash. Sq. and said, "I guess I gave you a workout." Then he wanted to know if I was gay or just horny. Males can ask the strangest questions. Another guy once asked me after I'd knocked myself out for him, "Why men?" Anyway I didn't point out to the one who asked if I was gay or just horny that I was both or that he being also horny didn't suck. The other ex-Marine was a bartender in a Bowery kind of bar on Bleecker. I went in late one night after a night of rejections. There were a couple of old timers and me. The bartender was in his thirties and in good shape. He said it had been a slow night and said how about you. I didn't pretend, looked him in the eye and said "very slow." He called "last call" and the old timers left. I started to but he said, "You got time? I got to do my books." He lowered the lights and locked the door, poured himself a shot and me another beer. He tallied up and we had another drink and the bullshit became personal. He'd been a Marine and liked "cunt." "Cunt," he told me, was anywhere he could stick it. He liked broads but fag would do in a pinch. He wanted to know if I had a place. He locked up and we got a cab and came up here. He fucked like a nigger and twice during the night. The next morning was best because I got into the act. The whole thing was great sex. I liked the humping OK but my big pleasure is sucking dick. Especially in the morning. His cock tasted and smelled from the earlier sex – scum-sticky and the odors of my box (a word I like). I've had some good times but that had to be one of the best. Also he was friendly, not nasty. If that's what I wanted it was alright with him. He left about 11 and said he'd be seeing me. I went to the bar a couple of times but he was never there and I never hooked up with him again. The first ex-Marine was younger. Both were healthy. In descriptions there is a lot of repetition unless a guy is a beauty or a dog. Most of the ones I've had are normal and that's alluring enough for me. Four H's: healthy, hetero, horny and hung – or combinations of these.

My butt-fucking history is limited and started with the black youth who picked me up on Wash. Sq. So. and I got in his car expecting to suck. He wanted to screw so OK. In a vacant lot in the twenties in the back seat. He screwed me doggy-style. I don't remember pain as I do on later occasions, which seems odd when you're getting your pussy started. It was a slam bang beginning. He took out a handkerchief, wiped his dick and handed it to me (the handkercheif). There was cream trickling down the insides of my legs and I swabbed that first and dried my shit-hole. The handkerchief was soaked with scum, a light shit stain or two and a little bit of blood. We dressed and he drove me back to the park. I don't remember what I did after but I didn't really rinse until I got home later. Next day I had a pleasant ache and that's how I lost my *last* cherry. It was a no bullshit fuck and my pussy didn't hurt till next day. This coon ripped me off the nice way, straight up the twat. None of the coons I had seemed likely to steal money. They didn't even ask for any. Let me know if more is needed. Getting my brain sucked could turn out to be harder work than getting my holes filled and much harder than getting my dick licked.

VI. "MAYBE I COULD USE YOUR BATHROOM."

I'd been out of town, was tired from the trip and had a couple of suit cases. Outside the station I hailed the first cab to come along without checking out the driver as I usually do. I settled myself and bags in the back, gave my address and realized that the cab driver was as beautiful as any I'd ever ridden with. A man about 28 with

9

broad shoulders, strong features that telegraphed a built-in "fuck off" to queers. So I didn't try to start a conversation and thought about how good it would be to get home and go to bed. He pulled up to my building. I paid the fare and tipped him and started to get out. He got out and said, "I'll give you a hand." I said I could manage but he took my suit cases, locked his cab and followed me into my building. At the door he said, "Maybe I could use your bathroom." That line from other cabbies has meant "blow me" but not this one. I let us into my apartment, he set the bags down and I pointed to the john. I had taken off my coat and when he came back I dug in my pockets to reimburse him for carrying my suit cases. He put out his arm to stop me, saying, "You've already tipped me." And then his hand was feeling my groin. And then he opened my pants. I was too surprised to move. He slid my pants down my legs and then my underpants and then, his arms around my legs, slid himself down in a crouch, shoving my cock into his blow hole. The first suck went the length of my prick. This handsome straight-looking cab driver was a firstrate dick licker. Clean cut, no nonsense, no slobbering. All the force of his powerful body was contained in his suck hole and my prick was soon screaming to spit. "I'm coming," I managed to warn him and he let up on his sucking, moved his hole to the base of my dick and was quiet while I scummed him. He stayed down on it while my prick melted and then he removed his suck hole, wiped it with the back of his hand, rose to his full height, gave me a mock salute and went out the door.

Howdy Sports Lovers.

In *Short Circuit* (Atheneum; 1983), Michael Mewshaw mentions that Jimmy Connors, the tennis player, "never walks around the locker room without a towel tied primly around his waist." Seven pages later, Mewshaw reports that on court, Connors grabs his groin so often a reporter asked him why; that he once spread his legs and motioned for an umpire to suck him off, and that he habitually uses hand and body language too obscene too describe here. It is odd Mewshaw placed these two sets of details seven pages apart, rather than together. They provide a suspicious contrast between Connors' obsessive display of his groin when clothed and his reluctance to show it naked. The details of his public performance rule out decency, shyness or modesty as reasons for never revealing his meat in the lockers, and thereby force into prominence other possible reasons for keeping himself covered.

It is my theory that our athletes in general are not well hung; if they were, why would they undergo such strenuous training and competition to achieve a recognition of virility that could be achieved more easily and aesthetically at any urinal just by waving a normal "or preferably larger than normal" dick.

For example, we have the case of a well known Southern athlete who has set new American records. But I doubt that his dick will ever break any records. Just before the race, when his name was announced and he turned to face the pool and the camera, he pinched his swim brief between his thumb and forefinger, pulled it out and down to loosen its hold and thus free his groin for better display, but still failed to show an acceptable bulge. Nor did it help when he flicked his dick with a finger. Like swimmers in general, he appeared to have between his legs the genital equivalent of a macaroni and two walnuts rather than a banana and two eggs.

Further evidence that many athletes feel they can win more hero worship through violence than through dick display is the revelation in *Time* that they use anabolic steroids even though these drugs can produce sterility and, worse, impotence. *Time* quotes a Dr. Robert Dugal: "Male athletes who use it [the drug] take the chance of becoming eunuchs."

One youth who has no need to bother with athleticism is a short, thin, dark-haired sex hound I saw displaying and manipulating a huge hard on for almost an hour in the Penn Station Men's Room, an inspiring sanctuary I retreat to whenever I'm in that squalid neighborhood. An appreciative audience gave him a recognition of his virility as enthusiastic as any accorded the tangled, sweating athletes upstairs in Madison Square Garden. Inspired by his leadership in exhibitionism, I provided leadership in voyeurism; after making several trips to the men's room during his show on the pretext of taking a leak, I finally just stood out in the open, away from the urinals, and stared blatantly as he blatantly performed. Other men soon followed my lead and formed a group around me. When the youth finally ended his performance and left, I followed, sensing that he would make a good subject for an interview; but I lost him in the crowded and confusing Long Island station, as sordid a place (except for the toilets) as the Island itself.

He was of course more admirable than the prudes, athletic or otherwise; more courageous and more intelligent. For the obscene and prolonged display he put on requires an overwhelming confidence that can come only from the knowledge that, though he is terribly outnumbered by the prudes, he is still in a strong position because he's right and they're wrong. The group of men who joined me in watching him stood as silent but convincing evidence that the public will respond favorably to the real truth on those rare occasions when they have a chance to see it. But usually the public only has a chance to see such attractions as Tommy Tune; tap dancing is the greatest menace in modern homosexuality, greater than the threat of Godless Communism, for Christ's sake.   — *B. McD.*

11

The Joy Of Heterosexuality

By Boyd McDonald

I. SENATOR CALLS US "SICK."

Henry Jackson was afraid that homosexuality would bring an end to what he called "the human race." But the Senator, like priests, had an exaggerated notion of how hard it is to reproduce; he didn't marry until he was almost 50. Then he did have children. He made up for his late start by wallowing in his hard-won status as a hi klass hoity-toity hetero; he called homosexuals "sick" and told a group of hecklers who asked about gay employment rights: "Go and have your own rally. Our people want hard work. We don't want gay work. We don't want gay jobs. You have your gay jobs. You just do your thing and stay away." Jackson's death last September recalled an episode of heterosexual hard work in his own state, Washington. According to William Arnold in *Shadowland* (Berkley Books, 1982), when Frances Farmer, the movie star, was locked up in Western Washington State Hospital in Steilacoom, she was "held down by orderlies and raped by drunken gangs of soldiers." But it is not this sort of thing, according to the Senator, but rather homosexuality that "is the first beginning of a breakdown in society." The redundancy alone, apart from the redneckery, gets a "U" (Unsatisfactory).

II. UROLOGIST JOKES ABOUT AIDS.

Congressman Lawrence Patton McDonald died about the same time Henry Jackson did and, like the Senator, he gave a stronger performance as an anti-homosexual than he did as an avid heterosexual. The Senator spent the first half century of his life as only a latent heterosexual and Dr. McDonald's first wife complained in divorce proceedings about his sexual adequacy. The fascinating thing about him was that he was a urologist and thus, at least before he went to Congress, devoted his career to the human genito-urinary system; I had deduced from his public behavior (he joked about AIDS and supported anti-homosexual legislation) that he had some interest in dick. His death at age 48 was even more tragic than Senator Jackson's at age 71. Had he lived, he could have examined many, many more penes; I always wondered what the plural for penis is. Good night, sweet prince.

Patrick Buchanan, the plump contralto who once did PR for organized crime (the Nixon Administration), has attacked homosexuals in the column he now writes but he objected to publication by *The New Republic* of Mrs. McDonald's unflattering testimony about the doctor's sex drive. And though Buchanan wrote that death from AIDS is God's punishment for homosexuals, I assume he would also object to including Dr. McDonald's death on the list of divine punishments. The same fate (death) befell all of Buchanan's ancestors and awaits all of the surviving Buchanans, including Patrick.

III. TILL DEATH DO US PART.

I was more touched by a third death reported in the same papers that carried the obituaries of the Senator and the Congressman. I know from baby-sitting that three-year-old girls have their little ambitions and I wondered if this particular three-year-old enjoyed the last trip in her life, riding 30 miles with Jimmy Lee Gray to a woods. I wondered what she thought of on the trip. I wondered whether she knew, at that age, as her head was being held down in the mud, that she was dying. I wondered if she even knew what death is. Or what heterosexuality is. She had just had her first experience of it; Jimmy kidnapped her, sodomized her, strangled her and threw her off a bridge. He had already done seven years for killing a 16-year-old girl. This time, with a three-year-old, he must have felt even bigger.

Unwittingly, by running his story along with the obituaries of the two lawmakers, the "straight" press supplied the best possible rebuttal of their boasts.

IV. RONNIE'S "STRAIGHT," FATHER CLAIMS.

Since both the President and Mrs. Reagan have made unflattering comments on our sex lives, it is only natural that I should search their own for clues on the source of their superiority. I was surprised to see Mrs. Reagan included in Martin Greif's *Gay Engagement Calendar* along with famous homosexual men and women in history; I had assumed that anyone as ordinary as she lacked the sensitivity to be a lesbian. Upon reading the text I find that Greif does not – repeat not – represent Nancy as a lesbian; he included her merely because of her comments about homosexuality. They are too trampy to be repeated here.

Neither is their son Ronnie, the President insists. In a new book appropriately entitled *Make-Believe* (Harper & Row, 1983), Laurence Leamer writes that the President, in answer to universal rumors that his son is gay, told an interviewer that he had checked and had found that Ronnie is "all" male.

The same can hardly be said for the President himself; he has a crucial male part missing. In 1967 a transurethral prostatectomy was performed on Reagan and about 30 prostatic "stones" were removed; as recently as last year he still reported occasional "discomfort" while pissing.

V. THE WINDS OF WAR.

As happened so often, Hitler was constipated at the end of September,

1944. He refused to let his doctor, Theodor Morell, give him an enema. According to *The Secret Diaries of Hitler's Doctor* (Macmillan, 1983), the Fuhrer "took an irrigator and tried to administer one to himself in the W.C.; the patient sitting upon the toilet bowel for the purpose. But the enema liquid did not stay in, he said, and he had to eject it immediately." Somehow, by 7:30 P.M. September 30 Hitler had had a legendary bowel movement, one of the great bowel movements in history, one in which everything that can happen in a bowel movement, did. "There had been four bowel movements between four and six," the doctor wrote, "two of them weak and two very violent. In the second one, after releasing a blockage there was an explosive watery evacuation. The third and fourth were extremely foul smelling and especially the fourth."

Even when the war was clearly lost and Germany was ruined, the Fuhrer's flatus and feces remained two of his principal interests in life. He engaged in "intense contemplation of his own bodily functions, and particularly...his gastrointestinal and digestive tracts." He discussed his digestion with "Frau Christian and Miss Schroder," two workers at his headquarters who were summoned to take late night tea with him. Once, Morell writes, "As I was leaving, the Fuhrer had me called back from the adjutants' room and told me...he had had a substantial bowel movement."

The book reeks with relentless references to his "frequent belching," "intestinal gases," "bad breath," "a lot of wind," "violent flatulence," "agonizing winds," "constant diarrhea," "laxatives of increasing savagery," "flatulence...on a scale I have seldom encountered before."

Before a conference with Mussolini, Hitler's abdomen on July 18, 1943 was "taut as a board, full of gas;" but during the flight to the meeting he "let off wind, which resulted is some improvement," and by the following day, he had "slept well and let off a lot of wind."

"Grinning generals" talked of his diarrhea at the daily war conferences during the summer of 1941, but there were no grins on the faces of the High Command who stood behind him in photographs. The book's revelation of their leader's acute flatulence throws new light on their strength of character; its revelations about Hitler's belching and diarrhea add startling touches of reality to hitherto vague descriptions of state occasions and war councils. To be with him was perhaps as much an ordeal as an honor.

The jacket reports that David Irving, editor of the book, "was on the trail of the missing Morell diaries for 15 years." His search was a labor of love; his publication of the book is a major breakthrough in the literature of Hitler's flatulence.

Hitler himself remained as unmoved as his bowels by the millions of deaths he caused. He was able to respond only to the death of someone he knew, such as one of his beloved valets. But near the end, the tragedy of war was finally brought home to him: transport in Germany was so fucked up that the samples of his excreta regularly sent by his doctor for analysis could no longer get through.

No one could ask for a more absurd, more debasing report on his gastro-intestinal system than that which Irving has painstakingly put together. The pity is that we have only a verbal record of the Fuhrer's flatus, not, so far as is known, a recording of the sound itself. The sound would be a perfect aural summary of him; his symbol, his quintessence. For Hitler, a typical heterosexual, had a gastro-intestinal personality – that is, he felt that his desires, just like his flatus and feces, should be released. For example, he had a desire to exterminate whole types of people, principally Jews and homosexuals, and he did try, simply because he wanted to. But his efforts finally were no more successful than his efforts to give himself an enema, and he died, as he had lived, full of shit.

Delivery Man Delivers Regular Loads But Writer Wants Him to Suck

MASSACHUSETTS – Enjoyed that letter in Issue No. 40 of S.T.H. on the South Carolina man and his delivery guy, because it brings to mind how I came out. After several attempts during five years to find a delivery driver to cop my cherry because I was hung up on that uniform and the bodies that filled it (and wanted one of those bodies to bring me out) I made overtures to at least four by groping and propositioning my intentions. Well word got around and several others toyed with me (I thought they were sincere). I thought finally I got the real vibes from this driver to enter my life, but decided to play it cool just in case he was like the others. He made clear that even though he was warned to be careful of me he wanted it too. Although he was four years younger than me he was a little more mature in certain instences [sic] . He is even taller and thinner than me and looks like a combination of a singer and actor (the Midnight and Rhinestone Cowboys). I threw caution to the winds after – while helping carry some bundles with him on the elevator of one of the buildings he was delivering to – he suddenly came closer to me, pressed up and ground his groin against mine. The next day he took me to a place he found where I lost my oral cherry in a freight elevator and swallowed my first taste of cum. I was addicted and for at least once a week, after the repeat the next day, while he delivered bundles to businesses on the route, he dropped loads into my hot mouth. I also discovered he was a "weekend warrior" of the National Guard. I even blew him while he wore that uniform too. The second shock of my relationship with him came when he asked for some mony *[sic]* to help him pay off his loan to a shark. He promised he would pay it back as soon as he could. As of yet he has payed *[sic]* very little because after two years he was fired from his delivery company because he was caught stealing (like our politicians do) – misplacing a valuable package. So now for several months the other stages of his work has been construction jobs and driving cabs on weekends. I have sucked him off in those garbs too. So as you can calculate, he has been five people to me – a delivery driver, a soldier, a hard hat and hackie, and a thief. The latter, robbing me of my oral virginity and a UPS customer of some package. But he has yet to complete the theft of my anal cherry. Despite the fact that I feel "at home" with his joint in my mouth as he blasts away, I would like him at least once to return the gesture and not make it completely one sided. I have asked him but get the story he has hangups and he will try soon to do it and fuck my ass too. My patience is very thin and I have been out of practice not knowing how to ask another guy to plow my chute or if he would be interested in a lovable, friendly, not too swishy 35-year-old late blooming gay who wants a sincere 2 way friendship and permanent love relationship. Anybody out there to answer my plea or should I be a little more patient with my ex-delivery Cowboy hustler and see it through.

[I think this writer may have a hard time finding reciprocation from the uniformed and blue collar sorts he likes, for they normally find that their uniforms make them eligible to play the role of trade. – B. McD.]

Writer Has Seen Runners "Throw Up Their Guts;" Suggests Boxer "Pass Gas."

Criticizing Roberto Duran, the boxer, for walking out in the middle of a prize fight because he had "cramps," Dick Young, a New York sports writer, wrote: "You got a belly ache, you pass gas." Young mentioned that he had "seen Les MacMitchell and other trackmen throw up their guts then go out and run a mile, two miles."

Youth Sees Parents Fuck

FROM A SUBSCRIBER – I had the hots for my father's cock from the first time I can remember even being aware of cock. From the day that a stranger seduced me into sucking him off in a shack when I was six, I thought a lot about my dad's cock. I tried to see it whenever I could and, when I did get a look at it when we were changing for swimming or on like occasions, I always felt more than a twinge of pleasure at the sight. And then, when I got to be 10 and started having my own hard ons, I often though about what his cock looked like when it was hard. It wasn't until two years later that I found out. Circumstances (financial) in our family brought about a unique combination at the time. I shared a bedroom with my parents. It isn't necessary to go into detail as to the why, except to say that it was legitimate and, in concept, innocent. But for me and I strongly suspect for them it became anything but innocent. By the second week that I shared their room, I was sharing their sex life also. At first it was merely by eavesdropping and, from what I heard, picturing the scenes on the other bed. I'd lie there listening and jacking off. Then one night, it wasn't so dark in the room; I could see the forms of their bodies as my father humped up and down over my mother. From then on it was never quite dark in the room. They started to leave the window shade up and there was enough light from outside for me to make out their activities. I thought it was an oversight on their part. I got to see that fucking wasn't the only trick in their bag. There was also quite a bit to do with having their heads between each other's legs. I was in a paradise of lust. But it was to get even better; about three months after we had moved there, the city installed mid-block street lamps. The one on our block cast considerable brightness into our bedroom. That didn't faze my parents; they still didn't bother with the shade, nor did they curtail any of their activities. They fucked and sucked with abandon, like I wasn't in the room. And I got good looks at all of it, my father's stiff cock ramming into my mother's cunt and him with his face against her twat and his tongue eating it out, to say nothing of my favorite performance, the the times when she went on his dick with her mouth and sucked down the entire length of it. I was like a fucking maniac. Sometimes I'd shoot off during their performance and then would jack off after they were done. I shot cum all over my sheets and wiped it up with my Jockey shorts. I desired them both. I would have gladly put my prick in my mother's cunt and fucked her, or would have lapped her pussy for her. Even more, I would have sucked my father off. Every time I saw his stiff prick I'd think about it going down my throat and shooting hot cum into me. When he was fucking my mother I'd think about it being my mouth instead of her cunt.

17

It went on like that for over a year. I was almost totally obsessed with sex and with my parents as sex objects. I had no guilt or conscience pangs over watching them; nothing could have made me stop; it never occurred to me at the time to question my parents' part in the whole thing. A long time later I began to suspect that they were not innocent, that they knew I was watching and were themselves turned on by it. When it ended (we moved into a larger house) I missed those nights. After I sucked off my father's friend when I was 14 a big change came over me and I was never the same boy again. I became introverted, stopped hanging around with other kids and stayed by myself. I was obsessed by sex, I thought about it practically all the time. I was convinced I was different, that there wasn't anyone else like me in the world. The first outlet I found was our family dog, a large male Boxer. I discovered that he liked to lick my cock and so whenever we were alone I'd let him lap and lick it until I'd get so worked up that I'd have to jack off. Then I'd let him eat my cum. When there wasn't anyone else home, I'd take off all my clothes and lay on the floor so he could lick my cock. One day, after I was stripped, I got on my hands and knees and the dog jumped up on my ass with his front paws. He began trying to fuck me in the ass. He wasn't getting his cock anywhere near my asshole but I was excited by the idea so I lifted my ass higher and moved back toward his humping cock. His dong was ramming against my ass but wasn't getting close to getting in, but I loved it. I was then 16 and just about all the time walking around with a hard on. And no opportunities except using my hand on it.

I had seen a couple of those dirty comic books. I started making my own comics. I'd trace pictures of guys and women in bathing suits or underwear from advertisements, making them naked and then drawing big cocks on the guys and tits and cunts on the women. I wrote dirty talk on them. I drew one character who was me; I was the star, fucking every woman and sucking off every guy. One of the characters I drew was my father's friend who I'd sucked off. I also drew my parents. I used everyone's name and the dialogue was frank stuff. With their names on it, it was dynamite. I had several sheets of it and stupidly kept them in a drawer under my sweaters. I went to get them one afternoon after school and they weren't there. I was scared shitless and stayed in my room the whole afternoon. All during supper, I expected my mother to tell my father she had something to show him after supper and she wanted me there. But she didn't. After school the next day, the pictures were back in my drawer. Mention of them was never made. It was a harrowing experience; I was convinced I could be locked up as a dirty pervert. But if my mother thought so, she never let on.

[Youths craving sexual relief, like the one in this letter, are not the only ones who are frustrated; men eager to provide relief are also frustrated. Today many people, including obviously the author of the above letter, can see that his yearnings were healthy, and that it is the men who forbid sex, such as the Pope, who are sick. Sexual health is the one field where the sick (including many doctors) attack the healthy, and often win. – B. McD.]

Priest Likes Authority

[EDITOR's NOTE: A reader in Connecticut lent me this letter, which he received from a priest in Chicago, for anonymous publication.]

Mr.——:
Forgive this intrusion upon your time. It is forward of me to assume you have the time for this letter. I do apologize that I should take up your time. ——— of Canada forwarded unto me your name and address – with the very brief note saying we may have common interests. Since I know nothing else, it is necessary for myself to describe myself & explain. I am 41, 5' 7", 140#, white male in service to others. In the possibility of you even visiting Chicago Illinois may I extend a welcome and beg I may be of service unto you. Since I am a screwed up old fag I do the most excellent service under verbal abuse. Some of the varied tasks I perform, out of the joy of masculine company, are the absolute clean licking of any dirty boot; the service of always being ready to be a urinal or licking ass clean – whether on a trip, at home, etc. On several camp trips my master was so relieved of the bothersome necessity of seeking toilet paper – and during the trip had no need to stop to piss. For one of the visitors, have entertained him with another asshole like myself. After serving him refreshments, the two of us assholes put on an exhibition using belts on one another, like a prize ring. In this case it was determined that I would be the winner, so the prize was the privilege of allowing the visitor to use my mouth as his portable urinal. The loser left out of this pleasure was designated to suck his cock. I am indeed not young or handsome – but my talents are most varied to compensate. I have served as a spittoon, a urinal, boot licker, bathing and combing master, rub downs, exhibiting myself with others, sucking cock when handsome cocksuckers are not available or always ready to bend over for a good screwing or belting. While this does not cover all talents, I hope it may offer an idea. Should you ever visit Chicago – and I may be of some small service – please call upon me.

/s/ Your Humble Bitch.

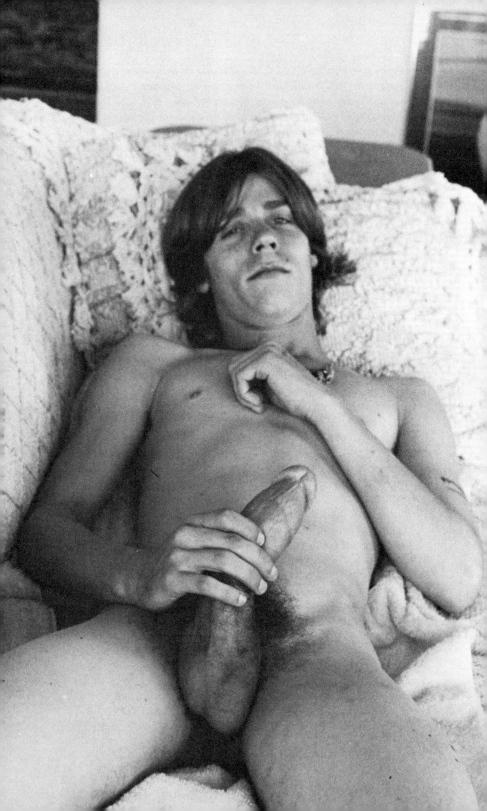

A Professor On The Prowl

I. A DRIPPING DICK IN FLORIDA.

LONDON – Now that Florida has had me, both as performer between the sheets and as exhibitionist (no visitor to my hotel was spared the sight of my semi- and sometimes fully-erect cock and delectably bronzed buns by the pool), I have returned to the sleaze of London. I crave admiration, delight in arousing cock juices, revel in any power I exert over men whether by my asshole perfumes or my perfumed prose. Which is one reason I love America. In both the U.S.A. and West Germany (I wonder how East Germany would respond), men feed my ego wonderfully. In Key West, the epithet which was constantly applied to me was "hot." "Christ, are you *hot*," seemed to be a typical greeting from sundry strangers in bars or on streets. This was not a question though I probably was perspiring freely at the time, my crotch hair and armpits dewey, my crack fully lubricated with sweat.

One bodybuilder, whose courtship (for 12 days) consisted of performing breast-busting feats and thigh-stretching exercises with occasional manly smiles in my direction, finally on day 13 sidled up and humbly enquired, with a gentle hand on my naked crotch which immediately swelled my dong to an impressive fat plum-headed gift for the muscle world, whether he stood a chance. I, who have given out my cock and quim to some of the most mediocre specimens on a middling day and every so often turned gerontophile (not, as you might think, for 25-year-olds but for really geriatric types) in my bid for carnal pleasure, being asked by a photographed, prize-winning beauty with not only white hairless bum mounds (golden-haired crack and tiny but stretchable hole) but a juicy, ever-stiff and often-dripping uncut cock, if he had a chance! He thought I was "beeyoot-iful" and let me know many times but I sucked his cock off twice and pressed my hole into his face even more avidly, the more he piled on the praise. I yearn for your approval, your advice on what scum to send you. Your approval will always evoke my murkiest memoirs for as long as you desire them. And thank you so much for that tight-bunned beauty on your stationery [Jim Lassiter, the A.M.G. model]. What a garden of perfumes in his holes, pits, and crevices.

I am now totally convinced that Conteh [an English boxer] is a shameless exhibitionist: two nude photographs of this beauty in non-gay papers and naughty underwear advertisements and now the story of his public nudity in an American hotel. Now that he has wisely decided to shelve the serious side of boxing, I can hope he will devote himself to whoredom, from which he could make as much cash as he can ever dream of. The shower shot [published in the

English press] is modest enough – no parted buns, but profiled globes and a gentle lather of soap on them to symbolize the sperm of his admirers or perhaps just to indicate that he is cleaning the shit from his shit-hole. The *Daily Mirror* is splendid, I think. Such titillatory subject-matter restores my faith in the gutter press, which has a tendency to try to crawl up to street level from time to time instead of rubbing our noses in sweaty jocks and failed sportsmen's arses.

North Dallas 40 [a 1979 picture now shown on television] confirms all your most mordant criticisms of sportsmen and professional sport in general and since it also features beefy, beat-up, and simply gorgeous Nick Nolte in jockey briefs and pissing in his bath as well as much ass and jock and several studs crapping in open stalls ("No wonder they call this the windy city," one character observes just in case some less imaginative members of the audience could not conjure up the scents of manly evacuations), I stayed late in the cinema scanning every name on the credits but unaccountably yours was omitted. Shame, since your attitudes were so justly celebrated throughout this soft-core porno piece. I now have decided I would probably not like to service an entire football team since they would be quite unsexy, having shoved all their crotch cravings into macho head-bashing during play, but I would dearly love to have Nick Nolte lower his heavy bottom onto my face and stay there till asphyxiation sets in.

The southernmost point of your fair country is a place of great beauty, natural and unnatural, some of the gays being genuinely bee-yoo-tiful, many being whorishly exhibitionistic (shorts pulled so high the balls dangle within sight, the cheeks exposed as far as the crack), and one beauty wearing see-through slacks with no underpants (sheer heaven when the thin seam failed to touch its proper object and left his shit-crack exposed), but there is a wholesomeness that makes the promiscuity somewhat too bucolic for the genuinely sleazy.

I must admit that the New Yorkers, or at least two of them, did their best to bring raunch back into Paradise. I had one nice stand-up suck-off with a NYer (his short, fat-headed dick deep in my throat, my longer, thinner finger right up his hole to shoot-off point) after a mere "hello" to him on the way to my bedroom and another was deeply into sniffing my unshowered armpits, balls, and highly aromatic crack as well as offering some good tasty dripping dick, terrific muscular thighs, buns with a deep sweaty crack, and the most impressively thick and springy pubic bush I've seen in my life. I sometimes shoot an even better load when I see densely hairy crotches and/or male-cunts though the appeal of hairless balls and fannies is far from lost on me.

I will not bore you with my successes as they were usually unkinky and worryingly healthy with protein-rich cream from the cocks of many of your states served up with much groaning and thrashing about but not much ass fun given or taken (fucking, yes, but not much licking and sniffing).

II. ENGINEER SUCKS ASS.

I am so scared of flying that I try not even to lust after the always faggoty stewards even when (as did happen in one case with British Airways) they have been published nude in a gay magazine in case at last my iniquity is punished with aerial disaster. However, I have enjoyed two pilots thoroughly, both British Airways, though I have no loyalty to any particular airline. Both had a convincing masculinity about them and both had delightfully short, unimpressive cocks which I could swallow along with their tight scrotal bags. One had ginger hairs at his crotch, between his thighs, and in between his freckled, white buns, and had a powerful asshole smell which I could inhale from a safe distance while licking his balls. Since then, I always imagine that the underpants of pilots must stick to their sweaty seats and be unbelievably rich in personal odours after, say, an eight-hour Atlantic flight. The airline should run a raffle for the captain's briefs to while away those terrifying or just boring hours and perhaps even I might forget that man is not meant to fly.

I met an American engineer, stationed in London, in my local public lavatory. I was in a playful mood that night and decided to wear no underwear other than a skimpy jock strap and my specially ripped-seated jeans. My sex game for the evening was to make up my mind to offer myself freely to the very first man, be he of whatever age, ugliness or unattractiveness (a screaming queen being the most nightmarish thought), who indicated he wanted me. I was in luck. The guy is about 45, ordinary-looking but surprisingly nice, and a terrific suck and lick artist. When he got me home to my place, he said he was so excited he didn't know where to begin. I told him to take his time and taste everything he wanted for as long as he wanted it. His tongue went deep in my asshole and eventually was coated with my jerked-off sperm. Maddeningly, he doesn't verbalize about my hole. He just sticks his nose or tongue in and proceeds to moan and sob and every so often to raise his head to say I'm incredible or fantastic and have the best ass he's ever got into. Maybe I'll get to the stage of asking him for somewhat more accurate and scientific descriptions and will then report to you.

III. A WIFE 'N' 2 KIDS.

My most devoted admirer once answered a sluttish advertisement of mine. He instantly appealed to me as he wrote that he was not just plain but amazingly ugly, being totally hairless on head and body,

23

and also old (late 50s). I immediately wrote and invited him to feast on my nakedness when he was next in town and kept him supplied with pornographic descriptions of the joys to come and pictorial evidence. He is married and has two kids. Since the first encounters, when he worshipped me by laving my every inch of skin and having me piss all over his Kojak-like face as well as into his mouth, he writes to me at enormous length and claims that he loves me as he has never loved before. I assure him that I have the loyalty of an alley cat, that I guarantee nothing, that I will not be bought, and he showers me with presents, mainly money (200 pounds a visit). Fortunately for him, his visits are about twice a year so I can't retire on the gifts. I frankly enjoy being entertained in a smart restaurant where I know very well the other diners are justifiably suspicious of his amorous gazes and my cool acceptance of same and rightly guess the sordid nature of the liaison, but perversely he loves the same exposure and though I behave with all the sincerity of the average tart he seems to find my frankness about said tartiness strongly appealing. In truth, I like him − a lot − and I am proud that I give him a good time. I even believe he does love me and that he would leave his wife and country for me but I can't see the point of that for either of us. He isn't as ugly as he promised, dammit, and he gives me, naked, a good time fully clothed. He gives me brazen underpants, bottles of whiskey, meals, and money and I give him a damn good exploration of my various juices and bodily fluids.

IV. STUDENT RATS ON TEACHER.

You ask about my boyhood friend who jerked off the kilted soldiers. I am quite sure that he was telling the truth. Why? Because he was very stupid, incapable of inventing a story, and not given to boasting, just to matter-of-fact descriptions of any sex he got. Any story that could be checked out did tally, as I would sometimes ask a school-pal who was claimed to have been interfered with by him and they would become pink and ashamed enough to suggest that there was no fantasizing. He pulled out his fat cock with me one night and tried to get into my pants, but I was in my prudish 15-year-old phase and fought the predator off, whereupon he gave out the word that, contrary to his expectations, I wasn't queer. He was a strange guy, not attractive (to me, that is), and almost mentally deficient (this being accompanied by such honesty and generosity that people liked him even if they feared his frankness), but he turned out to be very talented in music, and to classical music he became almost as devoted as to whoring. Eventually he became a music teacher. As he also adored young boys with the passion that he had once lavished on kilted rough trade, he used his pedagogic position to promote his pederasty. He wrote to me that he had formed "a lovely little choir." Anyhow, one day a relation told me that he had had to give up teaching because he had had a nervous breakdown and was now living at home again. When I went to see him, he was very far from mental ill-health. The true story was that one member of the little choir who played with their impressive prongs nightly after school hours and who surrendered their sweet fannies and little playthings to his hands, mouth, and prick, told his parents. This sounds like the kind of idiocy that only a true queer could have perpetrated, an act worthy of me in my disgustingly hypocritical youth. The headmaster promised there would be no legal proceedings if he resigned and guaranteed that he would never teach again. As far as I know, he takes only private music pupils now and many of them have dropped their pants for him.

V. "HE ASKED ME TO TASTE IT."

My first seducer: the first really queer seducer who got all my parts working properly was about 30, short, dark, handsome, Italian by birth, disconcertingly like Perry Como (who could have me even now any time he raised a finger to attract my attention). I came up to visit him with the guy I described in the last paragraph (he was then a music student) and his lover. I must have known I was being set up for total ruin but chose to pretend I didn't notice this. He seduced me slowly but thoroughly. The first evening, he showed me albums of naked boys and men, photographed and mounted (in several senses, no doubt) by himself. His eyes rested on my crotch throughout my inspection. When he showed me soft-porn magazines, I was delirious with delight and could scarcely conceal my trembling. He told me to come back alone next night.

This time his white jeans seemed even tighter over his delectable buttocks. When he had got me hard in my pants with more magazines, he kissed the back of my neck. I loved the sensation but retreated from him. He tried to get his mouth over mine but I kept removing it but raised no resistance to his kisses on my eyes and ears and neck and nose.

"Oh, darling, I love you – rape me, my dearest," my thoughts said, but I was like a frigid bitch in his arms. He walked me home and in a park in the dark started kissing me again. He forced his tongue into my mouth and I longed to suck it and drink his saliva but I fought it. I was in ecstasy to feel his breath and tongue and teeth and lips, but raced home protecting my already over-rated virginity. A night of masturbation, of longing, of terror that I wouldn't see his bare arse or taste his tongue again, let alone his tool.

Next day, I wrote to him, for some reason using the third person of myself and indicating that this character had made a mistake to be so modest and retiring. He wrote back with an invitation for that night (of the morning when I received the letter).

When I got there, he planted his mouth on mine. He laved my tongue with his, sucked on it, put his tongue to the back of my throat. I began to prod my own tongue into his mouth and ran it along his teeth, under his tongue. He stripped me naked and told me how lovely I was (I don't think I was then, but I was chicken still – just). When he invited me to strip him, I nearly fainted. At last my first willing stiff cock, all for me. I had never sucked before and when he asked me to taste it, I started licking the head but then started gobbling the lot and working like a real cocksucker. When he parted his thighs and told me to lick his balls, I got one of my biggest thrills because while I worked on his scrotum I could get such a clear view of his arse. I just never guessed that a queer could get so close to another's arse with his *face* – to have my nose and mouth and eyes only inches from his slit seemed unbelievable. Imagine my surprise and joy when he not only sucked on my nipples and prick and balls but got me to raise my bum in the air. "What for?" I sweetly enquired, terrified even now of rape. "Close your eyes and you'll find out," he insisted. A pause, then hot breath on my inner sanctum and then the supreme thrill – a tongue in the very centre of my arsehole. I went wild. Then it occurred to me: if an older queer is allowed to lick a bottom (a thought that truly had never presented itself even to my filthy imagination), perhaps a younger queer gets to lick the other man's bottom. The idea was so wild, so perverse, I nearly had a heart attack asking if I could do the same to him. He squatted into the divine position – ass up and parted. My first sight of the promised land, all hair and hole. I kissed the cheeks and rubbed my face against them. I looked into the canyon and was pleased to find it was clean and deodorized. I shut my eyes, stuck out my tongue and moved slowly forward. When my tongue hit fur, I licked and tongued like one possessed, as indeed I was.

I did far more work on his hole, nipples, armpits, and balls, even if I never swallowed his cum as he did mine or fucked his hole as he did mine, than I received. So good was I at rimming and sucking that he decided I had had lots of experience and was a fraudulent virgin. It may have been that or just because he was fucking tired of my tongue and naivete that he quite smartly dropped me after a week of ensuring I was actively as well as mentally homo. He got quite a kick out of telling me about the latest virgin he was instructing, much younger and therefore much better; he told me he was a better lay in any case and that I'd better find somebody else to play with as he liked variety. Every so often after that, if he had nothing around to screw, he would ring me up and ask me over. I would run there and do whatever he wanted, and when it was over he would drop me for another few months. He also did quite a few nasty things (which bordered on being nice) like once quite loudly farting after a session. This caused me some chagrin as I had been so deep in his hole with my tongue. "What do you expect with all that spit up there?" he coolly enquired. "I'm sure you fart when you get home, don't you?" I was stunned to think that a man would even imagine that I farted, let alone accuse me of such anti-social behaviour. I think he had a good time taking me off my high horse and I fucking well had it coming.

VI. SPYING IN THE TOILET

July was spectacular enough to merit several letters but I'll pick on highlights. JUNE 30TH, FOLKSTONE-BOULOGNE CAR FERRY: when bored by the prospect of yet another Channel crossing, try the men's shit-house. You might be lucky as I was and find one cubicle with tactful little holes bored into it on either side. The voyeur's role therein is tough, since you have to look for your opportunities carefully and since small holes may not show you the precise portion of the anatomy which you most yearn to see, and yet the whole business of spying on a man or youth while he drops his pants to shit is intensely pleasurable. Victim No. 1 turned out to be a young, rather repressed-looking Scot (part of the fun was in later walking around the ship to attach faces and ages to bare thighs and fannies). I concentrated on his bare white thighs while he shat but he was one of the few who stood up to wipe his crack. When he did, his old-fashioned shirt-tail stood out at a wide angle from his virginal-smooth buttocks and I salivated as I looked up his thighs to see neat fuckglobes as he busily wiped himself clean.

The second show was given by a French teenager. In this case, I concentrated on his face as he relieved himself. The tautening of his facial muscles, the grimaces and then the relaxation of his eyes and mouth indicated the stages of the shitting process. When he stood up, there was a kaleidoscope of flesh and white-paper and shirt colours but for one brief moment he stood still with his firm arse framed perfectly.

Possibly the most thrilling moment of my voyeurism was a uniformed gentleman in his mid 30s – a bit of rough trade, tattooed, charmingly nonchalant about appearance and personal privacy; he roughly pulled down the navy-blue trousers, yanked his canary-yellow briefs to ankle level, and squatted. His calves were bulging with power and his thighs were meaty. His cheeks were squashed against the seat, bulging outwards under the weight of his trunk. The legs were hairless and very muscular, the ass impressive (though I didn't get a full view of it). His farts were like cannon fire, loud explosions, three in number, well spaced out, his turds large and noisy as befitted this bit of beefcake. Seeing him later serving in the duty-free shop meant another trip to the same toilet to find relief with my hand.

VII. "HIS GREASY TWAT."

JULY 1ST-10TH, ST. TROPEZ: Take a walk along the immense beach, as I did on my first day, and you can sate (temporarily) your curiosity about "straight" cock and arse. Many men were parading their pricks and butt meat in total nudity, many were caressing their girlfriends, their thighs pulled up somewhat to hide their troublesome hard ons but their arseholes in danger of exposure thereby, and some just sat looking at the parade of cunt and cock with their own splendid truncheons hanging between spread thighs. I made a great point of checking out all the so-advertised hetero meat, of turning round to inspect the buns of any large-cocked male sauntering past, to let them know how exciting I found their cocks and fannies. Their blatant exhibitionism is all the more interesting since full nudity is forbidden and some gendarmes stride up and down the beach fining offenders each day of summer. I can't see why the cops don't just wear their cute hats and a large gun over their bushy prongs, nothing at all over their law-enforcing fannies.

When I got to my bit of beach, the professedly gay area, I stripped to the buff and lay back exposing my charms to some avid voyeurs.

Among my sexual adventures arising from the beach eye-cruising were:

GILBERT: 42 years old, bodybuilder and clothes-shop owner, with whom I went into the bushes behind the beach. He was very excited. He kissed me while pulling his bathing trunks down. He was big, uncut, with a very slimy, spunky cock-head, the goo oozing into his still rolled-up foreskin. He sucked me well but I wanted that heady brew in my mouth. I got to my knees, pulled the trunks all the way to his ankles, and rammed his prick all the way to the back of my throat, my hands clasping his bottom and fingering his hot hole, and occasionally playing with the hairy ball-bag. He shot off again and again and again, his legs convulsed, his belly heaving, his breath snorting. Even when I let his fuck-stick go, cream was still collecting at the head for my tongue to savour. He entertained me to an expensive meal twice thereafter so I must have done something right.

GEARY: American though looked totally German, with blond hair, blue eyes, golden body, surprisingly hairy ears, from Hollywood, about 26, in clothes design. Affectionate and good company, having a fairly sharp eye for the pseuds on the beach and a good grasp of what is fun in bed. Sucked well and was sucked well, I believe, but such bitter spunk. Never tasted a more acid brew, which is sad as he is quite a dish.

EGON: *Really* German, sportsman with mighty thighs and calves and breast. About 28, from Dusseldorf, choosy about his sex partners, he convinced me, by having sex only with me during his two weeks. Huge cock, really impressive, which I had difficulty in swallowing without biting, and a hairy rump which responded to licking. He also licked arse well (the other two were cock-crazy but didn't get into bottom fun)....I persuaded him to fire two loads into my greedy throat, while I fingered his twitching and unfucked hole.

NIKOLAS: Argentine, of Greek parentage, 27, dark moustache, well-defined body, smooth white arse cheeks. To get him into bed, I had to agree to have his lover as well, a Frenchman slightly older and certainly bigger in body, Jean-Claude, with smooth body, mountainous bottom, big cock. Nikolas proved a most able lover, diving into my parted fanny as soon as I started sucking on his pal's cock and begging me to fuck them both. Nikolas had to climb off my erection eventually as his hole couldn't quite accommodate it (surprising, since his lover was fairly big but with a smaller cock-head), and urged me to fuck Jean-Claude. I looked between the smooth large buttocks at the hairless light-brown fuck-hole, fingered it a little and then used KY to slip up the hot channel. I shagged him until I was becoming bored and withdrew from his greasy twat, to find that I had a small deposit of French shit on my tool. Much as I love to see some attractive number dropping his shit down a lavatory, I don't appreciate contact with the stuff and felt relieved when Nikolas cleaned me up. The Argentine then pushed up the vacated fanny-hole and got a good hard rhythm going. I concentrated on licking his bottom for him and when he was coming up the French rectum I felt him jam his hole against my tongue for maximum pleasure. Jean-Claude's own spunk splattered over my pubic hair and thighs. Once the latter gentleman was sleeping off the fuck, Nikolas began climbing onto my erection again. He bravely squatted down on it while facing me, knees up against his chest, ass gamely sliding up and down my prong. His face looked remarkably similar to the French teenage shitter on the Channel, pain and pleasure fleeting across it. I managed to suck his fat dripping prick while he fucked himself and got a glorious mouthful as reward for my work on him.

VIII. ASS-LICKING ON THE BEACH.

11TH-16TH JULY, VENICE: The place for boys of easy virtue who fuck for love rather than profit is the Lido to the right of the public beach as you face the sea. Their love is for themsleves and their splendid bodies but what worthier love object could you expect them to have? A Venetian will go with you to show you how good he is, to receive your praise for his body and technique. I satisfy their vanity by sincerely praising them and worshipping their charms.

Thus, I had a lovely piece one afternoon. I had been admiring his built body, the sheer power of biceps and chest and ass and thighs, the length and girth of his dick. The fact that I had sucked off a large-cocked Italian youth in his sight worried me in case he thought I was too whorish to deserve the gift of his spunk but I needn't have worried. He followed me into the pine forest, the big cruising ground, and then I obediently followed his rolling buttocks, so taut beneath the bikini trunks, as he picked his own spot. He stripped bare and I found he sucked excellently and kissed beautifully, his tongue which tasted of stale tobacco and dryness of summer driving me berserk. I gobbled his fat dong and licked his balls and thighs till he let the gusher of spunk flow into my enraptured mouth. When he had softened, I released him and he allowed me to get my own rocks off by fondling my balls and nipples as I wanked. I went behind him, gently pushed him forward while I knelt to examine his hole. He made no resistance as I pried the globes apart and beheld a bright pink well-cleaned shit-hole. I stuck my tongue up him, kissing his fanny lips tenderly till my balls tightened and I had to stand up unsteadily to fire spunk onto the earth. This charming pastoral scene was completed when he came to me with a large bunch of leaves for me to use to wipe my dripping dong, holding them out in his large labouring hands like Adam in the Garden.

Next day, I received my own worship. I was standing naked putting suntan cream on my back when a stubbly-faced short but cute Italian of roughly 40-45 came up offering to help. He smoothed the cream into my back and continued to caress my buttocks. He then knelt down and began to kiss my hole. An older man had caught sight of the ritual and stood transfixed. He came closer as I spread myself on my towel and allowed the first Italian to explore my bottom with tongue and nose. When the voyeur was right upon us, my explorer moved back a little to show off my charms to the other, holding my cheeks apart to show the hole. "Che bello!" the older man breathed. "Che culo!" and he pulled his prick out to show his enthusiasm. One showered me with admiring kisses as the other sucked hole and cock. The older man standing back a few feet to watch the activities suddenly cried out and jets of milk flew from his prick, poured out. The other man then shot all over my back and rubbed it in with the suntan cream. His next request was that he should photograph me. I gladly assented and now an entire film of my cock and arse is somewhere in Italy being enjoyed, I trust.

After that little episode, I dozed off and awoke to find a rather grubby gentleman of no great age but a rather unpromising body and visage close to me gazing at my butt. He had a sun hat on, wore filthy jeans, had a sagging belly and overlarge breasts, had band-aids on his face where he had been attacked in Sardinia in a camping site, he told me. I was ready to do my grande-dame performance and ignore him till he went but little knew the mistake I would have made. He inched forward and began running his fingers tenderly over my slit. I liked the feeling and allowed him more liberties, till he had sprawled over the sand between my thighs and had his face lost in my bottom. His tongue was wonderfully sinuous, creeping farther up my fanny-lips than I had ever felt. I began to raise my bottom wantonly, uncaring if anybody saw us at play, longing for deeper and deeper tonguing. I then squatted down in a shitting position and he clambered under my bottom to penetrate me still further with his devoted face and tongue till I dared take no more risks as people with whom I work in London were on the beach and even I was afraid of seeming too bizarre if they came upon my anal worshipper burried in my very willing buns.

IX. A SNEERING YOUTH.

22ND-23RD JULY, PARIS: I stayed in a jeweller's flat, but he was in Cannes at the time. However, he took a plane up to spend one hour with me in his bed and caught the next plane back to Cannes. I hope the suck-off and rim I gave him made the trip worthwhile. In the afternoon I went to the notorious Club Continental near the Opera. Though I had excellent sex with yet another Argentine and yet again ended up bringing a bit of novelty to the bed of himself and his French lover that night, I found these baths, though splendidly appointed, fairly dreary. Much ego-tripping, including one well-built youth who got his rocks off by sitting in a cubicle with the door open jerking off his impressive tool and sneering at anybody who approached him there. I watched him do his little number with five separate men and did find it a dismal little performance, as I did all the tentative sucking and groping in the steam. However, my Argentine was a real find. He kissed arsehole divinely and sucked nipples and cock like a dream.

Back in Scotland, I found the local cottage, to use the British term for men's room, surprisingly active two afternoons ago and shall make a point of returning before I leave this town. Three stiff pricks seeking pleasure in one hour is not bad for a tiny seaside place of about 15,000 population, even if some of the cock is presumably imported.

I saw little of Wimbledon but remain enamoured of McEnroe, who looks as if he would have dirty underwear and a fairly cheesy cock. I would be delighted to service him and the other unclean-imaged tennis star, Jimmy Connors. I've never appreciated the sex appeal of Bjorn Borg, particularly in comparison with my own gorgeous Swede resident in London, whose magnificent mountainous white buttocks, thick but fine blond hair, strapping frame and lengthy, slightly smelly dick make him a homosexual dream come true.

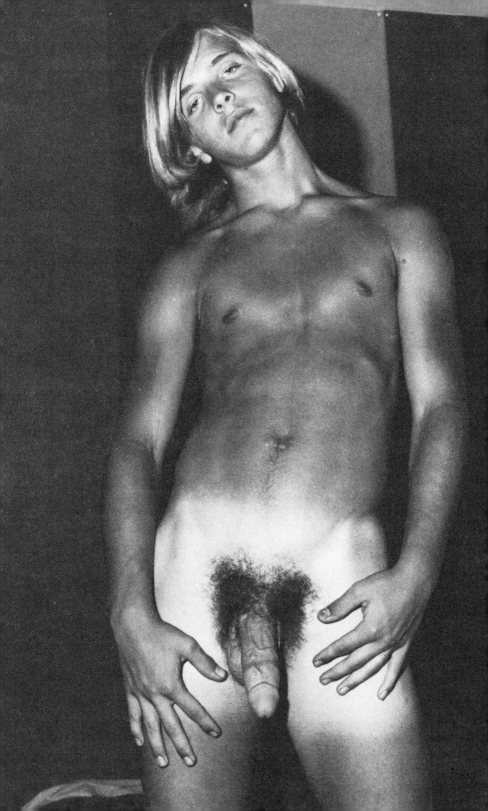

"You Little Shit, Why Did You Stop"

MISSOURI – When I was 13 or 14 years old, I walked into the attic room I share with two brothers and saw my brother Budd lying on his bed, his shirt open & his jeans & underpants down around his ankles, playing with his big hard cock. I froze on the spot & couldn't take my eyes off Budd, or more specifically, I couldn't take my eyes off his big pink cock. Budd said I could come over and feel of it if I liked. It felt silky and spongy hard. He put his hands in my hair and pushed me closer. The smell was terrific. Budd said, "Suck it, suck it" and tried to push my head down, but I pulled away and moved back. Budd said, "Come on & suck it; you know you want to." He said the way I looked at it he knew at once I was a natural born cocksucker. Now I knew that word "cocksucker" was an epithet of contempt and derision & so I started to leave. Budd must have realized that he was using the wrong approach, because he changed his tactics by asking me if I liked him, and when I said "Yes" he said it would make him very happy if I would give his cock a big kiss. After a few minutes more of persuasive talk from Budd, I decided to make Budd happy & give his cock a big kiss. I kissed the big pink spongy head & again Budd tried to push my head down on it. He said that wasn't much of a kiss, do it again. And to tell the truth I wanted more, too, although I really didn't quite know what I wanted to do. Budd reached over & felt of my own cock which was quite hard & told me that my getting a hard on meant that I liked what we were doing. Budd played with my cock a little while & I was filled with boy lust. I felt feverish all over. Budd told me to lick his knob and I did, flicking my tongue over the big smelly head. Then he fed me more of his cock and I didn't object anymore. I liked it. I would gasp and choke and he would say "take it easy" & soon I had my head bobbing up and down on most of his six-incher. I managed to keep this up for a few minutes steadily and he cried "Keep that up, I'm gonna come!" At his words, I quickly took my mouth off his cock and moved away. Budd said, "You little shit, why did you stop, it was just getting good." I said I didn't want him to come in my mouth. He carefully explained that swallowing cum would make me grow hair on my chest and around my cock and balls. He said that at school I was known as a sissy (this was true) and that cum would make me grow into a he-man. Of course I wanted to grow hair on my chest & around my cock and balls, and of course I wanted to be a he-man. So I happily went down on Budd again. Budd had cooled off some and was no longer ready to cum, so I had to start all over, but this time I had a real incentive to suck, and I soon developed a rhythm and bobbed my head up & down with a minimum of choking. When Budd came, there was so much of it &

it spurted so fast, I thought I would really choke, but I took a big swallow, recovered, went all the way down and didn't waste a drop of the slimy stuff that was going to make me a hairy he-man. After the first time I have never been able to get enough. And I did develop into a hairy brawny he-man (wife and kids, for example, and a hitch in the Army) who is also a hairy brawny cocksucker.

Ethel Smith Wore Wedgies

[The following review ran first in The New York Native.*]*

The Gay Engagement Calendar 1984
by Martin Greif

Each year, Martin Greif is able to add to his gay engagement calendar comments about, and photographs of, famous men and women who "came out" or were pulled out of the closet during the previous year. He also has a mammoth roster of historic sex hounds – kings, warriors, popes and so on – to rotate, so that his calendars each year seem as fresh as a new pack of Trojan-Enz.

His comments and illustrations are gorgeous and there is a little space left each day to jot down memoranda, be they trivial (Sunday night at the 54) or vital (get tuna at the A & P). His subjects similarly range from the ordinary (James I, Paul II, H. Jones Baker III, Murad IV, Gustavus V, Edward VIII) to the legendary – he reveals, for instance, that Ethel Smith, the 1940s organist (*Tico Tico Ti, Tico Tico Ta*), wore wedgies, and that the nude picture Sylvester Stallone made was Jerry Douglas's *Score* (1970). I haven't seen it but it can't contain any physical parts more offensive than his drooping eyelids.

Among numerous newcomers this time are, surprisingly, and most welcome, Bobby Morse, star of *How to Succeed in Business without Really Trying* (1967), to whose irresistible smile Greif pays a graceful tribute, and, not surprisingly, Tony Perkins, star of *Psycho* (1960) and *Psycho II* (1983). Presently overplaying the role of heterosexual, Perkins has appeared as an anti-porn crusader in Times Square, where I used to see him strolling more tolerantly, and he told *People* in 1983 that what he modestly summarized as some homosexual experiences were unsatisfactory (thus insulting, in a single sentence, thousands of men). Possibly by coincidence, Perkins's transfer of his desire from men to women came when, after a decade of learning in therapy how to have natural sex, as opposed to his unnatural homosexual acts, there was not much call for his age group among men who like youth and beauty. It was but natural at this age that Perkins should be more popular amongst women, who are trained from infancy to feel that only they, not men, must be attractive, and that they should learn to value a man's other qualities, such as his money and publicity. (In fairness to men, I should add that many of us are as appreciative of a man's fame and fortune as are women.)

Not long before his death, George Cukor, the director, put another newcomer up for the club: Clark Gable, who, Cukor said, used to be a gay whore (Cukor of course did not use so technical a term). Gable appears to have his own teeth in the early photograph Greif uses; later when, like everyone else in Bev Hills, he had false teeth, he could have been even more skilled at his original occupation, but by then he was far too rich to justify homosexuality on grounds of economic necessity.

Nancy Reagan's appearance in the book gave me a nasty start at first; I had assumed she lacked the sensitivity to be a lesbian. But upon reading her entry I find that Greif does not claim she is; he includes her merely to commemorate her remark about homosexuality. She's a *haaaaaaaard* woman.

My dear if David Bowie, the rock and movie star, is as straight as he claims, why, in the photograph Greif uses, is he wearing knee pads in his long underwear? Knee pads are worn only by a tiny élite of homosexuals who have an advanced obsession.

Unhappily, a *Playgirl* photograph of Fabian which, Greif writes, "indicates that his member in repose is far, far longer than his name," is not reproduced here. Nor are any other nude photographs. This isn't that kind of book. It's an ideal gift book, racy only in the text. It seems authoritative, but the arithmetic doesn't work out well for Greif's rumor that Cleopatra sucked off a hundred Roman soldiers in a single night. Fifty I can see, but a *hundred?*

Next year, if he wants to, Greif can add, among others, Tolstoy, whose "homosexual affair" was publicized in 1983, and, if any of them die, the movie stars whose initials appear in the 1984 calendar. Greif says, "you and I and they know they're gay." They are C.G., R.S., R.H., T.T., C.R., J.N., W.B., F.G., C.C., R.T., G.H., V.J., G.K., B.L., R.D. and H.H. What about P.N. and all the rest?

Greif is human, hot hilarious and liberated – not from sex, like the common ordinary gay liberationists, but from their quest for mass respectability. He has a bigger gay roster in print, a best seller in fact (*The Gay Book of Days*), and it would be useful if he would combine all the people he has the goods on into one big gay who's who. His roster includes many people, dead and alive, who demonstrate the brains, balls, humor, artistry and valor of homosexuality through history and up to today, when it is finally conventional heterosexuals who have become a beleaguered, boastful and belligerent minority. – B. McD.

"He Trembles When He Sees A Stiff Cock, and I Like That"

MASSACHUSETTS – Some years ago I met a guy who said he was a cab driver. He was solidly (though not particularly muscularly) built, had dark hair and eyes and an intensely animal approach to sex. All that I like, and we ended up in bed every time we met. The fact that, as he later admitted, he really was a schoolteacher instead of a cabbie didn't change that. Anyway it developed that, like me, he had a real thing about Vaseline. We'd begun by rubbing it on each other's cocks. From there it would get on our legs and bellies and everywhere else and we'd keep adding more and more to our cocks. In our sessions we'd go through a whole large jar and the sheets would take two or three washings to get it all out. But it sure was worth it. Actually I think half-dressed sex is a lot more obscene than naked sex. And baggy clothes turn me on a lot more than tight ones. I have a ratty old pair of coveralls that I bought at the Salvation Army. Some day I want to wear them to a porno movie house – just the coveralls, a leather jacket, a pair of socks and boots. Nothing underneath. They have a button fly and when I get a hard on it works its way through the front. The coveralls also have openings at the side, so anyone can reach in and jerk you off easily. But most of all I love corduroys – the baggier the better. I have one old, heavy, dark-brown pair that really make me feel raunchy when I wear them. I've pissed in them because I figure if other guys like the smell of piss as much as I do it will turn them on. I've also cut a hole in the crotch so that I can be fucked without taking them off. The hole is far enough down that it doesn't show when I walk, and I can wear them on the street. The only time I tried to use this sartorial glory hole, however, it was a failure. I was on an unused dock down near Christopher Street in New York. At the time it was a very popular fucking spot. I made my way from one dark corner to the next and eventually ended up in an alcove in which you couldn't see a damn thing except faint silhouettes when anyone went by its entry. There was a guy in a leather jacket already in there and we started fucking around. After awhile he asked me whether I had ever pissed in anybody's mouth. I said no. He asked would I piss in his. I said it would be difficult with my hard on but I'd try. Finally I was successful, although I didn't have a lot of piss to give him. The guy, it turned out, was with a buddy, and pretty soon he was feeling me up from behind while the first guy was sucking me from the front. As soon as the second guy discovered the hole he knew what was up. He tried to fuck me through it but he just couldn't get everything lined up right and finally pulled my pants down. Now I'm not used to getting fucked and don't like pain, so fucking me takes a little doing. I started to lose my hard on and the first guy, noticing it, said, "He's no man!" and pulled his buddy's hand around so he could see what he meant. That apparently only made his buddy want to fuck me more – and I was determined that I would be fucked, pain or no. In fact the idea of being raped by a couple of leather queens kind of turned me on at that moment. Well, I did get fucked, and I enjoyed it. But I didn't get it through the hole in my corduroys and I didn't get my hard on back. I avoid programmed sex, and prefer to go with the impulse of the moment. Recently I got in touch with a blind date and we had a scene all set up. I kept getting a hard on in anticipation for days before we met. But there were a couple of flaws in our plans: we both like guys who are bigger than we are (which is tougher to find for me; he had a slight build, while I'm 6'1" and 170 pounds), and we both like dominant-type guys. We met, kissed and sucked; I liked it but I lost my hard on. He eventually jacked off. Then we took a shower and rested for awhile. I got feeling very affectionate toward him, which hadn't of course been planned. Finally I picked him up (not difficult) and carried him into the bedroom and deposited him on the bed and sucked him off. It was great. He had a sleek cock just the right size for sucking – I can get the whole thing into my mouth with no sweat. And with that slim body I felt like I was sucking off a kid. I really liked it – and afterward he said that although it wasn't what he usually likes he really enjoyed it too. But that part certainly wasn't anything like the sort of sex we'd planned, yet it was the best part for both of us. There's a moral there somewhere. I was jerking off in a booth of my favorite public john today. This particular booth has two peepholes: one looks down the row of urinals and the other is at the groin level of the guy on the toilet next door. There was nobody next door. You have to be careful in this booth now because the door is missing. An elderly guy with a big paunch that I've seen a number of times there came and started to watch me. He trembles a little when he sees a stiff cock, and I like that. Then somebody came in from outside and the guy retreated to the urinals and I got a good view of him playing with his meat. The other guy circled around and lit in the booth next to me. Soon he had his cock out and was whacking away at it. I could see a fair-sized cock, some rather wiry arm muscles, a tattoo and a pair of pointed shoes, but not much else. The old guy came back and started feeling himself up as he watched me whacking and peeping. Then the guy in the next booth knelt down but he neither stuck his cock under the partition for me to suck nor reached under to get a feel of mine when I knelt down. This buffaloed me for a moment. What the fuck did he want? When nothing came of our kneelings we both got back on the seats and whacked and peeked some more. Then it hit me – maybe he wanted a finger up his ass. Next time out I tried it but he kept his ass up against the toilet seat so I couldn't get at it. But he did give a good feel of his balls and the root of his cock. Apparently that was all he wanted. I kept on fondling for awhile as the old guy looked on, but then somebody else came in and we both got back on our seats and the old guy went to the urinal. When I looked through the peep hole he was waving his cock again and when I looked through the other peep hole the guy I had been working on was wiping off his cock head. Eventually a donkey-dicked (I know because I saw him furiously waving his meat at the urinal from time to time) friend of the old guy came in. They cramped each other's style and my Dirty Old Man left. Hell. I sat there playing with my meat and fantasizing about him. He was dressed in red permanent-press pants, a baggy tan suit jacket and a loud tie off a bargain rack. Now that doesn't turn me on at all. I wished that he had been dressed in old, baggy corduroys. That would really make him look like an obscene old lecher. I wondered if he had someplace to go and imagined a small room over a shop on the main street where he would take me to look at his collection of dirty pictures of small boys doing nasty things to each other. I'd look and start getting a hard on. His eyes would be riveted on my jeans and as my cock started to push against my pants his hand would go to his own groin and start playing around. Then he would reach over and open my fly, his hand trembling as he did so, and smile that funny little lecherous smile I've seen on his face in the can a number of times...

The Joy of Heterosexuality: I

The family that vomits together, stays together, is the heart-warming message of a *People* article. Starting in 1979, Randy Moffitt, a pitcher for the Toronto Blue Jays, "constantly felt weak and nauseated...It got worse. The nausea turned into frequent bouts of vomiting." When a doctor told him he had no physical disease and it was all in his mind, Randy grabbed him by the necktie and diagnosed him as "full of shit." When Randy's wife was pregnant, she says "it got to the point where it seemed like *he* had morning sickness. I'd be in the bathroom gagging and he'd come in right behind me and throw up." (The Moffitts evidently had only one bathroom, not a good idea in a two-vomiter family.) But finally doctors discovered that Randy did, after all, have a disease: cryptosporidia enteritis, an intestinal parasite usually found in animals but rarely in people and thus, rarely in *People*. A horse lover, Randy believes he may have picked it up from a horse. But "the parasite...vanished as mysteriously as it appeared," and after a long period of being what his wife called "real grumpy and snappy at everything," the Moffitts are now back in each other's arms. Pam says, "I hold him sometimes and say, 'It's nice to have you back.' And he says, 'It's nice to be back.'" Sounds nice.

"That's A Fine Young Peter You've Got There, My Boy. Will You Let Uncle George Kiss It?"

SAN FRANCISCO — This is just a friendly letter to say hello and shoot the shit. I've lately discovered a newish publication which appears to be a further manifestation of the kind of thing you pioneered with S.T.H.: *First Hand*. I first saw a copy during a recent trip to New Orleans. Browsing through a small bookshop on the fringes of the French Quarter, I spotted it in the section at the back. As soon as I flipped through a few pages, I knew it was for me. I took it back to my hotel room and had myself a glorious time jacking off to a couple of stories. As good as much of *First Hand* is, nothing will ever take the honored place of S.T.H. I was overjoyed when one of my favorite bookstores in San Francisco first stocked copies of those Gay Sunshine Press anthologies of S.T.H.: *Flesh, Meat* and *Sex*. It's by no means a porny shop, but offers a wide array of "straight" material. And there, for the average browser to examine, were anthologies of your matchless work.

I first arrived in San Francisco in 1960. At that time there was nothing remotely resembling the present gay scene here. In less than 20 years, there's been a full-scale revolution. I was downright shocked the first time I went into a bookstore and beheld a magazine showing on its cover a hot-looking guy with a hard cock in his mouth. During the early years of that revolution, I went to my first male porny movie, at the Nob Hill Cinema. I'll never forget the moment when I entered that dark theater. Up on the screen, a gorgeous young stud was jacking off. I sat down and watched a long series of movies in which every possible homosexual act was displayed. Somewhere during that amazing show, a man sat down next to me and he soon proceeded to begin fondling the bulge in my pants, unzip my fly, bring out my cock and suck me off, while my eyes remained fixed on the screen. When it was over and he'd fondly licked and slurped my cock for a long while, he sat up and said, "Thanks. That was great." He got up and disappeared into the darkness. By now, of course, shit, when I can find both S.T.H. and *First Hand* in an ordinary bookshop, we've come a long way baby.

I was born in 1931, the youngest of three kids. I grew up in a solidly middle class atmosphere. My brother was six years older than I. He was athletic and handsome, with a swimmer's body, olive complexion, black hair, strong features. I used to watch him laying back on his twin bed across our room and stroking his uncut cock. It seemed enormous to my kid eyes and I was fascinated to see him fondle and stroke it. Watching him handle himself in that way filled me with wonder and admiration and my little cock grew almost painfully hard. I was uncut too and the tender head of my cock was so sensitive that it hurt like hell to slide the foreskin back and touch it. While I was still hairless down there, he sported an impressive bush of wiry pubic hair that made me yearn to have a patch of my own. The first time I saw my brother come, I watched him do what struck me as a most curious thing. He gathered the flesh of his foreskin in a pinch and it swelled up as his cream gushed into it. Then, still holding that strange-looking bulb, he got up and went into the john. He stood at the toilet and let go his grip and out fell large gobs of odd-looking pearly stuff. I asked him what that was and he told me, "It's my jizz." I hadn't the foggiest idea what jizz was and I asked him where it came from. He said it was made in his balls and that I'd be having some jizz of my own in a few years. He was about 14 at the time, and I was eight. From that day forward, I had an overpowering fascination with cocks and balls and jizz. I can't remember how many times I watched him jack off but it was almost a daily ritual. Once, as I was standing near his bed, taking in the horny scene, he told me to take mine out and show it to him. I was a bit bashful about that, since mine wasn't nearly as big as his. But I did as he said and he reached out and gave it a squeeze that almost made me faint. I wanted very much to touch his and asked if it was O.K. He said sure. That first touch was enslaving. He and I never shared more than that. He made me promise that I'd never tell anyone what I'd seen him do.

You've already published the story of the first time I got my cock sucked, by a painter who gave me a lift in his Model-A pickup. There was an old man who lived down at the end of our road, whom everybody knew as Uncle George. He drove a big white car and was always giving people rides. One afternoon he gave me a ride from our small village, where I'd been working at a grocery store, and he invited me to his house for a glass of cider. Fine with me. There were elaborately framed paintings on the walls, lamps with long fringes, an elegant clock on the mantlepiece and a large Atwater Kent radio that looked like the door of a cathedral. Uncle George brought me some cider and began asking me various questions about my family, school, the weather, etc. After awhile I had to piss and asked him where the bathroom was. He pointed down a hallway. As soon as my stream began sloshing into the toilet, I got the shock of my life. Uncle George was standing right behind me and he reached down and took hold of my cock, even as I was pissing. The flow stopped instantly and I was fully hard in only a few seconds. He chuckled. "That's a fine young peter you've got there, my boy. Will you let Uncle George kiss it?" I could only gasp and tremble. He lowered the lid of the toilet, sat down and quickly began giving me the second blow job of my life. At that age, I had a hair-trigger dick and in less than a minute my balls were pulling up tight and I shot my load of cream into Uncle George's hot mouth, nearly swooning with pleasure. For several years after that, I got regular blow jobs from Uncle George. It was always the same: he'd smilingly stop to offer me a ride and we'd have a glass of cider or root beer and he'd ask: "And how's that nice peter of yours today?" I'd tell him if was just fine, thanks, and whip it out for him to feast on. Once he told me, "I'll give you ten dollars if you'll do a big favor for me." That was a lot of money and I asked what he wanted me to do. "I want you to hold my peter and make me go." He sat back on the sofa and hauled his cock out. I was expecting it to be as aged and wrinkled as his face was and was surprised to see that he had a very impressive and strong-looking cock. It was cut and it was about 7" long. He handed me a tin box of Sweet Pea Talc and asked me to powder my hand with it. Then he spread his legs and I took hold of his throbber and began stroking it. He began to breathe rapidly, taking short gasps of air, and he spoke George! You're such a good boy! Oh, sakes alive! Such a good boy!" He seemed to be on the brink of a heart attack, so tense and rigid he became, and with a gigantic groan, he began shooting his load of cream. It didn't come spurting out but rather in slow, watery gushes which ran over my hand. He stayed in that rictus of ecstasy for a long time, still repeating: "Such a good boy! Such a good boy!" I got a towel from the bathroom and he wiped himself clean. He gave me the ten dollars and thanked me warmly for being "such a good boy." I had another hard on and asked him if he'd please suck me again, and he genially complied, right there in the front hallway.

As I grew up, I had a number of regular jack off buddies, and there were a few who liked to have their cocks sucked and even a few more who liked to return the favor. One of the latter still gives me a call when he's passing through town and he stops by for a glass of wine and a blow job. The last time I saw him was only a few months ago. He's the same age as I, 52, married, with four kids, a member of various civic bodies, active in his church, supports a local softball team, goes fishing and has even held elective office. For the record, he has a fine 8" and a pair of tremendous balls. He enjoys sixty-nining and he's an expert cocksucker. I've been married too and I have two kids in their late teens. My wife and I have lived apart for many years. Since we separated I've been exclusively homosexual and it's been a good life. I'm a respected and responsible person in the community and am often called on to help out at charity benefits and civic functions. I pay my taxes, do my work, cherish my friendships, cook great meals, play a hell of a good game of pool and I jack off almost every day, quite often to the perfect stimulation of S.T.H. I merely want to live freely and happily with the truth and with the many joys it can bring.

Likes to Strip While Men Watch

[I saw the subject of the following questionnaire at perhaps the most sordid room in all of New York — Studio 54, where he was a contestant in Blueboy *magazine's 1983 Man of the Year Contest. He did not win the contest — surprisingly, if his dick is as big as he represents it — but he has a winning insolence, and I sent him the questionnaire after scoring him high in the butt, thigh, calf, belly, chest, arm, face and personality categories. His dick is the one thing I didn't (and wouldn't have to) see; he was wearing a jock strap. He struck me as well worth sucking off but, as happens sometimes, he evidently doesn't want to get sucked off (conversely, some men who do aren't worth it). He gives minimal answers to my questions, but since he apparently gives far more than the required minimum sexually, I decided to print the questionnaire. — B. McD.]*

What kind of career are you planning? Chiropractor.

As a student, have you done any part-time work? Help at baths — masseur.

Do you, or does any photographer, sell nude photographs of yourself? Yes.

Are you interested in a temporary career as a nude model? Yes.

Are you interested in a temporary career as a stripper? Yes.

Are you interested in other show biz careers, such as acting on TV or in pictures? No.

Do you enjoy have men watch you undress? Yes.

If so, where? Baths.

Have you ever been in any situation — such as an apartment facing other apartments — where voyeurs could watch you undress? No.

Would you like to be? Yes.

What did you have to do to win your local competition and represent your city in the national Man of the Year contest? Suck off three judges.

How many male beauty contests have you been in? 2.

Do you enjoy having the judges and audience see and admire your body? Yes.

Is that why you entered the Blueboy contest: No.

Where have men seen your body? Baths mostly.

When you go to a bath, what do you wear? Nothing.

Do you caress your dick as a sign that you want to get sucked off? I want to get fucked not sucked.

What is the length of your dick hard? 9¼".

Do you live with someone? Roommate.

What type of living arrangement would you like in the future? Roommate.

What kind of underpants do you wear? None, too hot here!

Do you like to sniff underpants? Other young guys.

How often do you shower? Frequently.

At the end of a work or school day, do you change clothes when you get home? Yes.

If so, what do you wear around the house for dinner, watching TV, etc.? Jock sock.

What kind of friends do you like? Young, hung studs who want my ass.

Where have you met the friends you have? Baths, beaches (NOT bars).

In college locker rooms, have you seen much flesh you admire? Yes, I came out 6 mos. ago.

Can you give a brief summary of your experiences with women? I had 20 before I came out.

Can you give a brief summary of your experiences with boys and men? It would take a book.

At what age did you first jack off? 12.

How did you learn about jacking off? Other boys told me.

Did you ever, as a young boy, jack off with one or more friends? No.

What do you think about while jacking off? I don't!

How often did you jack off per week as a young boy just starting? 3.

As a high school boy? 7.

As a college student (today)? Don't need to now that I'm out.

What kinds of positions do you like for sexual intercourse with others? I want a cock in my ass.

What kinds of sex do you like – e.g., do you like getting your cock sucked? No.

Your ass licked? Yes.

Fucking? Yes.

Apart from bedrooms, where have you had sex? Outdoors, baths.

How often per week do you have sex now? 14-21 times – baths are great!

Do you plan to take advantage of your youth and looks and have as much sex as you want now while you can? Absolutely.

How important is sex in your life? Is it just a minor interest? Major force – very creative.

Do you like to watch yourself undress in front of a mirror? Yes.

Do you get a hard on when you see yourself naked? Usually it's hard before I take pants off.

Do you like to pose in a mirror in any kind of erotic garment, such as a jock strap? Yes.

Can you cite any sexual position which you've especially enjoyed? Any position where a huge young cock is plowing my throbbing asshole.

Duke Was "Queer," Duchess a "Fag Hag."

The Duke of Windsor, briefly King of England before he abdicated his throne "for the woman I love" in 1936, was "queer," according to Noel Coward as quoted by Truman Capote in the *Daily News* (New York) column written by "Suzy" (Eileen Mehle). Coward told Capote that the Duchess of Windsor was "a fag hag to end all" and that the Duke hated Coward because, Coward said, "I'm queer and he's queer, but, unlike him, I don't pretend not to be."

Brad Davis Jacks Off

Greeting Marcia Pally at an afternoon interview for *The Advocate* in his hotel suite in Manhattan, Brad Davis, the star of *Querelle* and *Midnight Express*, said that he "was really tired this morning because I didn't get any sleep last night, but now I've had a nap and masturbated, and I feel much better." I find that men who can't say "jack off" are not much fun, but perhaps Davis used the medical term out of deference to a lady.

Great American Terlets

MANHATTAN. – Thanks for your marvelous journal [S.T.H.]. There is a very active men's room in a building in the City University system of New York. They keep sealing up the glory holes but intrepid sexualists keep re-opening them. I had laid off this particular situation for fear I was noticed as an outsider but decided to check it out again after about a year and found it more active than ever. Spent 2½ hours there yesterday and it was quite a trip. Here's my report:

A SUCTION BLOW JOB.

11:00 A.M. – Got the best seat in the house. The glory hole booth farthest from the door. Shortly after my arrival No. 1 arrived. We eyed each other, showed our cocks, and I stood up and showed my torso. He began jerking off and unbuttoned his shirt. He was tall, blond, sun-tanned, and had about 8" of stick-straight dick. Small head but rosy red. He played with it for awhile then stuck it through the glory hole. Just as I got my tongue on the head someone else entered. No. 1 got nervous, annoyed I later learned, and left.

11:30 – No. 2 entered. We eyed each other, I showed him my cock, he began to play with himself. He gestured for me to put my cock through and I did. He began to give a really good suction blow job. Working hard with his mouth and giving me some good sensations. Several guys came in and we had to cool it, briefly. Then I gestured for him to give me his cock and he did. It was small, about the length of a long middle finger, with a little rosebud glans. Stiff, though. I got down on it and, truth to tell, I enjoy small cocks like that better than the hefty ones because you can really work on them inventively. I gently licked the head, coaxing his piss-hole open with my tongue, rotating that rosy orb in the front of my mouth, then ran the whole stick down my throat. He loved it. Began to groan and moan and murmur, "Thanks." I really went to town, inspired. I not only went up and down with my mouth but got my whole body into it, adding a twist here and there. Suddenly I felt the cock stiffen even harder, felt the muscles on the underside of his dick begin to work and began to taste the sweet jism trickling into my mouth. I kept sucking at the same rate; he kept pumping it into my mouth, no sign of withdrawing. I kept at it until I felt that I had all the juice, then took it out of my mouth and licked the head again and scooped up a few stray drops. Then I stood up, looked over the partition and touched his cheek and chest. We smiled at each other. He said, "Do you want to come now?" Surprising. This guy was really liberated and joyful and just plain nice. Many guys run off as if they had just been in touch with a monster or become monsters themselves. I thanked him and replied, "Maybe another time." He left.

BACK TO THE GLORY HOLE.

12:00 Noon – No. 3 entered. A 19- or 20-year old student. He pulled it right out and began to play with it and jerk it off. I immediately gestured for him to stick it through so I could take care of it – it was a thick 6" – but all he seemed to want to do was play with it for me. I reciprocated. Then the door opened and another guy came in and headed straight for the booth on the other side of me, the one without a glory hole. I cooled it for a moment until the new guy began making foot signals. Then I decided to peek into his booth from the front. Lo and behold! It was my first, the beautiful No. 1. He opened up, I played with it for a few moments and when I started to go down on it he whispered, "Let's go downstairs – that guy (the one in the booth) gives me the creeps." We went to the next floor, got into the end booth so we could cover up if someone came in, and went to work on each other. He played with my dick for a few moments, squeezing it, licking it, then I began to lick his. He said, "Careful, or I'll come right away." I laid offf for awhile so we could hug, kiss, and just enjoy each other. Finally I began to suck it and really enjoyed feeling that hard stick jamming into my mouth. I try to rub a dick like that against the back part of my palate, keeping the dick covered by stretching my mouth forward and working my tongue on the underside of the happiness hinge and sometimes flicking my tongue onto the balls. It certainly worked with this guy. Suddenly he said, "Oh! I'm gonna shoot!" He held it so I could get my mouth on the glans and get all the juice but he made it impossible for me to take over his dick as I usually do once a guy starts to come. (After all that work I feel that for those few moments I own the dick. I feel the same way when someone blows me – not only the load, but the cock are his property for a few moments.) He finished and the rod was still hard. We kissed and he said "Thanks." We parted. I went back upstairs to the glory hole.

STRUGGLING WITH A HUGE COCK.

12:45 – The glory hole booth was empty, No. 3 was in the booth on one side, and just through the glory hole was a good-looking 35ish guy with a huge wang on him. He was jerking it and willingly showed it to me hard, continuing to play with it and stroke his balls while I gazed. I frantically signaled for him to stick it through but he didn't seem to want to even though he stood up. Finally he opened his door and came out into the little hallway in front of the booths, still jerking away. I came out, as did No. 2, and I began playing with No. 4. Finally I got down on it – by this time he had moved directly in front of my booth – and began working. A big dick like that is hard to deal with; you can jet your mouth around it but there are certain practical, physiological problems involved in getting it far enough down your throat to do a job. I struggled with it, regarding it as a learning experience – the only way to learn how to work with big dicks is to suck a few – until finally he began to jerk it again. I was afraid that that was if for me but when I began to suck the head while he jerked, he got right into it. He used my mouth to twist his dick around in while he jerked. Loved it. I reciprocated by doing a really good glans job. I sucked it a lot, trying to get good suction going, using my tongue a lot and sticking with it no matter how hard he jerked. Finally the heavy breathing began and before I knew it a nice stream of hot spunk was shooting into my mouth. It was soupy thick, spurting to the back of my mouth, and delicious. I took every drop I could get, grabbed his balls to keep him from withdrawing, but finally it was over. He just went back into the booth and got dressed and left. By now I was a bit tired so I rested while No. 3 – the ubiquitous No. 3 – sat down in front of the glory hole and played with himself. I watched occasionally but didn't pay much attention.

NOISY SUCKING

1:30 – After a bit another guy came in, a bit hesitant, and headed for the far-end booth on my other side. Foot taps. I peeked through the crack in his door and couldn't resist the dick. He opened up and let me take the head. It was medium thick long – about 8" or 9" – and very veiny. No. 3 of course came to watch, which made the guy nervous. Finally I suggested that he transfer to the glory hole booth, which he did. He stuck it through and I got another chance to use and develop my technique. This dick posed different problems than the others. Its thickness was manageable but the length was another question. I ran it down my throat a few times, then began a steady suck, developing as much suction as possible, rubbing the head against my hard palate, twisting around to give a corkscrew suck, stretching my mouth forward to keep the dick as fully covered as possible. Finally he withdrew. Damn! But he began to jerk it instead. I gestured frantically for him to stick it back through, so he'd understand that I wanted the load. When he got close he rammed it into the hole and I took the start of the load but it was so intense for him that he pulled back before I could get all the spunk. What I got was thick, very thick, almost chunky, and sweet. He fixed up his clothes and split.

1:45 – No. 3 goes back into the glory hole booth but by this time I am tired of him. Again, a guy enters and goes to the far booth on the other side. Foot signals again, same story as before except he too said, "Let's go downstairs." I follow him and am pleased to see that he is a middle-aged guy, not old looking but aging, with a mane of hair and a cool demeanour. He never looks back to see if I am coming, he just proceeds to his destination, which is the same booth where I sucked off No. 1. He quickly pulls out the cock and while it is not impressive it is again the kind of dick it is easy to suck. I get down on it and really do a job – heavy suction, so lots of noise; get a lot of saliva on it and start a fast pace, run the glans onto the hard palate, twist a lot, giving a good corkscrew suck, deep throat it a few times without losing a beat, flick out my tongue to get the balls. After a bit he grabs my shoulders and begins pumping, making sure to get the rod rubbing against the hard palate as I had already done. Good steady beat which ends in a small groan and a large, spurting wad of thick cock juice. I grab the balls, hang on and keep the dick far down in my throat, sure to get the whole load. He doesn't resist. Finally he withdraws, says thanks, and splits. I think he was a teacher or a staff member.

By this time I begin to feel uneasy again; I decide that enough is enough, don't wear out the welcome, split while the splitting's good, etc., and do – I'd been there over 2½ hours. This was the best cocksucking day I have ever had. One other day I sucked more guys but didn't get as many loads. To other guys who are as free as I, find glory holes as safe as possible, get in there – especially in universities – and suck away. Give good head; today's suckees are tomorrow's suckers. Long live the glory hole! Long live casual sex! Long live cocksucking! Why should Cardinal Spelman have (had) all the fun.

Youth Gets Sucked Off By Experienced Younger Boy

FROM A READER – Growing up in Kentucky, I had my first homo experience in a neighbor's backyard pool. Ronnie wanted me to pull my trunks down so he could see my 12-year-old uncircumcised, seven-inch cock. I think it was because I had pubic hair and he was too young to grow it. Anyway his little hands went crazy under the water pulling at my foreskin and rubbing my still hairless balls. I got hard immediately because no one had ever done that to me, I hadn't even done it myself but I knew if he kept it up something would happen. We got out of the pool, got a blanket and went out to the woods behind my house. I laid down on the blanket and Ronnie pulled off my trunks. He was quite eager because he had an older brother he practiced on frequently. My dick got hard without him even touching it. First he jacked it off for a few minutes then he took it in his mouth and I thought I was in heaven. He finished jacking off my slick-spitted dick and I came for the first time – on my stomach. Ronnie and I were friends till I moved out of the neighborhood. We got more involved with the neighborhood boys camping out and having all nite group jack off contests. I usually won.

"A Virtual Heterosexual Glee Club"

By Boyd McDonald

Like war, rape, manslaughter by automobile, child abuse, and brutality and violence in general, the manufacture of TV shows is a male heterosexual activity, however much the product may sound as though it were written by "sob sisters." The TV industry trade association awarded "Emmys" to many of these shows in a telecast from Pasadena at 8 o'clock Sunday evening, September 25 on channel 4. Since so many of the winning shows had so many writers (some as many as eight), the 35th annual Emmy award show displayed a large enough sample of white, white collar, heterosexual male Americans *circa* 1983 to permit drawing impressions of them but not, of course, conclusions about them.

They are physically but not mentally heavyweights; there was not a decent piece of ass in the lot. But paradoxically, though not loveable they appear to be beloved; their acceptance speeches cited support from mothers, wives, children and each other.

But the love most visible on the telecast was their self-love. The industry honored them with Emmys but the most florid honors of the evening were the honors they heaped upon themselves. No less than two winners said that they "had expected to be up here." Considerably more than two represented themselves as intellectual heroes and pioneers for getting their shows about heart-warming cops, loveable surgeons and men who really do love women on the air. But those are the only kinds of shows that *can* go on the air.

After prolonged thank-yous to a wide range of relatives and friends, many of the winners shared personal vignettes (these are not men who merely piss, they share their piss with lonely urinals). In sharing personal data with an audience which showed every sign of having had more than its share, the winners put on a show as poignant (and pointless) as any of the night-time soap operas they hack out. Even as one of them accepted his Emmy, his mother was in intensive care at a hospital; she was, he said, "older," her condition "not that well" and her eyesight at least temporarily impaired. His use of "older" speaks poorly for the quality of the show he wrote.

Another writer soon topped him by announcing that *his* mother had actually died while he was working on his show. But if they had reached the age where their mothers are dying, they still have their wives for support; one thanked his wife "for trying to understand me for 35 years." But there is no understanding of genius.

They also had each other. Two members of a large group that eagerly made its way to the stage – a virtual heterosexual glee club – embraced each other all the way down the aisle of the Pasadena

Civic Center; onstage, awaiting their turn to discuss their mothers, wives and children, they remained locked in embrace.

One ineffectual-looking little man said he'd spent his honeymoon in a hotel room with another writer; the show's schedule required it. His tone was, "Imagine anyone as straight as I being in a hotel room with another man." But such a situation was funny in another way too: the television industry lavishes mammoth amounts of money on these people, and if salesmen can have their own private hotel rooms when they're on the road TV writers certainly can if they want them.

The media on Joan Rivers, co-host of the show, was negative even though she was *ipso facto* less shitty on the Emmy show than she has been on the Carson show, where she told the joke about the homosexual who died and was cremated and his ashes put in a "fruit jar." On the Emmy show, Rivers mentioned that a homosexual in San Francisco had gone to the "Burger Queen." The funniest part of this jest was that her co-host acts like a real queen; Eddie Murphy announced after the telecast that he's not going to do any more TV but will presumably stick to movies. How regal. Murphy has also joked about our death – death from AIDS. The only other public figure I know of who joked about AIDS was Congressman Lawrence Patton McDonald of Georgia. He died, but Joan and Eddie are still alive to carry on his work.

A man is known by the enemies he attacks. Murphy sticks to the officially-approved list: women, whom he sometimes calls bitches; homosexuals or, as he puts it, "faggot-assed faggots;" Jews, and blacks (although he's black). According to *People* magazine, when some of his black fans started putting down white people in general, he shut them up; there's no future in that. After two years with his face pressed against the butt of power, that of the white heterosexual male, Murphy has the flattest nose in show biz. But he's a cute little coward; he'll go far. He's right in thinking movies more prestigious. But there was at least one way in which the Emmy awards for TV shows had more klass than the Academy Awards show for movies: nobody on the Emmy show scratched himself. In the last Academy Awards show, there was sufficient scratching to raise the question of whether next time the Academy should set up a de-lousing station backstage to rid certain stars – I don't think I have to mention their names – of head lice and crab lice in their pubic hair.

700 Vomit on Long Island.

More than 700 Long Islanders became ill after dining on contaminated clams from the Great South Bay and suffered nausea, vomiting, dizziness, coughing, and headaches.

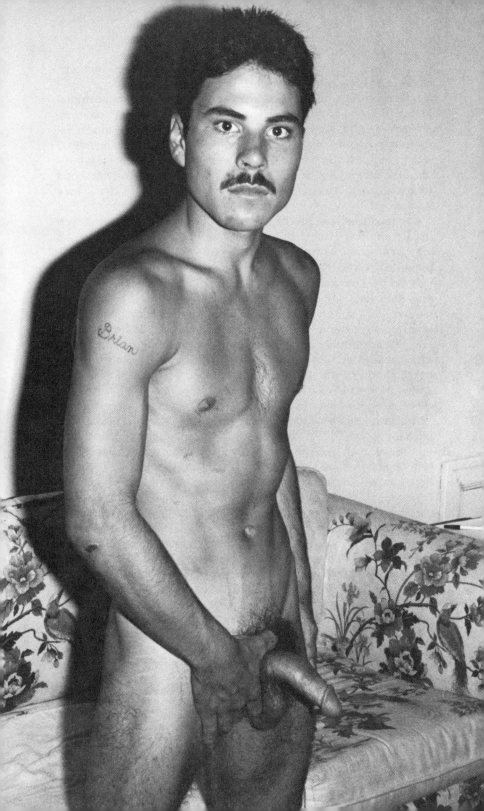

Fucks Cops, Fireman, Trucker, Hard Hats, Soldiers, Married Men

MANHATTAN – Thank you for the back issues [of S.T.H.]. The Marine interview on pages 6-8 of Issue 42 is more interesting than the other one on pages 25-27, which has been widely reprinted, including in *Meat*. I like the Marine "Professionals" [whores] in Issue 49.

I believe that Marines are available but I haven't been so lucky. I haven't lived near any major Marine encampment. I could kick myself for not being more aggressive in propositioning a Marine last summer when we were both flying from New Mexico to California seated next to each other. He wore only a T shirt and jeans – no underwear (I could see down the back of his pants when he leaned forward, revealing hair at the base of the spine and down the ass-crack).

I am Oriental, being of Japanese descent. I was born and raised in Honolulu and have lived in NY since 1970. I am masculine, 37, 5' 4", 125, not macho or huge. I seek tall, muscular, rugged-looking WMs who need to be ass-fucked regularly. Prefer blue-collar, uncut, tattooed, into wearing jock straps. I would especially like to fuck a tall, muscular WM Marine, who takes it like a man. B&D, WS, light SM.

I had sex for the first time while I was in the Army with a lifer who had been busted in rank. He was an older guy and I also was considered older, having already gone through graduate school when I was drafted. He was of Italian descent, with a slender body, taller than mine. Things began when I commented about a "kinky" fuck book lying on his bunk one morning. One thing led to another and he wanted to make out in the barracks. Because I didn't want to risk getting caught in the act, I asked him to wait until the weekend when we could go to a hotel in town. I will always be grateful that he started me out trying a lot of things: kissing and touching, sucking and fucking, rimming and tonguing all over. Before we got startd he wanted a drink and proceeded to get drunk. I broke it off because of that.

I had my eyes on a muscular dude in the company. I can't recall how I made my intentions known but I kept up friendly chatter. He worked out with weights and I complimented him on his body. He finally agreed to get together in town on New Year's Eve after I, as company clerk, got him off from KP. At the hotel, with some booze under his belt, he gave unmistakeable signs for getting it on. I was surprised and pleased. He let me suck his cock, which was small in its flaccid state but grew in size and hardness with encouragement from my tongue and mouth. He allowed me to insert my finger in his ass. He asked me if I had brought a lubricant. I was really caught off guard: I was unprepared and he was not a virgin. With difficulty, I got my cock up his tight asshole (he admitted it had been awhile).

I shot my first load of cum up a (his) butch asshole and took his cum in my mouth. That was sweet! He left sometime during the night after asking for a "loan." Asking for money became a pattern over a period of about a year, with four or five meetings. He didn't need to have alcohol, though. On post, he allowed me to press my thigh against his and to fondle his crotch in the dark when we went to the movies. One time he left his T shirt in the hotel room (deliberately?) and I smelled it from time to time before I eventually returned it. On another occasion he sucked me briefly, wondering what it was like. He hated the frigid winter temperatures where we were stationed so I reluctantly processed his request for a transfer to Vietnam. After he left the post, we corresponded. I sent him a plane ticket to visit me in NY after he returned home, but he sent the ticket back. His letters eventually stopped and after a few Christmas cards, communication between us ceased entirely. He was my first crush so I'll always remember him: his beautiful body with developed pecs unobscured by body hair (he shaved regularly what little he had) and especially his big creamy white high round firm ass cheeks, which, when spread, revealed a delectable rosebud to be rimmed and fucked.

Over 10 years later, I'm currently fucking a married construction worker of Italian descent who "hates/loves" it. He doesn't like kissing or showing affection, but he's one of the very few married men who doesn't dash off after cumming. He's only partially hard when I'm fucking him but his moans are unmistakeably out of pleasure. I enjoy fucking him from the rear, moving from a prone position with his ass pushed up until he's on his knees, the trunk in a vertical position with my hard cock impaled in his ass. When he's on his back, legs up and spread, I watch him fold his right arm back, pumping his bicep, and bite himself lightly. I jerk his big cock stiffer and vary the tempo of my fucking, all the while watching his facial contortions, hearing his moans and heavy breathing. When he comes, he does so forcefully. Lying on his back, his hands folded behind his head, his torso curls upward, like doing a sit-up, contracting his abdominal muscles, while in my mouth I can feel his cock contracting as he spurts out his load of cum. In the calm of the aftermath, both of us smoking cigarettes, he lets me stroke his chest, stomach, crotch, armpits, legs, and ass cheeks.

ITALIAN SANITATION WORKER WANTS TO SUCK 2 AT ONCE.

For over five years, I've been seeing a married guy with the most provocative ass. His visits are always brief (as are his Jockey shorts) and he needs to be tied up securely before I can fuck his gorgeous firm white ass. He insists that I use a condom. He has superb control over his sphincter muscles, alternately loosening and tightening them like a vise. He can almost cum just while I'm wrapping a leather thong around his balls and the shaft of his cock. He also likes to be spanked but I enjoy "teasing" his cock even more. This involves jerking it until he signals me that he's close. Then I stop. I vary the pressure, technique, and rhythm, repeating the process several times before allowing him the relief of orgasm, which is always convulsive.

Last year I fucked my first NYC cop. I didn't know he was a cop until after I fucked his ass. I was telling him about my fantasies, including fucking a NYC cop, when he volunteered the information. Previously I had fucked a state sheriff, a county parole officer, and a Port Authority cop. The latter is notable because he had a deeply-recessed asshole with a tunnel-like approach that makes aiming a cock up the ass effortless (I sometimes lose my hard on trying to get my cock up an asshole). I fucked him long and hard; under the influence of poppers, he just pushed back and enjoyed. He had a sensitive left nipple which when licked, sucked, or bitten made his cock even harder – it first came to notice when he was a kid having sex with an older woman. He mentioned that he is often propositioned while assigned to the tunnel toll plazas. Only once, he says, did he call a guy who gave him a telephone number.

The parole officer was really into having his asshole stuffed. He liked dildos, vibrators, a bardex pump (which has a balloon that is inflated after rectal insertion), as well as a hard cock. My favorite item is a string of five red rubber balls. The best part is seeing each one disappear into the asshole after pushing it in to its widest diameter: whoosh! I never got my fist up his ass but he easily took four fingers.

I recently fucked another NYC cop who wanted to be tied up first, but the thrill of having a cop seems to have evaporated. I saw him one recent Saturday morning and am reminded of a truck driver who calls me from time to time on weekday mornings when he's making deliveries in the neighborhood and pops over for a quickie. He called the other morning and for the first time actually said that he needed to have his ass fucked. Unfortunately, I had to get to work. On the mornings when I can accommodate him, he likes to have his enormous well-shaped uncut cock and big loose-hanging balls tied up with a leather thong or to have a ball-spreader used. I fuck his ass and suck him off. He puts his work uniform back on and continues delivering.

One of my all-time favorites is a 6'5" Irish NYC fireman, a great fuck who is embedded in my memory because once, while he was on his knees and I was pulling his nipples, he said, "Make me hurt good." I nearly came when he said that. Tall guys are always easier to fuck on their backs. They can bend their legs easier and longer.

I have tried group scenes from time to time. The most unusual one occurred this past July with a married engineer from Philadelphia and a woman at Fantasy Manor, Club O. The engineer usually likes to be tied up, fucked, and cock-teased. He's tall and during the summer sports a terrific tan line with a nice white ass. He expressed a great desire to be fucked by a guy while eating out a pussy. After looking over the premises of the club, I secured him to the wall of one of the back rooms and started tying up his cock and balls when a woman came over to us and struck up a conversation. We explained our goal to her and she expressed interest. My friend's cock got harder and harder as we were talking. She finally agreed to participate. Accompanied by a male friend, she joined us in a private room. I tied up my friend's hands behind him as he lay on his stomach. The woman positioned herself with her crotch in his face while I proceeded to fuck his ass. I could hear her moaning while her friend just sat there and watched. Eventually I flipped my friend over on his back, the woman re-positioned herself with her crotch over his face and started to blow my friend's big cock as I continued to fuck him. He came in her mouth but he hardly remembered anything that happened, he was so excited. It was my closest sexual encounter with a woman and for my friend it was a fervent fantasy fulfilled.

Things don't always work out the way you want them to. I invited my Chinese friend to join me and a real hunk: an Italian sanitation man, about 6'2", 190 pounds, bearded, a great body, and a favorite of mine. The hunk likes to suck cock and doesn't mind being fucked, jerking himself all the while. He wanted to suck off two smaller guys at the same time. It was his show but after we all got undressed he backed out and I haven't seen him since. It's regrettable because I liked the way he sucked – he seemed to enjoy it so much.

Sports Builds Character

Steve Pisarkiewicz, former University of Missouri football player who became a quarterback for the St. Louis Cardinals, was arrested in Hazelwood, a St. Louis suburb, for exposing what the *New York Post* called "himself" to an 18-year-old woman while driving a car. The episode recalled a similar one earlier when Lance Rentzel, then on the Dallas Cowboys team, was arrested for exposing himself to a ten-year-old girl. The chances are the two players didn't have much to expose; it is a truism in psych that men who display their pee pee things to strangers normally are unable to get hard ons and engage in normal intercourse, such as blow jobs, fucking and so on.

Tony

FROM A RESORT TOWN – When Tony walks into the local bar I fall in lust. He is dark, strikingly dark, with flashing eyes, red-red lips, and a commanding presence. I'm with the hotel gang and learn that he is a new waiter. He's with a girl but I catch his eye and hold it. That's enough for me for the time being.

The next evening after work I go down to the hotel help quarters. As I get there I see a pretty, pretty boy come toward me so, even in the throes of my new infatuation with Tony, my instincts work and I stop him to ask if this is the place I know it is. His room turns out to be next to Tony's. Tony isn't in. Kevin – the one I stopped – is in. He exudes sex. He is 16. He takes off most of his clothes while we talk.

Tony comes in with his date. I pull out Kevin's light, to listen. Kevin joins me on his bed next to the wall. We listen to our neighbors, joke quietly about their noises, and talk about women. Kevin's never been "in" one. He asks what you do first.

We're in the dark with hips, thighs, legs touching, pressing together. My hands wander over his chest and nipples, to show him what to do first.

His roommate comes in and I move to leave. Kevin, bulging in his underpants, squeezes my knee and says, breathlessly, "What's your name? When will I see you again?"

Tony double dates with me and two waitresses at the Inn where I work as bartender. They're nice. From the South. I had been dating both occasionally. Pretty girls I like being with, but Tony adds something else.

Tony is 16 and looks like what everyone imagines the perfect classic Greek to look like. His Italian father, an interior designer, met his English wife in Paris where both were studying. Tony's curly hair is in ringlets, his eyes are dark and liquid, his lips are sensual – everything contributes to make him a person of unusual beauty. He smiles easily and beautifully. He is reserved and his voice is soft and rather weak but somehow it doesn't matter. It makes him seem as if he needs someone.

Tony knows he is good looking but he likes to be appreciated, so I tell him how good looking I think he is.

Kevin isn't jealous, isn't consciously jealous, but competes by being sexy as hell. One night he decides to change his clothes when I arrive. He tackles me when he is naked. When I get a hard on wrestling with him, he calls me a homo and grins happily.

Tony comes in to tell us one of the hotel guests wants to paint his picture.

A very cute boy named Jimmy comes in. Jimmy is a football player in high school, as Tony and Kevin are also. Jimmy plays with Kevin's hair until Kevin cracks.

"Cut it," Kevin says. "If you want to blow me, just say so."

Tony turns up at my bar almost every night. When I get off , we cruise for girls but never get around to picking any up. Instead we drink and flirt.

Kevin likes to be called "sexy" and reciprocates by living up to it. After running my fingers all over his nearly naked body one day I say, "Kevin, do you want to sleep with me?"

With the sweetest and happiest smile he's got, he answers, "I'm no homo."

Tony isn't jealous, not consciously, but begins a few maneuvers of his own. One night he plays with the change in his pocket next to me in a booth at the local bar. When I drive Tony back, we stop in to see Kevin. I stay to play with Kevin's husky body and tell him about the evening. When the night watchman goes by, Kevin sneers, "That goddam queer. He tried to make me."

Yet when Tony leaves to go next door to his room, I unbutton the top button of Kevin's pajama bottoms and run my hands over his chest down to his pubic hairs. He lies there smiling, his face averted, and says, "Boy, that feels good. I'm getting hot."

Tony and I go on a trip to Moosehead Lake to visit two guys — twins I had met at Pond's End, a secluded local bar run by a gay friend of mine. I knew it was going to be a gay weekend; Tony didn't. The twins had been born and brought up in Moosehead where, in their 20s, they inherited a lot of property. They were very masculine lumberjacks. They took trips to the gay spots of the world on occasion and were so unusually attractive in their completely masculine way that they gathered a following of friends who were willing to travel all the way from Fire Island or Provincetown or wherever to the foresaken woods of Maine to visit them. We are met by two guys from New York and one of the twins at a dock and we go out to a cabin on an island mid-lake.

Everyone assumes Tony is gay so they do nothing to temper their conversation, which in turns becomes campy, swishy, gay, and funny, since both of the New Yorkers are born entertainers (one of them is a piano player on Fire Island). The twins and I are an appreciative audience; Tony shows little reaction, but flashes his beautiful smile at me if I look at him questioningly.

At the end of the evening, Tony and I go to bed together. I cuddle up to him and put my arm around him. I fondle his cock and it soon gets hard. When he comes, I come pressed against his hot ass. Saying nothing, we fall asleep. When we awake I ask him to look at me. He does. I ask him to smile. When he turns on his sparkling smile I know his attitude toward me hasn't changed much.

A beautiful weekend follows, a wild gay weekend in this deserted place 20 miles from the nearest village (whose population is 12 in the winter).

On the drive home Tony has no questions and little to say about what has gone on.

"They sure are a bunch of characters," he says. He thinks the Fire Island pianist is very amusing; he envies the other New Yorker's personality, his deep voice. Gradually I get him to comment more freely. He's impressed that two such totally masculine guys as the twins can also be totally gay. He likes me. He's glad he went with me. So if this is his first exposure to gay life, it was a fortuitous one.

Kevin is in bed when we get back. His light's out but I caress him. His face, buried in the pillow, says, "Hi, Peter."

"How did you know?"

"Who else would go feeling for my balls?"

He sits up, turns on the light, and throws off the blanket to expose his beautiful body for me to admire.

Tony has a fan club. From the girls at the hotel it has spread to the girls at the inn because he's up here a lot to see me. He gets notes, requests for pictures. They discuss him with me and try to decide which movie star he looks most like. I love it.

Kevin said he slept with Tony last night (to let some British sailor have his bed).

Tony has fallen in love with Betty, a new waitress; sees her all of her free time, which also, alas, is all of his. I am depressed at no longer seeing him and go to Bar Harbor to pick up a sailor. Kevin is also in love with Tony. We comfort each other.

Tony comes in to apologize for not seeing me for so long. He thinks he's getting tired of Betty. He gives me picture of himself.

Dana Mathes checked into the hotel when my parents were visiting; my observant mother first spotted him and remarked on his good looks. Dana, 16, is indeed handsome and terribly aristocratic-looking – perfect posture, impeccably tailored, but there's something more, the sum *is* more than the parts because Dana has an aura that immediately makes itself felt; as he nears people, they turn in awe to stare. He has great dignity and doesn't smile often. I'm terribly impressed but I can't fall in love because he's too perfect, too unworldly, too unreachable.

Getting Kevin and Dana together was interesting. They are both 16 but there the resemblance ended. Dana's family is rich, lives in a large duplex on Fifth Avenue. He was at St. Paul's and has the accent and diction. He seems detached from what is going on around him. Kevin's family is poor, from a depressed city in New Jersey. He quit school when he was 16; his accent borders on Brooklynese; his diction is tough-guy. He's always thoroughly involved in what he's doing. But they were fascinated by each other and approached each other warily and politely, rather like meeting a person from another planet.

Since Kevin and Tony continue to put down several obvious gay guys working at the inn as "queer" and "homo" in front of me, but not purposely to annoy me, I begin to realize how the all-American boy mind classifies people. They put down queers but a gay guy they like is different. Not being affected or effeminate, I get classified differently; my remarks, groping, sucking (all of which of course they like) allow them to classify me as just a normal bisexual oversexed uninhibited male.

But I want to search deeper into Tony, with whom I've become definitely in love. One night when I park outside this dorm and he makes no move to get out, I say, "Tony, do you want to get blown?"

"If you want to."

"I want to because it's you. I want to please you. But I don't want you to think I just like cocks. I like girls too." (I do but not in the way he thinks I mean it.) And I go on about my gay life and pretend bisexuality.

Tony tells me about an affair with his prep school roommate, whom he loved; how he likes gay people and wants to know more about gay life, and adds, quite easily, "I've always liked boys better than girls, up to now. This is the first time I've ever really gone out with girls. But I think I'm heterosexual now and I really don't want to have any more sex with boys – except if you want to blow me, that's O.K."

Tony says the man who wanted to paint his picture had him over for cocktails and tried to make him. He says the man asked him to take off his clothes so he could see his body. Tony did and stood naked while the man admired him.

"Did he try to feel you up?"

"He *did* feel me up but I don't think he's queer. I think he just likes bodies. Except he got awfully excited feeling mine so I said I had to go. But he still wants to paint my picture."

Years later I ran into a young guy who had the same name as the artist. I told the story about how years before I had run into a painter with that name who had tried to seduce my boyfriend. He said dryly, "Yes. That was my father."

On Tony's last night at the hotel, we got drunk at Pond's End. We became very affectionate, putting our arms around each other constantly and not giving a damn about occasional glances from "straight" customers. When we get back to Tony's dorm, I go in without asking him. I blow him. He comes almost immediately and we sleep until his roommate wakes us for Tony's last shift. Later, Tony says none of the kids said anything about our sleeping together.

As soon as I get back to Boston after my summer job is over, I call Tony. He drives down to school and I take him out for cocktails to the Harvard Club, dinner, and on to several gay bars where we run into several of my gay friends. They are all interested in Tony and decide to have an impromptu party back at Randy McVey's. Each in his own way tries to seduce Tony and he loves it. So do I – proud to be the one with him. But when one of them suggests to Tony that he might like to go lie down for awhile, I grab him and flee.

Back at school I start to blow him but he tells me to take off my clothes. I do. He does. After rolling around doing various things, I turn him on his stomach and start greasing his asshole. He has evidently fantasized about it and he gets a hard on and lets me continue even as my cock hurts him. It was his first time. I fuck him gently and lengthily and he loves it. Right after I come in his hot ass, he comes in my hand with my cock still in him.

This marks the beginning of a new relationship with Tony. he is honest about liking to be fucked. He tells me that his roommate at prep school and he used to blow each other and he used to think about his roommate's cock up his ass but didn't really know it could work. Since Tony was 16 and 17 then and voted best-looking boy in the school – by the other boys – I envy his roommate.

We continue to see each other frequently and visit gay friends of mine because I love to show him off and he likes to be admired. We stay together because we both look forward to the fuck.

Once, when I'm leaving Tony off at his parents' house, he asks me to "see" his younger brother. The boy was in bed but Tony brings him down to display him, beaming with pride. The boy, at 15, *is* perfect. A small boy with the most beautiful girl's face imaginable: perfect porcelain complexion, small delicate features, dark eyes and red, red lips. Tony says, "Do you think he looks like me?"

I take this question as an excuse to devour Vincent with my eyes, comment on his every feature, and walk around him admiringly as he stands before me in his pajama bottoms, lips slightly parted, dark eyes looking back into mine unwaveringly. I'm physically weak when the show is over and Vincent goes back to bed.

A couple of years later, when Tony gets married for the first time, I'm invited and Tony tries to get Vincent to sleep with me when I stay at their house for the wedding. Vincent is sweet and polite and very attentive all weekend, but he does not sleep with me.

Before the wedding, Tony had stayed with me until he got an offer he couldn't afford to refuse. A prominent rich man fell in love with Tony. With a bit of my permission but mostly without it, David, the rich guy, invited Tony to live with him, offering a handsome allowance.

I saw Tony after this but it was hard because he was now David's.

But I kept track of him through David, with whom I stayed friends.

Tony was unintentionally comical in telling me about his relationship with David. Neither of them liked the other all that much, but David was hot for Tony's body and Tony was hot for some of David's money. Once Tony came out with this:

"I'm really not trying to screw David or anything but that bastard had better get me a new car."

Tony's life became secure but complicated. He had all the money and cars he wanted, but his heterosexual side kept insisting upon its rights. So Tony got married — several times. Each wedding was sponsored by a generous and tolerant David, who gave them handsome wedding presents and then stopped Tony's allowance. This was not something Tony could become accustomed to so he'd go back to David, who'd welcome him with a new car and arrange the divorce. This sequence happened several times. Finally David fell out of lust and Tony fell out of life, out of our lives at least, having been spoiled by too much attention and too little love.

A Golden Treasury of Great "New York Times" Writing.

The following paragraphs are reproduced as they appeared in *The New York Times:*

Anita Loos, the screenwriter, playwright and novelist whose name was indissolubly linked with her book "Gentlemen Prefer Blondes," died yesterday at Doctors Hospital in Manhattan...

"Gentlemen Prefer Blondes," an idly written spoof of a romance between the professed sophisticated and intellectual H.L. Mencken and a mindless blonde, gave Anita Loos lasting celebrity as the creator of a minor American classic.

An idly written spoof of a romance between H.L. Mencken, the professed sophisticate and intellectual, and a mindless blonde, which was published as "Gentlemen Prefer Blondes," gave Anita Loos lasting celebrity as the creator of a minor American classic. Although in her long career Miss Loos had many substantial accomplishments ... it was with "Gentlemen Prefer Blondes" that her name was indissolubly linked...

[EDITOR's NOTE: I think I get it: it was with "Gentlemen Prefer Blondes" that her name was indissolubly linked; the book gave her lasting celebrity as the creator of a minor American classic, and it was an idly written spoof of a romance between H.L. Mencken, the professed sophisticated and intellectual, and a mindless blonde. Right?]

A Fucking Priest

FROM A READER – Finished reading *Sex* last night. I especially like middle-aged sex since I've found it to be the best, less frenzied and desperate.

Two years ago I went through an amicable divorce. Although I had a great many gay experiences before marriage, the 16 years I was married I didn't fool around.

Once free, I had a guest who was in town for his father's funeral and at the wake a good-looking priest (51, white hair cut in a butch trim, 5'10") walked in on us as we were embracing in a non-grieving way. I was embarrassed when he put his arms around us and consoled us because he could see my hard on through my pants.

The following week, after my friend had left, the priest called and asked if I had left a pair of gloves at the church (it was in November). I hadn't and didn't know how he'd gotten my telephone number or remembered my name, but I responded yes because there was something in his voice which told me he wanted to see me.

I arrived at his office after work about 6 p.m. He got the gloves. I told him that they weren't mine and he said they had a Lost/Found in the basement we could look in.

The room was musty and small. We brushed against each other looking through boxes which contained everything from rank jock straps to silk scarves. I was getting horny from our nearness and the strong masculine cologne he was wearing so I decided to make a tentative move. I told him I hadn't lost anything, I just wanted to see him again. He said he knew that, he hadn't found any gloves – they were his.

That was all it took. I put my arm around his waist and pulled him to me. We smiled into each other's eyes and softly kissed. We rubbed our crotches together. He told me he lived with his 85-yr.-old mother, invited me for dinner at his house, and after she went to bed we went to his basement bedroom and stripped.

His bed was heaven. It was a king-sized four-poster with a royal purple satin comforter and silver-satin sheets and pillow cases. We took turns chewing each other's nippes, kissing, and sucking cock. Then he said, "Do you want to fuck me?" I said yes. He said the only way he could let me do it is if he was out of control – forced. I asked him if he wanted me to and he sighed YES, please. He got up and returned with a box full of what appeared to be satin sashes for bathrobes. Within minutes I had him spread-eagled on the bed, ass up, according to his instruction.

He told me to gag him with a large bath sponge and to anchor it in place with a sash. I did so and found a tin of Vaseline in the box. Placing the pillow under his basket, I spread his buns and began chewing around the ass slit. He went wild. He bucked wildly and spit the sponge out.

"Gag me tighter, damn it!" I did this time because I was as excited as he was. My rimming continued and his asshole flowered, trying to suck my tongue in. I reamed his ass (very trim for his age). When I came, I removed the sponge from his mouth.

I untied him and rolled over and placed my hand on his hard on. "Jack me off, please," I did and took his load as he came. He got up and packed away the sashes and other items, then showed me to the guest apartment where we slept spoon-fashion the rest of the night.

In the morning he had me dress in a satin dressing gown from Korea and have breakfast with him and his mother. He gave me the robe as a present and said we couldn't see each other again because people might talk. Less then a week later he realized that it was impossible not to see one another. We saw each other once a week until he was transferred to another state.

II. EX-MARINE HAS BUTT TATTOO.

During high school, for a couple months, I stocked shelves at a small grocery owned by a man nick-named Happy. Happy had plenty reason for his constant smile; he was sucking off several teenagers a night who wanted beer and were underage.

Happy was repellant, about 5'5", approx. 300 lbs., with huge melon-sized breasts atop his beer-swollen stomach. His body smelled foul. I worked for him because I needed the money and I had a crush on the day worker, Buckner, who was an ex-Marine with tattooes. But-terflies over each nipple, Marine Corps insignia on his left bicep, a rose on the left buttock, and the American flag on his back. When he stripped off his shirt it put me in heat.

He'd show me what needed to be done, then he'd take off for his trailer with a six pack. One day after I finished work I stopped by his place on a feeble excuse. He was lying on the bed watching TV and told me to come in. The place was a pig sty – empty TV dinners everywhere. I stepped in and was delighted he was only wearing a baggy pair of boxer shorts. He told me to get myself a Pepsi out of the refrigerator. He asked me why I was there and I told him I didn't like working for Happy. He didn't either but his wife had walked out on him and left him lots of bills to pay.

He got up and closed the door and stood in front of me. It was hot; no circulation.

"You one of Happy's boys?" he said.

I said no.

"Don't lie to me."

I told him it was the truth. He stretched out on the bed. "You can't keep your eyes off me, can you, kid." He pulled his boxer shorts off. "Like what you see?"

I didn't answer.

"We had ways of treating your kind in the Corps." He told me to suck his cock, which by now lay long and hard on his hard stomach. I was afraid and got up to leave. I wanted him a lot, but my fear stopped me short. He laughed and put his shorts back on.

I quit there about a month later after Happy got over romantic and got mad at me because I wouldn't let him suck me. Buckner was around for years and many times I wish I'd let him have his way.

III. SHORT JAPANESE GIVES LONG BLOW JOB.

When I was acting in a show in Chicago in the 60s a Japanese-American man became my stage door Johnny. He pursued me with flowers, candy, scarves, gloves, and cologne before I agreed to a date. His height (just 5') was a turn-off. He was also chunky (not fat) and 20 years older than I.

On our first date he took me to dinner after the show, gave me a present (a beautiful sheer white silk kimono), and asked me to spend the night with him. He had a gorgeous lake front apt. decorated in stark Oriental style. We both changed into kimonos and lay on the floor drinking sake. He had me lie back and relax. For several hours he made love to me with his mouth. He licked my lips, chest, armpits, buns, toes, feet. He tongued my ass, flooding it with his saliva, then tenderly crawled atop my back and slipped his small unclipped cock into my sopping wet asshole. He set up a pleasant rhythm and flooded my asshole with his warm male juice. He pulled out, cleaned my asshole like a vacuum, washed his cock, and lay down beside me. I cuddled him in my arms and we slept until awakened by an Oriental houseboy who brought breakfast. I started to throw on my kimono and my admirer stopped me. He instructed the houseboy (in Japanese) to shave us and sponge bathe us.

After breakfast, my benefactor had to go to his office and asked me if I could spend a week with him. I told him I had a performance 5 nights a week and 2 matinees and he said he'd arrange for a cab to deliver me. I agreed.

That afternoon I got to know the houseboy. He told me the older man was his grandfather and each year his grandmother went to Japan to visit relatives for a month and his grandpa took a male lover while she was gone. As far as he knew, his grandfather never saw men the other 11 months.

After my performance and dinner, Mr. Y took me home and we looked at his artistic male Oriental pornography. He slowly sucked my cock, avoiding climax again and again, lingering at the edge of coming as I moaned from the pleasure. Repeatedly his tongue whipped my piss slit. Finally I came.

By the end of the week I had experienced a knotted silk handkerchief and balls on a string shoved up my ass and removed at the time of climax. Before I left I was offered money for my time and I refused it (an insult – but I didn't know at the time).

For several years after, I always looked Y up when a show I was in played Chicago. He usually took me to lunch and had a gift for me, but my time never again coincided with his wife's visit to Japan.

IV. A TRUCKER'S ASSHOLE.

Hitchhiking was a favorite pastime of mine from ages 12-22. On crosstown trips, it would often take the entire trip for the driver to ask for my phone number. On long distance trips, truck drivers were the Knights of the Road. If they liked the service I gave them, they'd arrange with their buddies to take me on too when I wanted to go. For the price of sucking a horny cock, I could travel America free.

Most truckers just flopped out their meat and had you wolf it down. Very few were into butt-fucking and very few were gay or good looking. One of the most memorable lifts I got was a leatherman from Los Angeles to San Diego. He was tall, skinny, and in wonderfully aromatic tight black leather – boots, chaps, shirt, hat. Outside Torrey Pines we pulled off into the woods and in a secluded area he removed my shirt and went down on my nipples. I was primed for being screwed. We stripped and he lay down, his ass up, and told me to remove the plug from his ass. It was an enormous butt plug. He told me wearing it on a motorcycle trip was like being fucked on every bump. I removed it and with the lube already there, hopped on and gave him the real thing. After coming, he shoved the plug back in, explained he was a bottom man only, and we lay in the woods, his arms around me, while he finger-fucked me until I shot again.

V. "HE STARTED CRYING."

The Boy Scouting years are the most dangerous to throw young men together. They are so sexually ripe and eager for experimentation. At the root of many bondage lovers is a Boy Scout experience. Circle jerks were a norm for many Scouts I knew – measuring cocks, distance you could shoot, number of times you could come. Sadism was rife.

In our case we had a rather effeminate fat boy in our troop. One summer six of us went for wilderness training in the woods for a week. We canoed into our campsite and I got stuck with Porky. The week became one of "making a man" of Porky. The first thing we did was make him strip and bury his clothes. For seven days he didn't wear a stitch.

Faced with a pasty, plump body which had never seen sun, we staked him out for half an hour in the sun and rubbed cooking oil on his body. He cried, so one of the guys gagged him with a Scout kerchief. When his body was practically sizzling, we turned him over for the other side. The only place he didn't have some pinkish burn was at the wrists and ankles where he'd been bound and the sides of his mouth where the kerchief had bound his mouth effectively.

We all went swimming bareass and late that afternoon we split up to set up our 2-man tents in various places in the forest. Porky was quiet as we made our camping site. I could tell the sun had gotten to him. I sprayed his body with Solarcaine to kill the pain of the sunburn. After dinner we returned to the tent. Porky's sunburn wouldn't allow him to sleep in his sleeping bag and I felt sorry for him. He started crying after he thought I was asleep. I put my hand to his lips, then petted his hair until he fell asleep.

The next day we all went fishing in teams of 2. Porky and I caught the most. After we had all gutted the fish two of the guys jumped Porky and staked him out again. They rubbed fish guts all over his sunburnt body, shoved them up his ass, shoved some in his mouth and forced him to swallow them. He retched and they left him there, the flies covering his plump body.

I'd had enough and told the guys so. I untied Porky and went swimming with him. When we came back the other guys told us we were a couple of queers and they didn't want to have anything to do with us. I took our provisions from the supplies and Porky and I took off, portaging to another lake.

Once there, we made a makeshift tunic for him from his sleeping bag. We had a great time, telling stories, and I suddenly realized I liked the fat kid. That night we opened my bedroll and slept on top of it. We both stripped and shared his tunic (bedroll) for a cover. Neither of us could sleep and we tossed and turned until we found each other staring into our eyes. Porky started to say something and I pressed my dry lips to his wet mouth. I had had sex with men before but I could tell he was a cherry. He was shocked but made no move. I kept my mouth on his for a long time before he opened it. I eased my tongue in his mouth and licked his teeth and gums, then pulled out and kissed his cheeks and neck before rolling away, my back to him. Wordlessly he put his arm over me and pulled himself close. I could feel his hard cock pressing against my thighs. I lifted my legs and trapped the cock between them, then reached down and rubbed the cock head with my saliva-coated fingers. I rolled my legs, causing friction to his trapped pecker. He caught on to the rhythm and shot quickly, his cum coating my thigh.

By now my pecker was swollen to the bursting point and I crawled atop Porky and thigh-fucked him. After I came we fell asleep spoon fashion.

In the remainder of our time alone we explored each other's body. I never screwed his plump ass because I didn't want to cause him any more pain.

When we returned our fellow Scouts called us fairies.

In the years after, Porky lost weight and married, then gained some of it back. He became very out-going and popular. We've always felt like brothers but we never had sexual experiences again.

SUCCESSFUL SUCKING
IN TODAY'S SOCIETY:

Theatregoers Wait in Line to Use Youth's Suck-hole

[EDITOR's NOTE: The following letter gives an inspiring glimpse of that aspect of Times Square (and of life in general) that I've always found more attractive than the attractions on stage. The men in this article seem more human, more liberal, and more valiant than the prancing pervuts who keep in step so beautifully in The Chorus Line, 42nd Street, *and so on. Tap-dancing is fascism set to music, and the sound of feet tapping in unison is as menacing as the sound of Nazi jack boots marching. Tommy Tune, the tall Texan who's tops in taps, is typical of the mechanized robots who are so successful in that other — that middle class — Times Square. But while he's tops in taps, and could no doubt do a magnificent number to the tune of "Me and My Shadow," he's bottoms in balls; terribly pretty, but not as attractive as the men portrayed below. Nor is the piss-elegant pervut who stays home typing up book reviews for* The Body Politic *with "one wonders," "one wishes," "one suspects," "one hopes," and that pretentious absurdity from Freshman French, "sense of déja vu." – B. McD.]*

MANHATTAN – I was in an all-night movie on 42nd Street early one morning. It was a huge old-fashioned theater and the audience was mostly male. Although some of us were there to get it off or try it on, a lot more of us were there to sleep it off or with wine in paper bags to keep it on. Some were late night or early morning workers and some were there to see the picture (usually a double bill of third-run movies). In other words sex was by no means the sure thing it can be in a gay flick house.

About 3 o'clock, having seen both movies, I needed to take a leak, so on my way out I headed for the piss house. It was located off the lobby at the bottom of a long flight of stairs and to the left.

To enter I had to brush past several men and I thought there was a rush on the pots but once inside I saw that this was not so. The urinals were along the wall to my left and except for a couple of guys standing near them they were unoccupied. I could now see that the men in the door were part of a line headed across the room where the shit stalls were located. The line stopped to the left of the first one, the one without a door. I walked over to the urinals, took my leak, and turned around for a better look.

At first I couldn't see much. Standing in the stall with his back toward the room was a heavy-set middle-aged man with a flapping top coat on who seemed to be taking a piss, but I could see two sneakered feet pointed outward from pot, so the old guy must be getting sucked off. As I watched, he began fumbling with his coat, turned, stepped out of the stall, and went out of the room. I could now see that the other occupant was a youth of about 19 with curly black hair, wearing jeans and a windbreaker, sitting fully clad on the toilet seat.

Then the man at the head of the line stepped in. He was a husky man about 30 and because he had only a windbreaker, not a top coat, and had slim hips, the view was better. He whipped out his dick the way you do at a urinal and dangled it before the youth, who drew him closer and began to suck. I looked down the line. There were about 14 guys all ages from 20 to 60. A few looked promising, especially the one who now headed the line, a well-built young man in his 20s and another about midway down. Most were ordinary. All the men had the resigned look of people standing in line, be it at the bank window or the supermarket checkout counter. The guys watching along with me had the vacant stares you see on men standing around a construction site.

When the guy getting blowed was finished he stepped out and the promising one stepped in. I continued to watch, filled with admiration for the audacity, stamina, and democratic spirit of the dick licker. He was now polishing off No. 4 and hadn't rejected one. I wondered how long he'd been there. He was eating the fifth man when there was a commotion at the end of the line and the line broke up, some of the guys heading for the urinals and a couple of them standing as a camouflage in front of the service station. An old man with a bucket and broom wearing a dirty tan jacket with the name of the movie house on the breast pocket had come in. He headed for the urinals, swept up a few cigarette butts from the floor, and tottered out without even a glance toward the suckathon, where #5 had finished and #6 was starting.

The line quickly re-formed and a couple of the watchers joined it. My own prick was urging me to do likewise but although the cocksucker was working fast the line was growing and it was getting late (or early). I watched the youth fill his suck hole with a seventh hunk of meat and headed for the door and the street.

Ba, Ka And Ca-Ca

By Boyd McDonald

[This piece first appeared in The New York Native*]*

Ancient Evenings by Norman Mailer. Little, Brown, $19.95

What a waste; Norman Mailer has spent a lifetime turning out common, ordinary heterosexual copy while all this time, it now turns out, if he hadn't been such a slave to convention he could have been writing red hot homosexual books. Now old and grey, he says the hell with it and comes out with the most homosexual novel ever written by a known heterosexual.

Most of the homosexuality in the book is abusive; at age 60, Mailer still seems trapped in fraternity-type sex, in which the so-called "straight queers" indulge in forbidden but desirable homosexual acts by using the device of treating homosexuality as a punishment. The book has probably the longest rape scene ever written. "You could see five men working on one fellow who had already been turned into a woman, and one poor captive was even put into harness like a horse while our soliders played with him as they would never dare play with a horse. This Hittite could not even get his mouth open to scream – it was filled to near choking. Picture the fury of the man who straddled his head." And so on and so forth.

In fairness to Mailer, it should be mentioned that he also includes rape of women: "The rush was so great in the fires of this night that many a man could not wait for his place at the front, and so took the girl between her cheeks, while she was busy up forward, and thereby made a three-backed breast, a copulation of serpents. Now, a new man was at her mouth, and another in the third man's bottom."

But what is striking about the book is that it takes an enthusiastic attitude not only toward raping men – which after all is conventional and is a daily occurrence in many prisons – but also toward being raped by them. Both of its two narrators have been forcibly used by men. Both liked it, and want more. One of the narrators finds a pharoah's sweat to be sweet smelling and even enjoys kissing his asshole: the pharoah, Usermare, "lay back upon the bed, and brought Menenhetet's nose near the divide of His buttocks ... 'I was drawn forward by the tip of my tongue. Like the paw of a dog scratching the earth for new mysteries, so did it quiver to kiss the buttocks of Usermare...' "

Again out of the fairness, I should point out that the pharoah is not the only one the narrator sniffs out: "I put my nose into that place out of which all children are born and smelled the true heart of this woman."

The book is probably the most olfactory book ever written; a certain egg "smelled a little like ca-ca on certain mornings, yet even as I could like such a smell one day or another – if it came from me – so did I like the egg." (In addition to his "ca-ca," elsewhere called cock, prick, member, Sweet Finger and even the Victorian proud shaft, the narrator also has a Ba ["soul of my heart"] and a Ka ["my Double"] which space limitations, compounded by severe boredom, prevent me from going into here.) Again, "by the smell of the stuff he now ate, his nose must be traveling through the anus of a goat."

The ordinary press has commented on the book's shittiness; the book's jacket claims that Mailer did research for it, but much of the research could have been conducted in his own toilet or at assorted garbage cans. Tyre apparently was the B.O. capital of the ancient world: "In all the stink of those decomposing snails, human bodies were sweet. Even old sweat smelled like perfume next to such putrescence, and of course no one bathed, not when water could be measured in gold." Somebody "broke wind from his buttocks with every God he named, a cacophony of caps, pips, pops, poops, bellows, and on-booming farts." The inclusion of the phrase "from his buttocks" suggests that the book was not edited, or perhaps even read, by its publishers, as does the paragraph in which the pharoah's visits are placed at "usually in the late afternoon" and, nine lines later in the same paragraph, "usually in the late afternoon." With the author and the publisher obviously not paying close attention to the book, I didn't see why I should have to; but even I noticed that Mailer at one point refers to woman's grandfather as her great-grandfather.

But these are minor flaws in a work where even the pharoah – the one man I'd thought straight – "now brought forth from beneath His skirt an erection of prodigious length. Already, it has pushed His garment forward like the prow of a ship, and, now, since He could not conceal it, He parted the folds of His skirt and showed it forth to the populace. No cheer heard in all the day was like that one." He even goes down on a statue: "He put His mouth around the gold member, the very staff of the God Amon. 'No man has ever penetrated My mouth,' said Usermare, 'but I am happy to kiss the sword of Amon, and know the taste of gold and rubies.' Indeed, on the tip of the gold member, on the knob itself, was a large ruby." Obviously Amon was circumcised.

Even the pharoah's pet lion seems gay: he "now gave a great broad grin at the sight of me, rolled over on his back, spread his legs, showed me the depth of his anus and the embrace of his front paws and invited me to roll on his belly."

Promiscuous homosexuals have always known that there is a lot of homosexuality in the "straight" life. In recent decades many commentators have made this official. But most heterosexual writers express their fascination with homosexuality by denying it. *Ancient Evenings* should have a citation in the history of sexuality, if not the history of literature, as a detailed report of the homosexuality that exists in the mind of a heterosexual.

"Billy Let Me Lick His Crack"

By a Prisoner

PENNSYLVANIA – You have given me the initiative to commit these various experiences to paper; something I've wanted to do for a long time but never had the motivation to do so. Before I forget this small incident I'll write about it now because it involved Billy, who was with me when we first met Joe, a man who took us in his house one rainy night when we were camping out in a tent for fun. I had sex with Joe and didn't think at the time Billy knew about it.

It was the next summer, a year later, and I had been helping another younger guy also named Joe fix up his 50 foot schooner which was tied up alongside the Quaker Cane Sugar Refinery at Front & Fairmount Avenue on the Delaware River in Philadelphia. Joe lived on the boat and while he was away at work I made various repairs on it. Billy lived about a block from me and we usually seen each other every day. This particular day I was leaving my home to go down to the boat and Billy asked if he could come along. I said sure and he asked if he could swim in the river. I replied that it's safe near the boat and to bring his trunks. We took the bus and arrived there about an hour later. I unlocked the cabin door and Billy said, "I'll get a little swim now and then I'll help you with the painting." There were three steps going up to the deck from the cabin and as I was about to climb them I glanced back and watched as Billy took off his T shirt and pants, that was all he had on. His back was turned toward me and I stared at his butt, it was full and round and I was thinking, I'll bet he has a tight ass-hole. Billy, sensing that I hadn't left, turned and seen that I had been looking at his butt. He reached down and grabbed his cock near the base and shook it at me saying, "This is what you want." I guess I stood there with a goofy look on my face. I did want to suck his cock and taste his hot cum. "Why don't you suck it Jack? I won't tell anyone." I wanted to. Then he added, "You and Joe did something last year when we were in his house and I never said anything about that." This confused me and I went up the steps and on deck. Billy came up a few minutes later in his swim trunks and I could see he had a hard on. He must have played with it to get it hard so he could entice me. He looked me in the eye and smiled, looked down at the bulge in his trunks and returned his eyes to mine again. I got the message, it was as if he had said, "Come on

73

Jack, you want my cock and I want you to suck it." He said, "I won't be long Jack." He jumped in the river for his swim. I was hard now, thinking about Billy's hot cock and the load of cum stored in his nuts, and I went down to the cabin to jerk off. I sat there on the bunk pulling my prick but stopped before I came, changed my mind and buttoned up my pants. Billy came down to the steps to the cabin and pulled his briefs off. I handed him a towel and looked at his cock, now shriveled up from the water. He watched me looking at his cock and it began to grow. "Fuck it," I thought, "I want to suck that cock." I went over and took Billy's cock in my hand. "Can I?" Billy acted dumb now and asked, "Can you what?" "Can I suck your cock?" He didn't say anything but nodded yes. He told me to sit down. I did. He straddled my legs and put his cock against my lips, reaching behind my head and holding the back of it with both hands as he slid his cock in my mouth. He began thrusting his pelvis forward and back again, holding my head, fucking me in the mouth. Twice, when he put it all in my mouth too far, too fast, I gagged and almost choked. He finally thrust foward and held my face buried in his groin, spewing forth his cream. It was thick and had a biting taste to it, but I loved it. He let my head go and pulled his cock from my mouth, lay back in the bunk with legs spread and eyes closed. I played with the insides of his thighs, running my hand up to his balls and cock, toward the crack of his ass. Billy reached down and stopped my hand. Seeing that I wasn't going to get far that way I had to try something else. I knelt down beside the bunk and put my mouth around the head of his cock and began sucking again, then I sucked his balls. "Raise your legs up Billy." He did this without any objection and I began licking under his balls, my tongue seeking the crack of his ass. Billy let me lick and suck his crack, even raising up and spreading his cheeks apart so I could suck his hot hole and lick it. I reached down and pulled my cock out and began jerking off. Billy came again and I came. Then suddenly, as though nothing ever happened, he pulled his pants up over his still wet dick and said, "Let's paint." I pulled my pants up from around my ankles and said Okay. That was the first and only time Billy let me have sex with him. Strange.

The Joy of Heterosexuality (II)

From *The New York Times*: "A 15-year-old girl, who had been raped by an uncle when she was 12 and sexually harassed by her father and her mother's boyfriend, fingered the scars on her wrists and said she was afraid to return home. So she had repeatedly escaped so she could stay in the corrections system."

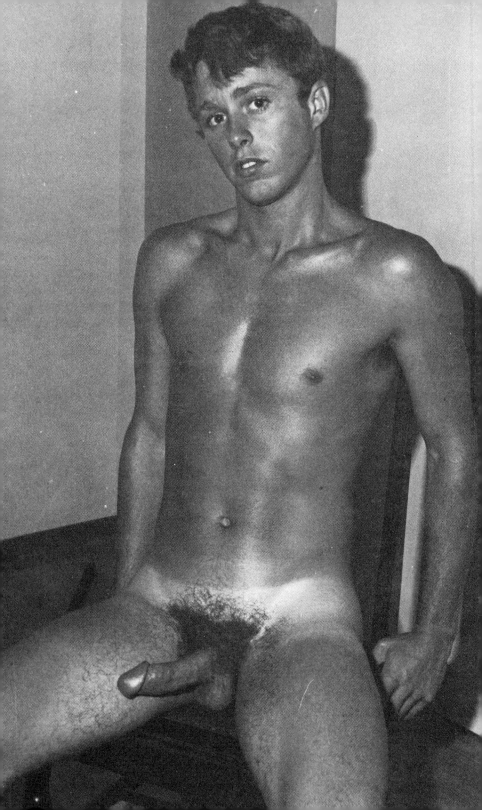

National Defense:
Cream of the Navy

By S. Donaldson
Former Sailor

NEW YORK – The English go crazy over Navy uniforms (it is said that touching a sailor's collar brings good luck, and ladies would come up and ask if they could touch me; gay guys likewise, sometimes without asking, and often not the collar). I got invited to a party with about five guys, including an Australian and a Canadian and the rest English; they were into leather and they got me stoned on hashish and we had an orgy. I even fist-fucked one of them, a new (and not since repeated) experience for me. I wouldn't let them try it on me, though.

I occasionally heard the Italian sailors who were attached to the NATO HQ in Naples talk about going up to Rome to make money off sex with the gays there. In southern Italy and in Greece it seemed to be quite an institution for the unmarried young males, especially the servicemen (who were always poorly paid – the Greeks got the equivalent of $5 a month spending money), to have sex with the foreign tourists for money.

In Naples there was a group of about 30 gay or bi American GIs – sailors, airmen, and soldiers, but mostly sailors – which got together for big parties. An invitation to these parties was much sought after by the gay Italians, but we seldom let more than half a dozen of the locals in.

There were no gay bars in Naples and the only one I ever heard of in Italy was in Rome and was for foreign tourists and rich Italians; it was just off the Via Veneto and too expensive for me. There were a couple of times I dropped in on it and once I met a young Italian I wanted to make it with. He told me it would cost 500 lire, or 80¢. When I agreed (not considering this to be real prostitution, just a cover) he took me home to a sumptuous villa on the outskirts of Rome, with gardens and servants. I met a lot of interesting people who picked me up on the streets (which is where most of the cruising is in Italy). The Italians never seemed to be able to comprehend how a guy would want to switch sex roles; for them you had to be either macho, in which case you were not *omosessuale*, or you were a flagrant queen, and you were not to cross over. Those who went with foreigners were more sophisticated about this.

One time in Naples it was my birhtday and I got very drunk, passing out in a park near Fleet Landing downtown. I woke up in the apartment of an Italian whose thing was making it with American GIs. He proudly displayed for me a Marine dress uniform jacket which some grateful jarhead (he said) had given him. He paid me $10 without my asking for it.

While in Naples I met a Navy officer who was gay. He was attracted to me and invited me to go up to Firenze (Florence) with him for a weekend, which we did; he had to get far away from the military in order not to be seen fraternizing with a non-officer. He wasn't so good in bed but I enjoyed talking with him. I also made it with an officer while I was stationed in Norfolk [Virginia]. I met him through someone else and spent the weekend at his house.

It was pretty easy to get picked up in Naples or Rome, and when I went to Rome I seldom paid for a hotel or pensione because I would count on getting picked up by someone, but sometimes it was a long wait. Finding a place to make out is a real problem in Italy, especially Naples, because all the unmarried men are expected to live with their parents no matter how old they are. As a result, there is a lot of outdoor activity.

There was one guy, Gino, in Naples, an artist (painter) who spoke good English and considered himself a "citizen of the world." He had a studio of his own. He picked me up one time and took me back to his studio. We drank wine and talked and he did a sketch of me until I was very drunk and lay down on his couch. He sucked my dick while I was half-conscious and I never acknowledged it nor did he refer to it in the morning. But he did invite me back. I made many visits to his studio after that and met his family and some of his friends and went out to eat with him and we became friends. For several months, though, he would only get sexual when I was drunk, and I would passively let him blow me. Then one morning he had his mouth around my hard dick when I woke up, and he asked me to fuck him, which I did. He also met my friend Joan and had dinner with us. After that I fucked his ass occasionally and we were more open about it, but I never even hinted to him that I was capable of going the other way; I liked it just the way it was. (I do this often, finding it easier to play straight trade than explain why I don't feel like reciprocating.)

Capri, one of the most beautiful and expensive places in the world, was also a good spot for a sailor to get picked up by rich foreigners who had villas there. In Rome the favorite open-air sex spot was the Coliseum, which was open at night, and where straight couples also went. It thrilled me to celebrate life in a place which once was dedicated to death.

II. DECEIVED BY A NIXONITE.

While I was stationed on the East Coast, Stateside, I had a regular girlfriend, Kathy, whom I would see in New York City. I did a lot of hitchhiking on weekend liberty between Norfolk, Washington, Baltimore, Philadelphia, and New York and my base (I was stationed at different times in different places along this area). I had a *lot* of sexual adventures Stateside.

One of the most memorable occurred in Norfolk when I was staying at the Navy YMCA, having gone down there on leave after boot camp. In the Navy Y downtown (since closed), there were peepholes in virtually all of the old wooden doors to the rooms. It was the afternoon and I was nude in bed resting before going out to supper. I was dozing when the door flew open and a big tough Marine charged into the room wearing only a pair of jeans and shoes, jumped on me, and within a few seconds was straddling my head, his legs pinning down my arms, and jabbing a big red dick in my face. I was totally astonished but I opened my mouth and he started fucking me in the head, coming off very quickly and flooding my mouth with come. Then he withdrew, pulled me over onto my belly, and using spit for lubricant, forced his still-hard dick up my ass. This time he took longer fucking me. He had slammed the door closed but anybody could have watched us through the keyhole as he hadn't hung a towel over it. He was really hungry for sex. After he came off, he jumped up, put his dick back in his pants, and hurried out of the room, not having spoken a single word.

It was in Brooklyn that I had my first experience with "water sports." A guy picked me up there and when we got to his place he asked me to piss on him while he lay in his bathtub. He was paying me $10. It took awhile for me to get over being piss-shy but I finally did and pissed all over him while he jacked himself off. I thought it was an easy way to make $10.

I did a lot of hustling while in the Navy Stateside (and some overseas as well), staying in the "butch/trade" role. One thing I learned early on was that a lot of the johns would be turned off if they learned that I could go either way, so I played it straight. Another thing that turned a lot of johns (and others) off was if they found out that I was educated and well-read, so I played it dumb. Actually, I enjoyed playing the part.

One time I was in a Washington hustler's bar and this old guy offered to drive me all the way back to the base, quite a distance, if I'd stay and talk with him instead of catch the bus. So I did. We didn't have sex, just talked, and then late in the evening we got in his car and headed out of town. About halfway, it started snowing, and before long the Interstate was impassable. The car was sliding all over the highway, so we got off the road and checked into a motel. I called the base and they told me to get in when the road was cleared. So we ended up in a double bed and he got to suck me off after all.

Another time I was sitting on a stoop in Georgetown in DC and a middle-aged, well-dressed guy stopped and talked with me. He then invited me to a party he said was going on at his house, with good weed and girls. So I went with him, but when we got there I discovered we were alone. I said, "Where's the party?" and he replied, "We're it." I got very angry at that. He tried to placate me by offering me Cambodian weed. He worked for the White House and had signed photos of all the Nixon people all over the townhouse and said the Cambodian stuff had come back through diplomatic pouches. It was really dynamite, so after I got high as a kite I didn't feel so much like kicking his ass and I let him take me back to Georgetown peacefully. I wouldn't let him touch me, though. This was hardly the only time when I've run into fraud and deception on the part of guys trying to pick me up for sex.

III. FUCKED BY A TEXAN.

When I was in the Navy I discovered to my surprise that getting cherry was not difficult at all. There were a lot of gay teenagers who had never been fucked before and were just coming out. They had a very romantic image of sailors, which I took advantage of. Normally I prefer fucking mouth over fucking ass, but a cherry was something special and I worked hard at getting them. Kids thought it was romantic to give up their cherry to a sailor. I'll never forget one time I went out to a studio apartment in Queens with a kid about 18, of very limited experience, and a delectably smooth ass. I fucked him in the mouth but he couldn't handle it (I fuck very strong and hard in the mouth) and I couldn't get off. I was horny enough to climb the walls and was pretty strong, and he wasn't, so I overpowered him and held him down and fucked him. He struggled hard but couldn't throw me off, and he cried, too. I fucked him till I came off (which wasn't long), then I rested on top of him, keeping my dick up his ass, which was incredibly tight, till he stopped crying. Then I started fucking him again (my dick never got soft), real slow, and took my time about it, stretched out on top of him and holding him down. He kept saying it hurt and asked me to take it out but I ignored him. I guess I shouldn't have forced myself on him but that's what happened. After I came the second time I again stayed in him and on top of him, then fucked him a third time, after which I stayed in him some more, though by then my dick was soft and it didn't hurt any more. I must have stayed in him for at least an hour, more likely an hour and a half. When I finally got off and we both got cleaned up, he offered me a drink and we talked for a long time. Before I left he gave me his phone number and asked me to call him!

I did a couple weeks later and went out there again, fucked him again though he still resisted and said it hurt, and that second time I spent the night and actually went to sleep with him under me and my dick way up his ass. In the morning he begged me to come see him again. I saw him a total of three times, then he went and joined the Marine Corps.

I got a lot of cherries as a civilian too, but it was a lot easier being a sailor.

By the way, the first guy who ever fucked my ass without it hurting was a sailor I met in New York, a Texan with Spanish blood in him. I met him on West 45th Street and I'm not sure who picked up whom, but we went to his hotel room after spending a couple hours talking in various bars. He was in uniform and was the first sailor I ever made it with. This was '65, in November. I developed an immediate infatuation for him and I think it was on account of that that it didn't hurt when he fucked me – and he had a big, thick,uncircumcised dick, too. I spent the night with him and went around town with him the next day; that evening I took him with me to an orgy I had been invited to. He participated by fucking several gay guys and then left. I think it was this guy who first told me a saying I was to hear many times, and he told me gently because he knew I was emotionally involved with him: "You never see a sailor twice." And I never did see him again.

In the summer of 1966 I hitchhiked out to Chicago. While wandering around, I spied a young Navy ensign on the other side of a broad downtown street and started to follow him around. I followed him for many blocks before I got to talk to him. He was 23 I think, sandy haired and very handsome, especially in his officer's uniform. He didn't tell me to get lost so I tagged around after him for the rest of the afternoon and evening, had dinner with him, went with him to some bars, etc. I told him I was interested in him sexually but he said very firmly he didn't go that way. At that point I should have left him but I just couldn't so I stayed with him, even as it got towards midnight and he started looking for a hotel to stay in. He finally found one that suited him and to my astonishment got a room for two. He said it was too late for me to find a place on my own. I was 19.

After we got up to the room, we got ready for bed (there were two beds, which he had specified to the desk clerk). I was almost asleep when he came over and crawled into bed with me. We had wonderful love-making till dawn. He told me he hadn't had sex with a guy for a year and a half and had to be very careful because he was a Navy officer. In the morning he had to catch a plane for the West Coast and from there go to Vietnam. He said on the ship he was on he shared a cabin with another ensign and he thought his cabinmate also was gay but wasn't sure and didn't want to risk finding out. I was quite in love with him, infatuated, you know. He was from Texas too. Neither one of us slept that night; the time was much too precious for both of us. In the morning when we got dressed he took out his high school ring and gave it to me as a memento. It had a beautiful red stone in it.

IV. CUDDLED BY A CHRISTIAN.

Then in the summer of 1967 I hitchhiked out to San Francisco, blooming in the Haight-Ashbury "Summer of Love." At the YMCA down near the waterfront I met a young sailor from the Philadelphia area named Frank, a devout Catholic, a beautiful, lean guy with dark black hair and deep brown eyes. I invited him up to my room (from the lobby where we met); we talked for a long time. I succeeded in getting him into bed with me but he wouldn't have sex. We just lay there embracing each other for a long time. His religion wouldn't allow him to have sex and he said he was just interested in girls. He was on leave and he liked me, so we spent most of the following week together, exploring San Francisco. It was very romantic and I fell in love with him quickly. He was very warm and tender. It was like a movie. When we finally parted, still without having sex, he gave me his address. I wrote to him. long letters, and he wrote back, and out friendship grew, though it was frustrating. After a year or two he got out of the Navy and went home and I visited him and his family several times, for I still loved him. And he also came up and visited me in New York. We loved to walk around together and hold hands. He was a regular guest when I was living with my friend Sharon, who was also quite fond of him. I had a long talk with him while deciding whether I should enlist in the Navy myself. Then he got a place of his own in Philadelphia and became a lay member of a Catholic order; he sometimes went to the gay bars in Philly to minister to the gays; he didn't drink. He eventually decided he was bisexual but that his way was that of chastity. In the 70s he got more and more spiritual. He lived selflessly in poverty and devoted his life to helping other people. A beautiful, beautiful being. And for all his dedication to chastity (which involved great struggles) he never suggested that his way was best for anyone else; he never condemned homosexual activity in others.

So I had been emotionally involved with three Navy men and had had many sexual experiences with sailors before I enlisted and became one myself.

Before I enlisted, I had been living with Sharon. She had a girlfriend in the same building named Joan. I was attracted to Joan but didn't make it with her because of my relationship with Sharon. After I joined up, Joan left for Paris. We kept in touch and when I got settled in Naples I invited her to come down for a visit. At the time I was sharing an off-base apartment with three other sailors, including David, who was my lover. His ship was in when she came down. David had a car, so the three of us went driving all over the Italian countryside. She didn't know that David and I were anything more than good friends and David was very good about it; he really seemed to enjoy her company and didn't intrude when we desired to be alone. I fucked her at every opportunity. Later I got leave and spent a week with her in Paris. I had a great time between the great food and the great pussy, and I also enjoyed just being with and talking with Joan. After I got out, though, I lost touch with her. David later enrolled in the same school I went to so we got in touch again and are still friends, though it's been almost a dozen years since we were lovers.

At Daphni near Athens, Greece, they hold a wine festival, 60 varieties of Greek wine, all you can drink for the price of admission, which was about $2.50. Daphni was very popular in the Fleet and towards the end of the evening the grass was littered with drunk and passed-out swabbies. I managed to make my way back to Athens when the festival closed at midnight. There I wandered around the Plaka entertainment district. I entered a public pissoir there about 2 or 3 A.M. to piss and passed out, in uniform, on the floor of the john. When I came to I found myself nude in bed with a guy in his 30s who was sucking my dick. He did a good job of it, too. I found out he was a German photographer who had seen me in the pissoir and carried me home, put me to bed, and taken my clothes off, all while I was unconscious. I had brunch with him and fucked his ass and then left.

I also made it with a Greek sailor in Athens. He was very friendly and I took photos of him. Also made it with a Greek soldier. He said he had to be paid for sex, but he was willing to settle for about 15¢ in Greek money. Both of these Greeks were only interested in Active (penetrating) roles, especially ass-fucking.

Naples must have the ugliest whores in Europe. One in particular was called Humpty Dumpty because she always sat on a wall about ¼ to ½ mile from the base. One night I was hanging out with a bunch of Marines, about seven or eight of us, and someone suggested we pool our cash for a joint expedition to see Humpty (the cheapest as well). I was in the right mood so I went along. She would disappear with one of the guys into the bushes behind the wall while the rest of us waited up at the wall. When my turn came I had a hard time getting up for her because she was ugly as an old sow and I had to use a rubber, which always turns me off. But I eventually did and closed my eyes and fucked her while thinking of another girl. Afterwards I wondered if it was worth it, but I hadn't had any pussy in quite awhile so I didn't feel too bad about it.

While I was on leave I visited Amsterdam and wandered around the Sailor's Quarter, also known as the Red Light District, where prostitution is legal and run by the city and the girls recline on couches placed in the windows. All the fees were standardized by the city — 25 guilders ($8) for a quick fuck with her pants pulled down but not off, 50 guilders if she took all her clothes off or gave you a blow job first. So you could window-shop and pick out the best one. I did and she led me up a narrow flight of stairs to a small room, where she provided me with a rubber (sigh), pulled her pants down and reclined on another couch. She was good looking, a dark-haired girl, so I was able to overlook the rubber and get it up to fuck her. I came off pretty soon, though, because it was so exciting to be able to fuck a good-looking girl and I was pretty high off the experience for the rest of the evening.

V. WARNED BY AN OFFICER.

I grew up in the Navy, son of a career Navy man, so I've been around sailors through most of my youth. I always loved the sea and ships and admired the sailors, so it was only natural for me to enlist in the early 70s.

Sailors believe they are the horniest guys on earth. I was told that this was a fact by my instructors in boot camp (Great Lakes); they said that a true sailor has to be able to "fight anything, drink anything, and fuck anything." Very early in boot camp we watched a TV lecture by an officer warning us young boots about homosexuals. He said: "You may hear various terms for these people once you are out in the Fleet, terms like 'sea pussy'..." At that point the whole room broke up.

My home town is Norfolk, which is the biggest Navy base in the world. On a weekend when the Fleet is in, there would be tens of thousands of sailors and Marines wandering around and not enough girls (other than professional whores) who would go with them. When I was in uniform and in Norfolk, there were two gay bars there, downtown, and neither one was off-limits. The area is full of "seafood queens" who love sailors. It was common for sailors and Marines to hitchhike back to the base from downtown late at night on Bousch Street, where the gays would cruise in their cars and pick them up – usually with a detour on the way back to the base. In the mid-70s the city fathers tore up the whole of downtown Norfolk and redeveloped it for banks, etc., so that the night life dried up and went to other parts of the city and neighboring cities like Virginia Beach. So all that action I used to know there changed.

Sailors know they radiate macho sexuality and deliberately enhance it by getting uniforms tailored very tight. The old Navy uniform with its 13-button flap emphasized the sailor's dick. The sailors, by the way, call that flap the "Marine tablecloth," implying that the Marines eat sailor dicks when their flaps are down (open). The gays call the sailors "seafood". A lot of guys would get designs embroidered on the inside of their trouser flaps so they could display them when they took the flaps down. Also favored are silk flap linings on the inside (worn without underpants).

Sailors take a lot of showers and are very clean. They may choose the Navy because they know they can always get a shower in the

Navy, not sit around a muddy or dusty field. They tend to walk with a swagger that comes from being on a rolling and pitching vessel. They are pretty uninhibited but not quite as uninhibited as Marines.

It is extremely common for sailors to form pairs of buddies, who really love each other though they won't have sex except by having a threesome where they both make it with another person (a woman or a gay guy), often at the same time and watching each other. It's not unusual for a group of sailors or Marines to all fuck the same girl, and occasionally also have sex with the same gay guy.

The common belief is that sailors especially like getting blown and Marines like to get fucked up the ass. Mostly I find sterotypes not very accurate, but this one has a lot of truth behind it. Sailors do seem to be very oral. It's common to hear sailors say they prefer a girl to give head than pussy. And they do love to get their dicks sucked. The American sailors don't seem to be much into fucking ass; maybe it offends their sense of cleanliness. When a sailor comes from liberty after getting his dick sucked by a guy, he might tell about it quietly or keep it to himself. The Marine, on the other hand, may burst into the barracks telling everybody, "Boy, did I get a knob job from this fag tonight. You shoulda seen him go to work." I've known a number of straight Marines who have volunteered for the experience of getting a dick up their ass, not as a regular thing but just to see what it feels like. The Marines are so indoctrinated with their own machismo that nothing seems to threaten it, whereas straight sailors stick more to the "male" role.

Different Navy ratings have different reputations. The HMs (medics), DTs (dental technicians), YNs (clerks), and SDs (stewards) are the gayest — all the HMs I never got to know well, in fact, turned out to be gay, or at least bi.

I suspect that ego plays a big role with sailors who go with gays. For the ordinary sailor, life in the Navy has a lot to do with being a number, part of a mass, always taking orders from somebody, and being treated with contempt by civilians. Then along comes somebody — a gay — who treats him like a king, tells him what a handsome stud he is, shows interest in everything about him, and finally even gets down on his knees in front of him. Now it's the sailor's turn to be in command, give orders, be the big man — "Suck that dick!" It's powerful stuff and leads some sailors back again and again. There's a lot more than just sex behind this symbiotic mating of straight sailor and gay civilian, this intermingling of two very different subcultures from the periphery of American life.

Naked In The Emergency Ward

By a Prisoner

OKLAHOMA — Dyral was a counselor and enjoyed the same cluster of male night clicks and surrounding as I. I could tell he had the gay blues when I excepted *[sic]* the complimentary drink at the Taj Mahal metro area of the city. I had just jumped off the one man stage in my jock strap when Sugar handed me the drink from Dyral. I was always shy about taking offers from male clients because I was affred *[sic]* it might be the vice. Dyral and I went for a drive about the beautiful city looking at the night at work. I knew Dyral wanted my prize pocessions *[sic]* for he couldn't keep his blue eyes off my large black meat basket, that throbbed in my jock under my blue jeans. Yet I played it kool for this period of my life I was a black male hooker in the better male lounges where business men came to get a breath of fresh air from the closet of every day stress and I was glad to be the preferred cup of tea. Dyral and I made it to his dwelling at about 2:30 that morning. I drove. We enter the house from the back entrance and made our way up to a red velvet bed room. Little did I know that Dyral mother was asleep in the adjointing bed room just a wall away. I could tell Dyral had the thing call middle age gay blues when he told me he would kill him self if I wouldn't belong to him as his lover on our first night. Dyral had written me a $400.00 check and put a $3000 diamond ring on my finger the first night. And I tryed to ease the pain in his heart and told him I would give him vast considerations. But he could not buy my love he had to earn it. And make me feel like givin it freely. Dyral was crying and I knew things were bad because his head was smoking with wiskey. He was sloppy drunk. And I hated drunks. I had almost fell asleep. When I opened my eyes Dyral was just about to finish off a bottle of Scotch and a bottle of some type of sleeping pills. Then I knew the guy had it bad, but I didn't know what. And I knew he wasn't bullshitting about killing himself. I reached for the telephone to call the hospital for an amalance, but Dyral faute me off the phone telling me no one loved him and he wanted to dye. And I knew I only had a few minutes to get him to the hospital to get his stomach pumped. I had to wait until he was asleep for he would fight to keep me from calling the doctor. I tryed to weak Dyral up for five minutes but he was out like a light. I found my way to the kitchens ice box and found some milk and a glass. Made it back to the bed room and forced his mouth open and held his nose so he would have to swallow the milk. I got about 4 glasses down him. I grabbed a blanket and threw it around Dyral nude white body and struggled to get him across my shoulder. I made it. I packed him to the car and layed him in the front seat. I was half way to the hospital before I recognized I and Dyral was nacked as hell. Only Dyral had the blanket. Then I was afraid as hell. Me in the South buck nacked in the car with a buck nacked white almost dead. I didn't have time to think in that fashion. I made it to the emergency enterance and had a guy go in and sommons a stracher and doctor. The male entern asked after he saw us nacked what in the hells going on? I stated look theirs no time for a lot of questions, this guy has been drinking a hell of a lot of buzz's and took half of this bottle of pills. I still don't remember bringing the pills but I had them tight in my hand. I took the blanket after the strecher came for Dyral. And I felt like a fool sitting in the hospital nude and answering all the questions to the doctor and police. The doctos knew we had had sex but I explained to the doctor that this could not get out to the public, the sexual activity, for Dyral would lose his job. I dated Dyral until I thought he wasnt sueciedal from my conceptions. The last time Dyral and I were together we were at the Bam-boo and every thing went private at 2:00 and the doors were locked from the inside the bar. I was the only black spot in the joint. When all of a sudden Dyral stumbled over to me and snatched me around to face him and snatched my pants down and started giving me head at the bar. I didnt know what to do. I had never had such a thing happen before. And I stopped seeing Dyral after that and gave him back his ring, for he was too much to take.

Lust in the 7th Grade.

Too often, today's youth are bad news. It is a pleasure to report something good about them for a change. In East Montpelier, Vermont, according to UPI, a ring of 25 boys in the seventh grade sold "sex magazines and posters" or rented them out for "15 cents a peek." The youths are to be commended for their healthy attitude towards sex, which they achieved naturally and with no help from their educators. Someone less healthy (a teacher) ratted on them and they were brought into the office of the principal, Lyman Amsden, who told the UPI that "we had an office full of embarrassed little seventh graders." But it is Amsden who should be embarrassed – embarrassed and ashamed. The inability to enjoy sex is something to be ashamed of, not proud of, and what the prudish majority regard as their superior virtue is not virtue but a flaw stemming from the fact that they are too cold, too conventional, too homely, or too frightened to enjoy the beauties of God-given flesh. Just by pulling down their pants and Jockey shorts and displaying their bare butts, the East Montpelier youths and other youths could present to each other images as beautiful as any that can be bought in the sex magazines; but I suppose it is expecting too much that that be *that* healthy.

An American In Paris Suck-Holes

SAN FRANCISCO — My brother shared a twin-bed room with me when we were kids. He was six years older, a good athlete, and a champion swimmer. I was only seven or eight the first time I caught him jacking off. He was on his bed, his legs spread, and his big uncut cock in one hand while the other slid around his body. He didn't make any effort to hide what he was doing and even seemed to enjoy having me watch him. After awhile, his stroking picked up speed, and I could see that he was growing more and more tense, closing his eyes, bending his head back, and thrusting his groin upward. Then he made a strange gasping whimper and his cum began spurting onto his body. It shot and shot and I was fascinated to see the effect the experience was having on him. When it was over he looked at me and said, "Don't you tell Mom and Dad about me doing this. Don't tell anybody."

Once he said, "How big is yours? Show me." I was embarrassed to let him see my little prick but I pulled it out. He reached out and squeezed it. It felt good. He said, "You'll be growing a big one pretty soon." I asked him what that white stuff from his cock was and he explained, "It's jizz. It comes out of your balls." He reached under and squeezed mine gently. I watched him jack off many times after that and I even got up the courage to ask him to let me feel his cock. He told me to go ahead and I kept at it until I made him shoot his load. When he joined the Navy at 17, I missed watching him there on his bed with that lordly cock of his. It was two years before I saw him again. He was now 19 and I was 13 and I'd already shot my first load. His first night home, I couldn't wait to be alone with him and show him that I could come, just like he could. When we went to bed I put on a show of jacking off but he said something about "kid stuff" and just turned out his light and went to sleep.

I soon sucked my first cock and an older guy picked me up hitchhiking and sucked me off for the first time. I've been a devoted and dedicated cocksucker-suckee ever since.

II. JACKS OFF WITH BOYS

The first time I saw a cock other than my brother's was in the locker room at school. After softball the boys went into the locker room to shower. I'll never forget walking into that shower room and seeing about 15 guys all naked, sporting cocks of every size and shape — long skinny ones, short stubby ones, cut, uncut. A kid named David had five inches soft.

When I saw a guy soaping his crotch without getting a hard on, I couldn't believe it. I couldn't get my self all slithery like that without having a hard on. At this stage I played with my cock constantly – in school, in church, in the back seat of my dad's car, in elevators, in the pool, and, of course, in bed; nothing I had ever experienced had ever given me such ecstasy and I couldn't get enough of it. There was another kid named Carlton who had the same problem as I – a few seconds of soaping his crotch and his cock stood up fully hard. It used to embarrass him and the kids would make rude remarks about it, just as they would about me.

It was with Carlton that I had my first contact with a cock other than my own. We were at his folks' place on a Saturday afternoon and I said something about the way we both got hard ons in that shower room. I said, "Watch." I just reached down and lightly stroked my crotch and the bulge stood out at once. He asked me if I liked to jack off. I told him I loved it and he said, "Let's do it." We took our cocks ot and stared at each other as we stroked ourselves. I couldn't resist moving to him and reaching out to feel his hard cock. He did the same to me.

From that time on I had an urge to jack off with any kid I could. By the time I was in my late teens, I made it with dozens of guys I knew and even with a few strangers.

When I was in my first year of high school, there was a guy named Keith who was not only one of the best athletes we had but who was widely reputed to be "doing it" to Helen, a girl with big tits who was the vice president of the Student Council. Keith got his pubic hair long before most of us and just about every boy in the shower room regarded him with awe. Although he wasn't especially handsome or bright, he had something that none of the rest of us had: a pubic bush and a full-grown set of cock and balls that absolutely radiated potency and excitement.

At my high school in Oregon there was a swimming pool in the basement of the field house and we swam with nothing on. Between that pool and the locker room, I got a good look at the equipment of just about every guy in school. One of the guys in my class was named Roy. He had beautiful black hair and his skin was fairly dark. He was well built and he sported a handsome cock and balls. Once I was walking out of the showers after a swim and Roy was standing in front of his locker, naked, toweling his head. I stopped and stared at him, wishing it would be OK just to go over to him and suck his cock. He caught sight of me looking at him and I'm sure he knew what I was thinking. He looked down at his genitals and then back up at me and he grinned. But he turned and got his shorts on.

That note of yours in S.T.H. about Jimmy Archer shooting basketballs in the high school gym before game time while wearing only a jock strap reminds me of a guy in my high school, Jimmy Porter. I have a vivid memory of watching him do situps wearing only a jock

89

strap. One thing I remember especially was the expression on his face. It was consummate self-assurance and calm pleasure. And, just as you related about Archer, Porter was even more exciting in his jock strap than the times I saw him completely nude in the shower.

There was a YMCA in Portland that had a large complex of locker rooms, massage rooms, and several rooms to store gym equipment, mats, towels, weights, etc. I worked there occasionally, taking care of the towel room. There was a guy named Johnston who swam at the Y almost every evening. He was around 30, chunky, with a good-looking uncut cock. One Thursday evening I was waiting for the last guys to leave so I could throw a load of towels in the washer and go home. Without much else to do, I sat on a large box and began playing with myself. Pretty soon I had a hard on and I took it out and was having a nice time. I kept glancing up to make sure nobody could see me. At 17, I jacked off a lot and I often did it right there in the towel room. I could stand at the counter with my cock out and nobody could see below my waist. It was fun to look at the naked bodies coming and going. This time instead of standing behind the counter I was sitting on that box. Suddenly I noticed that Johnston had stepped into the room and was standing there smiling at me. I tried to hide myself and pretend that nothing was happening but he said, "It's OK. Go ahead and finish." He fondled his own cock. It swelled a little but it didn't get hard. He dropped his towel in the basket, said good-night very genially, and walked out to get dressed.

III. JACKS OFF IN CAR.

In my junior year I switched to a new high school. The head track coach was a demon about good physical conditioning and our locker room was a supermarket of goodlooking bodies. Our best distance runner was a guy named Joe. I remember watching him many times and marveling at the graceful and powerful way he moved his body. One afternoon in the locker room Joe came in after running a few laps and there was a wonderful sweaty glow about him as he stripped off his shoes and socks, shirt and shorts, and stood there in only his jock strap, talking with a buddy. As he talked he casually reached down and scratched his balls through the pouch. Then he bent and stripped the jock strap off. He ambled toward the showers and the globes of his ass were beautiful. I wanted very much to get a closer look at Joe in the nude and I took my clothes off to take a shower, although I'd already taken one just a short while before. It got me very excited to see him slathering his crotch with soap and manipulating his beautiful equipment.

While I was in high school there was a club, sort of fraternity, that invited me to a rush party. It was held at a road-house restaurant near Portland and there were about 50 members of the club, with ten rushees. After dinner there was a dirty movie. The first thing I saw on the screen was a woman with enormous tits who was busily shoving a medium-sized salami in her cunt. A door opened and in walked a guy in overalls. He was black and he had a strange look on his face. The woman did nothing to cover herself, but went on screwing herself with the salami, and then she opened her mouth and beckoned to the man, who stepped up to her and shoved his big cock in her mouth. After a bit of sucking, the man took the salami out of her cunt and unceremoniously shoved his cock into her. He fucked her like a machine for awhile and then pulled out to shoot his load on her belly. They showed a couple of other films, the last of which featured a woman who took on two young guys at once.

When the movies were over, the lights came back on and I caught sight of a guy named David sitting a few feet away with a huge bulge from the hard on in his pants. When the evening was over I spoke to David, who lived not far from my home, and asked him for a ride. In the car, we got to talking about the films we'd just seen. He said, "Boy, I never saw anything like that before. It got me hot as hell." I said it made me get a hard on, and that I'd noticed the big bulge in his pants back there. He said it's not that big. I asked him to show it to me. He looked over with a curious expression. "You want to see it?" I got an inspiration and quickly whipped out my own cock, which was hard. He took out 8" of hard meat. I asked if it would bother him if I jacked off. He said hell no. He parked in a vista-point above the river and said, "Let's have a race." I didn't need more than a minute to come. He came about a minute later, sending large squirts of his cum up in arcs. He wiped himself with his handkerchief and I used my shirt-tail. Then he drove me home.

By the time I was 11 or 12, my fascination with cocks was total. I checked out every guy I saw, thinking what he must have between his legs, and I was a confirmed crotch-watcher. I also developed a passion for a particular kind of face, like that of the young Montgomery Clift. I can remember studying a picture of him and creating an intense fantasy in which the picture came to life and Monty looked at me and grinned in a lewd and knowing way, took out his beautiful cock, and told me it was mine to play with as I chose. My brother had a friend named Wally who came as close as anyone I've ever seen to Clift's magnetism, and I once had the thrill of feeling his cock get hard. By this time, I'd touched a few other boys' cocks, all boys my age — but Wally was 17 or 18 and he had a big, manly cock, not like the boyish peters I'd experienced. Several of my brother's friends were at the house for a party and Wally asked me to show him around the house. Up in the room I shared with my brother Wally he said he felt dizzy. I think he'd had too much beer. He sat on my bed and looked at me with those astonishing eyes. His lips were perfection, quite as sensual as the head of a cock. He said, "Whew! I thought I was going to pass out." I sat next to him. There was a hefty bulge in the crotch of his slacks. I felt scared, since he surely knew what I was thinking as I looked at it. He said, "Go ahead and feel it." I put my left hand on the mound. When I'd fondled it for just a short while, it was at full hardness and I could feel the outline of the head. "Here," he said, "take a look" He unzipped his fly and brought out his cock. It was glorious, I was just about to take hold of it when my brother's voice came up the stairs. Wally whispered "shit" and stuffed his cock back in his pants. My brother came up and he and Wally went back downstairs. I went to the bathroom, locked the door, and jacked off.

IV. SUCKS SAILOR IN BUS.

When I was 16 I spent a few days at a coastal resort town in Oregon and took a Greyhound bus back to Portland. There were only a few passengers, all seated toward the front, when I got on. I went to a right-side seat near the back. Just before the bus pulled out, a young guy in a white Navy uniform hopped on, toting a canvas bag. He moved along the aisle, hoisted the bag into the overhead rack and said, "Hi, how's it going." His accent was southern. I said great. As he swung into the seat beside me he said, "Mind if I sit here?" I told him it was fine. As soon as the bus was out on the highway the sailor introduced himself: "I'm Charlie. Glad to meet you." I told him my name and we talked for awhile. I asked him about the Navy and he gave me a run-down. Presently he stood up to get a brown paper sack from his gear. It contained a pint of Southern Comfort. He uncapped it and offered me a drink. I've never liked that stuff and I don't suppose I ever will, but I didn't want to turn his offer down. I took a slug and passed the bottle back to him. He took a huge guzzle and slid the sack under his seat.

Eventually, to my surprise, he grabbed his crotch and said he had a case of the stonies. He'd spent the night with a girl who turned out to be a prick-teaser; she would let him "mess around a bit" but wouldn't put out. He said his balls felt like they'd been kicked by a mule. I said, "Well, when they get like that, you can always jack off." A little later he said, "Hey, if you don't mind, maybe I'll take care of this condition of mine." I said it's a free country. He began undoing the buttons on the flap of his pants. Soon his pants were open and he reached into the slot of his boxer shorts and hauled out an uncut cock with a pointy end and big meandering veins on the shaft. He manipulated about a six-inch hard on and told me it was fine with him if I wanted to join in. I brought my cock out, already hard. We sat there stroking ourselves. I loved the way his foreskin slid back and forth, revealing the bare head of his cock, then covering it. He said a guy in Atlanta "sucked it for me, and he said it tastes pretty good." I really wanted to do it but I was scared the driver would spot us in his mirror. But I glanced forward and felt it was probably safe and slid down in my seat as though getting in a comfortable position for sleep. When my head was far down enough I bent to my left and quickly took his cock in my mouth and cupped his balls in my right hand. He began rolling his hips in short, rapid fashion. When he was ready he suddenly grabbed my head and he shoved his dick as deep in my throat as he could. I felt a series of hard jolts as he shot his load. It made me gag briefly but I took it.

When I sat up again Charlie thanked me and said, "I tried to get that damn cunt to do that to me last night but she wouldn't. I was hoping he'd return the favor. I had my hard cock in my hand. He said, "Hey, I'm sorry, but I ain't no cocksucker, but if you want me to I'll jerk you off." He reached over and took hold of it. He stroked my cock harder and faster than I'd ever done myself and I came in only a short time, squirting cum all over my shirt and his hand. I used my handkerchief to wipe the gobs of cum from my clothes. He merely wiped his hand on the side of his seat.

Not far from the end of that ride, I saw him groping himself again and asked him if he could come again. "Sure, if you suck it for me." The bus was only a few blocks from the terminal when Charlie shot his second load in my mouth.

V. GETS SUCKED IN EIFEL TOWER.

I spent a few hours with a note-pad writing down the names of as many guys as I could remember having sex with in my whole life. A few of them have special meaning, since they involve much deeper relationships than mere tricking. The range of ages is large, including youngsters I played around with when I was still a hairless kid. It's a multi-racial list and I can boast of several delightful experiences with blacks, hispanics, orientals, and a full-blooded member of the Celilo Indian Tribe. Of course, a few of these entries relate to frightening situations. The worst of that sort happened in Paris, while I was there as a student. Walking home after dinner with friends, I crossed the Esplanade des Invalides. In a stand of ornamental trees I spotted a man in the shadows. He was leaning against a tree, lewdly fondling his crotch and staring at me. I decided to check him out and walked toward him. I stopped several yards short of him and he put on a little show in which he ground his hips and slowly undid the buttons of his fly. He hauled his cock out, a thick, blunt one, and placed his hands on his hips. I figured it would be pleasant to suck it for him, as he obviously wanted me to, and I moved into the shadows with him. He reached out and began shoving me to the ground, taking a painfully firm grip on my shoulders. I sank to the ground and was engulfed with the most powerful aromas I've ever experienced from a guy's crotch. I enjoy normal man-smells but this guy was something else. It was a prodigious stink and I wanted to get away from it. Then, speaking a language I didn't understand but took to be either Portuguese or some Spanish dialect, he barked a few harsh words at me, took me by the hair, and started slamming his groin against my face. I've never been into S/M, but merely enjoy a good blow job or an occasional fuck. If that guy expected me to get a thrill out of his brutality, he was dead wrong. I took his nuts in my hand and gave them a healthy squeeze. He quickly let go of my hair and shoved me away and spat on me as I scrambled to my feet and got the hell out of there.

Most of the other names recall delightful experiences. In Paris, I had an American friend with whom I occasionally had sex. One afternoon we decided to have a look at the city from the top of the Eifel Tower. When we got into the elevator for the long, slow descent, we were the only ones in the car. Phil dropped to his knees, opened my pants, and said, "I'm going to make you come before we get to the bottom." He took my soft cock in his mouth and began licking and sucking, and it hardened quickly. I wanted to give him a load of cream but we were approaching the level of the tower's restaurant and Phil had to get back on his feet, since people could have seen into the car.

Looking over that list, I also came across a name that made me feel a bit kinky and embarrassed. It's the name of a patient at the state mental hospital. I'd gone there to do some research for a paper I had to write for a class in sociology while I was in college. I spoke with a couple of staff members and was encouraged to meet some patients. One of them was a wonderfully handsome fellow of about 19. He looked like my heart-throb, Montgomery Clift. His name was Lee. We talked for a few minutes and he offered to show me his room. As soon as we were inside his small room he closed the door and said, "Listen, we won't have much time. I need to suck you off. Take it out...please?" I was definitely not against having my cock sucked, but I hesitated. "Is it safe here? You don't have a lock on your door." He said, "Don't worry. It's OK." He slid the chair from under the small table and told me to sit down. Surprised and dazed, I did as he said and he just got on his knees and took my cock out and sucked it for all he was worth. It didn't take me long to shoot my load and Lee devoured it like a starving man. When it was over, he looked up at me and said, "God, that was good." He said, "There was a guy here for awhile who let me do that to him but he's gone and I haven't had anybody to suck for a month." I said, "Do you want me to do it to you?" He said, "Oh, Jesus, would you?" We changed places. His cock was surprisingly small, no more than 4½", uncut. But it tasted wonderful and he gave me a fine load of cum.

I just got a call from a guy who was once my lover. He wants to come over and pick up some things that have been stored in my basement for the last few years. He's a nice guy and we're still fond of each other. I owe him a lot because he's the first guy who ever made me love being fucked. I get goose-bumps when I remember the first time he screwed me. By the time he slid that magic muscle into my ass for the first time, I was not only ready for it, I was begging him to give it to me. It was a masterpiece of a fuck and I regarded him with complete awe as he took me to heights I'd only dreamed of before that.

VI. GETS SUCKED IN PARIS BAR.

It turned out that the Esplanade des Invalides was a good cruising place. Along one side of the Esplanade there were some trees in a formal array with a long carved granite railing, about chest high, that divided that grove from the grassy center of the Esplanade. One pleasant summer evening I was walking home from a show and as I passed by those trees I noticed two shapes in the near-darkness. It looked as though one was standing against a tree, the other kneeling in front of him. I stopped and leaned against the railing to watch the scene by the tree, about 20 yards away. No doubt about it; the head of the guy on his knees was moving back and forth and the standing figure was clasping the shoulders of the cocksucker.

Presently, another guy stepped out of the trees to my left. First he looked at the two guys I'd been watching, then he looked at me. He reached down and groped himself. Then he stood there with his hands on his hips, glanced again at the other two guys and back at me and then slowly turned and went back into the trees. It was too interesting to resist, and I left the railing and followed him. He stopped near a tree and when I was only about ten feet from him he began opening his fly. He slid his hand into the opening. For awhile I stayed a few feet away. I copied his gesture, opening my pants and reaching in to play with my cock. My French was good enough to understand "Je veux le voir" (I want to see it). I pulled my hard on out and he said, "Oh, c'est beau." With a gesture I indicated his crotch and he pulled out his own hard cock. It was an average 5" or 6", uncut. He moved forward and gently explored my cock. I returned the favor and we stood there swapping squeezes for awhile. Then he looked around, sank to his knees, and began sucking me. He was a good cocksucker. He took it to the hilt and he excited my balls with his fingers. I came in a hurry. Before he stood up he lavished kisses and licks on my cock and balls and whispered, "Delicieux." I was about to go down on him when another pair of figures appeared nearby. My friend quickly tucked his cock in his pants. The others stood near the railing and looked at us. My friend said, "J'ai peur...au revoir." He quickly moved off in the opposite direction. I guessed he was afraid that the guys who stopped to look at us were police.

A young French guy I'd met took me to a bar in La Place de la Croix Rouge. Before we entered he warned me that some pretty strange things went on there. As we moved through the tables to find a place to sit, I noticed that the crowded bar was entirely populated by men. Two guys at one table were locked in an embrace and kissing passionately. A guy reached out and groped my friend's crotch and then mine as we passed. Apparently it was a gesture about the same as shaking hands. I got a hard on at once.

Jean-Pierre and I sat down and ordered drinks from a tall, hunky waiter. I looked around and spotted a guy standing against a wall. Another guy was on his knees kissing the mound at his crotch. This was my first time in a gay bar. Jean-Pierre said, "This is nothing – you should see what goes on back there." He pointed toward the archway at the rear. I told him I very much wanted to see what goes on back there and he said, "Go ahead."

I was groped about five times as I headed for the archway. One guy, feeling that I had a hard on, said, "Mon dieux, un cheval." The corridor led to a complex of rooms. The first was merely a dark chamber with nobody in it. The second had a couple of guys standing against the wall. At the end, on the right, was a much larger room with several mattresses on the floor. About eight guys were grouped around two others who were fully naked on the floor, locked in a 69. One of them had a very big cock. A few of the guys in the group had their cocks out and were stroking them. I took my cock out and joined the voyeurs. Somebody groped my ass and the guy to my left reached over and played with my cock for awhile. Then he went down and sucked it. I was so excited I came in a very short time. A guy on the other side of the circle shot his load on the two in the middle, grunting and groaning like an animal.

When I went back to rejoin Jean-Pierre and described the scene in the rear chamber, he laughed and said that things "really get serious" after midnight and that there's a non-stop orgy there until about six in the morning. I was horny to suck Jean-Pierre's cock and I took him to the first room back there and had a fine time with him. His cream was quite salty.

VII. GETS HAND JOB FROM EMBASSY QUEEN.

I had a strange experience with an older guy who worked at the American Embassy. I was 23 and the man who helped me with the permit I needed for a "restricted" country had the softest voice I ever heard; I had to keep asking him to repeat. He also spoke with a fruity undertone. When all the details had been handled he asked me if I'd like to join him for a cocktail. We went to a bar near the Embassy and Irwin asked me all sorts of questions about my studies, my background, my family. After a couple of drinks he said, "If you aren't busy this evening why don't you come to my place – I've got some marvelous veal." I was certain by that time that he wanted to get into my pants. He had a very pleasant apartment near Les Invalides. He poured drinks and in his Virginia accent spoke in French to the middle-aged woman who was his housekeeper and cook, telling her that we'd have dinner at 8:30. When she said "Bien, monsieur" and went back to the kitchen, Irwin, who was a bit drunk, told me: "She's really a jewel. Does everything for me and it costs next to nothing."

It was only 6:30. Irwin poured more drinks, opened a cabinet, and brought out a large leather brief case. He set it on the coffee table and sat down next to me on the sofa. He took a stack of photographs out of the case and placed them before me. "I got these from a friend of mine who's a collector." They were all shots of naked men and women, all shapes and sizes, sucking, fucking, playing with themselves. When I came to a shot of two young guys with big cocks, each with a hand on the other's hard on, I remarked, "They sure have big cocks." Instantly, Irwin reached to my crotch. I had a hard on and I figured I'd let him have his fun, although I wasn't interested in him. He fumbled with my zipper and belt and brought my cock out. I asked if it was all right, since his housekeeper might come in. He said, "She doesn't give a shit, and she knows when the door is closed I don't wish to be disturbed." He played with my cock, saying, "Beautiful. Your cock is so beautiful." He jacked me off and asked, "Do you like it? Am I doing it right?" I told him he was doing it fine and I rolled my hips and really got into it. Pretty soon I started spurting and Irwin bent over and gobbled my cock, making ecstatic noises as he took my load of cream. I really enjoyed that moment, and told him so.

I asked Irwin if he wanted me to help him get off and he asked me just to sit there and play with myself while he jacked off. He pulled his cock out, a thick, stubby affair with an immense head, and stroked it with only a finger and thumb. He gave a quick series of gasps and shot his load into a handkerchief which he took from the pocket of his jacket. He put himself back together, returned the brief case to its place, and we talked. We never got around to dinner; he was just too drunk. I left by 8 P.M., leaving Irwin passed out on the sofa.

VIII. STRIPS IN PARIS PARK

S.T.H. came in today's mail and I came shortly thereafter. What got me off was the delightful story about the two guys in the park in Boston. I had just such an experience in Paris. One evening I went for a walk along the Seine. Near the Esplanade des Invalides, I spotted a French sailor. He was leaning against a lamp post and I homed in on him like a pigeon. He was about 21, fairly short, well built, and his crotch bulged attractively. In my rather shaky French I asked him if he'd like to go for a walk and have a drink with me. I punctuated the invitation by groping my genitals. He smiled and said, "Let's go." We ambled into the Esplanade and headed toward a bunch of trees. By the street lights near the walkway I caught sight of the prominent swelling in his pants. He was obviously ready. He stepped into the shade behind some bushes and I began rubbing his gorgeous bulge at once. His cock was steely hard. He reached forward and groped me in return. My meat was straining and the touch of his hand nearly had me squirting. We opened each other's pants. Neither of us had undershorts on and our cocks were soon sticking out proudly. He looked around to see how safe it was and then began stripping off his uniform. I was a bit scared, since the place wasn't all that private. But the prospect of being naked with him was too good to pass up. I got my clothes off in a hurry and went to my knees to suck him. I can report that French cock is just great. He had about 6", uncut, and the flavor and aroma were rather like mild camembert. I urged him to fuck my mouth and he obliged with rapid thrusts that made his balls slap my chin. It didn't take him long to have a glorious orgasm that gave me the first taste of French cum. Superb! His shudders and bucking as he shot his load were thrilling. I was jacking off hot and heavy, there on my knees, keeping his cock in my mouth. As I came he chanted in a whisper, "Oui! Oui! Oui!" and I shot my wad on his legs and feet. I licked him clean before he dressed. We sat on a bench and talked for an hour. When he said he had to go I told him I'd be glad to see him again. He took my phone number and address. Two weeks later I got a call from him and we arranged to get together the next evening for dinner. After a light dinner we went up to my place. We had our clothes off within seconds of closing the door. He asked me what I'd most like him to do and I told him to jack off on my face (always one of my favorite things). He knelt, straddling my chest, and gave me a glorious show as I licked his nuts, his asshole, his cock, and gazed up at him. After he squirted his load he sucked my cock for awhile and then took it up his ass by sitting on it. We were sex friends for the rest of my stay in France. He now lives in Chartres, is married, and sends me occasional letters in which he tells of his periodic romps with young men. I have a son, 17 years old, and a daughter, 16. My wife and I split up ten years ago, after ten years of marriage.

"His Hole Was Nice And Pink"

SOUTH DAKOTA — You asked about experiences with some of the cowboys out here. I had some years ago when I moved out here but this summer I had a very unusual and good one.

I have a friend who has a ranch in the center of the state. It is quite a large ranch and has some wild areas, woods and a creek and sandhills, stock dam, etc. I visit there now and then when I want to get away from the office. Also, I like camping so I drive down and pitch my tent and camp out for a weekend. Usually I am all alone so it gives me a chance to get the cobwebs out of the brain and just breathe deep and relax.

Last July I went down there for a week of camping. He had a guy working for him who really turned me on. He was good sized, beefy and a happy, really pleasant guy. I could not believe it when I was told that he was only a teenager, he was so big. Needless to say, I found him very attractive, though I usually do not have anything to do with that age group.

As you probably know on a ranch when a man has to piss he doesn't go into the house or the outhouse, he just walks in the barn and pisses where the cattle and horses do. So I went into the barn for a piss and the kid was right there with me. I was a bit amazed when I saw what he pulled out of his overalls. His muscles were not the only thing big. He was not the least bit embarrassed and let it hang there as he pissed. I noticed also that he was very interested in my cock. We stood there talking and shaking our pricks and then went out.

Later my friend tells me that the kid is pretty lonely on the ranch, doesn't have anybody to talk to, etc. So I ask if the kid can go camping with me. Fine. The kid is overjoyed. We drive down into the woods in my friend's pickup. On the way the kid, Dave, asks if he can talk to me without me telling anybody. I say sure, of course. He asks me if it is all right to jack off and I tell him it is good for him, which it is. Then he tells me about this friend who is sticking his cock in his brother's asshole. Can a guy do that? I assure him that it is physically possible and very enjoyable for both. Then he asks about sucking. He tells me that he gets real worked up at school when he sees the guys naked in the showers. But he quit school now. We get to the camp and it is very obvious from the front of his overalls that he really has a hard on, but he doesn't make any move to cover it up.

After we get the camp settled, he wants to go swimming. We bareass in a stock dam, and I am very happy to see him naked. It turns out that all he wears is overalls, a shirt, and boots. He is bareass in a minute, and so am I, except he still has the big hard on. Then he starts talking about guys having sex with each other and do I think that is wrong. I see now that the kid is really gay and needs some help. We got out of the water and Dave still has the big hard on. We are standing near the truck, letting the sun dry us, and his cock is about six inches from belly. I figure, take a chance and see what happens So I gently wrap my hand around his prick and he sighs. He asks if he can play with my cock and he starts to stroke. It is great. He is really hot and I am afraid he is going to cum. I ask him what he wants and he asks me to suck him. So I sucked him off for the first time and he came right away. Big load, thick. Then he sucked me, took to it like a duck to water and just kept licking and sucking it.

We went back to the tent and spent the afternoon just enjoying it all. He had been wanting it for a long time and hoped that some older man would take him and answer all his questions. His ass was beautiful, full, smooth skin, and his hole was nice and pink. He had blond hair and very little in his asshole. I rimmed him for a long time and he loved it. Finally I gave him what he really wanted and let him fuck me. It was great even though he had never done it before. Needless to say, we spent a lot of time talking about male sex and also enjoying it. I was surprised that he had no hangups, was not embarrassed, had no guilt feelings. However, he told me he had been thinking about it for a long time but could not figure out how to meet anybody. Also, he was scared of approaching a stranger. He comes to see me about once a month now; he was here last weekend. And he is beginning to accept himself.

He has not contacted anybody else because he is not quite there yet. But he will be all right in time and will be able to be positive about his homosexuality. He will make some guy a great lover and in the meantime I am happy to fill the bill. Last weekend another friend was over and Dave had his first three-way. He really enjoyed it.

I am meeting some other new guys now and then but this with Dave was a bit unusual. Also, my regular friends drop around but there is nothing unusual there. Even though there are no bars, baths, etc. out here there is still a lot of good action. You just have to have the right kind of friends.

Take care of yourself.

/s/ Love

"They Took Turns Fucking My Mouth"

CLEVELAND – Let me fill in some of the details about that encounter with the guy I told you about. We were walking down the aisle of the movie arcade. Every time I got to a different aisle the guy I scored with was there too. I walked up to a booth to look at what was playing in there. This guy smacked his lips and asked if I'd like to watch the movie with him. I said yes so we went in and closed the door. He then started to rub my groin and unzip my pants. After that he took my pants down and gave me a very smooth blow job. When I go to this place to look for something to eat, I usually make sure the guys I want see me lick my lips. I mostly go there to have my filthy mouth fucked. Whatever blow jobs or asshole I get is added delight. You asked me if I can take being fucked in the mouth laying down with a guy laying over me. Yes I can. It's a little harder to do but I try to be a good screwhole for those I score with. To some my lips are cunt; to some others my lips are like a hot tight shit hole and my ass hole is like a pair of puckered lips. One time a black guy and a white guy had me in bed with them. They took turns fucking my mouth while on top of me. One then the other, again and again. The white guy watched us two blacks. He got excited seeing nigger prick fucking nigger suck hole. He stuck his white dick in the other black guy's butt then fucked my mouth until his cream shot in my mouth. He stayed hot and had the other black guy jack off on his white meat. So, then the white used the black guy's slime to lube his dick so he could fuck my coon ass again. I loved it, filthy scummy slime bag that I am. Sometimes when I am alone in bed I amuse myself. That in itself isn't so unusual. However, my disgusting fantasies both alarm and excite me. I usually have my left hand around my meat and two or three fingers of my right hand in my shit hole. I think about what it might be like to be beaten with a rubber hose. What the feel of the hose slammed on my nuts would be like. I think about crawling on all fours with a man behind me who's got his arm up my butt cunt. The last vestiges of sanity evaporate when I think about jamming my filthy dick in some helpless asshole. I have fucked two boys who came on to me. I always wanted to be a fuck hole when I was a little boy but I didn't know how to go about getting what I wanted.

Tolstoy Did It

According to Malcolm Muggeridge in a review of *Tolstoy and Gandhi* in the Sunday *Times* Book Review (New York), the diaries of Leo Tolstoy show at least one "homosexual affair."

Sucks Brother Off
Before Wedding

When I was 8½ my brother Donald, who was about 13 then, decided he was going to have my cherry. It happened one night after we had gone to bed and my other brothers were still out for various reasons. He told me to turn over on my stomach and spread my legs. My being a sickly child, and him being so fucking healthy, naturally made me quiver with fright. I instinctively knew what he was about. I was curious enough to go along with his wishes, and yet fright filled my very being.

He proceeded to smear Vaseline all over my ass and shove some up my tight, hot hole. Even his finger hurt that still virgin ass. Beside being virgin myself he was hung like a horse. At that age he must have had at least 7". To a virgin asshole that is quite a bit.

He crawled between my legs with that fuck pole of his. He located the hole and started to push. Naturally I felt like he was making a new hole. I must have been very resilient from a very early age because he did get it in eventually the whole length. I felt, however, like I truly had a telephone pole up there. The pain was excruciating but for some reason I enjoyed the thrill of debasement. I knew instinctively that I was a fucking slut. He fucked for what seemed like hours, and with the mixed feeling of pain and whoredom I survived.

Whenever my parents would be absent from home, out would come his cock, hard as a fucking piece of steel, aimed at my asshole. He was just too butch for me to dare to raise my hand to him for fear of having the living shit beat out of me. I figured the best thing for me to do was to remain as passive as possible to keep from riling him up.

There was this one time when my folks had gone to visit some friends and left us home alone. Naturally I begged to go along but I did not dare to say why. They no sooner left the house than I ran out of the house like a streak of cat piss and up into the woods to get away from him. He knew where I had gone and eventually found me. He had brought some rope with him and tied me to a tree. Out came the cock, as usual, and he told me he was going to piss in my mouth. This was more than I could stand. I wouldn't open my mouth for him to do it so he started to belt me around. Eventually I allowed my mouth to be opened. As I look back I sort of half-assed enjoyed the filth I was called upon to do. It was just his rough tactics that scared me. With his cock firmly implanted in my mouth the piss started to shoot, filling my mouth with what seemed like gallons of his hot, salty piss. I swallowed and swallowed. Then he threw me down onto the ground and with some spit tore my asshole open with that fuck stick of his. When he was through using me he left me alone in the woods crying and wishing I were dead. I wanted to get away from it all but I did not dare to tell anyone and if I did – who? I could not fight him off myself and I was afraid to tell my parents.

Sometimes he would just have me put on some women's panties and stand there and do the hula while he jerked off. After he came he would tell me to lick the cum off his cock. After that was done he would very gruffly say, "Get the fuck out of here." I guess I would be safe in saying that he was sadistic.

This went on for many years. Eventually I started becoming the little whore of the neighborhood.

When I turned about 17 he stopped harrassing me. Then as I started coming home late from dates and movies or whatever I would make sure that he was in bed before I went up. He was always "asleep" so I daringly slipped my hands under the covers and played with that huge cock of his. Immediately he would get this ferocious hard on. I stealthily shoved my head under the covers so as not to "awaken" him. His cock just throbbed for attention. Slowly I would slip my mouth over the bulbous head and start a slow, steady deep-throat job on him. He never once "awakened" in the four or five years of this cocksucking era of our lives. When he shot his cum into my mouth he did not quiver, moan, or anything. I always knew when he was coming though because he always had to shift himself in his sleep and make sure his legs were wide open so I could be sure and finish my performance. He could not fight the urge to let those balls of his pour forth all the cum he had stored up for me that day.

The night before he got married I sucked him off. What a wedding present. So, at about 24 years of age, that all came to a close. Just when it was good, the asshole decided he was straight. I imagine he tried shit like this with his first wife. Being the prude she was I doubt she would go along with it.

I remember when Donald was in the Navy I would be elected to brush his uniform off with him in it. Naturally I would brush his front longer than the rest of him. By then I was just so into cock that I could have been immersed in them and not have had enough. I was blessed in the fact that I came from a very horny family. Donald was a handsome son of a bitch. Black hair and a swarthy complexion. God, if only he had not been so rough to my asshole. But there was always that fear of getting the shit beat out of me. He knew he had me scared and he used that to the hilt.

II. SUCKED OFF 9 TIMES IN 1 DAY.

Once when I was about 25 I got raped by a young powerful guy that

104

I had taken home to blow. I always say that was the best sex I ever had. Rape at that stage of the game was enjoyable. God he was good. He knew just what to do to a willing asshole that kept saying no. He took me with force and I fought him right to the bitter end and – thank God – he won out. When he got through with my asshole I knew I had had it. The bastard never came back though.

One of my best times was when I had this young couple that both had nice bodies and he about a 7-8" fat cock. The were in their early 20s. I came across them fucking in broad daylight in a field. Naturally I got to snooping so close that I got caught. Not being too bashful they asked if I wanted to join in. Well I did. She straddled my face in a 69 position. There her cunt was right above my face. He slowly slipped his cock into that fuck hole of hers and started to work it over. Every so often he would pull it out and shove it down my throat. To know a cock has been in a cunt drives me wild. When he shot his cock was way down my throat and not in her snatch. This went on in other positions before he shot a second time. I even ate her cunt once while straddling her face and he fucked me up the ass.

I love dirty talk. Strange as it may seem I do not find the word shit in the least bit sexy, but the best cocksucker I ever knew loved to eat my shit first. That guy could suck marrow out of a dead man's bones. When I blew my nuts with him the whole town must have heard me. I am not one of the silent ones. When I shot with him though it felt like my guts, liver, and everything else was coming out. He sucked me off nine times one day. One day he died and that was the end of that saga. I found one that came pretty close but no one could fill his shoes.

I love an audience. I was cruising this nice-looking 30ish white guy at the steam baths Christmas Eve two years ago. This 30ish black guy was looking at the white merchandize also. I knew from long ago that the black guy had a long fat cock to spread someone's asshole with. The black guy asked me what the white guy was like, thinking I'd already had him. The black said he'd like to have the white fuck him in the ass. The white guy would have nothing to do with him. The white wanted to watch someone fuck me, then he would fuck the one that fucked me. I consented to let the big black buck throw a fuck into me. We left the door open and got about as lewd about it as you can imagine. The white prancing by the door lit up with lust when he saw us. He wandered in and got down close to where the action was to see as much as he could. The white kept uttering filthy oaths at us and telling us what to do. Naturally we complied because we both wanted more action than just the two of us. Pretty soon the white guy crawled up behind the black and stuck his big cock up his ass. By now there were other stragglers coming into the room. There were about six stiff cocks just sticking out there waiting for whatever. There was this one nice-looking guy standing there that had a nice body and a horny piece of hot cock jutting out from under his towel. I managed to maneuver him over next to my face and sucked it voraciously down my throat. While I was sucking on this delectable piece of manhood he was saying filthy things like "eat that fucking meat," "suck the come out of my balls, "swallow my meat," "tear his ass open," and so on. With the double fuck, cocksucking, and occasional sniff of Rush I could not begin to describe the heaven I was in. Both fuckers were waiting for the other one to shoot before they wanted to drop their loads in our assholes. I was praying for a stalemate. If it never ended it would be too soon. God, I didn't think I'd be able to walk for a week after this. Someone always manages to fuck things up. The guy I was sucking got so fucking hot he blew his nuts. With his moaning, groaning, and dirty talk, like "I'm coming, you cocksucker," it was more than these other two could take and they both shot.

It had been sort of unusual because the other guys in the room seemed to pick up on the conviviality of the scene and they were mouthing obscenities along with everyone else. What a lewd scene it all was. Everyone thanked everyone else and wished each other a merry Christmas and went on their way.

My ideal would be to be sucking some gorgeous guy's huge cock while he lays on his back and slings his legs up over my shoulder. Then while I am down there stretching my throat muscles around his fat cock to have another guy come up behind me and start fingering my asshole with lubricant. All the time I am trying to get out of this predicament but the guy I am sucking won't let me up even with all my "fighting" to get out. Then the guy behind me sticks some Rush under my nose and I just go out of my fucking tree. I practically swallow the guy I am sucking on while the one behind me rams his cock in clear to the hilt. All the way out and all the way in. While all this is going on more and more guys come into the room. As soon as one is finished another crawls on. Eventually I am just awash with cum and I can feel it running out of my asshole and down around my balls. The sight of cum leaking out of my ass makes some of these guys so fucking hot they can hardly wait for the one ahead of them to finish so they can crawl on top of me. All the while they are shouting dirty, rotten, filthy things in our direction. Things like:

Fuck that dirty slut
Feed him that fucking pork
Ream his ass out good
Fuck his guts out
Give that cunt your balls and everything

Then when the one on the bottom has held back as long as he can he gushes forth with "take my cum you bastard, swallow it you cocksucker." After he has shot and left the room then some of the others roll me over on my back and start to fuck my asshole with my legs wide open for all to see the cocks that are ravishing my cunt-hole. One by one others climb up on my face and start fucking the hell out of that. They show no mercy as they fuck their hot, fat cocks down my throat. Meanwhile I am trying to fight them off but I am losing miserably – thank God. Some of them shoot all over my face. One guy pisses up my ass while another pisses down my throat.

I love to have people standing around and egg on the ones that are doing all the action. Then when they get sufficiently horny from all this, they become part of the action while others line up and await their turn. I would gladly hire a hall and charge people $10 a head to come in and watch. I'd be a millionaire in a year.

III. "HUMILIATED AND HAPPY."

One day I went to Loring Park for the usual hunt. I met this gorgeous guy that wanted a blow job. Naturally I told him I could more than accommodate him.

Home we went to my place. Once there we started to disrobe. I was well satisfied with the merchandise I had brought to my home. He was somewhere in his very late teens or early 20s. He had a stocky, muscular build and was about 5'10" tall. His cock was perfectly shaped and about 8" long and on the fat side.

He lay down on the bed and spread those muscular thighs of his for me to crawl and grovel between. I took out my teeth, crawled onto the bed, and licked that gorgeous piece. I sucked, licked, and generally juiced up the head of his cock and then slowly started to lower my cocksucking mouth down and around the whole length of that stick. His groans and moans just drove me up the wall. I was so fucking hot that I could have shot my wad if a fly had landed on my ass.

I played with his beautiful balls by rolling them gently around in my hands while I increased the fervor with my hot mouth. By now he was rolling, moaning, and writhing around in the bed. His balls were so tight against his body that I could hardly get at them.

I wet a finger while doing all this sucking and slowly eased it up his hole. This brought even more delight to his already ecstatic face. He was beside himself. This guy knew how to be sucked and he knew that he had a first-rate cocksucker on his cock.

When he got close to coming he told me to stop. He just lay there and said "God, what a fantastic cocksucker you are." This made me very happy. There are so many lousy sex partners out there that I prided myself on knowing what I was doing and being good at it.

He spread his legs and we got back into the blow job. As I continued my ministrations on that lovely cock, I got him to fever pitch once again and then to prolong his coming I told him to roll over and stick his ass up in my face. He complied with my wishes and even took his hands and spread his ass cheeks. I massaged his prostate with my finger and licked his balls and asshole while I gently and slowly massaged his cock, which was as strong as steel. Looking between his legs gave me one of the most enjoyable sights a man in heat could enjoy.

I rolled him onto his back and started sucking that gorgeous cock again. "Eat me, eat me, eat me," seemed to fill the air. The cock was swollen with lust by now and the veins were well raised along the entire length of the shaft. It was ready. At this point he wanted to shoot so bad I'll bet he would have fucked a skunk. "Oh God," he said, "make me come. Suck it. Suck that fucking meat. I got to come. I can't stand it."

So with my asshole pointed heavenward I took his cock down my throat clear to his balls and sucked for old glory. Soon I heard the most glorious words in a cocksucker's life: "It's getting close. Don't stop." When he came, I thought he would fuck my brains out as he held my head and hollered every dirty word in creation. I thought I would suffocate before he relaxed enough to let go of my head. He was one in a million.

As we lay there recuperating, he kept raving about the beautiful blow job I had given him. After a short while his cock started to liven up again, although it never had lost its swollen appearance entirely. I started to work on it again and he said he wanted to fuck me. I did not especially want to get fucked by him, although it would have been an honor. He crawled out of the bed and stood there and told me to lie down with my ass up in the air. I did not have any good reason why he shouldn't fuck me; I just did not feel in the mood for a fucking. Probably because I was having a ball sucking him. He just got on the bed and turned me over like I was a feather. He forced his way between my legs while I "fought" him. I must add that it is terribly hard for a dyed in the wool whore to ever fight off a man. God is it fun to fight for your virtue when you don't even have any left. His stiff cock found my asshole and in it went clear to the balls. Without any preparation, it felt like I was being torn from asshole to belly button. The fact that he was gorgeous made the pain easier to take.

He rode my ass regardless of how I felt for what seemed like a half hour. My asshole was getting stretched and reamed like never before. This guy knew how to fuck as well as be sucked. All the way in, all the way out, short jabs, long jabs, around and around. There was not any fuck motion he overlooked. Being a good whore I just loved it when he said, "You've got a good ass there. It was made for fucking." He had no regard for how it felt to me and I can truly say, it was one of the best fucks I ever had. When he was through I was thoroughly humiliated, sore, and happy.

As is the case so often, I never saw him again. Too many gay men say nothing – absolutely nothing – the whole time they are in bed. I love my men to use dirty talk when they are having sex with me.

Married Men at Play

[EDITOR's NOTE: There are still some people, such as the United States Government, who regard married men as "straight," and I always welcome letters like the following one which describe what goes on behind the facade of Holy Matrimony. The author of this letter is a divorced father; his visitor is still married. Another thing I like about the letter is the visitor's age – there is no shortage of young meat in these books and I like to publish accounts of older men too. I don't have the author's exact age, but he is considerably younger than his visitor. He practices law and has, according to his photograph, an unusually long prick.]

TEXAS – Don't know if you can use this, but I'm sending it along. I'm busy so don't have the time to write, but wanted to get the enclosed item to you.

He turned out to be an average looking 58-year-old, almost bald, with a bit of grey hair around the rim of his head. He has an athletic build and is in good shape for a man his age: very little discernable belly. He drove me out to a convenience store to buy a roll of Polaroid film and some beer. We drank beer and chatted while he loaded both the Polaroid and the movie camera he'd brought along, an old Bolex that takes 100 ft. of double rolls, meaning that when they split the finished film, you have 200 ft., which runs about 12 minutes on screen.

He was a little nervous, never having been with a guy before, even just to film him jerking off, which is what he wanted me to do. He had a mess of lights, bluecorrected for Kodachrome, and he set them up in a fairy professional manner, with a few tips from his subject, a former film student at U.C.L.A. He was quite the director, actually, saying he wanted "continuity," so would I sit on the edge of the bed and take my clothes off, as that was what a man would be doing in "real life" when he's preparing to jerk off.

I must be an exhibitionist because I enjoyed taking the cues, taking my clothes off slowly and deliberately and tossing them on the floor. Then he had me stroke my stick. When he saw that I was having difficulty getting a hard on, he took off his own clothes and came over to where I was sitting, offering me his cock, which was about 6 inches but thick. I started sucking him off and he moaned, and I could tell it was a genuine moan of pleasure. As far as I know, I'm the first man who's ever given him a blow job and, as he later admitted, none of the women who've gone down on him have done so well as I did. I told him that's easy to explain: "Women don't have cocks, so they don't know how to make one feel good."

Anyway, I kept stroking myself as I was blowing him, and I got a hard on pretty fast then. He pulled away and started filming me jerking off. My cock got super hard, the way it is when I'm most turned on, so much so that when I took my hand away from it, it jerked about spasmodically, which it will not do unless it is really erect and turned on. He shot about 30-40 feet, then said, "Lean back on the bed – I want to try you."

I could tell it was something he'd never done, because his teeth got in the way, but as he got into it, saying, "I kind of like this," he got better and better, and he even managed to get abut half of it into his mouth before long. He kept saying things like "You've got a monster on you" and "one hell of a big cock." He took some more film, then let me suck him some more, and then I had him lie on the bed with his feet pointed toward my head and showed him how faggots sixty-nine. He really got into it, then. Being older, he was slow to cum, very slow. He took more film, then we sucked some more; then more film, then more sucking. Finally, he started to jerk himself off, and he moaned and groaned and I kept putting my lips around the head of his cock as he was jacking off, so he got the point and said, "I'll give it to you." When he was on the verge of cuming, he stuck it into my mouth and I deep-throated it, sucking like crazy as his cum unloaded furiously into my throat. He came and came and I swallowed every drop.

Then more film and more film and more still. He told me that his son shoots film on the same camera and that if the processed film came back from Spectra in one of their "Processed Film" envelopes, his son might open it thinking it was his. So would I mind if he used my return address on the order? I said fine. That way, I will be able to see it, too, and can merely forward it to him.

He shot me jerking off in every conceivable position; that is, *he* shot from various positions; all I did was merely lie on the bed and jack, jerk, jack. He managed to time the thing quite nicely, so that after I finished myself off, he had about five feet of film left. When I came, I spurted in every direction – not the usual spurt, spurt, spurt type cuming, but a fountain-like thing, like a spray, and voluminously. He told me that it would show up very well on film because he had shot it with the dark brown headboard of the bed in the background for contrast. "It looked nice and white." He kept two of the ten Polaroids and gave me the others. My cock looks enormous in them. In all, we were working for about four and a half hours. I had blueballs from jerking off without cuming for so long. And that night, when I got back from the theatre, I saw that my cock had swollen up something fierce. It was sore, but it's better now.

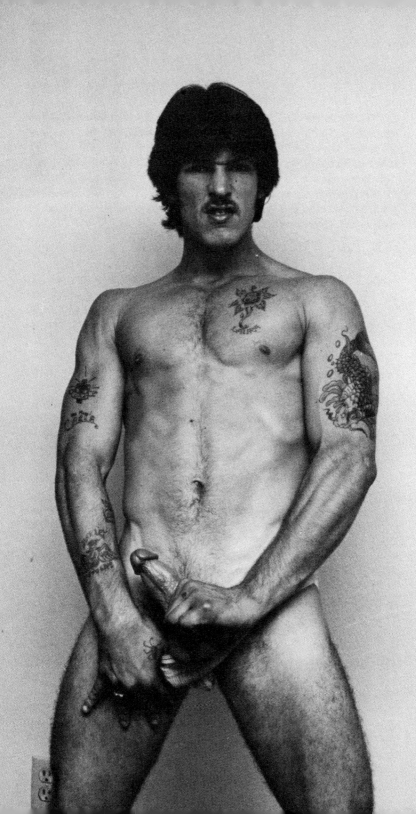

Boy Ass

By a Prisoner.

[EDITOR's NOTE: Most of the boys in the following series of letters are underage. I do not publish articles about adult men seducing underage boys, which is against the law; I do publish memoirs like this one, written by adult men about their own boyhoods. I have not corrected the punctuation and spelling; I wanted to retain the authenticity and purity of the letters as written. The men who write for S.T.H. can do something much more important than spell correctly – they can write honestly and courageously.]

NEW JERSEY – What I write is true incidences in my life. I started my active gay sex life when I was a young boy. I had a lover named Andy. I was having sex with Donny, a friend. He was the one that got me into hustling with no front teeth. I was sucking older teen boys' cocks at three dollars a suck. Would jerk off men I met at the movies for three and go down on them for ten. So my experience in sex is a lot. Well I think I'll write about Eugene.

A friend of mine is a Catholic priest and he is also gay. He dropped Eugene over at my place and told me he lived on the streets. When I met him, he had pete-male [petit mal] epilepsy. He was a dirty little boy. When I looked into those warm brown eyes I saw love. I stripped him and put him in the bathtub. I emptied his pockets and put his clothes in a bag and threw them away. I checked out his hair as he sat in the tub. He asked me to wash him. He kissed me on the cheek as I washed him. I turned and kissed him on the lips and he smiled. He wore a towel as I fed him. It was like he hadn't eaten a full meal in years. He over-ate and made himself sick. I gave him a bi-carb and held him in my arms. We sat and watched T.V. and he fell asleep. I put him in bed and locked the door and went to the store. He wore a size 14 in cloths. So he would have new cloths when he woke up. I didn't have sex with him the first night. I just snuggled up to him when I went to sleep. I woke up with his legs around me. He had been sleeping in a junkyard in old buses. His father found him in bed with a man and threw him out. This is a five-three ninety pound kid on his own and trying to make it on the street.

When he had a seizure, his eyes would get dreamy and his head would shake back and forth. He was an almost completely helpless boy. What he needed was love. He loved getting butt fucked. His way was sitting on your lap. He'd fondle you until your cock head got wet. He'd then rub the head against his ass hole, then slowly lower himself on your cock. He'd be facing you with his small cock and balls rubbing against your belly. That position he could get hugged and kissed as he fucked himself on your cock. He is very good. He'd soul kiss you all the time he was getting butt fucked. You could feel the sexual pleasure he was getting. His breathing would get heavy and his tongue would move faster against yours. When you shot a load in his ass he'd push down and moan.

Gene needed a lot of loving. He was neglected. His father and mother didn't believe in hugging and kissing their son. They were afraid they'd turn him into a sissy. Gene told me he started giving blow jobs in school. When his cousin Tony, 12, was baby sitting Gene talked him into letting him suck his cock. Well it was Tony's first blow job, so he sucked Gene and turned him over, and butt fucked him. Gene loved it. He said when Tony's cock went in his ass, the thrill all over his body almost made him pass out. From that day on he couldn't get enough cock. If you start getting butt fucked at six your ass is well broken in at 11.

When I met him he was a very loving boy, whose parents didn't love him. But his friends loved him. Father Tim couldn't keep him. That's the reason he left him with me. There is another thing – I have the patience of a saint. Gene had to re-learn how to wash himself. He had an emotional shock from his parents throwing him away. His only "sin" (?) was that he loved boys and men. He gave me his love and sexual satisfaction. His love was lost to his parents but I grew to be a better man for having known him.

He didn't leave my house for his first four days. I knew I'd have to wean him away from me. I was not going to let him go until I taught him to survive. I taught him how to cook. I taught him to be proud of himself. Since he is gay and doesn't seem to get enough sex, I taught him how to suck a big cock. A friend of mine who's hung pretty good stayed over a night. Sam has an ass hole fetish. He loves licking ass holes. So using Sam's cock, I showed him how. First you lick the cockhead, put your tongue in the slot, lick the shaft, lip the head, then take a deep breath and put it deep in your mouth. Taking the deep breath prevents you from upchucking and choking.

I did make him happy in three months. He was showering by himself. He could cook. I talked him into calling his cousin Tony. He like Gene wasn't welcomed in his house. He's also gay and is living with the guy who owns the restaurant he works in. The thing is the man is a straight with compassion. Tony had finished high school and was going to cooking school. Gene would go to live with his cousin if I would visit at least once a week. Our last night together was pure love. He started sperming when he lived with me. He stayed naked from the time he woke up in the morning. It was a Saturday morning. After breakfast he gave me a blow job and after he got my sperm he got in his favorite position on my lap. His unquenchable thirst for sex kept my cock sore for two days. His cousin Tony at 17 was Italian, tall dark and handsome. He has a sweet tasting cock.

When I first sucked him I was still sore from my day with Gene. This guy who owned the restaurant was one of the best men I have ever met. He knew Tony is a homosexual and he let Gene move in with him and Gene told him he is gay. He looked at me and asked me, "Are you one too." "Yes," I said, "I am a homosexual and have been one since I was a boy." He smiled, shook my hand, and said, "Tony told me what you did for Gene, and I am proud to meet you." I can't give his name; but he gave me hope, if he can accept a person for what he can do, not his sexual identity. Let's hope he is not a rarity.

II. NOT HANDSOME, BUT ATTRACTIVE.

Well I'm happy you are looking for more true stories. So I'll give you my two Sams.

I was 16 when I met the older Sam. I was staying with my uncle Mike and sleeping with my cousin Cary. They have a house outside of Atlanta Georgia. My cousin Cary is straight but jerks me off as I do his. Well he is the one who helped me get a drivers license. He got me a good price on a Harley, so I loved him for it. It was red with gold pin stripes and it was one beautiful bike. Cary had one too so he showed me where we could race. I was racing him one Saturday morning and this guy pulls up to us and points to me. He said kid you're pretty good did you ever think of going pro. I'm looking at this guy, around mid-30s, dirty blond, scraggly hair, hazel eyes, around six foot, and said, "You're not kidding are you?" "No, with a little training in about a year you could have your first race." Cary said, "I know you're the one who raced last night at the track."

That night after showering I looked at Cary and said, "You are my luck." We are only a week apart in age, he's an inch taller. I looked at him, his dimpled smile looked back at me. There is a family re-semblance. We have the same nose and cheek bones and dimples. We lay in bed jerking each other off. "I think he wants you to leave with him after tomorrow's meet," Cary said. "I'll go with him if he offers me a job to work with him," I said. The funny thing was Cary's cock was like mine and it felt like I was doing myself.

Well Sam took first that day and I did leave with him that night. We drove until about 10 P.M. and he pulled into a trailer park. When he put his hand on my leg I looked up at him and said, "You want to have sex?" "Yes" is all he said and we 69ed.

Nine months later, I had raced pro twice and came in the money once. We were outside Denver in a trailer park and he told me to take a day off and play. I was 17. The bike I raced on was still chained to the pickup. I still had my street bike, the red Harley. I went out exploring and came across a ball field with guys my age playing softball. They let me play and I became a little kid again.

There was one boy with a funny laugh, he had brown hair and green eyes and the nose and high cheek bones of an Indian. After the game he followed me to my bike. "Right fancy motorcycle you're riding," he said. "I did jazz it up a bit," I said. "Can I ride with you?" he asked. I told him to hop on and I'd give him a ride home. It turned out his name was Sam too. He said he was a half-breed: "My father was a Ute and my mother Irish." He had a noble face, not what you would call handsome, but still attractive. His pleasant smile and funny laugh made him good to be with. He was 15 and only about 2" shorter than me.

He showed me where he lived. The house was run down. I guess with his mother working as a barmaid and he in high school, there wasn't anybody to fix the house. "Why don't you stop for awhile," he said. "I'll give you something to eat."

He took me to his room. What was amazing, it was neat and clean. He brought me a tray of food and handed me a few magazines. They were sex magazines, boys our age having sex together. He stood in back of my chair. "You like it don't you?" he said. He had his hand on my shoulder leaning over me. I turned my head and planted a kiss on his lips. I got up and took him in my arms. He quivered when I ran my hand down his back onto his high muscular butt and fingered his hole. Our penuses were rubbing against each other as our tongues played in each other's mouthes. We finally lay on his bed in a passionate embrace. We groped for each other's cocks. As soon as his and my cock felt the tongues, we were so hot we shot our loads. His penus was about the same size as mine and what all gay teen boys want to do is suck their own cock or one like it. I licked the shaft and went down to his pinkish hairless balls, kissed each one. He was doing what I was doing for him. I kissed the inside of his legs under his balls. I ran my tongue up the shaft of his penus, tongued his foreskin, ran my tongue over the glistening head, licked up the cheese from the head, ran my tongue in the piss slot. He shivered when I did that. I slowly began to suck on his cock. It felt good throbbing against my tongue. I could feel the muscles and veins with my tongue. I'm going to give him the best blow jock he ever got. He too was sucking my cock. The joy I felt when his penus pumped his delicious boy sperm into my mouth. I rolled his boy juice around my mouth before swallowing it. When we finally relaxed we said almost in unison, "wow you're good." We pissed and went into the kitchen and had a glass of juice.

III. AN ARMPIT-TO-ASSHOLE BLOW JOB.

"You know, I thought you were gay when I first saw you," Sam said. I said, "Sucking your cock is almost like sucking my own." He said,

"I was thinking the same when I had yours in my mouth." He filled the glasses again with apple juice. I think I really saw Sam for the first time as he had the glass to his lips. His coloring was fascinating, tan with a pinkish glow. I told him his Indian part gave him a glow and makes him sexy. He asked if I wanted to fuck. I said sure but first I wanted to do something. I lay my cock on his and maybe there was a hair difference in size. I knew my size – it was a round five inches. He took a bottle of Wesson Oil with him up to his room. We flipped a coin who would fuck who first, he won. While he put oil on his cock he said, "it doesn't have a smell." He oiled my ass hole. He rubbed the head of his cock on my ass hole, then pulled his foreskin forward, then pushed his cock all the way in me. I raised my ass to accept all of it. Then I put my hands on his ass holding him so I could enjoy the feeling of his penus in me.

He took his time. He slowly started pumping his cock in and out of me. Oh did that feel great. He lay on me, his head resting near my head. He kissed my neck as he butt fucked me. He said wow that feels good. After he came he lay where I was laying. I oiled my cock and rubbed some oil on his ass hole. I pulled my foreskin back and my cock popped in his ass hole easily. I copied what he did, I lay there with my cock all the way in his ass without moving and tongue kissed him, then started pumping my cock in him. He was better than I. While I butt fucked him he would tighten and loosen his ass muscles. Oh did he please you. I've been butt fucking and getting butt fucked since I was seven, but Sam was the best ever. Then I felt my sperm was building, that good feeling you get in your balls and that tingling feeling you get in the head of your cock. Even after my cock squirted I liked him and left my cock in him and kissed him.

My man Sam kissed me when I got back. He's a good cook. That night it was game hen and wild rice stuffing. Sam didn't drink, so there was a lot of different juices in the fridge. He did drink tea. I took a shower after eating. I knew he was clean because he showers after practice. "How's the track" I asked after sitting next to him as he watched T.V. "Some soft spots I'll show you in the morning," he said. I told him I was scared when I came home because I came close to hitting a baby girl. "Hi, baby," I said, "what's your name." "Judy," she said, "and I'm this many." She held up three fingers. A woman of undetermined age had the look of a drunk and picked up the little girl. Sam took me in his arms and kissed me. "I know who you are talking about and I'll handle it." "You know Sam that's what I love about you, you know how to solve problems."

After the show was over we went in to a nightly ritual. He would feel me up and start licking and kissing my body. His giving me a blow job takes in the least time about 20 minutes. So that Masters-Johnson report is right, hets can learn from gays about sex. He would kiss my armpits, suck on each of my nipples, tongue my belly button, suck on each of my balls, lick between my legs, stick his tongue in my ass and lick it for a time, then go back to my balls. He would then lick the shaft of my cock, kiss the head, and take it deep in his throat. When he went down on my cock I already was in ecstasy and after he brought me to a climax we would hug and kiss and I could taste some of my own semen in our kisses. I then would lay on my bell, he liked to butt fuck me every night. I enjoyed the pleasure my ass gave him. I spread my cheeks welcoming his man's cock up my ass. I did the same to his cock as the boy Sam did to mine. It was easy, just tighten and loosen your ass muscles when he pumps his cock in yours. Sam sure liked what my ass did to his cock as my ass drained his sperm out of him. "You made me feel great tonight," he said. He brushed his teeth and went to sleep. Sam needed a lot of sleep, around 10-12 hours a day. I slept my usual 3-5 hours a night. He never questioned where I went on my own time. I told him I like to have sex with other gay teens and wouldn't have sex with another man. I kept my word.

One of the therapists is suing this place for sexual harrassment. She charged a former deputy superintendent with sexual assault. Yes a sex scandal in a sex treatment center. They are keeping it quiet, they don't want this to get out.

IV. 13 DICKS, 26 HOLES.

That Jerry Falwell is spreading lies across this country. He says AIDS is a plague sent by God on the gays. He leaves out that less than 2,000 men got it. In a population of over 230,000,000, that is not a plague it is a rare infection. What he doesn't say is what about all the diseases of all the other people. God curses them also. Yet this mad man like all others before him have followers who believe all the lies he spreads. I can take these phonies apart and put them back together again.

I do write more than gay sex. I was an activist on the street and I do mean the street.

Well I should tell you about the first sexy orgy I went to. The gay who was having it was one I first met. Bart, the most magnificent hunk of male beauty I had ever seen. He has dark curly hair, a straight nose, thin face, sensuous lips, big chest, narrow waist, a small thin line of hair that went down his belly and pointed to his joy stick. His cock was 5½", small head and a slim shaft. The head would push through the foreskin its glistening redness beckoning you to taste it. His balls were big and hairless their glowing pinkness guiding you to lick and suck them. His seman tasted so good that after you tasted his first load, you kept sucking for more. Wow was he good to taste and lick and suck and feel and fondle. He had air mattrices all over the rec room and living room. Besides me there were 11 others, so all together there were 13. I was not the youngest there was a pair of twins. The twins had whitish blond hair, very pale skin and were uncut. The twins veins showed under their skin, that's how pale they were.

The rest was older, my lover Andy, his hair is yellowish orange, his nose is a small pug nose, his body is covered with freckles, his eyes like Bart are green except Andy's have a reddish tinge to them. He has dimples on his cheeks and chin. He does stand out in a crowd. I am in love with Andy, he is my life, fun and all the good that comes to me. My feelings for Bart is just pure lust. The boy who had twins was their cousin. He had the same coloration they did, whitish blond hair and pale skin. His name is Steve. Bart had his boy friend Glen, he has light brown hair hazel eyes plain face, hairless except for pubic hair around his five inch cut cock. There were these German cousins Hans, Fritz, and Carl. Carl the youngest. They all were uncut and had the same washed out blond hair. They all had small noses and large full pink lips. Fritz was the only one with body hair and it was pubic hair. There were two other cousins one with auburn hair and blue eyes the other dark haired. Dan was the auburn haired one and Billy had dark hair, but they both had blue eyes. Dan had more pubic hair than Billy and they were cut. Their cocks were 4".

Then there were these two buddies. One was on the chubby side, his small cock stuck straight out, lucky they did not cut him, he didn't have much. He was funny looking, has small ears and nose and his close cropped hair made his scalp look pink. His name was Charlie. Henry was dark haired, olive skin, he had a baby face like boys under five have, he had pubic hair and an uncut cock, his balls were big for his age. Georgie was on the pleasantly plump side, he had medium brown hair and a nice smile, he too had pubic hair and his cock was an uncut fat one. Bart said the first things you guys do is everyone hugs and kisses everyone. Bart said, "Now we form a daisy chain." I had Bart's beautiful cock to suck on, one of the twins was sucking mine. I loved Bart's cock and balls, I pulled the foreskin back, kissed the head, giving the slot a lick, ran my tongue through his foreskin, licking up his head cheese. The smell of him was getting me heady. The twin was finger fucking me as he sucked and he can suck good. I pushed a finger up Bart's ass, he shuttered in the thrill of it. His cock was oozing pre-come, I loved the taste of it and feel of his big rod deep in my throat.

After we came Bart served wine and cheese, the little ones including me got it watered down. It is traditional food served at sex orgies. We sort of mingle at sex orgies. The twin that sucked me wanted me to fuck him. That auburn headed boy named Dan was feeling my ass and he said I have a high ass and he liked to fuck me. The twin lay on his side, held one leg up, and put my cock in his hole. I spread my cheeks for Dan. It was my first time as the middle in a sandwich. Dan's cock was just the right size to give me pleasure.

My ass was broken in by a 13 year old cousin when I was seven, so I could take a pretty good size cock. When Dan took his out his cousin Billy put his in, it slipped in easy. Carl the German boy backed his ass hole up to my cock and his cousin put his in the twin. Wow this feels great I was thinking my cock in Carl's ass, Billy in mine. The chubby boy put his little cock in my mouth. It didn't taste bad. Andy put Carl's cock in his mouth and Bart mounted his ass. I can't believe this, my cock is in one boy's ass, while another boy is in mine, and a boy kneeling is pumping his little cock in my mouth.

The chubby boy shot his load. It was just one shot and it tasted sweet. The oldest of the German boys Fritz jammed his cock up the chubby boy's ass. He fell to all fours and grabbed the boy's ass trying to get more cock inside him. Andy told me before I came here the only rule is you can't have sex with your lover. Anything goes, you don't ask, if there is an ass free, you can fuck it and put your cock in any mouth.

Billy dropped his load in me and when he pulled it out the dark haired boy Henry mounted me. Well, I was thinking, I'm popular. Carl took my cock out of his ass and the other twin started to suck me. Wow those twins know how to please. They are the best in sucking cocks.

Georgie put his cock in my mouth. It tasted good but his foreskin was attached to his head. I was squeezing my ass muscle on Henry's cock. All the guys started slacking off. We were getting over satiated in sex. I walked over to the table and picked up a plate of cheese and a glass of wine. The wine was full strength so I just sipped as I ate. After finishing the cheese, I carried the glass of wine to one of the upstairs bathrooms. A German boy was in the tub. I got in, soaped up, the boy washed my back for me, I rinsed myself off, got out and dried myself. Went back down to the kitchen, finished the wine, put the glass in the sink. Went back to the rec room, saw the twins wrapped around each other asleep and lay next to them. They smelled like flowers, I guess Steve used his mother's bubble bath to bathe them.

Well I hope you like my first sex orgie. I didn't remember all their names. Bart, Andy, Glen, Steve, Dan, and Billy are real names. The others I just made up. Glen was the only one I didn't have sex with. He's Bart's lover but I never cared for him.

V. "A PRETTY ASS."

You asked me about my status here. I am an open gay here. I know of only seven other true open gays. You would think in a treatment center where 70% is gay more would be open in their gayness, but no.

When I use to race motorcycles, Sam had a pickup where we put the bikes and pulled a small motor-home. Now you know what I did with the money I made as a boy hooker, it kept me alive for a year and a half before I earned any money.

I was riding my Harley and was cut off by a truck in front of a state police car. Well I got a cut on my elbow and the police insisted I go to the hospital. I had just turned 17 and it was a southern state. At the hospital there was another boy who had a cut hand and we conversed. While we talked a representative from the trucking company showed up. He offered me five hundred if I wouldn't sue. I said double it and give it to me in cash and I won't sue. He came back and counted out ten hundred dollar bills and I signed the release form. Well we both got to see a doctor at the same time and both got stitched up. He said his name was Fred. He was small for his age and on the plump side, his hair light brown and hazel eyes.

After we got our shots a cop came in to talk to me. Well the truck that cut me off almost hit the cop car. I signed his report as a witness. Fred and I paced the corridor as we walked off the tetanus shots. He said he was the baby in the family and his father left him home alone a lot. The state police had left my motorcycle in the hospital parking lot. When he saw my red highly chromed bike he let out a long "wooooow." He asked for a ride. Well I wasn't sexually attracted to him but when he held me as I rode him home it was a sex hold. He had his hands close to my crotch. I rode him up to his house and let him off. The house had a neglected look, not having a woman's touch in a long time. He told me to wait – it's lunch time and he would give me something to eat. I knew he wanted me in bed with him so I went along with his plan to seduce me.

The house looked better from the inside, it was neat and clean. He reached up to a cabinet and said ouch. He forgot about his hand. While we ate he joked, "I can't close my hand so I can't jerk off." I was wondering how long it would be before he mentioned sex. The cut was in the heel of his hand near the wrist. He had five inside stitches and three outside.

He offered me beer, wine, and even the hard stuff. I told him I don't drink because I race motorcycles. Now that impressed him. I offered him the best place to watch the races in the pits. Well I was waiting for the sex books. When you are seducing someone if they don't drink that comes next.

"Do you want to see something real good," he said. There were two. They showed boys having sex with other boys and men. All the magazines are in living color. One showed this hairless boy spreading his ass cheeks to a man's big cock. He could see my hard cock through my Levis. He put his left hand on it and said "I'll suck yours if you'll do me."

I had to help him with his pants. He like me is uncut and can pull his foreskin all the way back. I had what I have now, just over five inches. We were so hot as we lay next to each other on the couch, we just swallowed up each other's oozing cocks in each other's mouth. I hadn't sucked one that small in a long time. He sure was good sucking my cock. It is rare but we both came at the same time. His ass cheeks tightened and he started to pump his cock in my mouth. We stripped in his bed room and lay down on his bed. He had more sex books in his room, he even had a photo of himself. It showed him grinning with cum around his mouth, with his hand on some guy's cock.

He had a firm round butt and I tenderly stroked it. The muscles tightened and loosened as I caressed his ass hole with my fingers. He licked me under the balls, then licked around my ass hole, then put his tongue in. I was bent over him so I could tongue his ass hole at the same time. Only boys can do this contortionistic type sex. We both were giving out love moans.

I took a deep breath and took his whole cock down to the pubic hairs in my mouth and slipped a finger in his ass hole. The feel of a cock in your mouth is a great thrill. The muscles, veins, and the masculine sexual smell brings you to ecstasy.

We took a break and snacked in the kitchen. We were still naked. We talked about our sex lives. He asked almost all the boys in school if they wanted their cock sucked. They were giving him dimes and quarters for blow jobs. I told him my first sex was getting butt fucked by a boy baby sitter and I loved it.

Fred had one good looking rump so after I finished eating I got up, walked over to his chair, he got up, I kissed him and rubbed his behind. "You know you have a pretty ass," said I. "I sure do know my ass is pretty," he said giggling. We went back to bed and I pumped my cock in his pretty ass.

I asked if it would be alright if I ask my lover Sam over. When I told him Sam was a man in his thirties and had seven inches he said yes.

Between 16 and 20 I had at least 3 thousand encounters with boys and men. It is a good thing cocks don't wear out.

Straightening Out the Astronauts

In *The Right Stuff*, Tom Wolfe reveals that candidates for the astronaut program were briefed by U.S. Air Force officials on the right way to put their hands on their hips: "The thumbs should be to the rear and the fingers forward. Only women and interior decorators put the thumbs forward and the fingers back."

Great Moments in Television.

[The following article ran in Christopher Street.*]*

I. STEVEN FORD CONTEMPLATES THE SEAT OF A YOUNG MAN'S PANTS.

On June 14, 1983, between the hours of 12:30 p.m. and 1:30 p.m., a young, blond, name-unknown bent down to pick something up from the floor. A second and more handsome blond, Steven Ford, son of the former president, lowered his eyes and looked at the seat of the first blond's pants. Both of his globes, and the crack between, were beautifully outlined as they pressed against his khaki pants. This happened on the CBS television network, in the soap opera *The Young and the Restless.*

I had noticed Ford standing in his Jockey shorts in *Life* and sitting in *People* with his thighs spread in such a way as to display a distinct khaki-covered bulge, and after reading in Liz Smith's column in the *Daily News* that he had gone to a Third Avenue gay bar I decided it was high time I turned on *The Young and the Restless* to see how this hot stuff walked and talked. I hadn't expected such high-voltage sexuality. I was delighted. I wondered if the director had told Ford to look at the blond's rear end or if he had done it on his own; to do so would be only natural.

II. RICKY.

After all these years (Ozzie 'n' Harriet 'n' their two creamy sons went off the air one tragic night in 1966), Ricky Nelson made a brief appearance on *Entertainment Tonight* (WABC-TV), giving America a chance to see how one of its discarded idols looks today. He looks good. Disgracefully good. Now middle-aged, he is still preposterously pretty and still seems embarrassed by it. He is one of a small elite of men his age who can still qualify as a piece of trade. I have no reason to suspect that he wants to. It is a sad truism of the sexual marketplace that many of the men most obviously worth having are, for that very reason, not interested in being had; sex is often compensatory, and what would Ricky possibly want to compensate for? Still, when someone like Steven Ford turns up in a gay bar and indulges in ass-watching on national television, the imagination soars.

Ricky of course is no longer as traumatic as he was in his youth, when his every entrance, no matter how fully-clothed and wholesome, was unavoidably pornographic. He was almost amusingly, even comically beautiful; it is almost a handicap to be so scandalously good-looking. His very name is absurdly alluring. There are a few such creatures in life and in show biz and it is embarrassing, for them and for everyone. Ricky was always saved from seeming debasingly beautiful by his charming embarrassment and by the slight suggestion of a sneer in his lips, which offered the promise of an attractive contempt; we don't want our stars *too* nice. (But we don't want them to be assholes either, like Matt Dillon.)

There is no shortage of stars who are charismatic, but they have to sweat for it. Ricky was one of a tiny number of stars so astonishingly interesting that they didn't have to do anything at all, really, including act. Ricky could – and did – just stand there.

He spoke only once on *Entertainment Tonight*; he was there to publicize his daughter, who, it turned out, is a television star, and he made some little remark, possibly agreed-upon before-hand, just to prove that he has not become paralyzed. I wouldn't be surprised or, in light of his beauty, disappointed to learn that he is not very bright. He doesn't have to be. But he may be; perhaps he is so embarrassed by his beauty that he can't relax and talk well.

In recent years he has had a touring act in which he sings and plays a guitar; he has to do something, for neither he nor the public is sophisticated enough – or primitive enough – to participate in set-ups where he would just stand there like a carnival freak, doing nothing, while his fans would pay just to walk in and stare at him (even though to do so would be well worth the price of admission).

In the old days in Hollywood a real star was one whose face, like Ricky's, automatically made a sufficient number of millions of people wonder what his Jockey shorts smelled like; as I mentally undress Ricky I see flesh of a slight extra lushness, not man-made swellings of muscle from a gym like Travolta's but natural, smooth, milk-fed flesh with no visible muscles, full-bodied without being fat-assed. But his beauty was so statuesque I do not see any detail as gross as pubic hair.

Too often today Hollywood will put a man into a picture merely because he is a superb actor rather than, like R., a succulent piece of meat. So it is in life; how often have we gone looking for a piece of meat and found only a wonderful human being? How often have we gone sniffing around for sex and found only its unsatisfactory substitute, love? Love means never having to have a hard-on. What's needed are men who can sustain an honest quickie for five or ten minutes, not men who have only their lives to share or men who are willing to work at a relationship. After working nine to five blow jobs are work enough.

III. WILLIAM ATHERTON GOES STRAIGHT.

Yes, I am aware (though heterosexuals don't seem to be) that "straight" is a viciously ironic term for anyone as crooked as heterosexuals.

Heterosexuality is an acquired taste and William Atherton, an actor both literally and in the sense that all heterosexuals are, reported on the Susskind show that he has, with some effort and some help from something called "Aesthetic Realism," acquired it. [Applause]

Our society provides relentless aid for boys who want to become, or at least to seem, heterosexual: pressure from each other, from parents, school, television, employers, the cops. But some men require even additional help before they can have natural sex, as opposed to the unnatural sex they indulge in spontaneously. Aesthetic Realism is one such helpful organization. I don't know what Aesthetic Realism is. No one seems to. No one can describe it. Things that can't be described usually turn out not to exist, really. Atherton appeard on the Susskind show as one of the current crop of Aesthetic Realists, or former homosexuals. A former homosexual is like a former alcoholic; they may stop doing it but that doesn't necessarily mean they stop wanting it.

It must be confusing for a heterosexual: is it his sex life that is fun or the applause society gives it? Would actors act without an audience? Would heterosexuals go to bed with women if they had to do so furtively, without public displays of courtship? An undoubted heterosexual is one who, for some reason, must practice sex in secret; then heterosexuality is as authentic as homosexuality, for it is done out of desire, not for applause.

I had never heard of Atherton until I saw him on Susskind; it turned out that he was a star on Broadway in *The Caine Mutiny Court-Martial.* Of all the Aesthetic Realists I've seen over the years in their relentless appearances on the Susskind show, Atherton is the only one who looks aesthetic. But there is something faintly sickly about him; a more wholesome young man would simply enjoy such sexual pleasures as come his way without being so strict about gender and without seeking applause. Still, his face was arresting, as were his thighs (which is more than can be said for the last previous guest I'd seen on Susskind, David Denby, the homosexually-obsessed movie reviewer for *New York* magazine, who has the mind, and even the appearance, of a Boston nun), and I decided to watch Atherton in *Day of the Locust* on channel 11 at 5 p.m., May 29, 1983. The picture was released by Paramont in 1975, when Atherton, of course, looked even better than he does today. Near the end there is a tight close-up of his mouth opened wide, presumably in horror (I didn't turn the sound on, only the picture, for the real horror of this movie would be in its contrast to the Nathaniel West novel on which it is based). The open mouth filled the screen. I know I oughtn't to've, but this is the image I chose to remember Atherton by. It would make a smashing poster. — B. McD.

"How Big Is Your Cock?"

SAN FRANCISCO — I'll try to give you some answers to the questions you raised about things that happened during my teens...other guys I messed around with, etc.

One was a kid named Chuck. He was a very bright and pleasant guy. My only intimate time with him happened at his home one Saturday afternoon. He took me up to his room to show me a display he was was building for a science project. It involved a graphic demonstration of the way lenses can change the path of a beam of light. As Chuck was showing me the various elements of his work, I noticed some pen-and-ink drawings on the little table next to his bed. One of them was a self portrait that showed him astride a galloping horse. He told me that his uncle had some beautiful horses and that he sometimes got to ride one of them when his family went for a visit. He also said that one of those animals, named Topper, was his special favorite. He said that he'd seen Topper mount one of the mares and "he had a cock that was bigger than my arm." In a "joking" way I said, "Well, I can see your arm. How big is your cock?" He smiled at me in a funny way and said, "Well, Topper's is bigger but mine's straighter." That led to one of those "You show me yours and I'll show you mine" scenes and we stood there in the middle of Chuck's room with our hard young cocks exposed. He was right about the straightness of his cock. It was a six-inch bolt, rather lean, cut. He surveyed mine, which was much fatter, and said, "Yours looks like it could break a door down." I reached out and took his hard on in my fist and said, "Yours is like a spear to use against the infidels." He grabbed mine and said, "I'll have you a race. Let's see who can make it squirt first." We stroked each other at high speed and it didn't take more than a minute for us both to be blasting our loads. The spasms of Chuck's orgasm were the most rapid I've ever seen, like an automatic pistol that goes bang, bang, bang, nearly like a machine gun. After that I wanted to get together with him again but he wouldn't ever let it happen.

II. "WE TOOK OUR COCKS OUT."

Another guy I remember from that same period was named Bob. He and I were hired by a wealthy real estate developer to clear some brush from a tract of land that was being readied for a project. The first day, Bob showed up in a pair of cut-offs, a tight T shirt, and work boots. He looked as though he were a sex bomb that could explode at any moment. We hacked and chopped at that brush and we built a hug pile to haul away and burn. During a break we sat and talked and Bob "confessed" that he would sure like to get his rocks off. I asked him how he liked to do it and said, "Just jacking off...but it'd be better if you did it too."

We went into the shed at the back of the temporary building and took our cocks out. Bob's was much smaller than I'd imagined but it was still very inviting. I very much wanted to suck it but he was not into anything except stroking himself while watching me do the same. We flailed away at our hard ons and when Bob came he sank to his knees with a gasp and fired salvos of cum that went several feet.

III. "HE DARED ME TO SUCK HIS COCK."

When I was 16 one of my friends, David, had an old car with a rumble seat. On a weekend we drove to Seaside, a resort town on the Oregon coast. We spent the day on the beach and started for home around sundown. When we were near the turn that leads to the highway to Portland, where we lived, we saw two guys we knew hitch-hiking and David stopped to pick them up. One of them was another David and the other was Carl. We opened the rumble seat and I wanted to ride back there so the other David got in with me and Carl rode up front with the first David. It was chilly in the evening air and I unfolded an old Army blanket and stretched it over David and me. We were huddled together in that cramped seat and I enjoyed feeling his body pressed against mine. We were talking about nothing in particular and my right hand was resting on David's left leg and I felt him squirm a little when I squeezed him. He said, "You're getting me hot." I said, "Let's see," and I slid my hand up to his crotch. His left pants leg had a very prominent bulge in it and I gave it a thorough grope. He giggled and said, "You'd better watch out. That thing's loaded." He reached over and felt mine. The guys in front couldn't see what was going on with us and we soon had our cocks out and were playing with each other. David asked me if I jacked off a lot and I said yes. "Have you done it today?" "Not yet but I think I'd like to right now." He said, "Let's do it to each other." He had about six inches, with a broad, somewhat flattened shape leading to a head with a very sharp ridge. His nuts were fairly small. When I started working on his cock he told me just how he liked it: hold it well below the head and take short strokes. We worked on each other like that for awhile and it felt great. There was a towel on the floor and I grabbed it to have handy when we came. David took one end of the towel and I held the other. Pretty soon I felt his cock getting much harder and he was panting and gasping. His cock began throbbing power-fully and he shot his load into the towel. I felt the warm wetness of his cum on my hand. He had to stop stroking my hard on because he was so exhausted and I took over and finished myself off. When it was over we wiped ourselves clean and that was that. About three weeks later, in the rest room of the local movie theatcr, he dared me to suck his cock and I gave him a fine blow job. He wouldn't ever return the favor, but I sucked him off several times after that.

IV. "QUEERS DO THIS."

There was a kid named Wally, whose father was the local police chief.
I'd seen him naked in the locker room a few times and he had a very
big cock that I wanted to play with. I got my opportunity up at the
Scout camp one evening. Wally's sleeping bag got messed up when a
pot of soup was dropped and I told him he could sleep with me in
mine. We were tightly packed into my bag, laying on our right sides,
and Wally was behind me. I could feel his cock swelling against my ass.
He shifted his position a little to keep me from feeling that pressure,
but pretty soon he had a full hard on that was just too big to hide. It
must have been eight inches or more. I reached back and felt it and I
whispered, "God, you're like a horse." I let his hard on slide between
my legs so that it was up against my balls and I clamped down on it
with my muscles. He said, "I'm never going to get to sleep if you keep
doing that." I said, "You'll probably sleep if you go ahead and take care
of that." I reached under and played with his balls. He took hold of my
cock, which was yearning for some attention, and said, "You know, this
is supposed to be wrong. Queers do this." I said, "Well, let's just pretend
we're queers." I felt him rolling his hips and that big cock of his was
sliding in the crack of my ass and rubbing against my balls. On the
forward stroke, the head of his cock went well beyond my ball sack.
He began jacking me off as he got hotter and said, "OK, let's get this
over with." He fucked between my legs with rapid, powerful plunges
and I felt his body getting tighter. I was so excited I couldn't hold back
and I shot my load. He let out a long sigh and his cum began squirting,
coating my balls. We lay there, breathing heavily, for awhile. Wally said,
"Promise you won't tell anybody?" I told him not to worry and we were
soon asleep.

V. "I'LL BEAT THE SHIT OUT OF YOU."

When I was in high school, there was a guy named Keith who was the
star of the athletic teams. He played outstanding football, baseball, and
basketball, ran track, and had a large collection of ribbons, medals, and
trophies. I saw him naked in the locker room on several occasions and
his body was a wonderful display of vigor and magnetism. His cock
wasn't especially large but he had huge balls, so huge that they made
his cock stick straight out even when it was soft. Keith was dating a
girl named Della and it was understood that they were fucking at every
opportunity. Then they broke up and Della started going with another
guy. One evening I was driving home from a movie and I saw Keith
walking in the same direction. I offered him a ride and he got in with
thanks. As we talked, I told him I was sorry about the break-up with
Della. He thanked me and told me he was really having trouble with
the "stonies" without her around. I said, "Well, why don't you jack off,

like I do?" He said, "I do, but it ain't the same. It's better with somebody else." I asked him if he cared who that somebody else was and he said, "Right now, I'd stick it in a cat." Playfully, I reached over and felt the mound in his pants. He jumped and pushed my hand away. "Jeez, you go doing that and you'll get me sweating." I grabbed him again and said, "That's fine with me, go ahead and sweat." He took hold of my hand but he didn't pull it away this time. His cock swelled hard in only a few seconds. "You're making me hard. You ought to quit that." But he let me keep on with my fondling. I said, "Take it out and I'll suck you off." "You suck cock?" "Sometimes." He snorted: "That's disgusting." I kept on groping his hard on. "You like it, don't you?" He rolled his hips and pressed his cock against my hand. "OK, if you want to suck my cock you can do it, but if you tell anybody about it I'll beat the shit out of you."

I parked in a place by the river where there were plenty of trees as a screen and said, "Take it out." He quickly unzipped his pants and out came a handsome six or seven inches of uncut cock, veiny and drooling pre-cum. I played with it for awhile and pulled his gigantic balls out. When I went to kiss them, though, he forced me away. "Just the cock. Go ahead and suck it." I wanted just that, very much, but I was pissed off by his attitude. I said, "No, I changed my mind. Suck your own cock. I'm just going to jack off and take you home." I got out of the car, took my cock out, and started stroking it. He looked at me for awhile, slowly stroking his own meat. He watched me shoot my load on the ground and when I got back in the car he said, "You feel better?" I told him I sure did. I drove him to his place. He jumped out of the car and slammed the door as though he were trying to destroy it and ran into his house.

VI. "I PRETENDED TO BE ASLEEP."

In my mid-teens there was a guy named Doug who was the technical director of the civic theater in my home town. Late one night, after I'd helped with a frantic job to get the sets ready, Doug invited several of us to his house for spaghetti. I wasn't used to drinking and it didn't take very long for me to get fairly wasted on the glasses of jug wine that kept being put before me. Apparently, I fell asleep during the party and Doug conducted me to his bedroom and let the festivities proceed. When everybody was gone he simply went to bed with me and I woke up to find him sucking my cock. He was damn good at it and I was having a beautiful time. He had my cock in his mouth and a finger in my ass and I was writhing and squirming like crazy. When I realized what was happening, and who was making it happen, I could only go along with it but I pretended to be asleep. When I shot my load, he devoured it like a starving man. A little while later I was awakened by his snores, which were loud, and I got up and left for home. I had my dad's car and I knew he needed it in the morning.

VII. "HE TOOK OUT HIS DENTURES."

One afternoon, driving home in my Model A, a dog ran out in front of me and he was knocked flying by the front bumper. I was horrified and I stopped to do anything I could. He was a black Labrador and he had a tag on his collar that said, "Prince Joseph," with a name and address. I went to a phone booth and found a number for that name. The dog's owner came at once but the dog had already died. I was full of apologies and the man, who turned out to be a dentist, told me not to be sad. He invited me to his house and he showed me several photos of Prince Joseph. He thanked me warmly for taking the trouble to call him about the accident.

It took me a long time to calm down from my terrible feelings about the dog's death. I don't remember how it started, but I remember that I cried and the man held me in his arms and comforted me. Then he had his hand in my pants and was fondling my cock, which grew hard in no time, and he laid me back on the sofa and just leaned over and sucked me off. I remember especially that he took out his dentures and sucked my cock beautifully.

For a few years after that he called me occasionally and invited me to come to his house and every time he eneded up sucking me off. He always insisted on giving me money, usually ten or twenty dollars. The last time I saw him he said he'd give me $100, which seemed like a fortune to me then, if I'd jack him off. He wanted me to stand behind him and cover my hand with talcum powder and to hold his cock just so and bite him on the shoulder while I stroked his cock, which was a thick, blunt thing with a pointed head. I went through that just as he asked and he shot his load with what seemed like death agonies. After he came he just sank to the rug and he held his eyes tightly closed as he said, "That's fine...now just go away." I left in a hurry and I never saw him again.

The Danger of *Time* Style

Sensitive readers of the *Sunday News* TV schedule in New York, if any, were startled to find a question from a reader that began, "I'd like to know what actress Linda Blair is doing these days." But the rest of the question – "Is she in another film and how old is she?" – indicated that the reader was merely writing in *Time* style, which uses people's occupations as their first name, and only wanted information on Linda herself rather than, as it seemed at first, the name of the actress Linda is now sucking.

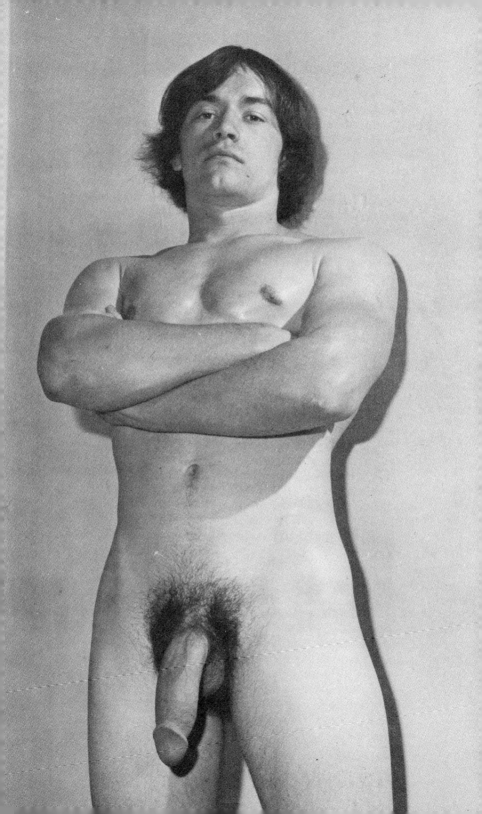

Butt-Fucking In A Changing World

ENGLAND – Here are some of my less successful experiences among the a-rabs. I'll write also of my awakenings to sex when I was a young boy, evacuated to a farm in England during World War II.

I nearly had my skull cracked by a cop's night stick in the Moroccan city of Rabat some years back. I accidently discovered a pleasing park in which to walk by moonlight and discovered in that park a very cruisy area, exclusively locals, nontrade, as Rabat is far from a tourist centre. I had only got to the interested looks stage when suddenly the whole area was alive with truncheon-swinging cops. One young man who had been smiling at me and massaging his basket was attacked by two cops simultaneously. I think I saw blood before I saw stars. I must have shouted something in English, because when I came to my senses a cop with sergeant's stripes was leaning over me, holding a cool wet rag to my forehead. Standing a few paces away were four or five of his men. The cruisers had fled.

The sergeant was talking in rapid French and I got the impression that he and his men were out queer-bashing and were embarrassed that they had bashed a foreign visitor in the process.

But the man was not going to admit his mistake. I was being attacked and robbed, wasn't I? He and his men had arrived just in time to rescue me, hadn't they? Like hell they had. But it was their word against mine and I had no witness to support my story that it was the cops and not the cruisy ones who had attacked me. They returned me to my hotel in a patrol car and by the time the sergeant left, he was behaving as though he deserved a medal for my rescue.

There was an even more fearful incident in Kennedy Park in Tunis a few years later. I had made contact with a ravishingly beautiful young man with long hair, smelling of country herbs. His robe was as delicate as his body. I wanted to take him back to my hotel but he said he didn't have the time and we could make love in the park. He leaned against a palm tree in a secluded place, holding his robe up under his arms, while I sank to my knees and worked on his weapon. Suddenly I was aware someone else was standing behind me. I heard a quick exchange in Arabic and for a moment thought we had a threesome. How wrong I was. My young partner dropped his robe, pulled his cock from my mouth, and scurried off into the darkness. Seconds later, I felt a knife pressed against my ribs. My assailant was standing behind me and I felt his breath on the back of my neck as his other hand began to search my pockets. I cursed myself for being such a fool as to be decoyed by a sweet-smelling country boy, for I was convinced he had refused to return to my hotel for no other reason than to set me up.

At last the mugger had what he wanted. He stuffed the contents of my pockets into his shirt and paused in front of me long enough to deliver a stinging blow to my face with the open palm of his hand. Then he was gone into the night.

A little later I heard voices shouting at me. I was surrounded by three uniformed policemen and my young friend; he'd called the cops and come in search of me. The next two hours were spent in a police station making a statement. They were very discreet, avoiding all questions that might be compromising; they knew damned well what we had been doing in the park but their main concern was to find my attacker. My total loss had been one pack of cigarettes, partly used, and about $10 in local currency, but the emotional loss was worse.

My beautiful friend, Salah, asked timidly if he could accompany me back to my hotel. He explained that he had refused earlier because he had to catch the last bus back to his village or his pa would be mad. But the bus had gone hours ago. How could I refuse? It was a wonderfully gentle night. The sweet-smelling youth calmed and comforted me as we kissed and stroked each other's bodies.

A few years later, in the same room in the same hotel, I had an experience that had started with a chance meeting on a beach. It was late in the season and a chill breeze kept me sheltered in the sun at the side of a shuttered concession hut. I was stuck into some paperback when I looked up to see a cop standing over me. He was not particularly young and not particularly good looking but as we conversed in hesitant French I got vibes from him. He was on duty and had a pole tenting in his pants and I couldn't see any place we could go for quick action, added to which I have always been careful about tangling with the cops. He asked me where I was staying and I told him the name of a small Arab hotel in Tunis. He said next time he was in the city he'd look me up.

II. BEAUTIFUL YOUNG TOUGHS.

A week later, I was awakened by a knock on my door. I opened the door to see two cops standing there with the concierge hovering in the background. The cop who spoke I recognized as the one I'd spoken to on the beach. He said they were checking on my passport, as I had been in the country longer than the average tourist.

I am not so green as not to know damn well that uniformed cops do not check passports. I had shucked my pants for siesta and was trying to put them on when the older of the cops, the one who had spoken to me on the beach, calmly opened his fly and yanked out a long length of soft meat. His companion, younger and dark-skinned, was grinning lustfully. I was not surprised when he spoke English; he looked the university type.

"You want to suck Arab dick?" he asked. I was nearly fainting with the excitement of all that leather, the holstered pistols, and the hand cuffs. I sat on the edge of my bed and the older cop dangled his meat a few inches from my lips. The moment my hand came up to guide it to my mouth, the younger one said, "It'll cost you." I knew I was in trouble.

"How much?"

"Let's see how much you've got." He rummaged through my belongings while the older cop stood with his fat meat dangling from the open slit of his pants. I was about to protest when he silenced me with a mouthful of soft cock. I didn't fancy sucking one while being robbed by the other and I spat the cock meat out. The younger one found my fold of traveler's checks.

"I suggest you sign these," he said.

I pride myself on being a coward. I signed all the checks, some $300 worth.

"My partner is in debt," the older cop explained. "He is trying to buy a house. Come. You want, don't you?" He pushed me to my knees and I realized that in spite of my fear and anger, I did want. I began sucking him and very soon he unhitched his leather and shucked his pants, making it clear he wanted to go all the way.

The younger cop took my checks and passport to a bank to exchange them for local currency. I was naked, face down on the bed, and the older cop was screwing me in just his tunic shirt, when the door opened and in the mirror I saw that the younger cop had returned. When he saw the action, he came to the side of the bed, unbuttoned his fly, and stuck his cock in my mouth. I could tell by the way the other one was screwing me that he was experienced and enjoyed homosexual sex; the younger one had an unpleasant straight arrogance. He was the "queer rolling" type I've seen in so many parts of the world.

After they both shot their loads, they adjusted their uniforms and preened in the mirror. It was the most expensive sex scene of my life ($300) but it was instructive. Since then, when staying in a city longer than 24 hours, I have opened a local checking account and any cashable documents worth more that $50 I have insisted the hotel should guard in its safe. I can even look back on that rip-off with some pleasure; two cop cocks spurting their load in me.

It was also in Tunis that I had an educational encounter with a gang of street kids. I'd spent a rewarding few hours in Kennedy Park and was returning late to my hotel, fucked into complacency. I hadn't the smallest coin on me, let alone bank notes; I'd spent my evening allowance and I'm not the jewelry-wearing type, not even a wrist watch. Suddenly I found a kid of about 16 padding along by my side, making his offer quite obvious as, in the dark, virtually deserted street, he stroked my butt with one hand while groping his crotch with the other.

"Me good fuck," he said. As I hadn't a cent to give him for his services, I rejected the offer, but the language barrier prevented any explanation. He shuffled resentfully down a side street. A few minutes later he was back with several other kids, on either side of me, behind, and in front. I was surrounded, not by the stereotypes of a Hollywood movie, but by a basically friendly gaggle of teenagers who were determined not to have their little personalities rejected by the foreign visitor. They were all feeling themselves up, laughing at their own vulgarity, trying to get a sexual reaction from me, and when it didn't come, their good humour turned to bad. One of them grabbed my arm, then another, then another. I was held by three while two others raided my pockets. The street was ill lit and there was no one in sight. I didn't call out for help. I had nothing to be robbed, especially my virginity. And I was excited by these beautiful young toughs.

Finding that I had no cash, they punched and kicked and spat at me and I might well have sustained injury had not a passing motorist pulled up with a screech of brakes. The kids scattered and I tried to recover my dignity, assuring the occupants of the car that I was not harmed and no, I did not want to file a complaint with the police.

When I finally got back to my hotel room, exhausted by the night's excesses, I had a hard on that was so urgent I had to jack off thinking about those hot-blooded teenagers and how I might have wrapped my hands round six smooth stems and drowned in a wave of spunk. I decided that it is almost as dangerous to cruise with no money as it is to cruise with more than one can afford to lose. Ever since then I have cruised with an emergency "bank" secured by an elastic band between my big and second toe.

III. SCHOOL BOYS' WHORE.

In the days before religious conflict took hold of the Lebanon, I was working for six months in Baalbek and staying with a Christian Arab family. They had two daughters and a 12-year-old son, Pierre. The son was cute but I was determined, for many reasons, not to lust after him.

There was a neighbor boy, Francois, nearly 16, who went to the same school as Pierre. As soon as I met him I knew he knew the score: he coyly gave me one of those "secret" handshakes, accompanied by an "I'm available" smile. I was getting my rocks off anonymously round the Roman ruins at night, mostly with very experienced tourist guides. Francois's parents asked if I would help him with his English and I found myself going to his house twice a week for language sessions in his study-bedroom. It wasn't long before Francois

135

was throwing himself at me, literally, in a rather old fashioned way, with every suggestive body contact, as he sat close asking questions about his English text. He saw I was getting hot and one day slyly opened his fly and let his meat spring out. His foreskin was a delightful surprise; he was a Christian Arab and apparently it was family pride not to cut their kids. It flashed through my mind that maybe little Pierre was uncut too.

But Francois had a cock discharge that wasn't semen or pre-seminal lubricant. He admitted he was getting pains when he pissed. There was no doubt he had a dose of the clap. I told Francois he had to do something about it and certainly not have sex with anyone till it was cleared up. Did he have any idea how he'd contracted it? Yes, he thought he'd got it from Pierre!

It developed that my host's cute son was a little whore who took it in the ass from nearly every boy in school. Francois told Pierre he was diseased. Pierre thought he was going to die. And both boys said they daren't tell their parents, it would be too shameful. I told them it was more shameful to leave disease untreated and they had to go to a clinic or at least consult the family doctor. They pleaded for me to say nothing to their folk and the more cunning Francois implied that if I told he'd say I'd interfered with them both. Stupidly, I took them by taxi to Beirut one afternoon when they cut sports and presented them to a specialist clinic for treatment, for which I volunteered to pay. It was an insane act of generosity. Some do-gooder in the clinic not only informed the boys' parents but also the police, and the police informed the British consulate.

I found a lawyer who was able to convince both lots of parents I was innocent.

IV. ARE BOY SCOUTS TOO QUEER?

I've been digging deep into my past to try to find out why I stayed being gay while other kids only played gay games for a few years, then drifted into dreary heterosexuality.

Do dirty young boys pervert innocent mature men? I asked myself that question after reading a recent Northern Ireland court report. Six wardens at a Government hostel for delinquent youths were accused of grabbing teenage ass. In their defence, they pleaded it was the boys who grabbed adult prick: and I found myself recalling my own awakening to sex.

I grew up in an English seaside resort town, the only child of middle class parents so over-protective that I was sent to a local college as a day boy instead of boarding and, for fear I might come to moral harm, forbidden to join the Boy Scouts.

I had a friend, Martin, who lived on the same street. Because he was two years older than I he was always in another class at school, so we saw each other mostly outside school. It was early in 1939 and I was 12 and Martin 14. He was mad about cowboy movies but I was mad about Tarzan. I think Tarzan then was Johnny Weissmuller and my Dad would take me to see every new Tarzan movie because he thought I liked the animals. I was too ashamed to tell even Martin that it was Tarzan I liked. The whole time he was on the screen, my eyes were riveted on his loincloth. I had never seen a naked man. I didn't really know why I wanted to see Tarzan's meat.

The school hired a swimming pool for an hour every morning for instruction, the young boys one day, the older boys the next day, and so on. One morning when we arrived, a football club was finishing a session and some of the men were still dressing in the cubicles that lined the pool. Three men had not drawn the curtain of their cubicle and were horsing around stark naked. They were in their late 20s or early 30s, I guess. When they saw me pausing to look at them, one man turned his back, the second quickly covered his genitals with a towel, but the third grinned, parted his legs, and thrust forward his pelvis so the giant dangling equipment kind of did a dance for me in its pubic bush.

A few weeks later, Martin said would I like to see his big sister make love with her boyfriend, who was in the Royal Air Force. It sounded like a sensational idea. We clambered on the garage roof of his dad's house with a pair of binoculars, borrowed, unknown, from his dad, and spied on big sister and her boyfriend through a small gap in the shades. We didn't see anything but Martin said that one night the gap had been wider and he'd seen his sister unbutton her boyfriend's pants and "play with his joy stick" while he put his hand up her skirt.

Then all of a sudden Martin asked, "Have you ever let anyone play with your joy stick?"

"No."

"It feels great. Want to try it?" He led me from the garage roof and into the back of his dad's car. It was quite dark. I felt him tug down my short pants. He made me lay on my back along the seat, grabbed my hairless little pecker, and proceeded to rub. I was real scared as it got stiff and tried to make him stop, but he was stronger than I and was kneeling firmly on my legs as he worked. He said I was too young to juice but that he had started juicing a couple of months ago. I closed my eyes and saw Tarzan leaning over me and felt his hot stiff cock in my hand. The next thing I knew was Martin's cock jetting some warm sticky fluid into my palm.

"Now you've been initiated," he said. "You can rub your own anytime you get the urge and you can rub mine for me anytime I tell you."

In the days that followed, every time we were alone Martin would make me masturbate him. I began to take a possessive interest in his prick, worrying about the spurts of liquid which I thought might be poisonous. Martin seldom rubbed mine again but I played with myself in bed every night. I once asked Martin to rub mine when I was very excited and he said to get the kids in my own class at school to do me. He mentioned three names and I realized that, like him, they were all Boy Scouts.

One day we had the run of his house to ourselves when his parents and big sister went out. He had stolen a contraceptive from his dad's bedroom and took me into the bathroom to show me how it worked. He was completely naked. Suddenly he rolled it off his prick and said, "I want you to suck it for me." I was thunderstruck. No such dreadful thought had entered my head till now. "It won't do you any harm," he assured me, "and if you do it good I'll give you a rub with a handful of grease. You'll love that." I demanded to know why he was so sure it would not be harmful to let him put his cock in my mouth and, rather reluctantly, he told me about the Scouts. It seemed that after every meeting the Scoutmaster left the Patrol Leader, who was 19, and his buddy, a Pathfinder of 18, to lock up the hut and put away the equipment. They always made a "fag squad" of the boys who had failed their tests stay behind and do the dirty work. Every evening at least one boy would be taken into the Scoutmaster's den by the Patrol Leader and the Pathfinder for "special instructions" while the others got on with the tidying up. The "special instructions," Martin hinted, meant having to "do things" with the big boys' pricks. More than that he would not say and he swore me to secrecy.

He sat on the W.C. pan, leant back, and parted his legs, instructing me to kneel on the tiled floor between them. "Open your mouth real wide and be careful with your teeth and let me feel your tongue working." I remember his hands clamped around my head controlling the movements up and down his stem and the spurts of hot liquid that gushed in my mouth when I was least expecting it. I struggled to spit it out.

Then he said he was going to give me a treat, like the Patrol Leader gave the younger boys, and to shuck my clothes and lay on my back on the bathroom floor. He produced a pot of Vick vapour rub (the mentholated ointment used for winter colds) from the medicine cabinet and massaged my cock with it. I thought he had burnt me. I struggled to get to my feet, but he was two years older and easily held me down as his hand beat my meat in the burning, slippery gel. It was wonderful.

Moments later, he was sitting across my chest and telling me to open my mouth for another lesson. He said very soberly that when you were 14 you needed to come four or five times a day; and if I did everything he asked me, he promised to keep our secret. He kept that promise, too. Now at night I jerk off with cold cream. I was mad at my parents for refusing to let me join the Scouts and be given "special instruction" by that 19-year-old Patrol Leader.

V. MR. CRITCHLEY SUCKS ASS.

That summer, Martin went to Scout Camp. I suddenly felt dreadfully alone. I decided to run away. I stole some money from Mum's purse and caught a train to the next big town. I had no idea where I was going to sleep. The wooded area of a large park seemed ideal. It was while I was looking for a comfortable hide for the night that I came across a soldier making love to his girl. They didn't see me but I had a good close up view of them from where I was frozen in the undergrowth. At last I saw what I wanted to see – a man's prick fully erect. He was about 25 and he knelt over her with his uniform pants off and his shirt rolled up, giving me a splendid view of what I regarded then as a monstrous piece of equipment. Moments later, he had her skirt up and her panties down and was riding his piston to and fro up her snatch. I thought a man's prick would never fit a boy's mouth.

Later, a policeman shone his torch on me. My worried parents were informed I would be returned safely to them the next morning.

After that, my parents kept me even more a prisoner in the house. Then Martin returned from Scout camp with the devastating news that the Scoutmaster and several of his friends had been arrested by the police for offences against the boys. A few days later the Second World War broke out.

For the next year Martin was like he had always been, making demands on me for my sexual services. I asked him about the Scoutmaster and the boys. Did the men do anything with the boys' asses, I wanted to know. I still had in mind my experience at the police station after I was found in the park. The police had asked me if any strange men had given me lifts in their cars and when a doctor came to examine me, he fingered my ass and asked was it tender. They thought some man had been using my ass like the soldier was using his girl's quim! Either Martin didn't know if the men had been fucking the Scouts, or he was sworn to secrecy. All he would admit was that the Patrol Leader sometimes made him suck cock and he hated it because the bastard made him swallow his load.

The bombs came. Martin was nearly 16 and I was nearly 14. Martin's parents had relatives who had a small farm in the West Country and they agreed to look after us both in the safety of the countryside if we helped about the farm. Letting me go with Martin to the farm that summer was the best thing my parents ever did.

Martin and I shared a caravan parked in the farmyard. Eddie, a hired hand, was not called up for the forces as he was considered mentally retarded. He was 25, a vast hulk of sun-tanned muscle. Certainly he didn't think too clearly, but he was a hard worker. He lived with his widowed mother in a nearby cottage.

One day while we were grooming the horses, I suddenly was aware that Eddie had opened his breeches and was beating his meat. It was thick. "You boys do this?" he asked. Very soon all three of us were jacking off.

A few days later, the farmer's wife told us that a Mr. Critchley, who was a traveler in veterinary products, had been bombed out of his weekend lodgings and she had told him he could use the third bunk in our caravan on Saturday and Sunday nights till he found better arrangements. Mr. Critchley, who at once asked us to call him Harry, was about 35 to 40 and smelt like a doctor.

During the night, I awoke to feel myself erect. The bedcover had been pulled back, my pyjama top unbuttoned, and the cord of the pants released. In the moonlight I saw Harry in his undervest and pants leaning over me. His delicate hands were touching me up. It was the first time an adult had molested me. I wondered if I should call the sleeping Martin for help. I was both afraid and excited. I decided to feign sleep. He rolled me over onto my belly and carefully pulled off my pyjama pants so he could get at my butt.

At first I couldn't believe it. But there was no doubt that the man had buried his face in my ass and I felt his tongue working up my shit-hole. At the same time, he had a hand under my belly, playing with my prick. Almost too quickly I felt my cock spurt its liquid into his hand. He brought his head up to my ear and whispered, "Will your butch friend object if I make him feel good, too?" – for he had apparently summed me up at once as Martin's passive partner. I told him I didn't think so. I lay on my side and watched as he slid a hand under Martin's bedcover.

Harry eventually paid us each a quid (a pound) to help him come. Martin and I discussed this and decided it wasn't so bad after all, particularly as it gave us more pocket money than we had ever had in our lives.

I didn't dislike Harry but I didn't feel drawn towards him. Martin had started talking about girls in the nearby town who let you fuck them for a quid; it was time he dated a girl, he said. Perhaps because of his desertion, I refused to suck Martin off anymore; he lost his temper and started to fight and, being two years younger, I ended up with my head gripped between his muscular thighs while he jacked off over my face.

The following Saturday, Harry arrived for his weekend armed with a chicken hawk's kit of gin, orange squash, and dirty photos. Needless to say, we were both anxious to try the forbidden alcohol, and the photos Harry had, while technically very poor by modern standards, certainly did the trick of turning us on.

Harry asked Martin if he had ever fucked me and when Martin said no, Harry told him how to go about it without even asking me if I fancied the idea. By this time the drink had made me unsteady and when Harry started to undress me I didn't resist. Martin was already shucking his clothes. I was placed face down on my bunk with three pillows under my belly. I felt Harry part my legs wide and then his fingers started to massage my virgin sphincter with soothing grease (he used udder balm). Martin kneeled between my legs. I felt a prodding weight on my sphincter. The grease prevented any resistance and his cock slid in one long thrust up my rear as his body collapsed over me. I felt a sharp, stabbing pain and yelled. Harry said, "Relax, relax and it won't hurt, I promise." I didn't actually like Martin's stiff meat up my gut but it stopped hurting and I stopped yelling. In spite of my fear and repulsion, I enjoyed it.

Sunday night I felt increasingly deserted by Martin: I was left alone in the caravan while Harry drove Martin into the nearby town to try his luck with cunt. I was awakened by Harry interfering with my cock again. He gave me a good blow job but I didn't want it from *him*.

Martin insisted he did fuck a girl that Sunday night and showed me the packet of rubbers Harry had given him, as though to prove he was a man. On Monday night, when we were alone, he got out the tub of udder cream and said my butt would be the next best thing. We had a bit of a fight and Martin said, "Look, do you or do you not want cock?" Martin had been my best friend for several years and I still liked him, so I gave in and let him grease up for another session up my rear. It still hurt as he entered and I pleaded for him to take it easy, but he seemed to enjoy his new-found aggression and his fucking was totally selfish. Martin got to screwing me regularly, and although my hole felt tender I wasn't feeling any more acute pain when he entered.

The following year, the Battle of Britain was won, the threat of invasion receded, and it was considered safe for me to return to the coastal resort town. By the time I was 16 I was hunting for the kind of sex I wanted in a town full of American, Canadian, and British soldiers and sailors preparing for the D-Day invasion of Europe. Do dirty young boys pervert innocent mature men? A whole international army was about to find out. I'll send this in my next letter.

Unnatural Act

"Anybody," says Auberon Waugh, the English writer, "can cultivate a taste for heterosexuality with a little effort." Unsaid, but implied, is that homosexuality is natural and doesn't require any effort.

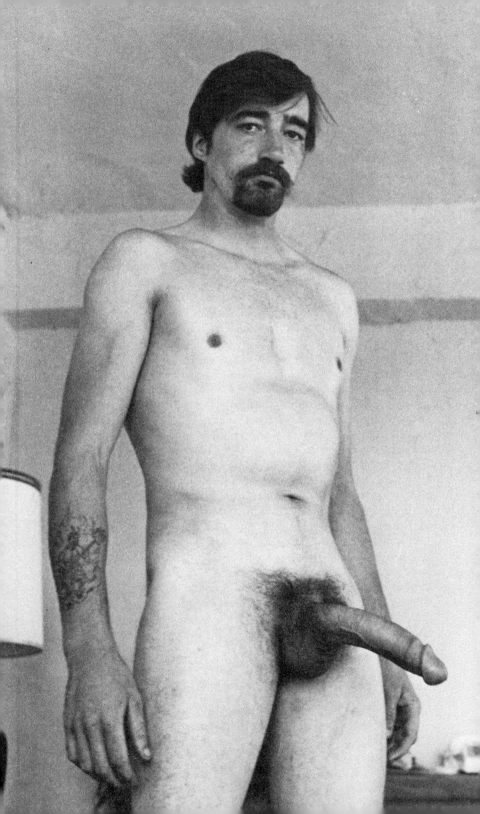

The Straight Life

Fatal Vision
by Joe McGinnis
G.P. Putnam's Sons
$17.95

Captain Jeffrey MacDonald, M.D. is superbly heterosexual, a real lady-killer, handsome, popular with men too (both "straight" and gay).

He lifted weights; he had what some thought was an embarrassingly large number of mirrors.

"We were brought up," his brother says, "in a school system and a locality and by a set of parents who thought that football was good, and sports were good, and Boy Scouting." The military was the most dangerous, and best, sport of all; as soon as he could, he enlisted. He liked the parachute jump training – "It's like are you man enough?" He liked "incredible warrior types" and the Green Beret exercise where they practiced the assassination of student leaders. The paratroopers were "hard core" and his wife, he said, "knows how I respond to these guys."

Presidents, especially presidents like Nixon and Reagan, cannot have too many troops like Jeffrey but America can, and does. He feels Americans "have a duty to do what was ordered by the president."

At 16 or 17, while "dating" Colette, he slapped her and she cried. Later they had the kind of marriage in which he would say, "Hey, what are you watching this for? The ball game's on." His buddy, Ron Harrison, another Green Beret, would spend several evenings a week with the MacDonalds; Jeffrey would say, "Ronald's out of beer, Colette" and "Ron needs some chow." Ron and Jeff were such good buddies there were rumors they were having sex and psychiatrists who interviewed Jeff later did conclude unanimously that he had a great deal of "homosexual material" in his mind. But anything psychiatrists say should be taken with a grain of Stelazine.

Still, what he told them about Fire Island is suspect. He said that when he was young he used to earn $200 a throw there by fixing up homosexuals with each other. But that isn't the way it works; not at all. His other anecdotes are incomplete too.

"This priest who was sitting next to me," Jeff told a psychiatrist, "began telling me how much he admired men in uniform, and the next thing I know he's got his hand on my thigh." Then he abruptly changed the subject.

When he was a sophomore in Patchogue, Long Island he met a Humble Oil engineer named Jack Andrews and went to Baytown, Texas to live with Andrews and his wife. "I think my husband Jack was just attracted to the boy," Mrs. Andrews says. But it became "a strain...it just got to be an uncomfortable situation," and after five months Jeff returned to Patchogue.

He thought the family physician, and his tweeds, attractive (his own father was dead). He decided to become a doctor. His ambition was to serve the more or less attractive young men at his college (Yale) but he wound up serving the more or less attractive young men of the Green Berets. Shopping around for a hospital to train in, he found San Francisco General the most attractive because of its "knife and gun club atmosphere." What made him join the Berets was a certain recruiter – Jeff was "extremely impressed by the physical appearance" and uniform of the officer. What he did was oversee the sanitation of the mess halls and latrines and file a monthly venereal disease report.

Just as our astronauts, according to Tom Wolfe, receive heterosexual training – they are told how a he-man puts his hands on his hips, as opposed to the way an interior decorator does it – the Berets had what they called "weddings" featuring a "sandwich" (a woman taking one dick in the ass while sucking on another).

Jeff didn't really need the training; he was making out, and had been since shortly after his marriage, with secretaries, nurses and airline stewardesses. He was a dreadful snob about them. He would call them "airheads" and say things like "Big deal, she was a secretary" – odd talk from a male who liked such non-intellectual reading as Mickey Spillane's *Kiss Me Deadly* and Rod McKuen's poetry and watched Glen Campbell, Tom Jones and Johnny Cash every week on TV. His favorite movie was a Troy Donahue-Connie Stevens picture.

When last sighted, in jail in Texas, Jeff had lost his looks. He still maintains that he is innocent of the charge that he violated the provisions of Title 18, United States Code, Section 1111, by killing his wife and two daughters in February, 1970. He was 27 then; they'd been married seven years.

I became convinced of his guilt the minute the *Native's* art director told me that a cops' organization was supporting MacDonald; normally a man doesn't win the approval of the cops unless he's really rotten. The author, Joe McGinnis, was neutral when he began work on the book; he wound up convinced that MacDonald is guilty. Nowhere in the book, from Jeffrey or from anyone in his family, is there any expression of the outraged innocence that even a man falsely accused of jostling a woman on a crowded bus would express. When his sister saw him for the first time after the murders, they just embraced and both said "fuck, fuck, fuck;" his mother testified in court, for some reason, that when her husband hanged himself there was a discharge in his groin, "probably semen or urine;" his brother is either crazy or crazed by narcotics. After the murders Jeff 'n' Ron and Mom went shopping and to the movies; then Jeff and Mom went alone to a beach resort, where he complained about the food; when he moved to California between trials, Mom followed and took a house 10 minutes away from his.

"Do you think I should wear a khaki uniform," he asked a reporter while preparing for the photographers, "or put on my greens?" To a photographer he said, "How about getting me some copies of those pictures. They were just great."

He is not totally insensitive; he doesn't like to talk about the 33 stab wounds in the body of his two-year-old daughter. That's a lot of stab wounds in a body that small. On second thought, in a body of any size. The nice thing about non-fiction is that you can get away with things that would be too corny in fiction; after the murders, Jeff gave medical lectures on child abuse.

McGinnis does not make any attempt to excite. He doesn't have to. His forte is choosing subjects that offer a huge amount of details which can be gotten by a man who, like himself, inspires confidence. In Mac-Donald's case, that confidence was misplaced. McGinnis actually lived with MacDonald while gathering material and MacDonald thought he was doing a favorable book. But McGinnis found too many lies and MacDonald now feels betrayed by the way *Fatal Vision* came out. McGinnis first came to prominence by traveling with the white collar rednecks who were promoting Richard Nixon and perhaps they too felt betrayed after seeing *The Selling of a President*. But anything to get a story and in both books the reader is the beneficiary.

MacDonald will be eligible for parole on April 5, 1991. By then he will be 47 and there will be a new generation of airline stewardesses. At present many of them provide a well known, but un-advertised, service for many travelers. Perhaps by 1991 the stews, now brought up to feel that it's important to relate to men, will know that there are better ways to spend a layover than with the Jeffrey MacDonalds of the world.

Fatal Vision is a bloody, true heterosexual horror story in the medical murder genre (the best since Tommy Thompson's *Blood and Money*), the story of an aggressive all-American with high self-esteem who went to all the trouble of becoming a physician only to ruin everything by making incisions on the wife 'n' kids. Talk about unnecessary surgery. I stayed up all night with the book. I gave it to two friends and they both stayed up all night with it too. But I wouldn't bother watching Robert Redford in the part (he's the one MacDonald wants). – B. McD.

[The above review ran first in The New York Native.*]*

What Is This Shit Called Love?

A Philadelphia correspondent writes that I have "bad taste." He has also written – twice – that he has acquired hepatitis-B from sucking ass. I regard the assholes he likes, from which he has sucked hepatitis-B germs, as being in bad taste. Neither I nor *S.T.H.* has ever given anyone hepatitis-B; to do so would be in bad taste.

–B. McD.

National Defense:
The Truth About Sailors.

[EDITOR's NOTE: John Glenn, the spinsterish Senator who at this writing is running for President, thinks homosexuals shouldn't be admitted to the military service – they wouldn't be good in "trenches or foxholes." If this were true it would be a compliment; American men should spend more time in sex holes and less in foxholes. But of course it isn't true, as the following questionnaire and numerous other military memoirs show. I never had any complaints about my military service, which is more than John Glenn can say; the other astronauts complained about his criticism of their sex lives. He was a non-stud even then and, like prudes in general, he doesn't like to see other men have what he doesn't have himself. If he still feels like attacking men, I'd like to see him have the balls to attack the men in power who are responsible for the sad condition of the world today.]

How often did you beat your meat in your early youth? In high school, up to seven times a day, more commonly once or twice a day. In the Navy, about once a day.

Please describe your body today and compare it to your body when you were in the Navy. My body hasn't changed much: medium build and height (5'8½", weight ranging from 150 to 160 pounds), 7½" circumcized cock. Short hair of course in the Navy, medium long now. I have often shaved my body hair off, a long process. Often short moustache in Navy. Brown eyes, hair. Medium thickness of dick. First measured it probably around age 13.

Have you ever examined your asshole in a mirror? Yes. A doctor friend of mine said it was "the prettiest asshole I've ever seen."

What kind of underpants did the sailors wear when you were in the Navy? Boxer shorts. Navy issue. Some guys wore civilian shorts, Jockeys, but all Navy-issue "skivvies" were boxers. You could wear any underwear you wanted as far as I knew, since you didn't stand inspection in skivvies except in boot camp.

Did many sailors spend an unusual amount of time wearing only their underpants, to the point where you suspected that they liked to display themselves? Yes. Remember, though, it is very hot on ship a lot of the time; in the boiler room it is regularly 140°. The boxers, by the way, had the effect of pressing your dick down your pants leg so when the trousers were tight (as they usually were) you could see the full length of it in outline, rather than the lumped-up effect given by Jockeys.

Did the sailors sleep in their skivviess or bareass? In skivvies. A few slept bareass, not many. I always did.

What did the sailors wear going to the showers? Most wore a towel, some went nude, some wore skivvies.

Was there much talk of homosexuals? Yes.

What words were used? Besides the usual civilian slang, there was the sailor term "sea pussy."

Were there many men in the Navy who were widely suspected of being homosexual? Yes.

Were they teased or bullied by the others? The way they were treated varied a great deal. Some were teased, some bullied, some left alone. Often it was difficult to tell how serious the suspicion was since it was a widespread mode of talk to straight-facedly discuss such things but not mean it seriously. I think in a lot of cases this was a cover, as humor so often is.

Were there any sailors who were openly homosexual? Yes. I know of two sailors who were fairly open on their respective ships and didn't seem to have any problems on account of it.

The Department of Defense, Senator John Glenn, and so on and so forth, say homosexuality is incompatible with military service. Since I, and most homosexuals of my age, were in the service, I find this attitude kinky. How do you, as a serviceman of the present era, regard the official position on homosexuality? Pure bullshit.

Please describe your first sexual experience with a girl. I was 19 and shy with girls at the time. She indicated she was ready one afternoon and we got into petting over where I was staying. She sucked on my dick a little bit but not long and then I put it in her pussy and we fucked for the rest of the afternoon. I couldn't get enough. It was stupendous. She was 22.

Please describe your first sexual experience with a boy. I was 9, he was 12, but I don't remember what we did. Second time I was 11, in the Boy Scouts, he was 12, we were on a camping trip in the swamps and I was visiting his cabin. He asked me to do him a favor. I agreed. He took out his little dick and told me to blow him. I breathed deep and blew air on it, not knowing what else the term "blow" meant. He told me to suck on it and I told him only if he'd let me rub my dick on him. He agreed, so I sucked on his dick for awhile (he wasn't pubic yet) and then I rubbed my dick against his back as if it were a sheet, like when I jerked off. I didn't think it was a very important event.

Did you hang out in gay bars much? Quite a bit. Good place to get free drinks, place to stay, and breakfast. I usually wore my uniform and was the center of attention – once won a bar's "Sexiest Guy in Uniform" contest.

Why did you go to gay bars? Boredom, horniness, ego, financial gain (hustling), find interesting people to talk to.

Did you often hustle – that is, play the part of trade and get sucked off for money? Yes. Helped to pay my way through college. I enjoyed it. It was as much for adventure as for cash. I was always interested in meeting wealthy gays this way, see their luxurious living places, taste exotic liquors and cannabis. Flattered my ego too. Met a number of famous people this way, movie stars, and a politician (known for public homophobia too, that one).

As you look back on your Navy life, does any unusually beautiful image of flesh come to mind? Yes, one, a Marine, 19, blue-eyed, blond, medium-build, muscular, intelligent (he was an aide to the Admiral), with a very fine masculine face, smooth skin, circumcised, about 7".

Can you remember any unusually repulsive or offensive sailors? My nemesis was a fat, ugly, young sailor I met in radio school, a whiny queen whom I fucked out of horny desperation, and who later turned me in.

Can you recall any sailors whose personality was especially attractive? There was one sailor I got to know in Naples (and visited in Texas after we were both out) who radiated charisma. Though he was uneducated and from a small town in North Texas, everywhere he went everyone was attracted to him, magnetized by him. He seemed totally unaware of this effect and was as nice a guy as you could imagine. He came from a very poor family. His gang in Texas when I visited him for several days treated him the same way. I did end up sucking his dick, just as natural as can be, and it didn't affect his attitude toward me one whit. He was just totally unaffected and totally charming.

In living close to a lot of men in the Navy, were there ever offensive smells from dirty clothes or bodies? I'm sure there must have been. None stands out in my memory. Sailors are well known for cleanliness and take frequent showers. I think some of them picked the Navy for just that reason – they could always get a hot shower.

Please describe your first sexual encounters as a young kid. I became very popular immediately after that incident I already mentioned, where I blew a Boy Scout when I was 11 and he was 12. I was called a "blowboy." I sucked dicks for a half-dozen or more Scouts and wondered why so many guys seemed interested in it. There was one fellow, another 11-year-old named Artie, that I especially liked, and he was in my tent. After the other guys were finished (I don't recall that any of them ejaculated), Artie lay back and had me lay down between his legs and suck on his dick. He wasn't yet pubic so he didn't shoot anything and I didn't know when to stop. I just kept sucking on it for a long, long time till I noticed he was asleep. Then I stopped sucking but lowered my head onto his crotch and lay there digging the body contact. He had his hands on my head while I was sucking. Eventually I fell asleep just like that. When word got around that I was a blowboy, a lot of the kids in school (6th grade) propositioned me, some seriously and some as a joke. In the boy's room they would grab my head and pull it down to their crotch, then let go. One time I was invited to a shack in the woods where about four boys had gathered. One of them finally got bold enough to pull his dick out and got it hard and told me to suck on it, but it was all red and purple and I got scared looking at it and refused to do it and took off. There was a second Boy Scout camping trip when I also sucked a lot of dicks. After that I got thrown out of the Boy Scouts on account of it; somebody ratted on me. I was 12 now but still not pubic. Then my family moved overseas (my father was in the Navy) and I did the 7th-9th grades in Germany, living in an all-male schulerheim or dormitory for schoolboys while attending public school. I had quite a number of sexual adventures then.

Do you have any brothers? Yes, three, all younger.

Did you ever want to jack off with any of them? No, but I taught one of them how to do it.

When you were in the Navy, which would you usually prefer: having sex with a woman or a man? Woman, if I had a good opportunity. Often settled for a gay guy instead.

Now that you're out of the Navy, do you expect to have much gay sex? If the occasion should happen to arise, but I don't think I'll go out looking for it. Still, you can't be sure you're not going to get bored. I have some gay friends and I think they will be sources of activity either directly or indirectly. More likely it would be threesomes with my gal and another guy I met in other social circumstances.

When you were in the Navy, what percentage of sailors went to gay bars to pick up a sex partner? A very small percentage. Some went in uniform, most in civvies.

How did you happen to know Marines? Wherever there's the Navy, there's the Marine Corps, except on small ships. And I had some doings with them before I went into the service myelf. At one base we shared the same barracks. On weekend nights when everybody was drinking beer, the Marines sometimes would wait on the top deck till some sailor stuck his head out of a window (usually a newcomer and often a victim of a set-up) and then try to piss on him from above. One night I was talking to a Marine, a tall, lanky fellow with sandy hair, somewhat intoxicated. After awhile I mentioned that I was up on charges for fucking a sailor up the ass. He was curious as to what it felt like. We went over and snuck into the chapel and I fucked his ass. He said it was an interesting experience but he doubted he'd want to do it again. I do recall asking him why he did it and he said he was bored to death and wanted to do something different, that he'd never done before.

You mentioned that sailors hitch-hiking back to the ship from Norfolk bars were picked up by gays. Did this ever happen to you? Many a time. Most often, the driver would invite me to stop over for a nightcap at his house or apartment. A couple times we went down to the waterfront and got out of the car and did it in the open air. In the car it was always front seat. Generally it would begin with the guy putting his hand on my thigh – to test my reaction – and then move up to play with my dick through my uniform trousers. I'd lean back against the door and he would work the 13 buttons (I met one talented guy who could undo them all with his teeth). I'd swing my legs up onto the set so that he was sandwiched between them, reach out with my arms and pull his head down onto my dick, and just push his head in and out while talking to him, sometimes humping up at him, till I shot off. I wouldn't let him get up till after he'd swallowed all my cum, and sometimes, when I was in the right mood, I'd just keep him down there – I had strong arms – till I came off a second or third time, sometimes just to relax with my soft dick in his mouth and his head cradled against my crotch, just for the contact, the touch. I never took my trousers down – that's what flaps are for, after all.

Please describe the Norfolk bar scene in your era. The gays who cruised straight sailor bars did not appear too flamboyant, too obvious. Sometimes a whole group of sailors would go off with one of them. If it was just one or two it would be more discreet – meet you outside. A convenient way of exiting was offering a ride somewhere. The sailor that went off with gays would sometimes be teased about it, but all in good fun. One technique I've seen many times is for the gay to have a sailor he trusted go through a bar and form up a party, picking reliable shipmates, non-troublemakers, who would meet out on the street and hop in the car or cars and go to the party. This happened most often in the hour before closing time. One incident I was told about happened in New York, where three gays descended upon a sailor bar in West 45th Street and got into conversation with a tall, strong, and very self-assured sailor and told him of their wish to invite a party's worth of sailors to their Upper West Side brownstone for drinks, late night food, TV, and cocksucking. He thought it over and told him, "Well, let's see what I can round up. Meet me out front in half an hour." As they were leaving for coffee elsewhere they saw him moving around the bar. Upon their return, there were enough sailors standing around on the sidewalk in front of the bar to fill four taxis, which were summoned and sent off to the guys' address. There they had a wonderful party, I was told by participants. Two sailors got sick and one threw up on a rug but they said it was worth it. The three of them sucked every sailor off – all, that is, but the organizer, who said he was saving it for a girl he knew that he'd be seeing the next day. He said he just thought it would be interesting to go to, didn't have anything else to do that night, and he wanted to see that everybody had a good time. Brunch was served at 2 P.M. and some of the guys didn't leave until late that evening.

Are sailors' pants tight to begin with or do the sailors have them altered to increase their allure? The Navy it seems has always realized the importance of well-fitting trousers. Plus most of the guys also get them tailored, especially overseas, where the the tailors know how to emphasize male sexuality. Also some had made-to-measure uniforms, especially gabardines (black "blues," really sharp), and especially anybody who was overseas, where such things are cheaper than in the States. I can remember a tailor asking me which side I wore my dick on. I don't think I asked especially for "tight," just "good fit."

You mentioned that Marines were less inhibited than sailors. Can you remember any details? I witnessed a Marine walk into the barracks and shout, "Man, did I get a fucking great blow job tonight. That fag could suck better than half the girls in China." The Marines were more talkative about their experiences with men. They would be more likely to walk up to you (being strangers) and ask you for a blow job.

Sailors are famous for threesomes – two sailors and an outsider, either a woman or a man – which psychologists regard as an indirect way for two sailors to have some kind of a homosexual thrill with each other. Did you have any threesomes? Many a time. When I was in college I picked up one pair of sailors at the bus terminal and took them up to my room in the dormitory and made it with them while they watched each other. After I was out and living with a girl I had several pairs (including one pair of Marines) for bisexual orgies. Another sailor and I when we were stationed in Europe picked up a beautiful 17-year-old peasant boy and spent the

151

night in bed with him (making sure he had a bath first), having sex most of the night.

Have you heard many sailors mention that they and a sailor buddy went with one homosexual who blew them both? Lots of times. The sailors often maintained that they got paid for it.

You mentioned that certain occupational classifications in the Navy were gayer than others. I don't think I ever met an HM who didn't turn out to be gay or bi. Of course it was a standing joke about the YNs, having secretarial jobs. The SDs were Filipino and I've been approached often by them. One Filipino used to get me drunk in the barracks late at night (he had his own room, being a First Class) about every two weeks or so and suck my dick while I was supposed to be sprawled out in a drunken daze (often not very far from the truth).

I've had reports from sailors that they've never seen sex aboard ship. Have you? On the destroyer-escort I knew a quartermaster (enlisted navigation asst.) who took care of the crew, discreetly. On a sister ship, it was a radioman, and the two of them shared an off-base apt. with me and a fourth (straight) sailor.

Can you recall any sailor who was caught having sex with another sailor or with a civilian man and was discharged for that reason? Yes, me. I fucked a gay sailor up the ass while we were both in training in the States. Much later he got caught (leaving gay mail around on his desk, which is stupid, but so was he) and he turned in a bunch of names, including mine, so I was brought up for administrative discharge. I fought it, since my Navy days were the happiest of my life, and it took them nine months before they kicked me out with a General discharge. I then fought the matter further and got it changed to a fully Honorable discharge. It was generally known around the base that I was fighting this case during those nine months and I got general moral support from the enlisted men, many of whom went out of their way to express it. A friend of mine who was a Hospital Corpsman (HM) also got kicked out. He was completely gay, but that happened before I met him so I don't know the details. He was also completely into sex with sailors and Marines and was living in Norfolk when I met him. I spent one summer sharing a house with him. He had a huge collection of skivvy shorts (boxers, USN and USMC issue with serial numbers stenciled on them) which he had hung up on one whole wall of this house, all from sailors and Marines he'd made it with. He'd replace their skivvies with a new pair and keep theirs, so they were trophies. I guess he eventually got tired of the Navy because he left Norfolk and moved to Jacksonville, North Carolina, home of Camp Lejeune (biggest USMC base on the east coast), and ran a massage parlor for the Marines there. One of my sailor friends who was on a tin can (destroyer) was sought for questioning because the snoops had heard he was gay (which he was), but his skipper flatly refused to allow the investigators on his ship, so they couldn't do anything to him.

Do you recall hearing about any sailors who beat up homosexuals? Certainly. Also one case of vice versa. I had one encounter before I went into the Navy myself. I was with my friend in Norfolk (see above question) and he and I picked up three sailors downtown and walked out to his place with them. They said they were horny and wanted blow jobs. But once they got there they got very hostile and it looked like they were going to try and cut us up. We were saved at the last minute when police arrived (on a routine mission, coincidentally), and they scampered away. My friend said they were latent homosexuals and he turned their names in to the Navy; he told me later they got kicked out.

Did you hear about any rude rejections of homosexuality by sailors? Any who made a loud public scene about it? Sure. That too. So commonplace I wouldn't particularly note the details.

Do you find sex with men as satisfying physically and psychologically as sex with women, but sex with women preferable for social reasons because it's respectable? Physically, I find a blow job from a guy as good, sometimes even better, than one from a woman. Fucking a man's ass can't hold a candle to fucking a woman's pussy. Psychologically, I think there's more satisfaction with women; one of the reasons I think I preferred sex with women while in the Navy was that it was more of challenge, harder to get (prostitutes excepted), thus gave more of a sense of accomplishment or conquest.

Do you think many sailors went with homosexuals because it was accepted by their peers, while if they weren't in the Navy, surrounded by men who did the same thing, they might not have the courage? No question about it. Also, while in the Navy you weren't home so you didn't worry so much about your reputation. If you're from a small town in Iowa it doesn't matter so much if half the gays in Naples talk about you – it isn't going to get back to anybody at home. A lot of the sex is also anonymous, which is a protection you couldn't get back home.

Did you see many hard ons in the Navy? Occasionally, usually clothed: sailors asleep in bunks, chairs, on deck. Sometimes at work (in the radio compartments), esp. when guys were reading fuckbooks. Sometimes in waiting rooms (like bus terminals). I think the most deliberate exposure of hard ons under pants was in bus terminals and other places with a pick-up atmosphere.

Opens Legs and Takes Cock

CALIFORNIA – I don't care much for the delicate, nothing-kinky types, I don't mind fems at all – some are great. But I like an unabashed stiff rod.

I've been off with a lover in his van sucking cock day and night. We went down the coast toward San Diego and stopped here and there to wade in the surf, naked when we could, bikini when we couldn't, but did a lot of laying on the sand at night, 69ing until we were limp. I love to suck cock and never get enough. Yum yum. I also love to get fucked by the right guy.

Here is an account of my first sexual experience. I was very young at the time and innocent as hell. But the experience possibly changed my life. It's hard to tell if I'd gone gay if it had never happened. Probably.

I lived with an aunt and an uncle and one summer they took a house by the beach for a vacation, near where some of their friends lived. My aunt was busy with the friends and I was usually sent to play on the sand in front of the house.

One day I wandered a bit, down to the nearby pier, where there were exhibits and rides, etc. I wasn't on the pier very long when a guy about 35 in jeans and a shirt came along and made friends with me. But I knew nothing about the world and hadn't been warned much. Anyhow, this guy was pleasant; he took my hand and bought me cotton candy and took me in to see some of the exhibits and I thought I had met Santa Claus himself.

After about an hour of that, he took me in a doorway, down some stairs and around to the back of a building that was built out over the water, part of the pier. There was a little deck area with some chairs and an ocean view. We sat down and he started talking – about what, I don't remember – but then he was unfastening my pants, and we were such friends I didn't try to stop him. He took my cock out and handled it, smiling and talking all the while, and I was liking it. Nobody ever did that before, of course. I hadn't even played with it myself very much.

Then in a few minutes he slid down in front of me, opened my legs, and took my cock in his mouth. Man! That really shook me. It felt marvelous and scared me a little all at the same time. But he kept sucking it and the more he sucked it the better it felt and the more I forgot everything else.

After awhile he asked me how I liked it and I said it was good, so he sucked me some more. That was the best time I'd had with my dick up to that time. He had my pants mostly off and he started sucking my balls too and I was having the time of my life.

Somewhere then he unzipped his pants and took out his big hard cock. I had never seen a man's prong before, especially hard. It was 3 times as big as mine. He asked me if I wanted to feel it and I did. I still remember the thrill I got when I curled my fingers around that cock. He didn't ask me to suck it but he let me handle it for a bit. Then he went back to sucking me again. The whole experience was so exciting I would have stayed there forever if he'd just kept sucking me. But after awhile he got on his knees in front of me and as he mouthed my cock he began to jack off. He took a long time at it but when he finally shot his load I managed to see it spurt out the end of his cock – the first time I knew that anything came out of a cock. That shook me up too.

Anyway, then he sent me home and I could feel his mouth on my prick all the way home and half the night. It was a marvelous feeling.

A day or so later I got the chance to go back to the pier but I never saw him again. Dammit.

II. 4 BOYS JACK EACH OTHER OFF.

I can tell you about a group of us, 4 in all, who used to meet in a lumber yard after school and play with our cocks. One of the guys and I met after school one day and I learned of the joys of sucking cock. I've heard of a lot of boys' experiences and some are far more exciting than mine. For instance, I talked with a guy I knew as a Boy Scout – years later we talked – and he told me that the Scoutmaster and another man took him on a hike one Saturday (we were in the same troop, so I knew these men) and up in the hills, they undressed him and played with him and sucked his cock for hours, got him to jack them off, etc. He said he never told a soul until he mentioned it to me. He did say he had a good time.

Now, about myself and the three playmates. We were all about the same age. Phil, the kid next door, was maybe a year older, and he was the leader, if we had one. We ran around together and played ball, etc., but what I remember mostly is the sex. (This followed the experience on the beach. A year or so.)

On looking back I think this must have been a particularly horny little group, or maybe it was Phil's leadership. Anyway, he had a few fucking pictures that he let us look at and get hot over. And he talked constantly about sex. Of course he had it all wrong. He told us in all seriousness that the man got on top of the woman and pissed into her cunt. He made is sound like he had heard his parents at it. (Maybe they did that. Who knows?) We all believed him, even though it sounded a little messy.

One of the four lived across the street. He had a sister who seemed our age. She was a tomboy. Once she showed us how girls pee. She took off her panties in a secluded place and we all got down on hands and knees and watched her squat and let go.

There was a lumber yard only a few blocks from where we lived and we investigated it thoroughly when no one was around. It was easy to get over the fence. One end of it was a huge shed filled with packs of shingles.

We began meeting there on Saturdays. We could be absolutely alone, no parents anywhere near. And Phil talked about sex and got us to take our dicks out to compare them. His was the biggest. It was an easy move from cock comparison to feeling the other guys'. And that was how I really learned to jack off. We would hang out in the shed, take our pants off, and masturbate each other for hours. It was the most fun we had.

It was a long time between Saturdays, so I was jacking off every night in bed. The kid across the street, Howie, told me he was too. He and I used to meet in his garage or mine or we'd run out to the fields behind our houses and jack off after school. Our house had a basement, open to the back yard, and Phil used to come over after supper and we'd go into the basement and jack each other off. We were a cock-happy bunch. It was about the only fun we got and it was illicit, which made it sweeter.

Then one day Howie told me he was fucking his sister all the time when his parents were out. I didn't know what to think, but he swore it was true. Phil thought it might be.

So, one Saturday afternoon, we got the sister to come over to the lumber yard. As I look back on it, she seemed very willing. We all took our pants off as usual and I don't remember that she was surprised by that. She took her panties off and then Phil laid her on her back and got on top of her. We all craned our necks, watching him put his cock into her. It went in all right and she grinned at us while he fucked her.

Then the rest of us drew straws. I was the last one to fuck her, and though it felt all right,it wasn't as good as a hand jacking me off. Of course the guys were slapping my bare ass and telling me to hurry up. When I got off her she said she felt great so we all fucked her again.

It was the only time she came to the lumber yard. Phil told me afterward that he had fucked her a number of times later in her backyard. I only fucked her once more. I met her in the street one afternoon and we walked out into the fields together and when we were out of sight of the houses, she asked me if I wanted to do it. So we laid in the grass and I fucked her. It was something I had to do. But I would rather have had a guy jack me off.

About that time my folks decided to move away. And just before we did, one of the kids from school, not one of our 4, came home from school with me one day. No one was home so we made a couple of sandwiches and when we ate them this kid unzipped my pants and got down in front of me – without saying a thing – and began sucking my cock. I was astonished, but I liked it. He sucked me for a long time. Then he went home. I never saw him again because we moved soon after. I have often thought about that kid. I sucked 2 guys off last night, for instance, and it was no more exciting than that time with him in our kitchen.

He was the last sex I had for a couple of years, except solitary jacking off, until my folks moved to Hollywood and I met Marty, a kid my age and a real horny, street-wise sodomist.

Athletes Stink

The "Athletes' village" (housing) at the IX Pan American Games was plagued at first by "no running water, erratic toilets and showers and cement dust from construction," according to *The New York Times*. The athletes were in all probability subjected to the stench of their unflushed urine and fecal matter and unable to keep their sweaty bodies and dirty shit-holes from generating an additional stink.

Cops Piss on Ferris Wheel

A half-dozen drunken off-duty rookie cops pissed on a ferris wheel at Coney Island, according to the *Daily News* (New York); "roughed up concessionaires" and "handcuffed passers-by." The cops pulled their guns on civilians who objected to their behavior but used only water guns on the woman proprietor of a water gun shooting gallery and then "manhandled" her.

Wanted: Dishonest Magazines

FROM A GAY BOOK STORE (LONDON) – Many thanks for the copies of S.T.H. It's certainly one of the most honest gay sex mags around. Now I have seen a range I have decided not to stock it. So please stop sending when we have got through the money [which had been paid].

Sexual Conquests In World War II

LONDON — In 1943, the threat of invasion over, my parents brought me back from evacuation on a farm to continue my education in the English Channel resort town where we lived. At 15 years of age, it was like arriving in a strange town rather than returning home; my parents were unaware of my fascination for men and the town itself was strange. The sea-front and harbour were a mass of barbed wire and concrete fortifications; most of the shops were shuttered for the duration. The civil population was less than a quarter normal: hotels, public buildings, and unused schools were packed with British, American, French, and Canandian soldiers and sailors preparing for the D-Day invasion which was 18 months ahead. My new school was run by old men and old women not wanted for the war effort. The playing fields had been plowed up for growing vegetables and my first lesson was in the art of planting potatoes. Our parents took us to school and brought us home — such as the fear of German air raids from fields across the Channel, less than 20 miles away.

I desperately wanted some sexual activity with someone. The nearest I got was rubbing the crotch of a boy sitting next to me one day in the darkness of the school's air raid shelter.

I began to fantasize about having an older brother. I stole a candle from my mum's power-cut emergency store and slid it up my butt nights while I beat my meat, pretending it was my big brother in me. I resented my parents having only one child.

The school started a scheme whereby soldiers and sailors visited one day a week in its pupil's homes. Most of the kids wanted a Yank, for they were known to be bearers of such gifts as Hershey bars, Camel cigarettes, and nylon stockings. I drew Vic, a 19-year-old British sailor, who came froma coal-mining family up north. Vic had close cropped sandy hair that went in all directions, freckles, green eyes, and a broken front tooth, and he was mine. The soldiers and sailors were given a midday-to-midnight pass once a week and the school gave us a "pass" on the day we were to be hosts, added to which the authorities chipped in with a few extra food ration coupons for the mums and dads.

II. SAILOR WANTS BUTT, NOT MOUTH.

I had a den over my dad's garage and after the family meal I took Vic there to play the latest Artie Shaw and Benny Goodman discs. He was scared of me because my education had taught me to talk with a posh voice and my dad, with a car, obviously had more money than his dad. Vic's dad worked on the coal face with his two older brothers and Vic found himself in the Navy because, being the youngest and less experienced, he was a surface worker and thus not in a reserved occupation. I played an Anne Shelton record (she was the sweetheart of the British

Forces) and he started talking about girls, how they were easy lays up north but the sluttish camp followers "only do it with the bloody Yanks who have all the money." I was too scared to tell Vic I could satisfy him just as well as girls. After his first visit, I beat my meat raw thinking that when he visited again I'd somehow be able to get my hand in his uniform.

Next time we were in my den listening to discs and reading copies of *Photoplay*. Vic whistled through his breath at a pix spread of Dorothy Lamour and said he'd like to poke a girl like that. I blurted out a question I was dying to have answered: was it true they put bromide in the soldiers' and sailors' tea so they *couldn't* poke a girl like that? Vic grinned and said yes but they didn't put enough in for him.

He asked if I was old enough to jack off. He said he had to. I was in a daze as he pulled up his jumper to expose the flap (held by only three buttons, unlike the massive row on an American sailor's uniform of that period) and moments later he was leaning against the wall with parted legs, flap open, cock out, beating his meat urgently with a rough pink hand. His cock wasn't long but it was very thick and as he beat it the foreskin slid to and fro over a gleaming wet purple head. It was a natural instinct for me to drop to my knees in front of him. He dropped his hand to let me have free access to his meat. The record came to an end and repeatedly scraped in the run-off. I was scared my mum and dad downstairs would hear it and suspect something and told Vic to keep putting a disc on the machine while I sucked him off. Bromide or no bromide, when he came he flooded my mouth with warm cum.

He told me that back home he had a mate his own age and if they couldn't make out with a girl they took turns screwing each other's ass, and the next week he asked me if I'd let him screw me. "I promise I won't hurt," he said. I dropped my pants and bent over the back of a chair near the record player, which was hand-wound, and tried to keep the thing going while he shoved his pecker up my ass.

"Now it's your turn," he said. It was my first fuck. He shucked his pants and bent his white butt over the chair. I was scared my mum would come up with a cup of tea.

I wanted to suck his cock again but I never did; he preferred screwing and thought cocksucking too queer. In a couple of months I was getting quite adept at plugging his butt after my first nervous attempt.

One of the kids had his big sister raped by an American Negro (as they were called then). For the first time in my life I became aware of black men. Were they black all over? Was their cock black? Did it shoot black cum? I was obsessed with blacks. Every time a black Yankee soldier passed in the street I stared. They never stared back, I thought then because I was not attractive enough to them, but in later years I realized the extent of white racism that kept them trapped behind the color of their skin. How wonderful it would be if one of them would rape *me*.

160

I wouldn't tell anyone about it and he wouldn't get into any trouble. How could I explain all this to him so that he *would* rape me?

The weekly fuck with Vic was not enough. I wanted more. Evenings were dull and long. There was no TV in those days and my dad refused to take me to the movies for fear of air raids. They tried to engineer my friendship with a neighbourhood boy the same age. I hated him. I tried to get in his pants for a mutual jack off and he told me to take a cold shower and have my head examined.

The confines were eased somewhat when they stopped escorting me to and from school. Even with a war on they sensed it was a crazy way to treat a boy of 15. Shortly after that I discovered my first cottage [men's room], built in a clump of overgrown bushes in a small public park half way between school and home. I needed to do a shit. The place had obviousy not been cared for since the outbreak of war. It was not till I'd solved the problem of a lack of paper by tearing a sheet from my then precious exercise book that I noticed the writing and drawings. The once white plaster walls were filled from top to bottom with mind-blowing ideas. I was scared to stay too long for fear my folks would ask why I was late home from school. But I went back the next day, and the day after, just to read the walls and beat my meat.

III. WEARS SHORTS TO THE MOVIES.

One day I left my gas mask in one of the cubicles (we all had to carry gas masks in little cardboard boxes) and had to go back for it, telling my mum I'd left it at school. I returned to the cottage just at the time the men were coming from work at the local brewery, which was just around the corner from the park. There were two men at the pissers as I tried the door of the cubicle in which I'd left my mask. "That one's occupied, sonny," one of the men said. I explained I'd left my gas mask in the occupied cubicle. The man seemed to find it funny. He banged on the cubicle door and shouted, "Open up, Ben, there's a kid here that's lost his gas mask." When the door opened, there was a man with a cock rearing up from a forest of black hair. I was stunned. "Here," he said roughly, thrusting the box in my hand. "Now clear off home sonny and don't hang around here again." I cleared off home, filled with exciting images of men old enough to be my dad, older maybe because you had to be old in those days to be in civilian employment.

I knew I had to stay late enough in the cottage on my way home from school to see the men from the brewery. But what was I to actually do? How was I to make friends with these hostile men? So I decided to stand at a pisser, beating my meat, hoping some man would come and join me. One did. A man wearing a drayman's leather apron came in. He must have been 50; his hair was flecked with grey. He stood two pissers away from me and had to lift his leather apron to piss, only I couldn't hear him pissing. My cheeks felt hot with excitement and he must have noticed I was rubbing my cock; he stood a pace back from the pisser so I could see his gnarled hand stroking his cock while his other hand kept the leather apron raised to expose it. I stood back a pace too. The moment he saw my hard on, he walked over to me and a hand as rough as the leather apron he was wearing wrapped round my cock. "That's nice, boy," he said. "Feel mine." My fingers could just close round his stem and the moment they did it throbbed. Suddenly, and too soon, I shot my load. "Get out of here, sonny," he said, "or I'll do something to you I knows I shouldn't." He virtually threw me out of the cottage. I was both pleased at my conquest and disappointed. What shouldn't he do to me, I wondered.

I was so desperate that one day in the cottage I let a rather repulsive fat man whose breath smelt of whisky take me in one of the cubicles. He made me suck his cock, which wasn't very big and tasted unclean. Then he fucked me and, either because he was so fat or his cock was so small, it didn't feel as though he ever got it in there. He made no effort to bring me off and I hated the experience.

But another time I met a boy about my own age. We played around a bit but he said he didn't want to come. When I asked him why, he confessed he was really looking for G.I.s, particularly the older, married ones. They paid a lot of money, he said, to "do things" with schoolboys. I was shattered, but intrigued. How much money for what things, I wanted to know. He said he got a quid (a pound, which in those times was a day's wages) for either sucking them off or letting them screw him. I almost told him if I had a pound I'd pay *them*, I was feeling so in need; but instead I asked where and how I could make contact. He said the best time was at night after the movie houses closed. It was easy to find some place in the black-out. I told him my folks would never let me out nights, so he suggested I try to Rex movie house for a matinee.

I hadn't any spending money but the next sports afternoon (the sports meets were so inadequately supervised no one would know if I was there or not) I got into the movie house for free through an emergency exit door that other kids were always leaving open for that purpose. The first thing was to find a seat before I was accused of not having a ticket. Almost immediately someone sat next to me. It was a G.I. Pretty soon he was pressing a leg against mine. I was wearing my football shorts, as I was supposed to be at the meet, and the next I knew his hand was on my naked thigh. I instinctively leaned back on my seat and parted my legs to let his fingers gain access to my crotch. He pulled my shorts down and gave my cock a wonderful massage. He put his hand on the back of my neck and forced my head down towards his cock, which was sticking out of his fly. I tried to resist but he whispered, "it's okay, no one cares till the lights go up." I sucked the biggest piece of meat I'd yet had. He nearly choked me when he came, grasping my head and holding it on his cock. He jacked me off, sat for a little while watching the movie, then went. It was after I'd left the movie house myself that I realized I hadn't earned a quid. But it didn't matter. I felt really satisfied. I hung around the Rex a lot after that. Quite often G.I.s would pay for my ticket out of sheer generosity, never attempting any sexual advances once inside, which I found disappointing. Once a soldier did give me a quid without asking for it, and I felt a bit insulted.

IV. GETS ASS LICKED IN HOTEL.

When the next school term started my sex life really took off. I had reached 16, which meant I was old enough to do night time fire watch (a civilian protection against the German air raids). One night a week I had to join a fire watch team, a mixture of underage boys and overage men. Foot patrols were sent out every hour, wandering the dark streets to make sure all was safe. Bruce Hampshire, a neighborhood garage mechanic with a bad reputation, let his hand wander over my butt as we walked together. I made no attempt to resist. He was a lean, masculine guy in his late 40s who had a son in the Eighth Army in North Africa. Finally he asked, "You fuck other kids?" It wasn't my specialty but I mumbled yes, wanting really to get my hand in his overalls. But he made no further advances, just groped my butt and said to wait till he got me together with Barry later. Barry was a boy my own age whom I knew, but I didn't know he'd gotten involved with men. About three o'clock one morning Bruce managed to get us together in the garage stock room. He turned on a heater for warmth and told us to shuck our siren suits. Barry's dick sprang straight up when he stripped. I was expecting the man to suck it, then fuck him. But he just watched while Barry and I took turns fucking each other. At no time did Bruce free his cock from his mechanic's overalls. The whole time he was feeling us as we fucked – feeling our balls, our butts, everything. He set me up with at least three other boys this way. One night I tried groping Bruce's cock through his overalls but he got angry and said he wasn't a "sodomite."

In an air raid one night I dived into the nearest shelter and found myself sitting next to a man about 50. He kept talking about girls, emphasizing that he'd never married one. He asked me if I was old enough to have a girl friend. He said his name was Gerald and he managed a small hotel and when the raid was over would I come back with him for something to eat. Something to eat turned out to be something to drink, and it wasn't long before Gerald had me ginned up in the tiny office at the side of the bar-reception desk. Servicemen were coming and going with a weird assortment of women, all of them smelling and looking like cheap candy; it turned out that what Gerald ran was not so much a small hotel as a house of assignation.

He asked if I'd had a girl; he bet I was a big boy who could satisfy a girl; how big was I, would I object to him finding out – and it wasn't long before he had his well-manicured hand in my pants. Terry, Gerald's butch partner, ran the reception desk while Gerald and I went to his bedroom.

Gerald turned out to be very nice, so anxious not to do anything I might object to that I thought we weren't going to get round to doing anything at all. I told him I could stay all night because my folks thought I was on all night fire watch. "May I undress you?" he asked. He was so excited his hands trembled as he removed first my shoes and sox, which he placed carefully under the bed, then my shirt, which he carefully folded. When he had me naked his careful hands so lightly frisked my skin I could hardly feel them. "Lovely," he said. "Lovely. Just part your legs so I can feel between them. So smooth, so wonderfully smooth. It's monstrous that soon you'll start to shave."

Being flattered made me feel great; I'd never met a man like this before and I'd have done anything for him. But all he seemed to want was to lay me on my back on the bed, with my legs parted wide, and give me a tongue bath from head to toes and then back again. My cock was hard, leaking, and Gerald lapped up the juice. Then he turned me face down, parted my legs wide, and resumed his tongue bath. He worked his tongue deep up my shit-hole.

He stripped; his white body was overly thin. He rolled a rubber on my cock, got on his back with his legs over my shoulders, and guided my condom-covered dick up his wide open asshole. I didn't give a damn how old he was; I was so switched on I fucked like a wild animal.

He eased me off his hunched body and, while I stood at the side of the bed, lovingly rolled the cum-heavy rubber off my cock and put the whole thing in his mouth and chewed it like gum. Then he licked my asshole again. I felt his hand under my belly giving me another hard on, then his head was there urging me to fuck him in the mouth. I shot into his mouth and fell asleep exhausted.

V. 1,000 COCKS AT THE Y.

I woke several hours later in the dark room to find a cock up my rear end, a hand jacking me off, another cock prodding my lips, another hand wrapping my own hand round a hard cock. My mouth was filled with cock – I couldn't ask who was there, or how many were crowded into that big double bed. I heard one guy say, "This kid really loves having his butt plugged." I just let it all happen.

I fell asleep again and when I woke it was light and only Gerald was in bed with me. "The bathroom's down the passage on the right," he said. "I'll fix breakfast." And what a breakfast. I'd grown up during the war and was not used to the basic luxuries, but Gerald supplied real oranges, real fresh eggs, real bacon, and limitless lumps of sugar. It was like the war was over.

I didn't need much persuading to return to Gerald's "small hotel" other nights when I played truant from fire watch. He introduced me to other middle-aged men with whom I had sex. It never dawned on me that these men might be paying Gerald for my services. I was flattered by the attention of men feasting on my young body. I was proud of my growth of fluffy pubic hair, proud of the fact that my cock was smoother but no smaller than the grown men's cocks. All it needed was a little flattery for me to take it in the ass or down my throat.

But I wanted a younger man, a soldier or sailor with a 12-inch prick. Preferably a black 12-inch prick. I told Gerald of my obsession with black cock and he said he'd see what he could do. One night he pushed a hefty American black G.I. into the room. I could tell as soon as the guy got to the side of the bed that he'd been drinking; his breath was heavy with the fumes and he called me a bitch and told me to get my panties off because he had a big "wang" for me. He told me to suck on it. I opened my mouth and got my first taste of salty black cock. As he grew accustomed to the dark, he pulled his cock from my mouth and bellowed, "This ain't no fuckin' girl." A black fist came flying toward my head. I fled down to the crowded bar and the next moment the bar was being wrecked as Terry and Gerald tried to appease him. As I got dressed and fled out the back door, a U.S. Army jeep disgorged M.P.s at the front door.

My folks were only too pleased for me to spend all the time I was not at my classes helping out at the local YMCA. Every night at the Y there would be a dance attended by possibly a thousand guys and fewer than a hundred girls. Jacking off in the toilets was commonplace. The older Britishers, married men particularly, could be good value if, like me, you enjoyed taking it in the ass. They appreciated a willing boy butt and I shall always remember one sergeant in the Royal Engineers, about 35 years of age, who had a couple of kids, who screwed me at least a dozen times over a period of months in one of the Y closets. He insisted so often he wanted a photograph of me that I had to get one done at the only wedding studio still operating.

Getting black prick, with which I had become obsessed, was the real difficulty at first. I got my mouth round a lot of Gurkhas cock – the Indian regiment – but this was brown, not black meat. But the Gurkhas were very tough and very sexy; homosexuality was second nature to them. The American blacks were really screwed up; their white troops treated them as inferiors, and they were scared to do anything. Often at a pisser I would let a black G.I. or Marine see my hard on but more often than not they would give me a guilty kind of grin, button up and get the hell out. But I did make out with quite a few. My first full experience with a black was in a crapper at the Y. He followed me in and we bolted the door. He was a G.I., young (how young I don't know; I've always found it difficult to judge a black's age), and scared the M.P.S. would catch him with a British kid. But as soon as he felt my lips around his cock he calmed down. Boy, was I in heaven. His pants round his ankles, he laid back on the toilet with his thighs parted wide as I explored that wonderful black cock and tough ball sack and coarse wiry pubic hair. That unique salty taste of Negro prick has remained with me for the rest of my life. He wouldn't leave the crapper till I'd gone out and made sure there were no M.P.s hanging around. He told me the safest place for action was late at night behind the Red Lion.

VI. NAKED IN THE PUB TOILET.

The Red Lion was one of many public houses (bars), which I was legally too young to enter. But I was not too young to use their outside pissers. All pubs in those days had somewhat primitive cottages adjacent, usually a couple of walls with drainage for the piss. During the war they were totally dark at night. One had to grope one's way to a pissing position and if a match was struck for more than a moment to light a cigarette there would almost certainly be a distant yell from an Air Raid warden: "Put that bloody light out." (A neighbor, a friend of my dad's, was taken to court and fined five quid for the careless use of a match.)

Anyhow, the Red Lion had a particularly fine urinal. It was in the side street behind the pub, under a railway arch, and not far from the entrance to the harbour. Like the famous Windmill Theatre in London, the Red Lion's urinal never closed. There was action there all night, every night. Occasionally, someone would quickly light a cigarette and in the momentary flame you could see the piss-cavern crowded with sailors and soldiers and marines, jacking off, leaning against walls being blown, or just waiting their turn. Sometimes a guy would come in strictly to piss; I once heard a guy say, "Get your filthy hand off me." His complaint was met with laughter in the darkness. I never had any refusal when I reached out in the darkness to feel prick.

When the weather was warm enough, I wore just my siren suit and nothing underneath. In the Red Lion pisser I let the older men peel off my suit, I was stark naked except for my shoes and sox. Bony hands would be all over me, eager tongues rimming and licking, while I handled unseen soldier or sailor prick in the piss-perfumed darkenss. It was a miracle I never contacted V.D. but I didn't. Some of the more sensible guys, mostly American, rolled rubbers on their cocks before they screwed me. Their medics were making them scared.

One night the warning siren sounded but no one ran for the shelters. There were at least two dozen guys crowded in that pisser. The ack-ack opened up. Pieces of shrapnel fell on the corrugated iron roof. Several bombs fell a short distance away. The searchlight beams occasionally reflected into the cavernous darkness. I saw two Yankee sailors making a sandwich of a pink-faced Royal Engineer. A young soldier grabbed my stiff meat and guided it to his butt. Either I was the last of many or he'd lubricated it with a lot of KY. It was wild, screwing and getting screwed to the sound of gunfire.

But promiscuity was not enough. I desperately wanted to talk to someone. One of the priests hanging around the Y interested me in religion and I started going to a Catholic church. I actually read the Bible and the more I read it the more I loved Jesus and the less I loved that church. I was convinced Jesus was gay and my favorite story was how he stopped the guys stoning a woman to death just because one husband was not enough for her.

I got into a conversation with one priest about masturbation but after half an hour of doubletalk I realized he wanted to get his hands on my cock without me or Jesus being angry with him. I didn't have any objection to priests wanting to do these things but I did object to his feeling guilt-ridden. After my cum splattered on his cassock I had to convince *him* that Jesus loved him.

One day I heard a friendly voice calling me from a line of women waiting patiently to buy some rarely seen oranges at a greengrocers. It was Gerald. He wanted to know why I stopped visiting him and that night I returned to his hotel. One of the men there stroked my butt and whispered in my ear, "What you say we find ourselves a quiet place upstairs?" The guy was in his late 40s, well kept, with a quiet determination behind his gentle facade; I was to find out later that he was a policeman. I said yes, which was how we opened one of the bedroom doors and saw Terry and Gerald in bed. They had fled their own party. At that moment, as I saw them wrapped in each other's arms, I knew what I hadn't got, what I'd never had, and what I so desperately wanted. This was one of the most beautiful sex scenes I've ever seen. My companion said the two had been together more than 30 years "and they've still got this thing going for them."

Eventually I found the real constant love of my life. We've been together for 34 years now. Yes, 34. When life keeps us apart we write long letters every day, including Sunday, which we mail together in the Monday envelope. Our closeness makes our promiscuity not only possible, but desirable.

Student Wrestlers "Suck Weight," Magazine Reveals

About 350,000 high school and college wrestlers in America "suck weight," *People* revealed. This doesn't mean that they give blow jobs to fat men; rather, before a match, in order to qualify for a weight class, they starve themselves, then compensate after the match by "pigging out" on food, to use *People's* swinish phrase. "Pigging out" is followed by "inevitable diarrhea."

"O.k.?" "O.k."

I was surprised to read in a letter to *The New York Native* from Arthur Bell that he'd gone to Michael's restaurant at 2:30, June 28, 1983 "to read my mail and have a coffee and muffin;" half-past two seems late for muffins, which I associate with much earlier in the day.

Bell's letter continued along less surprising lines (a woman in the restaurant, evidently a typical heterosexual, said she'd be glad when all gays were dead from AIDS; Bell called her a dumb cunt, she called him a prick, he spat in her face, the manager told her to leave, and so on and so forth; a typical New York encounter).

Bell's behavior was inspiring; in the spirit of Stonewall. I'd add this proviso: you get extra points for men. My most satisfying attempt to achieve this ideal behavior was at Roosevelt Hospital, where I'd gone for a routine blood pressure check. An unusually contemptuous doctor demanded answers to his questions in an even more barbaric way than most doctors; I gave him a quiet but vicious tirade that surprised both of us, ending with "O.K.?" After hesitating, he whimpered, "O.K." My performance made me feel healthier than any nostrum or bromide he could have prescribed. Doctors agree that it is healthy to express justified anger – healthy at least for heterosexuals, although many doctors would not include homosexuals.

I differ from Bell in a minor matter of style. Mistreatment of homosexuals is normally a job for sexually inadequate males. When a woman does this manly job, I suppose most decent people would instinctively call her, as Bell did, a dumb cunt, but I would call her a prick. For example, I assume most decent Christians think of Anita Bryant as a dumb cunt, but I've always thought of her as a prick.

In the same way, my style is to use the phrase "dirty bitch" for men and boys who abuse homosexuals; I believe they like it less than being called pricks. They would *like* to be pricks. Common ordinary heterosexuals like Pauline Kael, movie reviewer for *The New Yorker*, reserve the word "bitch" for women. But the women Kael so frequently calls bitches fight with people they know; it is only men and boys who call out names to perfect strangers on the street. What could be bitchier? Joan Crawford never called out "fag" to strangers.

– *B. McD.*

A Latent Heterosexual?

A man who signed his name "Plenty Bugged" wrote Ann Landers, the advice columnist, that he is a high school wrestling coach, is a homosexual, has never had sex with a woman and is having an affair with one of his wrestlers. But he is tempted to try women for a change.

HOLES:
The Memoirs of a Sex Artist

I. "HE WAS RAMMING IT INTO MY MOUTH."

MANHATTAN — About married men: they're fun. They want what they don't get at home. They live with women and usually bring out my femininity. On one occasion my masculinity. As you will see. Here goes. I was in school in the Bronx and walking home along Webster. His car was stalled and I offered to help. I pushed; he started the motor. He was a stocky Italian youth. He said, "Can I give you a lift?" I got in beside him. He said, "Where to?" I said I'd been out for a walk. He turned off Webster towards Third. We stopped for a light. He grabbed my hand and placed it on his crotch. "Want it?" I didn't say anything but I didn't take my hand away. "It's big ... it's nice." I squeezed a little. He turned off Third into a quiet neighborhood block. He parked. "Let's get in back." We did. I had school books and put them on the curb during the change. I sat in the back seat corner and before I could get in position his dick was out and he was ramming into my mouth. He was bending over me and going like crazy half-way down the throat. I did what I could with my tongue but it was his show. Then he squirted and I got his load. I was hot and kept on with the tongue but he pulled out, saying, "Gotta save some for the old lady." He asked me where I "hung out" and I named a bar near. He made a date for same night next week but never showed.

I was walking up Third in the Sixties (in Manhat.) and a man cruised me from his car a few blocks. I stopped to light a cig and he pulled alongside. "Need a lift?" I got in. "I'm looking for a blow job." I said, "So am I." He said, "Sorry, I got the wrong guy." I said, "No you didn't." We drove to my place. His wife was in the hospital expecting. He had just visited her. I let him have my pussy that night and my suck hole in the morning. He took my number but I never heard from him.

I only know they're married if they tell me. Like the guy I met one night in the White Tower on 86th after the bars were closed. He was a real beauty, dressed corporate, handsome, built and I took him home. He was separated and living with his mother and when we got home HE blew ME. We shacked up for a week. I was between jobs and next day we drank beer and he was afraid I'd be put off because he sucked me off. Aside from sex he was good company and as male as anybody would want outside the sack but that night I fucked him, at his suggestion. Funny, every man I've ever laid had a bigger dick than me. After a couple of days of fucking I was running out of dough, beer and butts — and cum. And all he wanted was beer, butts and my pecker. His body was a beauty — chest, stomach, ass, prick, and here I spent my time plowing him. In between sex we talked and he was screwed up with the wife and the mother and I was beginning to flake out. Once at the end of the week, I had to piss in the night and on my way to the john I found that all four burners on the stove were on. I turned them off, woke him up and said "this is it" or something like that. "If you want to take yourself off OK but don't take me with you." He swore it must have been an accident on his way back from the john, but you don't even go near the stove on your way from sack to shit-house. I called a fag friend, borrowed carfare for him and cigarette money and screwed him one more time (because he begged) and sent him back to his mother.

He wrote a letter a couple of weeks later saying he was doing alright and wanted to get together (not for sex). I didn't answer and a couple of weeks after that he called to say he'd landed a good job and would like to meet me for dinner (on him), that he was grateful and that it didn't have to be sex. I said no because of those open burners. I liked that week; his company, his suck-hole, his shit-hole, but don't want to face my number till it's up.

II. "I WANTED HIM IN MOUTH-FUCKING POSITION."

Had lunch at a bar restaurant where two boys (not together) had me creaming. One in garish green top and garish blue jogging shorts was young enough, blond enough to overcome this. I wanted to run my hands over that slim form and get him into mouth-fucking position. The other in tan cut-off corduroys with large hands, big Adam's apple and bookish glasses was unknowingly sending messages to my ass-licking tongue. I was ready to probe corduroy and all. That's the mood I'm in and am back home, where I'll soon jack off and both boys will star in the production – a sleazy triangle with tan cords and blue jogging shorts piled on the floor and their owners piled up on me.

Being a devoted cocksucker I don't look at my watch during blow time. When you are eager 20 minutes can seem like an hour. Some boys have asked me when I wanted them to come. Anytime is fine with me. When you are ready you are ready. If they aren't ready you ease up on the sucking and change pace. All I know is 20 minutes doesn't always cover it and some times 3 minutes does.

Some of the pieces I've had may seem like sullen, filthy creeps but they left my world (represented by both holes) a little better than they found it. I got what I deserved and I hope sometimes they did too.

You ask me how many wads of scum I have swallowed and what are the different flavours. Asking how many wads is like an earlier letter asking me to list every blow job. The answers to both would require the letter to be delivered by United Parcel rather than U.S. Mail. For awhile I used to keep it in my suck-hole swallowing as little as possible and then spitting it out and gargling. I soon came to my senses – my senses of smell, taste and touch – and cut out that shit. Men generally come in two flavours – bland and sharp. Closest thing I can tell you about the bland is a Swiss gin – Geneva. It's the best (to me) but both are OK right out of the piss-hole. One youth liked to pull out and come on his own belly so I could lap it up. It tastes a hell of a lot better from the tap. Which gets back to taste and smell. The main reason, for me, in being a cocksucker is that it satisfies those senses and that of touch. Taking it in the back door satisfies only "feel." I wrote about the pleasure of sucking off a partner in the morning after he had been in my shit-hole and/or suck-hole the night before. The taste of stale scum on his prick plus my saliva and/or my shit-hole was pleasure. Your Ontario writer is right when he talks about the taste and smell of ass.

I've never had pigs who tasted and smelled so bad I hoped it would all end in a hurry, only bores whose responses smelled that bad. I have found cock-slime (the juice that oozes out of a hard on before it shoots) rather tasteless. The feel of that meat in your suck-hole, the smell of that crotch and finally the taste when he shoots – having it slide down your throat, coming to rest in your belly – those are what I like.

III. "HE FLASHED HIS PRICK AT ME."

You asked for a letter on jacking off. In high school there were two boys I did it with. The first was my age, in my class and we were both sissies. He took violin lessons. I was not interested in using my height to go out for basketball. We were rivals in a way – I had more buddies who were all-boy and I got better grades. He was one up on me because he could toss out sentences with shit, piss, hell and damn in them (he had an older brother). Because of this talent I confided in him that while taking a bath I accidentally scrubbed my pecker longer and harder than necessary and came by hand for the first time. It told me it was natural and we started jacking each other off a couple of times a week – in his bedroom or mine or on Sunday walks in the woods. As high school went on we went on to sucking each other a few licks but always ended jerking. His was the first and only cock in my hole for a long time and my first sample of slime, although I never took his scum. Once he tried sticking his pecker in my asshole but we began to laugh at what seemed silly and continued to jack off. I mention the rivalry because it's why things never went any further. We weren't going to do anything the other didn't. At the end of high school he went into the Army and on leave we got together. This time, uniform and all, I'd probably have done him but I came and didn't finish. After the service we met a few times but now he said if we did it it would be one way and I wouldn't because of the rivalry.

With the second boy it was more "natural;" we just pulled each other's dicks and they squirted into handkerchiefs. They both got married and had kids.

After that for several years jacking off was my only sexual activity and by myself, which is really the best way. In these last few years it's been my main source of pleasure too. I knew a guy who knew a guy who was able to suck himself off. This would be even better than *beating* your meat. I now sometimes jerk off two or three times a day, flat on my ass in the sack with my meat in front of me. I relive in my mind good sex with men and boys and create in my mind new sex with the ones I never had but still remember. You are lucky I can't write while jacking off or you'd get the fantasy you don't want instead of the facts which I try to give you.

I said the first boy I jacked off with had an older brother. In those days I never paid him mind. He was a ne'er-do-well, boozed, womanized, kept flunking out of college and ended running a garage. We had neighborhood showers (courtesy of a local company) and the men used it as a change from taking a bath. A few years after what I've written I was using it when big brother came in, stripped and stood under the shower across from me. A fucking beauty. I don't know why I'd never noticed but I'd never seen him stripped. Broad shoulders, narrow waist, large balls, big prick, sturdy legs. With the water playing on his body, bubbling from his piss-hole, he was one of the most beautiful, sexiest men I've ever seen. That's all that happened. Two guys matter of factly taking a shower. I turned the cold spray on to douse my growing hard on. But he's one of the stars of my meat-beating act. Only then he leers seductively, fingers his meat and says "take it." And I do, right there under his shower. I tongue him all over that body.

My meat is not my long suit. Soft, I hang about 4 inches; when provoked I stiffen to just over six inches. More important, it works well. My six inches has fed many a hungry cocksucker, pleased a lot of assholes and continues to gladden my hand.

Most of the men I brought home had to be worked up, having lost their hards in transit. In cars they were hard but lost it by the time we got to my place. Working them up again was no problem and feeling cock harden in your suck-hole is enjoyable in itself.

I don't remember taking a man home when he showed it hard in a toilet. I tried to take care of it right there if he was interesting. If there's a shit stall in the toilet it's possible to do that. A queer sucked me off once in a shit stall in Grand Central. I stood on the toilet seat and crouched so that only his legs showed under the stall while he gobbled my meat. Men who show it hard in public toilets want instant gratification so why take them home.

In a bar the toilet is usually exposed so if a man exposes himself, there is no way but to find some other place to take care of him. I sucked one guy off in a bar toilet but it was after closing and he was the bartender and had locked the place up. Another time in another bar I was drinking beer with some guys and a man in building attendant clothes came in. He flashed his prick at me and the guys I was with didn't notice. He finished his beer and left. I excused myself and followed. He led me to a nearby apartment building and I ate his meat in the employee's room off the lobby. He didn't have to be worked on, just sucked off. I swallowed his scum and went back to the bar and rejoined my drinking companions with some lame excuse as to why I'd left.

IV. "THE PAIN WAS FIERCE."

I hailed a cab from outside a queer bar on the upper west side about midnight. The driver was a good-looking young man who spoke English like a Puerto Rican. As we drove across town I began to talk to him. I found out that business had been slow, I was his last fare and when he got off work he usually drove the car back to the barn where he played cards with some other cab drivers unless he had a chick lined up. "Which is it tonight" I asked. "Card game I guess," he said. We were silent after that and soon reached my building. "Want to come up for awhile," I asked after I paid him. He hesitated. "I am big." It was half question, half warning. "O.K.," I said. "O.K.," he said.

Inside the apartment he was out of his clothes and laying on his back on my bed in minutes. His body was long and brown and his prick firm and smooth, pointed toward the ceiling. He hadn't lied. It was big. "Will you take off your clothes," he asked. I did. "Do you have pomade?" I reached into the night table drawer and took out the KY. He reached for it, squeezed a large amount in his hand and held it toward my suck-hole. I lapped it up from his palm and licked the fingers he now offered. I then licked his prick all the way, heavy on his piss-hole. I was now on my belly and he knelt over me, his prick pointing toward my butt-hole, which he softened with sticky fingers. Still kneeling, he plunged his greased prick into my shit-hole. The pain was fierce and the room began to spin. He yanked his cock part way out and plunged it in deeper. My asshole felt like it was on fire. He rested his body on top of me, his arms around my waist, his outstretched hand rubbing my belly and my nipples. He was now fucking me steady and the pleasure of his movements seemed to lessen the pain. I was soon breathing as heavy as he was and my butt began to heave as it rose to meet each new thrust. My asshole burned like it had never been fucked before.

The screwing stopped as quickly as it began. I could feel the juice pouring from the head of his cock deep within me. The cabbie stayed in me until his cock wilted in his own sauce. He pulled it out and hopped to his feet. His meat was now soft and juicy and I wanted to taste it but I knew it was the wrong time. He went to take a shower while I lay on my belly letting my asshole dry. My dick, which had hardened and softened a couple of times during the humping, was getting stiff again. I wanted to postpone that pleasure so I pulled on my underpants and sat on the edge of the bed. The cabby came back looking fresh and alluring and got into his clothes. After I locked the door behind him I took my turn in the shower. I soaped up and began to clean out my shit-hole, which was puffy and sore. As I probed it my dick began to stiffen again and this time I satisfied it, slowly jacking off with my right hand as I fingered my butt-hole with my left and reliving the whole experience. After I came I finished my shower. It took 20 minutes just to clean and rinse my hole; it was that tender. When I finished I spread Vaseline on the wound and went back to a bed still warm and smelling of bodies. Nuzzling those smells, I fell asleep and slept like a baby until it was time to get up for work.

V. "I LICKED IT GREEDILY."

I came out of a gay bar on the east side intending to walk the few blocks home when a cab pulled alongside me, the driver a husky man in his thirties looking good. I decided to treat myself to a ride home. I knew he was aware of where I was coming from and after giving my address said nothing more. When we pulled up to my building I paid the fare and as I leaned forward to get the change he rubbed his crotch and told me, "I could use a blow job." "Right here?" "You live alone?" He turned on the "Off Duty" sign and came home with me. In the apartment he sat himself in an easy chair and let me remove his pants and his underpants and sink my suck-hole on his dick. He raised his legs so I could get at his balls and I was faced with the most alluring shit-hole I'd ever seen. It was tightly curled and pink and looked like a rosebud. I kissed it a couple of times and gave in to an urge to go further. Inside it was moist and tasty, becoming more moist and tasty the deeper I went. I had never eaten a shit-hole before and was surprised at how good it tasted. It had been well wiped but not washed. (I had always looked down on some friends who were shit-hole eaters but now I began to understand what I'd been missing. It tasted only faintly shitty, fresh and sweet smelling.)

The driver let me roam around in his hole for about five minutes. It got more juicy the further I reached. I felt at home and licked it greedily. He let me eat it for awhile but then said, "If you aren't gonna blow me, I gotta get back to work." I sucked him off and although he came heavily the dominant taste in my mouth was his shit-hole. When he left I jacked myself off to its memory.

VI. "HE SAID HE WAS SORRY."

I call myself a cocksucker and a queer and I enjoy doing that. You could say it was self-hate but I think it's because I *am* a cocksucker and a queer that that's how it goes. I've done it with sexual partners who seemed disappointed because I was depriving them of their right to so label me. One youth said, "You're the first one who ever said it." That language is for them to use next day – boy did I get blowed last night by this fag. I realize that the foregoing will strike you as literary but you have to know that I'm not a *stupid* queer.

One man called me such names a long time ago. I was sucking him off and he got excited and called me the book. Cocksucker, girl, cunt and so on. It excited me and when he'd released his load he said he was sorry for his language. It just made me hotter. So many guys say nothing or give you a vapid "You're the best baby" when they're about to shoot. I imagine women feel that way when a man gives them that indifferent "I love you" routine although I'm told women don't give a shit about sincerity so long as he says it. That's just *participation* but all the foul words are an expression of *pleasure*. It was voluntary. I hadn't suggested it. Another time with another guy I did suggest it. He said it all but it lacked free flow and didn't work. After, he said he'd been embarrassed.

In a bar I worked I knew this woman who was "in love" with a guy I found unattractive. He was a prick in the asexual sense. She told me that one problem she had was his dirty mouth during the act. That interested me and one night after they had split I got bombed with him and took him home. She was right. He used the same names the other guy did plus "pervert" and it was erotic as ever. I don't know why this "turns me on" but it does.

VII. "HE'D STICK HIS DICK IN MY BEER."

It occurs to me that I was a male slut. The pleasure of coupling is the satisfaction I get from all that is NELLY in me. When I suck cock or take it in the ass the NELLY is being fulfilled. I know there is part of me that is butch. Both facets of my nature are genuine. I've enjoyed being pseudo-wife to married guys. I've enjoyed being tonight's girl to studs. If the married man accepts me in that role – if the stud does – then a part of my nature is being taken care of. I don't begrudge a man for being heterosexual and a lot of them have not begrudged my homosexuality. I've never wanted a boyfriend or a husband as a way of life but for a one-nighter it was fine. The male part of me wants to take what's there and quit. I don't like the word "lover" but the marrieds and the horny bi's were just that. They brought out the fem in me to our mutual satisfaction and what's the big deal? I sometimes washed their underpants as against re-union but breakfast was something they gave me. You may use my stories but I doubt if you understand the fun involved. I enjoyed almost everything. After I stopped getting excited I could have quit but I didn't. Even the lousy jobs entailed sucking and cum in my mouth. Even the cock up my ass was gratifying even when there was more pain than pleasure. I identify with the guy who likes sucking dick. I have always liked sucking dick. Sex between two men is something that brings out dominant strain. If he's male he doesn't have to swagger and if I'm lucky my partner doesn't swish. This is just getting straight my queerness. Now for some items.

He was pudgy and raunchy. He was looking for a blow job. He loved to be sucked. He was trying to flag a hooker. They were working 86th [Street] then. He came into Wrights all night place (no longer there) and I was there. He wanted it sucked bad and I was there. We stopped at a deli for beer and came to my place. He was married, separated. His wife didn't like sucking him off. He liked women who did and took one to a movie where she went down on him. Most times he depended on hookers and queers. Hookers charged $25 when they were available. He played the horses and when he had $25 to spare they were busy. So queers were all right. Before we got together in Wrights his favorite was Fat Andy of the deli. From the first time we did a lot of slimy stuff. He'd stick his dick in my beer and I'd slurp it off. One night he poured a can of Reingold over his crotch and I drank it up. It ran over his cock, his balls, his asshole. No butt-fucking, just cocksucking. I carried on with him for about six months. Then I saw him on 86th with a broad and got the cold shoulder. I guess he finally found a broad who could take it like a queer. When he came into the bar where I was working about a year ago all that stuff was over. The fact that he didn't speak didn't matter. The possibility that he'd "finger" me did. He came in with a low gambler, since barred from the bar, and he could have fucked up my current image with the new crop of bartenders. In the old days I was his scum bag and I guess he just threw me away. Probably he didn't want his gambler buddy to know details and figured better let sleeping dogs lie.

I went home with a guy one night and all he wanted was a load of piss. He was fat and ugly and thirtyish. Wore glasses, well dressed in expensive conservative rags. He took me to place in the East 30s crammed with books and the "right" furniture. He talked to me about books, art etc. and keep feeding me beer. When I was ready to piss he wanted it. Wouldn't suck me off or anything. Just wanted to be my urinal. It was a cheap drunk and I don't remember how many times I pissed in his mouth. It didn't do much for me but the beer was good. I'm pretty shat out for now so I'll pick up the pen later. There's lots more but it gets exhausting. Cocksucking was much easier.

"Buckley is the Liberace of Literature"

By Boyd McDonald

[The following review appeared originally in The New York Native*]*

Overdrive by William F. Buckley Jr. Doubleday, $16.95

Overdrive is overdone; Buckley is the Liberace of literature but it is not his piss-elegance so much as his other sexual disturbances that make him seem so unwholesome. Since he is disturbed even by unauthorized heterosexuality, homosexuality is a really grave problem for him. But he has discovered, in the experience of a friend, that homosexuality can be "cured." He admires the "dignity" with which Robert Bauman announced at a press conference that the source of the homosexual desire for which he was arrested is alcohol and that after he stopped drinking "any tendency to homosexuality," in Buckley's words, "had gone with the alcohol."

Yet on network television Buckley called Gore Vidal a "queer" and Vidal is not a drinker.

Vidal, a distinguished business economist and juridical scholar, countered by expressing a fear that Buckley would land in jail after a Securities and Exchange Commission investigation of his family's shoddy little Catawba Corporation. But Vidal's fear, never perhaps heart-felt, proved groundless. After signing a couple of consent decrees (do the innocent sign consent decrees, ever?), the Buckleys got off with only a fine and no prison sentences.

Bauman himself sabotaged Buckley's heralded "cure" for homosexuality; not long after this book was issued, Bauman announced at a press conference that, having previously categorized himself as a former homosexual, he was now revising his classification to that of former-former homosexual or, in his word, "gay"; he and his wife are separated and he is now going to support, where formerly he opposed, "gay rights" legislation. If the Bauman experience proved anything, it is that it is heterosexuality that can be "cured."

If there is anything worse than a snob it is someone who tries to be snobbish but can't make it. Throughout the book Buckley talks about his servants much, much, much, much more than the authentically rich do; but at the end of the book, after hundreds of attempts to seem patrician, Buckley aborts himself by suddenly, and inexplicably, revealing that when he visited his mother in her "Park Avenue" apartment she was eating pizza, and eating it at a card table. What if a tenant, trying to impress an important piece of ass, brings him home at the same time a delivery boy enters the apartment house with a box of pizza? Can't a committee of concerned tenants be formed to prevent pizza deliveries to these buildings? I object not to pizza eaten in the closet, but to any attempt to legitimize it. Buckley's sordid revelation dragged *The New Yorker* which ran this book originally, down with him. *The New Yorker* used to be so good at being snotty. I never thought I'd see the day when it runs the autobiography of the son of a pizza-eater (especially one who eats it at a *card* table), an autobiography which finds a "cure" for homosexuality. Talk about the decline in the quality of snobbery. Yet the two subjects – pizza-eating and "curing" homosexuality – go hand in hand; show me a person whose mother eats pizza off a card table and I'll show you a person who is ill-bred enough to publicly and frequently judge the private lives of others. I had assumed that these people (the Buckleys are Irish Catholic) ate corned beef and cabbage, but Buckley's book shows that even that stereotype can be misleading.

Even worse than his view that homosexuality is a disease is his claim – made in his blue collar class *Daily News* column – that what he called a "homo" winked at him at a lecture (I assume "homo" is his redneck word for homosexual; comparable manners would be to identify him as a mick rather than Irish). I find it incredible that anyone would want to get into Buckley's pants; the pants themselves, to begin with, "have lost all memory of a crease," according to *People.* Obviously he wears his pants for excessive periods between cleanings, raising the question of how long these pants are worn without cleaning.

That this is a legitimate cause for concern may be seen in another of *People*'s revelations: that he has dandruff on his shoulders. If he is so careless in the personal daintiness of a part that shows, such as his head hair, what must be the condition of a part that does not show. The combination of seldom-cleaned pants exposed to other parts, would, if true, surely be enough to restrain any "homo" from making a pass at him; but even if the "homo" cited was not close enough to notice his dandruff and the condition of his pants, Buckley's face alone frees him from homosexual molestation (in one photograph in the book he looks like Gladys Cooper, the grand old English actress and mother-in-law to Robert Morley, the grand old English actor).

Would it be asking too much, finally, that Buckley describe activities at *The National Review* – a sordid enough greed-and-hate sheet in itself – without mentioning anything so coarse as men going to what he calls the "bathroom"? He writes that when the publisher of this periodical goes to the "bathroom" and finds that the light there has been left on, he instinctively turns it off as he would, in a dark "bathroom", turn the light on. While this gives an insight into the mind of the reactionary, I find it unbearably squalid.

To end on a more alluring note (the only one I found in this whole, miserably Catholic book), there is a sentence that, though poorly composed syntax-wise, contains data sufficiently inspiring to warrant quoting. In referring to a World War II troop train, he writes that "lower berths were for two men who slept head to toe."

Cocksucking In Contemporary Culture

By Charley Shively

[EDITOR's NOTE: It's easier to describe the sneering queens like Dennis Altman and George Whitmore than to describe the author of this article, who has a character so rare there is seldom any occasion to think up words for it. He's a giver, not just a taker; honest, valiant, unpretentious, bright, funny and hot. He provides comprehensive leadership in all aspects of the cause, both outdoor (street demonstrations) and indoor (publishing). He's important in the intellectual and political efforts of the cities from Washington to Boston. He's the most beloved of the gay leaders; most people are crazy about him. He has become a professor in a huge university not by being asexual and orthodox but by being honest; he gives his students and fellow faculty members a rare experience of reality. His courage comes from his obvious honesty not, like that of so many writers and professors, from the mere ability to keep in step as an academic tap dancer. His comments on America are shocking but not as shocking as the conditions he comments on. He is both a great mind and a great lay; he has an attractive heart. – B. McD.]

I. THE MAN IN THE DAZZLING WHITE JOCKEY SHORTS.

Hot afternoon, evening traffic traveling south out of Louisville, Kentucky, on the Interstate. I stop quickly for a young hitchhiker.

He explains that he's been on the road for 24 hours and only gone a little over 100 miles; he's from Hazard, has been living with relatives near Cincinnati, and is now on his way south before the winter sets in.

Turns out he's about 20 years old, he installs carpets for a living, and he's on the wrong road to get to Florida; but I say why not ride south with me & hook up with a road out of Nashville later. Quickly he falls to sleep. I hesitate to grope him & instead stop at each rest area along the way. I manage to get a good look at him: totally clean-cut, he's wearing black corduroy pants, a checkered shirt without an undershirt, and tennis shoes. No sign of even a half hard on.

When we get to my turnoff – I'm on my way to a conference in Bowling Green, Kentucky – I wake him up and suggest he might want to take a nap and shower in my motel room; then I could drive him on to Nashville later that night. He slips in a back door & I go off to a meeting. When I return he's asleep on the bed with his pants on but his shirt, shoes and socks off. His body is much more extraordinary than when I'd first noticed: smooth, tanned skin, a few freckles, and well-developed muscles; close cut sandy red hair; all very well proportioned.

I wake him up and suggest he'd feel better with a massage. First I start with the toes – rotating each one first clockwise three times and then counter-clockwise three times; then doing the same with the ball of the foot and then with the whole foot. He relaxes. Then I have him turn over and I work on his back muscles: they are extraordinarily well developed and tight. I knead carefully starting down the spinal cord from the neck, working and rotating the shoulder blades. The tightest place of all I find is his back muscles just at the line of the belt; he's wearing an embossed leather belt. To work on that muscle I have to loosen the belt; then I suggest taking the pants down; he acquiesces. He's wearing a pair of Jockey shorts dazzling white (they stay on) with not the slightest shit or piss stain visible. Now I begin massaging his thick muscular legs; they are also beautifully smooth and tanned. Then I work my way up to the buttocks; finding the gluteus muscles – especially the gluteus maximus that sort of rests spiral-like inside each cheek of the ass. For this massage I work my way inside the very bright white underwear. He's totally quiet and unresponsive until I get the buttocks going around and around; the muscles sort of dancing.

Reaching down a little lower, I then check for the root of the cock. I run my finger along the line that goes from the asshole to the balls and discover engorgement; more than the boy's muscles are hard. I turn him over, slip down the bleached underwear, and find the roaring hard ready to go. He doesn't say a word nor even seem to notice. I take his hands and put them on my head as I slowly swallow everything. His cock is standard size, about six inches, neatly cut, and his pubic hair is a little more reddish than the rest of his body.

He wants me to go slow, almost not move at all as I hold the cock deep in my mouth, occasionally working down to the balls, which like the underwear are very well washed, soft. I work my finger to his asshole, but it turns out he's very ticklish there so I can't go for the prostate gland, nor for rimming. The head of his cock is also ticklish so I have to almost hold it in my mouth without moving. With the cock in my mouth I turn him over on top of me; he just holds my head down on him and after about five minutes with just the least little massage he comes in a blast.

He says, "Oh, I didn't expect all that." Then he washed up and got his underwear back on; pushed his pillow up, lit up a cigarette and said, "You know I've been thinking, maybe I could just stay here with you" – the conference was three days – "and then go back to my mother's." I'd be driving back through the Cincinnati area. "Great," I said.

We settled into a steady routine. I'd come home at five and right away blow him; then we'd go get a bite to eat. One night we went into Nashville and had fast Mexican food. When we got back to the motel in Kentucky and were settled down I said do you want to do it again. He said no. But I noticed he had a very good hard on; so I just slipped off the underwear and went to it. I discovered that he didn't talk about sex at all, but he seemed to always be ready; two or three times a day.

There was a color TV in the room and when we weren't having sex we tended to watch all the shows. There was one on about the gay boy with two women roommates; he laughed vigorously at the antics – that night involving a cop – & I thought how strange to learn about the gay life so skewed; certainly not the usual Kentucky fare.

We returned to Cincinnati; I wanted to kiss him good-bye or go into the gas station men's room and blow him again; we exchanged addresses; he asked to borrow $10. He'd spent all his money on food in the motel. Since then we haven't been in touch.

II. HE SAID, "TAKE THE WHEEL."

One cold night around 1967 I was cruising Boston's "miracle mile" – which then was a general mixture of people cruising, hustlers and just plain hitchhikers. I caught the eye of this kid – about 18 years old. He was wearing a wool jacket checkered green and tan; light brown hair, thin body; dark brown trousers and brown snow boots – it was very cold and had just snowed about a foot a day or so before. Turned out we both had cars; so he said, why not come along in his car. It was a four door without those awful bucket seats. He said why don't you come home with me. I said. O.K.

He headed out into the turnpike going about 60 to 70 miles an hour and began playing with me and me with him. I pulled down his pants and began blowing him. He had a nice cock, about seven inches – pencil like, with a nice eraser on the top. He wasn't cut; he got very hard and hot as I blew him. When I came up for a moment he said "Take the wheel" and then went down on me. He was a wonderful cocksucker; a bit frantic, which added to the enthusiasm. So we went back and forth for about 15 or 20 miles. A couple of times I was just about to come and he would stop and say, "No, no, wait, I want to get you home." Likewise he'd hold back when he was about to come.

About 20 miles outside Boston he took an exit and stopped at a roadside truck stop and said, "You wait here, I have to take my mother to work, she's a rest home nurse and goes to work at midnight; soon as I drop her off I'll be back; I want to get you home and get into bed with all our clothes off." "Great" I said and got some English muffins and hot chocolate; I waited an hour and a half and then realized he was not going to return. I kept eyeing the hunky truck drivers going toward Boston, but nothing developed. Then I took to the road and put my thumb out; weather near zero. Luckily I only waited about 15 minutes until a woman stopped. She seemed very cruisy, said I reminded her of her son, and she went out of her way to take me back to the Block. Nothing, however, happened, and I hurried home to my lover who got off work at 2:30 (he was a bartender). I told him the car hadn't started because it was so cold.

III. "MORE WHITISH THAN PINK I THOUGHT."

One night in the Palace Cinema I saw these two numbers come in together; they were wearing black jackets and boots but not really heavy leather. One man was over six feet, well built, and the other shorter, more delicate. I thought these two must be lovers out for some kicks. But they cruised very funny. The tall one seemed uninterested in it all, so I figured he was just going along to please his lover. I approached the shorter one. His jacket was actually plastic and his pants were polyester – not exactly the serious leather type. I pulled down his pants and he jerked them back up and only let me suck his cock and balls. The balls were very smooth with virtually no hair; the cock was straight and slender, about seven inches. It was cut and the head had a nice heart shape; more whitish than pink I thought.

After a little sucking, he pulled his cock in and I thought, "Well, this one's no fun." But as he was walking away with his friend he motioned me to follow. We had been in the top balcony and I followed them down into a back corridor connecting the upper and lower corridors. There was no light here; lots of piss on the floor; many winos came to sleep off their night here and they couldn't bother going to the basement to piss. The floor was slanted so the piss all went to one end.

I began by going down on the smaller one; again he only let out his cock and balls. I was blowing away when one of them hit me in the back. I thought, Oh, great, they like a little rough stuff." I had a navy coat on so the hit seemed light. I turned to the tall one and began to open his belt and unzip his fly; the little one began hitting me. And I thought, "Oh, this one is very jealous." Then the two of them began going through my pockets and it dawned on me that a robbery was in progress. They took my glasses out of my coat pocket and threw them into the piss. I had only a little change but became annoyed so I started hitting and kicking them. This startled them and since I'm over 200 pounds, they reeled a bit from my fists. They ran down the stairs.

I went for my glasses. The theatre bouncer appeared with a flashlight asking "What's the trouble?" I said, "I'm looking for my glasses." He said, "What happened?" as I recovered my glasses. I said, "I think two men were trying to roll me." He said, "Come on down to the door. We'll maybe get them before they leave." When we got to the door they were a couple of steady customers, queens who hang out near the door hoping to get first try on any hot numbers. One of them had been interested in the duo and when she saw they were beating me she went for the security.

They said, "What happened?" I told my story, explaining I liked a little rough stuff now and then. The security man said, "Jesus, you fags." The queen said, "Watch yourself honey." And I explained that they weren't real leather at all, just robbers. Then the security man said, "You know you look familiar, what do you do?" I said, "I'm a poet." He said, "Oh, yes, you're the one who burned the Bible in public – why'd you do that?" I said, "It was only one copy; I don't know why people get so excited." Then he said, "You know my girl friend's a poet." And I say, "What's her name." He says, "Oh, she's going to school in New York." Then he says, "Read a poem." So I read the ending verse of "Repeater:"

> *Delicious penis*
> *delicious penis*
> *delicious penis*
> *comes in my mouth.*

The queens applauded; he shook his head and I went back to find some more cocks to suck in the balcony.

Petty Squabble.

The Village Voice (New York) ran a huge headline on page one:
THE WAR OVER
AMERICA'S MIND.
Can they really believe anything as trivial as the American Mind is worth fighting about?

Robert Redford Uses Night Cream

Robert Redford, the movie star, "creams and greases his face nightly," Cindy Adams revealed in the *New York Post*. Redford, she writes, has a "sure-fire, super-rich moisturizer."

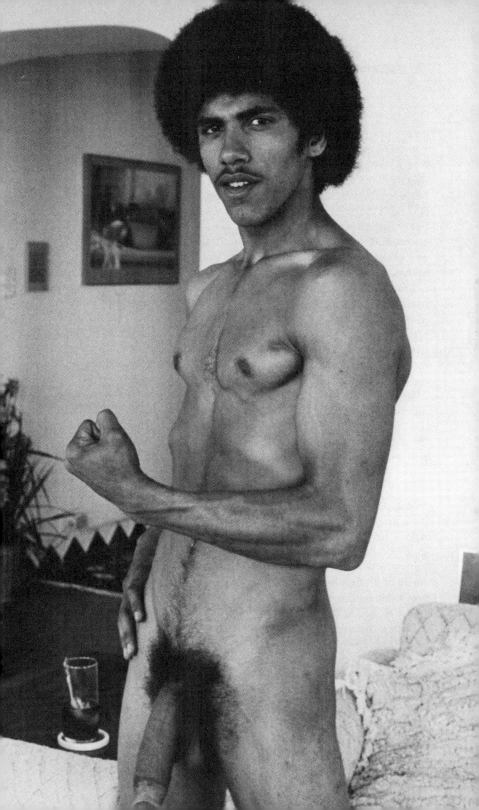

Memoirs of "A Natural Born Cocksucker"

I. SMALL BOY EXPLORES BIG MAN.

Even in early childhood I became aware of a strong homosexual drive. I had a sister who was 16 years older than I was, and she married a man older still. I remember an incident which happened when I was a small boy while my mother and I were visiting them shortly after they were married. Early one morning (it must have been Sunday) while my mother was still sleeping, they took me into bed with them. My sister did not interest me (I had been in bed with her before) but the strange man did. His sweaty body had an attractive aroma and I explored it eagerly, climbing over his feet and legs, hips and chest. I remember he lifted me in his strong arms, rubbed my belly and ass and cupped a hand under my groin.

I wanted to get into bed with him again but never had the opportunity. Years later it occurred to me that probably it was my brother-in-law who set for me my ideal of masculine beauty. He was a telephone linesman, tall, lean, and rugged, with a handsome face, attractive eyes, and dark curly hair. A real stud. He was always clean shaven so I was never attracted to men with beards or moustaches, and I always avoided effeminate men.

Several years later my sister and he were divorced. He went somewhere in the Middle West and I never saw him again. I learned from gossip that my brother-in-law had been a popular sex partner among the loose women of the neighborhood. I wonder if he ever let another guy suck his dick or asshole.

II. "I BEGGED HIM TO LET ME SUCK."

Not long after this incident an older cousin introduced me to the pleasures of cocksucking. He was stronger, more aggressive than I was — the dominant type. When his parents were away he would take me to their house, strip down, lie on the sofa, and get me between his legs to suck his cock and balls. I got to like it tremendously and often begged him to let me suck him off. Many afternoons we went to the movies together and when we were in the men's room urinating he would have me lick the last drops of piss from his prick and suck him until he got hard. With some success I prevailed upon other boys, my age or older, to let me do the same to them. We used to hide in obscure corners of buildings under construction after the workmen had gone home. Even now the smell of fresh cement and wet tile recalls those furtive half-scared fumblings.

III. SEES MOUTH FUCKED IN SUBWAY.

Then, for a decade or so I had no active homosexual contacts, though when I was capable of producing sperm I sure had a hell of a good time jacking off – especially in front of mirrors.

Butch type men always packed a wallop. When I saw auto mechanics in a garage, flat on their backs, their hips and legs projecting from under a car they were working on, I felt an almost irresistable urge to kneel down, open their pants and pull their cocks out. I hung around swimming holes and men's locker rooms to catch sight of guys bareass. I haunted public toilets to watch men take out their pricks to piss and then shake off the last drops of urine when they had finished. From newspapers and magazines I cut out pictures of naked or near naked swimmers and athletes and hid them away in a scrap book.

As a boy I was somewhat sissified but as I grew older I got jobs at hard labor on farms and in pipeline and road construction. I grew stronger and my physique developed to where I could pass for straight, though I was never much of a fighter. I was a mature man when the repressed homosexuality burst forth like a flood that has shattered a dam. It began in the subway toilets. In the men's room where I stopped occasionally I noticed guys standing at the urinals with a hard on who made no attempt to leave or even shoot their load. Then one day I almost fainted with excitement when I caught one stud, his pants down below his knees, legs bent so that his pelvis was thrust forward obscenely, ramming his cock down another stud's throat. The cocksucker was squatting on his heels and was frantically jerking off. They both realized that I was gay too, and continued as if no one were present.

IV. "YOU GODDAMN QUEER."

Seeing those two studs getting their rocks off in the East Side subway station opened up a whole new world of sex for me. Here was a chance to get at a man's cock for the asking. Too good to be true. I made a systematic tour of all the subway toilets in the four boroughs [of New York] but I discovered that only certain stations were very active and that these were best at certain hours of the day, like 5 P.M. when guys were going home from work, and Friday and Saturday nights and Sunday afternoon. I noticed, too, that holes had been punched through the partitions that separated the toilet stalls. It was exciting to sit on the crapper and see what the guy in the next stall was doing and watch for any signals of interest, see if he was playing with his prick or peeping through the hole to seek a contact; or sit with the door open to watch a guy standing at a urinal and wait for him to turn around showing his hard on. What joy if the man in the next booth stood up and thrust his cock into my open mouth through the glory hole or if the guy from the urinal walked over and stood directly in front of me so I could have access to his balls and asshole as well as his prick.

It was especially good in the summer months when the men wore little clothing. With their shorts and pants down to their ankles and their shirts lifted up to their armpits they were nearly nude in front of me. This gave me a chance to stimulate them to greater heights of sexual excitement by playing with their nipples, rubbing my hand over their legs and thighs, caressing their ass cheeks and tickling their assholes. I remember a guy I used to see frequently in a subway toilet at a station near Union Square. Scandanavian or German probably – tall, blue eyed, blond, sandy hair, a face somewhat square cut but good looking, strong chest and arms with smooth rippling muscles and a cheerful smile. A potent male. Enough to make any cocksucker cream in his jeans. One hot day in July he came into the toilet, nodded pleasantly, and remarked that he remembered I had sucked him off a few days before at a station further down the line. Because of the heat he wore only a T-shirt and thin pants and his bare feet were thrust into dirty sneakers. "Want a repeat?" he asked.

I sat down in a booth while he stood in front of me, dropping his pants and rolling up his T-shirt. His chest and belly were shiny with sweat. He had a beautiful prick, slick and tasty, that filled my mouth as soon as I clamped my lips around it. I worked on him as hard as I could, running my hand over his sweaty body, playing with his balls, probing his asshole. With all this going on he didn't hold out long. Soon, with a soft moan of pleasure, he squirted his come down my throat. I thought he was the kind that liked only to be serviced and never repay the compliment, but some time later I saw him squatting down sucking a teenager.

With practice my technique began to improve. After all, my previous experience with cocksucking had been with boys who were unable to ejaculate, but now I was dealing with mature men who apparently were used to being sucked off regularly, and they didn't hesitate to let me know when I wasn't satisfying them. One guy taught me how to twirl my tongue tantalizingly around the head of his prick, while another guy wanted a more slobbering approach, covering with saliva the underside of his cock, working up from his balls to the tip, then proceeding downward again, topside,until my tongue was buried in the wiry hairs of his bush. One stud that I was servicing suddenly ordered me to "tongue it!" Dutifully I twirled my tongue about the head. But somehow that wasn't what he wanted. "Tongue it!" he repeated, angrily pulling painfully on my ears. Releasing his prick to swing in the air, I looked up and explained that I didn't know what he meant by "tongue it." "Why, you God damn queer," he barked, "any cocksucker who is worth his salt knows that 'tonguing it' means ramming the tip of his tongue into a guy's piss hole."

I should have thanked him for the information since "tonguing it" is a sure fire way of bringing a stud to new heights of ecstasy.

V. CALLED "BITCH" BY QUEEN.

Until I was a grown man all my orientation had been oral. I had not been aware that a guy's asshole could be dilated so that he could be fucked more or less like a woman. I hadn't been in the subway very long, though, before I encountered this form of sex. In one of the subway toilets popular with gays I often saw an older man who, when the place had cleared out and we were alone, would go into a booth, take down his pants to expose his rear end, bend over the stool, and stick a finger up his hole. What could be more explicit? Somehow I wasn't very much interested. If I remember correctly, my first experience with ass fucking occurred in a subway toilet on Morningside Heights. I met up with two studs there – young, good looking, real hot numbers. I had been sucking on one of them before the other guy came in. Our little scene excited him and he didn't even bother to go to a urinal but unzipped his pants and pulled out his cock as he came over and stood beside us. I offered to suck both cocks at the same time but the newcomer refused. He stepped behind the other man and started feeling up his ass. He reached around the guy's waist, unbuckled his belt and I had to stop my cocksucking long enough to lower the man's shorts and pants. The sight of the bare bottom seemed to excite the newcomer. He spit on his fingers and then, to my amazement, stuck first one, then two fingers up the shit hole. The guy I was working on reached in to his pocket and handed a tube of Vaseline to the man behind him, who then proceeded to lubricate his rod and after that thrust a gob of Vaseline up his friend's ass, inserted his cock there, and started pumping away. Surprised and fascinated, I had stopped sucking, to the guy's disgust. "Chow down you lousy pervert," he shouted. "Keep that cock in your mouth. You dumb bitch, don't you know that a guy likes to have his prostate massaged by a prick up his ass while he's being sucked off?"

Sometimes real orgies developed in the subway toilets. Half a dozen guys would be standing around waiting for something to start the ball rolling so they could act out their sex fantasies. One guy would stand at the door watching through the slits of the ventilator to let the rest know if anyone were approaching. The excitement would build up until three or four couples started going at it hot and heavy. Heads bobbing back and forth in and out of guys' crotches; asses rearing back then thrusting forward to ram a stiff prick up a buddy's shit hole. It was always exciting to change off – to tongue a more succulent cock or to play with heavier balls; to find a rectum that would grip a cock more tightly. The air would reek of the smell of sex.

Sometimes the men who disliked the grime and foul smells of the subway latrines would take me to a vacant lot if it were late at night, or take me home with them, often stopping at a bar on the way. I remember many dreary, ill-kept rooms where men led me to suck them off. On the East Side, on the West Side, up in the Bronx. They hardly ever stripped down but would sprawl in a chair with their fly open for me to kneel down before them, or they would stretch out on a bed, fully clothed, not even bothering to kick off their shoes. Generally, they wanted me to leave as soon as I had gulped down their load.

I remember an older man, however, from the South Bronx who stripped for me when we were finally alone in his room. He said he was 54 years old but he looked much younger. He had a magnificent body and apparntly was quite proud of it — an ex-Marine, I believe. A black Irishman, a black Welshman, a Breton? There must have been Celtic blood in his veins. He was definitely not Hispanic, although he lived in a Puerto Rican neighborhood. He was stockily built but well proportioned, dark hair, an open, pleasant countenance, a stubble of beard on his chin and cheeks, powerful shoulders and back, heavy thighs, sturdy legs, fleshy ass. There was not an ounce of flab on him. A real hunk of man. He glanced up at me with eager, questioning eyes from the edge of the bed where he was sitting naked, quite aware of my interest in his anatomy.

"So you like my body, huh?" he inquired anxiously. I nodded my approval and replied, "You've got one hell of a build. I like it all, but especially what you've got down there between your legs." I knelt and lifted his heavy cock and balls in my hand. "Get your clothes off, kid," he ordered. "Get into bed with me and make yourself comfortable."

I was glad to comply. I peeled off my clothes as fast as I could and joined him on the bed where he lay stretched out full length, staring curiously at my own nakedness. "You've got a pretty good body yourself," he said. It was a warm day in late spring, so there was no need for any covering.

I started working on his cock, but he reached down and pulled me up so that my head was even with his shoulder. He turned over so that we were lying there stark naked, belly to belly, and gave me a bear hug that nearly cracked my ribs. He seemed to be starved for affection. I returned his embrace as hard as I could. I kissed his hair, his neck; sucked on his nipples, which seemed to excite him, since his prick stiffened perceptibly. I felt happy that I had found a "father figure," as the psychologists say (a naked and virile one to boot), whom I could snuggle up to. Finally he loosened his hold on me and I returned to his groin, almost reverently this time, and made a big deal about sucking him off. His cream was thick and heavy, the way he was. It was slightly acrid and I savoured it in my mouth before swallowing the load.

I lay quietly beside him for awhile, with my head on his shoulder. Then we got up and dressed.

"Thanks, kid, that was great," he said as I stood at the door ready to leave. "Good luck. Hope to see you again sometime."

"Same here," I replied and closed the door gently. As I walked down the dark echoing hall and the creaking staircase I wondered about his sex life. Had he fucked a lot of women? His build and easy-going manners must have attracted many of them to him. Did he run with queers, now that he was ageing, only because he found it easier and cheaper than getting a woman? Or had he only had sex with other men? I never saw him again so I will never know. However, our brief encounter remains one of my happiest memories from the "subway circuit."

VI. SEDUCED BY HIGH SCHOOL BOY.

I have never seduced a minor. The penalties for seducing a boy under age are one thing (have you ever read what happened to Big Bill Tilden, the tennis star?) And then the fixation I had for my brother-in-law made me prefer a man around 30 — mature but still handsome and athletic. However, one evening a high school student I encountered in a subway toilet in the East Bronx seduced *me*. He latched on to me and took me to a vacant lot for sex. He was a golden boy, with rich blond hair and skin a golden tan. He was a boy in the first blush of manhood. I doubt that he had to shave very often. He was vibrant with youth and strength: everything beautifully proportioned, a musculature that would have delighted an anatomist or a sculptor. In short, such stuff as dreams are made of. And of course the kind that goes out for sports — a high school athlete; good at the 100-yard dash or high hurdles very likely — 16, 17 years old at the most. Actually, as I said, I was the one who was seduced. It was surprising that he could find me attractive, for I must have been more than twice his age. Perhaps he, too, was looking for a father figure.

It was a large, vacant lot where he took me, a wilderness of scattered bricks, slabs of concrete, and broken bottles, but in a remote area of the city probably not patrolled very often by the police. Smart kid. He knew we were fairly safe. He found a dark corner under a high wall heavily shaded by a clump of trees where there was a sort of low platform constructed of bricks and concrete. It was a hot summer night and he took off most of his clothing, giving me access to all the secret parts of his body: cock and balls, asshole and armpits. I licked them all. He had a big cock that was hard and insistent as he plunged it into my mouth. He was exciting and came quickly. His come tasted like nectar. After a few moments' rest he insisted I get him hard again for a second round, but I was reluctant to obey his command. I suddenly had a hot desire to see him completely nude, so I asked him to remove his shoes and socks, but he refused. "Ain't I stripped enough," he said petulantly. I wanted to smell his socks, play with his bare feet, suck his toes, lick his soles, cup his heels with my mouth. He was adamant. I couldn't persuade him, and finally had to give up on that deal. I sucked him off again, but in spite of the excitement of his youth and beauty there was something cold and impersonal about him. It was a bit like making love to a statue. I preferred my ageing ex-Marine from the South Bronx.

Somewhere along the line I had picked up a foot fetish – only for those feet that were well formed and sexy, that suggested a hot bout in the sack. As for sock sniffing, that goes back a long time ago when I was in grade school. I attended grade school in the country, one of those one-room schoolhouses and a single teacher for all eight grades. I guess they've all but disappeared nowadays. When I was in the seventh grade there were two older boys – they must have been 13 and 14, or possibly older, who thought they were the two prize males of the countryside and even at that age strong as young bulls. One was a dark-haired Irish lad, the other blond, of pioneer American stock. Their nascent sexuality seemed to be too much for the teacher (who wasn't much more than 20 if she was that) and things got rather loose in that schoolhouse. These two bozos made no bones about kissing the teacher casually, often quite voluptuously, in front of the rest of the children, and at recess time the younger ones were sent out to play unsupervised while Rex and Ken stayed inside with the teacher, and with the door locked.

I remember making ineffectual efforts trying to get back in one day. I didn't know much about sex at the time but I was aware that something forbidden was going on inside. Later, when I was much older, I tried to imagine what kind of sex games they played. A bachelor uncle, a crochety old guy who loved gossip and scandal and who lived next door to the schoolhouse, confirmed my suspicions. "You know, don't you, what's going on at the schoolhouse?" he asked me one day while I was visiting him, and I told him about the younger children's being locked out at recess time. But nothing was ever done about it, as far as I know. My folks moved to a nearby city so I never found out how this rustic idyll terminated.

To show me up as a coward and weakling, the two older boys, Rex and Ken, would take every opportunity to humiliate me. In winter, or when it rained heavily in spring or fall, the men and boys in that farming district wore heavy rubber boots. At school, these two often took their boots off and went around in their stocking feet to be more comfortable. In addition to knocking me down or beating me up, and as an extra degradation, they would poke an odorous foot under my nose. I rather got to like it. They had strong, shapely feet and each boy had a slightly different odor. These smells came to be just one other attribute of masculinity, on a par with odors from the groin and armpit. It was all the more exciting when a toe or heel peeped coyly through a hole in the sock.

Then one day while I was pissing in the boys' toilet, Rex, the dark-haired Irish lad, burst in, and noticing my cock was still hanging out, he came over with a leer on his face and put his hand on my prick, stroking it gently; then he reached in for my balls, playing with them in one hand while with the other he rubbed my ass through my pants. He didn't take out his own prick nor ask me to suck him, as I hoped he would. Perhaps he was saving himself for the teacher. Suddenly he stopped his manipulation and left, leaving me half hard.

I had imagined that the two boys would marry local girls, settle down to farming and confine their sex to fucking their wives, but after that encounter in the boys' toilet it occurred to me that they may be bisexual after all and for extra excitement get each others' rocks off in true homosexual fashion.

VII. YOUTH IS DESPERATE FOR BLOW JOB.

Don't imagine that every time I entered a subway toilet a guy was standing around with a hard on, ready to stick his stiff cock into my mouth. Often I failed to score at all, even after long and anxious searching and loitering. I remember one such afternoon in late fall. I had made a tour of the toilets in the Bronx without any luck at all and was on the point of going home and relieving myself with a hand job while thumbing through a stack of photos of naked men, when in walked my dream man. Of Italian origin, apparently, with dark, lustrous eyes, black hair, dark skin. A mature man but with the lithe, powerful body of a Roman gladiator. I could smell his maleness. It was not a raw odor like that from secretions under a guy's foreskin, or stale sweat and dirty underwear, but the intoxicating scent of a clean, healthy man. He had been working and must have perspired. I noticed the bottoms of his trousers were crusted with cement – a construction worker, I would guess. He was hot to go. There was no one in the toilet at the time and he stood at the door to watch for intruders on our privacy. He knew instinctively what I was there for and without hesitation unzipped his fly and took out one of the most beautifully sculptured pricks I have ever seen and a gorgeous pair of balls. It almost made me cream just to look at them. He didn't treat me in any condescending way but seemed glad that someone was there to give him a needed blow job. I grabbed him by his narrow hips and sank down to worship his magnificent manhood. I applied all the arts of cocksucking I could think of: tonguing his prick, twirling my tongue around the head, licking his shaft up and down, taking the whole cock down my throat until it nearly choked me, plunging my nose into his thick pubic hairs.

There was something wild and supernatural about it all, as though we were eager participants in some phallic ritual of ancient Italy that transformed the sordid reality of a Bronx subway toilet into a craggy vale in the apennines. He never spoke. After he came, he caressed my neck and tousled my hair with large strong hands, hastily put his sex organs back into his pants, kissed me full on the lips, held the pressure a moment, and left.

Guys whom I sucked off in the subway toilets told me about other places where I could pick up men for sex. They mentioned cruising areas in parks, at the beaches, gay bars, the waterfront. And as time went on the subway scene grew more and more dreary. It was dangerous for cocksuckers. There was always the possibility of arrest by plainclothesmen; robbery by thugs as unemployment and the crime wave rose, and beatings from queer bashers. So I gradually transferred my activities to other places. Then years later the subway scene disappeared almost completely when the Transit Authority closed nearly all the subway toilets in the city. The number of blow jobs I gave in them must be staggering. After two years I counted over 500, and I am sure there were many more I had forgotten about.

However, before I leave the subject, there were three incidents that seemed incredible.

One day when I was riding in an uncrowded subway car, the guy sitting next to me kept brushing his knee against mine. At first I didn't pay much attention to it since I was used to being squeezed up against other men in rush hours, but this pressure was firm and insistent, also exciting. The implication was not to be denied. The guy was young, probably still in school, well built, and strong, so when he got off the train I followed him. He headed for the toilet and I kept a few paces behind. He had one hand at his fly even before he got the toilet door open. There was no one inside and he stood by the door jerking a huge hard on as I entered. I went down on him, started sucking lustily and presto, he shot a hot sweet load.

The second episode was not quite so hurried; it developed more gradually. I was riding along in the subway not particularly thinking about sex when I noticed a young man sitting opposite me, his head bent over a book – the intellectual type, but he did not wear glasses and was appropriately male. I built up fantasies of having him naked with me in the sack. As passengers got off, I moved closer and was able to make out the title of the book he was reading. It was Cabell's *Jurgen* and that fed fire to my sex dreams. Somehow I struck up a conversation with the boy. He admitted to being hot and bothered in the groin. So we left the subway and I went to a lonely section of a park where I sucked him off in a dark corner under a bridge. A good blow job; nice hard prick; spurts of cock juice; good balls and ass to feel up. After it was all over he cleaned himself up a bit with his handkerchief and we went our separate ways.

The most casual sex experience I ever had in the New York subways was on the platform of one of the stations along the elevated tracks. It was a pleasant evening in spring, the sun had set and it was already growing dark. In those days the high barriers had not yet been set up to prevent objects being thrown from the elevated stations to the injury of pedestrians and passing vehicles below, so I was leaning over the rail enjoying the cool air and the local scene. In the distance some of the skyscrapers in mid-Manhattan were visible. The city at night is always a fascinating spectacle. I was absorbed in the view when a man strolled down to the end of the platform where I was standing and leaned over the rail beside me. "Nice evening," he said. "Sure is," I replied hastily, trying to be friendly. I turned and sized him up. I liked what I saw. He was of medium height, rather stocky and square jawed, but with pleasant features and deep-set inquisitive eyes. I could sense strong muscles under the rough work clothes. The baseball season had just begun and we talked a bit about what the Yankees and the Mets had been doing and what their prospects were for winning the pennant. Then the conversation took another turn.

"Those guys must get hard up, traveling around the country the way they do. It must be bad for the rookies, too, who have no families. I wonder how they get their rocks off."

"Well," I replied, "I shouldn't think it would be difficult to find plenty of women in the large cities who would welcome the chance to sack in with a handsome young ball player."

"No, I suppose not," the stranger agreed. He kept glancing down at my crotch. I looked down at his. I noticed a considerable bulge there. With one hand I casually lifted my nuts, and that gave him the courage to put a hand between his legs and trace the impressive outline of his swelling cock. Then he got bolder.

"I have often wondered if those ball players didn't help each other out once in awhile up in their hotel rooms. Ya know what I mean, don't ya?"

"Yeah, I know what you mean all right," I answered, and put a hand on his shoulder.

One more question, a direct one this time: "Do ya dig men?"

"Sure," I replied, patting his belly and thrusting an exploring hand into his groin. He looked about to see whether we were alone and, reassured that no one was spying on us, he pulled out a massive prick. Even though there was no one about he wouldn't let me go down on him.

"Too public on an open platform," he said. "The station toilet has already been closed." But he did want me to jack him off. "My pleasure," I said wholeheartedly. It was disappointing not to take that gorgeous hard on into my mouth, but it did feel wonderful in my hand. He was uncut and I gave him an extra thrill by retracting his foreskin and rubbing a finger over the blunt head of his tool, tickling his piss hole. For extra stimulation I reached in and pulled out his balls, fondling them gently. I applied spit to my palm and started pumping. After a few moments he began to tremble as his sperm shot out, splattering over the rail and the platform. What a waste of a guy's come.

These three incidents came out of a clear sky. I hadn't been looking for any action; hadn't even been thinking about sex at the time, but fortune had thrust them upon me as a bonus to top off my long cocksucking career in the subways.

Boy Exhibitionist Hangs Wash Cloth On His Dick

FLORIDA — You asked how I learned to jack off, so here it is. When I was around 10-11, my best friend was the kid next door who was about 4 years older. We would bet each other who could stand something longer, like staying in one position or some sort of repeated movements or putting up with some sort of discomfort. He was older and stronger and could stand on his head longer and chin on a tree limb with one arm. He was into testing my endurance for foolish irritation.

He said several times he bet he could do something I couldn't stand for over the count of ten but I nixed him off. Once in my bedroom he bet he could get on my nerves by just keeping pulling up and down on the window' shade till I said Uncle. Then he asked me if my thing got hard. As I recall, there was only the merest suggestion of a hard on at that time. He bet me he could make my dick hard and that I couldn't take it if he did ten pulls on it. That time I said OK because I didn't believe him and let him open my fly and pull it out. To my amazement, it got hard with a few pulls by him and he kept it up and kept stroking with a big triumphant smile while I tried to figure out what was going on with my feelings all over my body. I told him it was like a spell coming over me. Pretty soon I pushed him away and said, "I can't take it anymore." So he was the winner and really happy and feeling superior. But I hadn't shot any cum, just something dribbled a little. There was no sex education in schools or at home at that time and I didn't understand the whole business.

But we started getting together every day or two for what we called "spelling" and we would exchange the same number of strokes. This was generally in our basements or behind the barn and we would count

196

the strokes. It would start out, for instance, with me saying, "Me first for 10." Then he would jack my cock 10 strokes and I would have to do the same to him. We didn't always cum but his cock was a lot bigger and harder and sometimes he would discharge a load or mine would leak a little.

That went on for a long time, maybe a year, while my cock was growing, and I finally would get a full hard on and shoot a good load. But his cock was bigger and set higher and he liked to show how he could make it jump or hold a weight on it or do various tricks. Our bathrooms faced each other across a driveway so we would take a bath at the same time and display our cocks and he would show how he could hold a wet washcloth on his cock and flip it, measure how long it was, etc. At about 15-16 he was a well-muscled athlete. He swam at the Y, where his father had taken him for training, and he liked to exhibit his body and skills, ball size, and cock, while I was learning from him and pretty far behind him at age 12-13. He was not a bad guy, but had a strong urge to teach a younger kid about sex and develop my nerve power and endurance. He later went into the Air Force, became a pilot and instructor, even gave me some flying lessons; but somewhere when I was maybe 13-14 he started running around with older friends and I was left out in the cold, though we kept up the mutual jack-off behind the barn for a long time.

Some of the other things that happened along the way were that he showed up with rubbers, claimed it made the sensations better. So we tried it and he put a rubber on me several times after jacking my cock up. Then he came one day and said he had seen a man sucking another guy in the Y steam room, so we should try it. The Y was for him the learning ground and everything that happened there was the way to go. He was a real Y man, always off to camp in the summer, told me about circle jerks, etc. We tried sucking each other but it didn't seem too great so we stuck to fist jobs. He liked to just take his cock out and be jacked off. After awhile I found I liked to drop my pants and feel the air on my balls and have him hold my cock and aim it while I shot. Later I wanted to try cocksucking again but he was picking up the idea of social disapproval of this and said no mostly, but he said it would be OK if we used a rubber so we did that a few times.

Then somewhere along the way he started bringing home fuck comics from school, like Popeye giving it to Olive Oyl with a supercock or Mutt and Jeff starting out with girls and ending up with one getting fucked in the ass. Then he started bringing home better stuff, mostly from England, like one with good photos in which a young English stud was making a career of fucking virgins against a haystack and priding himself on his cock size. I didn't need any more stroking to get it up — just one look at a fuck scene and I'd have to go behind the barn. And that was the period when a kid has to start wearing a jock strap because it's up all the time. I felt guilty about jacking off alone, particularly when it would hit 10 times a day or so. I discovered that rubbing my finger against my asshole gave it a faint smell which got me super-hard and I tried insertion of enema tubes, etc., but there was never any ass-fucking with my friend or anyone else at that time.

My friend was starting his first experiences with whores and he told me how it didn't go up till she inspected and washed it and then he was hot to go. He used to talk about girls and playing stink finger, which I didn't understand. Once in awhile he would take me along with some of the older guys, where I would hear talk like "She's awful, no better than a good jack off." So I knew the older bunch was still beating the meat too, so I felt OK about keeping it up.

II. BOY, 14, LIKES "DIRTY COCKSUCKER."

When I was about 14, a European refugee kid by the name of Albert moved into the neighborhood. I was not too friendly with him but wanted to exchange stamps and learn a few words of his language. He lived with his parents and Uncle Carl in a ground floor apartment about ten doors away. Occasionally we played together. I was taking piano lessons and Albert said his uncle was interested in music and wanted to meet me. I had seen his uncle on the street, a fairly short but muscular, square-jawed, blond guy with a determined walk, usually in work clothes.

One day Al said his uncle had a fine new hi-fi set and would probably let me hear some records on it. Next time I saw Carl come by I nodded "hello" and he came over to the porch. He said he would be happy to let me hear some of my records on his hi-fi and wouldn't I like to come up right now. I delivered papers and said I couldn't because I only had 10 mins. till pick-up time, but he insisted and insisted, and I really did want to hear his set-up. I was saving up for one of my own. So he won out and I went with him, carrying a couple of records I really wanted to hear badly on a good set-up.

He took me into a back sitting-room where the hi-fi was set up and told me to sit on the couch. I was nervous but he was friendly and said "Make yourself at home."

"Damn, it's hot," he said, and stripped off his shirt. He sat next to me, put his hand on my knee, said he loved music and admired my talent. He asked if I liked Albert, what other friends I had, whether we played together much, whether we went to the beach or pools – and moved his hand up my leg a bit. He was a smiley, strong-faced guy with a very direct look and manner. He said he thought Albert had a fine body and pointed to a sketch he had made on the wall, showing Albert lying in a rear view nude position. I really thought Albert was a puny and gawky kid but I said, "Yes, nice sketch."

Then he asked whether I had any *special* friends and I said "Yes, the boy next door."

By this time his hand was gently rubbing my thigh and he popped the question, "How often do you jack off, Pete?" That did it. I suddenly felt warm and relaxed, with a guy interested in me and my welfare and the smell of his strong breath and the look of his teeth as he smiled. Everything seemed OK and honest and I felt my cock expand against my pants.

Carl massaged my crotch and asked, "How big is your cawck, *[sic]* Pete." His accent on that word really went into my chest and balls. I said I didn't know exactly. He said, "Who's got a bigger cawck, Albert or you? Let's see. Take your cawck out, Pete." Christ Almighty, that felt good to have my cock out. I spread my legs and thrust it up. "Oh," he said, "you've got a beautiful cawck, that's a fine cawck, I really like your cawck." He stroked it and told me to stand up and drop my pants. Shit almighty, that felt good to stand with a jutting cock and naked ass and balls in front of a man like Carl with a muscular chest and strong male breath. I forgot all about the records, the paper route, and sickly old Albert. I would have liked to see Carl's rod but he told me to step over in front of a chair. He said, "I like to kneel to take a guy off." His hot lips with the pungent breath and the square-jawed mouth went down over my cock deep and he sucked fast, taking the whole length each time. He held my ass. I came very quickly. I came automatically. "Christ," he said, "I love the taste of your cum."

The excitement and tension of answering questions about my cock and jacking off, the friendly feeling of a guy's hand working up to my groin, then exposure of my hard cock, showing it to a horny cocksucker who wanted to initiate a kid into full cock-lust, better manhood, and full cock-crazed lewdness, to teach the uses of a man's body for pleasure – this was where it was at for me and Carl.

Thirty years later I can still smell Carl's foul breath that probably came from the accumulated sweat and cum and asshole juices of a couple of thousand hot men who had to jab their cheesy piss-rods into the hole of a dirty cocksucker. A square-jawed cocksucker's hungry lips to ride your shaft, a tongue to swab your cock head, and a deep raunchy gullet to suck out your cum and piss – ain't nothing better.

I had one more experience with Carl later, with me on the can calling him a cocksucker. For the next 30 years, every time I heard the word "cocksucker" my rod would be up and ready. I guess I've massaged my dick a few thousand times since then, thinking of old Carl and how he taught this boy what his cock really wanted.

Straight Queers

Forty of the 42 men arrested on sex raps in a men's toilet at D Avenue and U.S. 131 in Kalamazoo County, Michigan were married. Ages of the men ranged from 18 to 66.

Mother Finds Blood
On Boy's Underpants

CALIFORNIA – OK, I'll tell you about Marty [mentioned briefly in this writer's other letters]. I was about 14, I guess, when I met him his brother, Col (we never called him Colby). I lived in Hollywood then, which was not the run-down crap-filled place it is today. Marty moved onto our block. They came from Canada and Marty went to my school. He was slightly older than me, maybe as much as a year. Col was a year younger.

Marty and I took to each other right off. We used to ride our bikes all over hell after school. Right off the bat, Marty was talking sex – when we were alone. That's all he thought of. We would sit in the middle of some vacant lot where no one could come near us unobserved and he'd tell me wild stories about what he did in Toronto. He told how guys would get together and compare pricks. Then they'd jack off and then they'd fuck each other.

After a bit of this, maybe a week or so, I quess he was getting me in the mood; he started giving me pats and when I didn't object he was rubbing my cock. The first time we took our cocks out was in a shed behind my house. Marty pulled his out and it was hard, so of course I had to take mine out. Then we began playing with each other and pretty soon we were jacking each other off. Then he wanted to fuck me. I was leery of that so he told me he was fucking Col all the time. That astonished me, but I let him take my pants down to my knees, get behind me, and rub his prong against my asshole. He got off doing it but he didn't get it into me then. But I made him tell me more about Col. He said Col loved it, that they had been doing it for a long time, nearly every night because they slept in the same room. He said he had started by using his finger on Col.

Marty was persuasive. I have never known anyone quite like him since. He could talk you into anything. He did me, anyway.

He said he put some Vaseline on his cock to get it into Col and next time he'd use some on me. And he did. In his garage after school. His father and mother both worked and didn't get home till almost dark, so Marty and I were alone in his garage and of course he was after my cock right away. We started playing with them and then he wanted to fuck me. And by this time he had me horny enough to want it. So I got on hands and knees like he told me and he greased his prong with Vaseline and eased it into my ass. It hurt a little and felt like a phone pole but it went in, and when he had a lot of it in it felt better. In a little while it felt pretty good and my cock started to get hard. After quite a few minutes, I felt down under and he had most of it in me. Before he was through he had it in to the balls. I remember he said he was taking my cherry. I don't remember how long we did it; it seemed a half hour. I think Marty came a couple of times and he reached around and played with my peter a lot and I got off too. By the time he pulled his cock out I was really enjoying it. That night in bed I could still feel his cock in my butt.

When Saturday came around Marty suggested that he and Col and I should ride up into Griffith Park. It was only a few miles away. I was a little surprised at our taking Col along. Col never talked a lot. He was as different from Marty as moon and sun. But just as horny.

We rode around the park for a bit, then up into the hills on one of the paths. There was no one around except down in the valley. Marty found us a nice little shady spot off the trail and right away wanted to play games. He started by taking his pants off. His cock was nice and hard. Then Col took his pants off and they looked at me, so I took mine off too. Then we all knelt close together and played with cocks and Marty said we were both going to fuck Col. Col just grinned. Then Col surprised me. He bend down and began to suck Marty's cock. Marty and I had never done that. Marty grinned at me over Col's head and said he liked that. He did, too. Col sucked me, then back to Marty, then me again. Marty got out a vial of Vaseline, put some on his cock and got behind Col and worked his prong in – all sort of matter-of-fact. Col was still sucking my cock when Marty was fucking him.

After awhile Marty pulled it out and got behind me and worked it into my ass. This time it went in better and felt good. Col was under me, still sucking me. My memory of that day is not Marty fucking my ass but Col sucking me so much. He got me off a couple of times and sucked me for at least an hour – maybe longer. My cock throbbed for hours afterward from Col's sucking.

The next day, Sunday, I went to Sunday school like always. We went into classrooms on the second floor of the church. When school was over I went downstairs looking for Marty and found Col. He said he didn't know where Marty was. When I looked at Col all I could think of was him sucking my cock. He must have been thinking the same. We dawdled around as the grown-ups filed into church and finally went back upstairs. No one was there. We wandered down to the last class-room in the row, then Col asked me to sit down and when I did, he knelt in front of me and took my cock out. It was hard in a second and I watched him suck me. He didn't screw around, he went right after it. He got me to come in a hurry, then settled down to a nice long suck. It was really great. While he did it he took his own cock out and jacked off. He didn't ask me to suck him.

Marty was not one to be satisfied with one ass (mine, not counting Col). I didn't know it at the time but he was also fucking another guy or two, and one of those told his mother. The story I heard was that the boy's ass had split a little and there was blood on his underpants and his mother wanted to know why. So it came out that Marty had fucked him and there was hell to pay. Marty was pulled out of school and I didn't see him for awhile; I stayed as far away from it as I could. I didn't want my folks to think I was mixed up in it. I saw Col all the time, usually after school. He said the boy's mother had raised a terrible stink.

Anyway, I got Col aside a few times and he sucked me off, as hot as ever, and in a few months they moved away. The neighborhood was never the same. I sure missed them, because now I had a hankering. I would ease candles into my ass but it wasn't the same. I wanted the real thing.

II. SCOUTMASTER HAS "SWEET" WAD.

I was in the Boy Scouts soon and one of our leaders, a grown-up, was named Roul. He was one of two. We had about 30 kids in the troop, I guess. I was usually around Roul because I was attracted to him. He was a dark Latin type, probably Italian, and a great guy. He must have been about 25 then, unmarried, and always helpful, etc. I used to go to his house all the time on my bike; he lived with his parents. His father was a character actor in the studios and had another job to stay alive. Anyway, Roul and I were good friends, I thought, and when he began to put his arm around me and rub my butt now and then I thought it was great. One day I was in his house when he stepped out of the bathtub. He had a big prick and I got a hard on. He dried himself very close to me and I felt that big cock rub me a few times.

One Saturday a bunch of us from the troop went on a little hike with Roul and when we came back into town I went with Roul to his house to pick up my bike. He invited me in to take a shower. His mother was a radio nut and sat in the breakfast nook all the time listening to soap operas and such. His father was out. Roul suggested we shower together and I was all for it, thinking of his cock. As soon as I got naked and saw it I got a hard on. Roul didn't say anything, just got me in the shower and soaped me. The soaping included a good working over on my cock and I came in his hands. He was very understanding about it. And let me soap him, which included my handling his prick, which got hard.

He took me out and dried me and laid me on the bed. By then he knew he had me. I had a pretty good-sized cock and he started sucking it. I couldn't hold back. I came. Then he turned around and I had practically my first experience at sucking cock. I had done it long before, sort of, but this was really the first. I did the same things he had done to me except I could only get the big head of it into my mouth, not half or more as he could. But I was having a ball. I guess we lay there and sucked each other for an hour, easy. At about the end of that time he told me he was going to come and for me to swallow it fast. By this time I would have walked on live coals for him. So when he came I

202

gulped it down. His cream was sweet tasting and I got every drop and kept sucking it long after it boiled over.

That night in bed I jacked off half the night thinking about it. Imagine: I had sucked Roul's cock. I guess I was in love.

Him being a Scout leader, my folks thought nothing of him calling me or even coming by. There were always things to discuss; I pretended a great interest in the troop and my folks thought that was wonderful. It kept me from meeting bad companions, right?

About two nights after we had 69ed on his bed, Roul came by in his car and I went with him to a "meeting." The meeting was Roul and me. He drove to a public golf course, deserted at dark, and we parked the car and walked out to a grove of trees and laid on the grass on a blanket and sucked each other's cock for about 2 hours. Roul could take the entire length of my prick in his mouth and when he deep-throated it I was in heaven. He was a marvelous cocksucker with a huge appetite for boys my age (15). He probably got me off 4 times that night. I remember very well that I made him come twice and swallowed it avidly both times. What nectar! He turned me over after awhile and licked my ass, which felt great but surprised me. No one had done that before. He also sucked my balls and nipples. He told me we were very special to each other and I believed every word. When he kissed me I kissed him back — I was in heaven.

When he drove he home he parked a half block from the house, in the deep shade of some pepper trees, and we sucked cocks again.

About that time my folks allowed me to build a shed-house on the back of our garage. An uncle helped me get the lumber and hang the door, etc. It was a nice place, wired and everything. Our house was on a side street, with streets on 2 sides. There was a wall fence on one side but it was easy to scale. I could get in the shed from the street without anyone in the house knowing I was there. And so could Roul. (I had thought he was Italian but then I learned his parents were English. I never knew where his name came from.)

A couple of times a week Roul would call me and we would talk Scout business, then he'd say he would come to the shed at 8. So while my folks were watching TV I'd say casually that I was going out to the shed. And at 8 Roul would show up and we'd suck cocks for an hour or so. He had a big appetite, as I said. He never wanted to fuck me, but he began to suggest that I fuck him. And finally I did. I liked it, but not as much as Marty had the previous year. I was becoming a compulsive cocksucker. Roul used to straddle my chest and fuck his cock between my lips and that was paradise. I dreamed constantly of having his cock in my mouth. Sometimes when he shot his wad I would let the cream drool down the sides of his prick so I could lick it up and savor it. He was always telling me how wonderful I was. And when I had a mouthful of his cream he would suck my tongue.

Several times my patrol of Scouts went on overnight hikes – that consisted of me and Roul in a motel. My folks never thought to check up; I doubt if it entered their minds. I would come home from these suck sessions so worn out and fucked out I thought I would never be able to get a hard on again. I would tell my folks we'd had a long hard hike, etc. But in two nights Roul was in the shed again with his cock in my mouth and mine in his.

This idyll went on for about a year and a half before Roul was suddenly dropped from the Scout troop, accused of making passes at a younger boy. He told me it was all a frame up and untrue and of course I believed him. But now I am sure it was true. All the times he was sucking with me, Roul was undoubtedly doing the same with several others. He never admitted it but he moved out of his parents' house and I heard he was in San Francisco, working for the city. I never saw him again. And for a long time I had a really broken heart.

But Marty and Roul taught me everything and I'm grateful to them for the lessons – and the fun.

III. "HE MADE A PIG OF HIMSELF."

After Roul disappeared from my life, I was pretty empty for a long time. I wanted to join the Foreign Legion. I hear the Legion is full of cocksuckers. I would have been right at home. Anyway, I didn't have another lover for a long terrible time, not in the 3 years of hi school. I met a kid my age in school who I was sure was like me but it took me months to get close to him, and sure enough, he was. He lived with his sister; their parents were dead. We got together first in a movie theater and felt cocks and walked home in the dark and on a dark street I unzipped my pants and he sucked me off. Then I did him and didn't see him again for a month or so. I wasn't crazy about him anyway, I think we had sex once or twice after that but it petered out.

I did have some great sex during my senior year at High. I was on Hollywood Blvd. looking in windows one evening when a guy with a big dog sidled up and asked me to a party. I said, "What party?" He said you and me. He was about 26 and not bad looking so I went to his apartment with him. He was so eager to suck my cock that he was all trembling and could hardly get my pants off. I laid on a couch and me and the dog watched him suck me off. Then he gave me some beer and came back to my cock. He didn't care if I touched him; all he wanted was to suck me, He got me off 3 or 4 times and I had a lot of fun. He was a good cocksucker and ass-licker.

I did a lot of hitchhiking then, not having a car. And 3 times I got picked up by the guys who were hot. I remember the first guy very well. He was tall and slim and very friendly. He asked me if I liked girls and all the standard questions, then ran his hand up my leg. I let him squeeze my cock. He asked me if I wanted him to park. I said sure, so he did. He drove into a big parking lot, back by the fence. Got down in front of my in a hurry and got my pants open and my cock out in nothing flat. I had a big hard on by then and he sucked it like it was the last one left in the world. He was great. In those days, when I was 16, I could come over and over again, and this guy got me off several times. He made a pig of himself over it. He was jacking his cock at the same time and the car smelled of cum. I really enjoyed it.

The second guy who picked me up was younger and smaller and asked me before I got in the car if I was interested in having some fun. I said what kind of fun and then he showed me his cock. It was hard, sticking out of his pants. So I got in the car and unzipped. We drove along Sunset Blvd. and played with our cocks for a mile or two, then he pulled off into a side street and drove to a school, all dark and quiet then. He parked alongside some big hedges and got on his knees in front of me and started sucking and made me come quickly. Then I sucked him off, which didn't take long; he was ready. Then he had a cigarette and gave me one and asked if I would come to his house,which was not too far away. He said he'd drive me home later. So I said OK. He had a small bungalow, not bad, but all I saw of it was the bedroom. He tried to swallow my prick and balls whole. Then he wanted me to fuck him. So he laid on his back and put his legs up over my shoulders and I buried it in his butt and he jacked off while I fucked his ass. It was pretty good. He took me home about midnight, insisting on another good suck before he let me out. He was a lot of fun and wanted me to give him my phone number, but I was afraid my folks would wonder. (I sometimes told them I was seeing this girl or that but they too often said, how come we never see them?)

The third guy was wearing lipstick and smelled great. He was very coy and we sat for a minute or two when I got in. I think he wanted to make sure I wasn't going to get rough. But I liked him at once and told him I just wanted a ride, and I think he knew. I was a horny kid and I knew this guy wanted to suck me. So I made the first move for once and ran my hand up to his cock, which was hard as steel, and unzipped him. He pulled off the street and parked and we sucked each other dry. He was one of the best cocksuckers I ever had. I still remember his name, Marc, with a c.

I had one other experience in Hi school that was nice. An opera company came to town and I got a one-night job backstage, through one of my teachers. The stage manager loved me at sight, I think. He was subtle but his hands brushed against me. He was about 40, a wiry black-haired guy. He showed me the backstage and we ended up in his locked office with my cock in his mouth. It took him a long time to get his fill but I loved the ride. He was a great cocksucker; he had false teeth that he took out – the first time I ever saw that – and his gumming was beautiful. I was drained when I left him. I did the show and was paid a dollar and he begged me to come back the next night. So I did, after the show. He sucked me again, not as thorough as the first time. All this taught me that there were a hell of a lot of crazy-wild cocksuckers out there who were eager to get a young guy like me. I read in a book that some guys were selling cock but I didn't know where to go to do that. I thought at the time it might be an easy way to make a few bucks. However, I did make some bucks – not many – but all by accident. I met a guy on a bus, man of about 35 or so, who put his leg against mine, then rubbed my thigh, and finally offered me 5 bucks to go to his apartment. I asked for 10 and got it. He sucked me off and I went home. I got a summer job parking cars for about a week till they found out I didn't drive very well. But one of the guys was gay as hell and gave me 5 to sit in a parked car while he got me off. He would have done a lot more but I was leery of him. He was too eager.

I almost forgot Lakey. I was in the gym at school one day, just doing nothing much, and he came over (he was a classmate) and wanted to wrestle. We were in shorts and T shirts and when we started to wrestle he was really enjoying the rubbing, as I was. I got a big hard on and so did he and we got to giggling when we discovered it. We were afraid to fool around in the gym but we met after school and I walked home with him. He lived with his mother, who worked, so we spent 2 hours in his bedroom naked, sucking cocks. Unfortunately he was graduated in less than six months and left. But we had sex once or twice a week in his room while I knew him. He was my best cock for 3 years. We didn't get along well but we sucked good.

I got practically raped by a girl in my second year. She was in the glee club with me and I guess got a crush. I met her at a party and somehow got outside with her and she insisted on getting fucked. I did what I could. I don't think she was pleased but I got it in her and got her off. And went home and washed my cock thoroughly.

In between my high school conquests, I jacked off and jacked off some more. In all that time I only had one guy surprise me at it. It was in a public toilet. I thought I was the only guy in the place, so I sat in a stall and pulled myself off with the door half open for air. And just as I got off a skinny guy came up to the door with his cock sticking out of his pants, pulling on it. He had a high-pitched voice and asked me if I wanted to get sucked and I said no. I got out of there in a hurry.

Well, that's hi school. More later if you want it.

[EDITOR's NOTE: I've written this man asking for more; he appears to be an ideal S.T.H. writer, except for his inexplicable failure to let the skinny guy in the toilet suck him off. Skinny guys oft-times are the hungriest cocksuckers, although fat ones are fine too.]

BOOKS FROM GAY SUNSHINE

The Editor

Boyd McDonald is a native of South Dakota, a graduate of Harvard, an Army veteran (on the American side), a columnist for *Christopher Street* and *Mother Jones* Magazines, the founder and former editor of *S.T.H.: The New York Review of Cocksucking*. He gathered, edited and published the memoirs in *S.T.H. Magazine* – material from which was excerpted (along with new material) in the first three volumes of this series (*Meat/Flesh/Sex*), as well as gathering and editing the new memoirs for *Cum* and *Juice*, and for one S.T.H. anthology published by The Gay Presses of New York (*Smut*). He is continuing to prepare S.T.H. books for publication and would like to hear from readers who care to send their true experiences. His address is:

Boyd McDonald
Box 977
Radio City Station
New York City 10101

S.T.H., the magazine from which these anthologies grew, is now being edited by Victor Weaver. Under his editorship, it continues to provide one of the very few true histories of homosexuality in our time, written by the men who have sex. Readers of this book can obtain the 4 most recent issues of S.T.H. for $2 per issue (a total of $8 for all 4) by writing to: Victor Weaver, STH, Box 982, Radio City Sta., NYC 10101.